Books by Bellora Quinn and Sadie Rose Bermingham

Elemental Evidence

Breathing Betrayal
Burning Boundaries

Books by Bellora Quinn

AURA

Quinn's Gambit
Flax's Pursuit
Kellen's Awakening

Burning Boundaries

ISBN # 978-1-78686-181-8

©Copyright Bellora Quinn, Sadie Rose Bermingham 2017

Cover Art by Posh Gosh ©Copyright 2017

Interior text design by Claire Siemaszkiewicz

Pride Publishing

Elemental Evidence

BURNING BOUNDARIES

BELLORA QUINN
&
SADIE ROSE
BERMINGHAM

Dedication

To R and X, love J and M…thanks for the inspiration, guys.

Prologue

"I'm late. I know. I am so sorry." Doctor Ilmarinen Gale reached across the polished mahogany desk, still out of breath, to shake the proffered hand of the head of Internet Security at MI6. When that esteemed gentleman, Brigadier Edward Stern, gestured toward the vacant seat beside him, Mari sank into it like his strings had been cut, still babbling to cover his embarrassment. "There was some incident outside the Lithuanian Embassy. Lots of blue lights and police tape. We sat there for ages. Nothing was moving. My cab driver had to divert around the Tate in the end, and then we got stuck in nightmare traffic coming back along Millbank. Frankly, it would have been quicker to walk."

"My grandfather had the pleasure of working alongside your great-grandmother at Bletchley Park. We've been most eager, here at Vauxhall Cross, to speak to the latest member of her Elemental bloodline," the old man said with a genuine smile, making no reference to his tardiness or his breathless explanation. "It's a pleasure to meet you at last, Dr. Gale. Professor Karden told us a great deal about you."

Mari hoped he managed to keep the surprise off his face. His fingers twitched toward the lapel of his new Pierre Cardin suit jacket but he stopped himself from fidgeting and folded his hands back in his lap, pleased that the crisp blue linen had not crumpled in the unseasonal late spring heat.

"All good, I hope?"

"He had some issues with your timekeeping, Dr. Gale. But with the work you did for him? Yes, I think we can safely say, he was happy with that." Stern chuckled and rubbed at his slim, gray mustache with the back of one well-manicured finger. "You know well enough that no one in Karden's team is able to do the things with technology that you can. We were amazed that he was prepared to let you go, and very pleased that he referred you on to us. I head up a diverse, young team and they are already very excited about the prospect of working with you."

"I'd heard you already had an Interface," Mari ventured, put at his ease by the brigadier's calm, informal manner.

"Had being the operative word, Dr. Gale." Stern looked bitter for a moment. "She was poached by the Kremlin last June. Money outweighed prestige for her, I fear."

"Ah... I thought I'd heard that there was a woman working for Six." Mari nodded. "I'm not interested in going to Russia, by the way. Too bloody cold."

Too bloody dangerous! his conscience added, in Great-Grandmama Amelia's cut glass tones. *Especially for the likes of you.*

"I should hope not." Stern fixed him with a shrewd gaze that reminded Mari of his paternal grandfather, a man he'd always been very scared of as a child.

He shifted in his seat, lifting one hand to smooth his already immaculate blond hair, then forced himself to be still. He was the UCL's whizz-kid, not some teenager, fresh out of college.

"You got your PhD at Cambridge?" Stern observed, without referring to his notes.

"I did, sir." Mari nodded. "I worked on the development of artificial intelligence in security systems. Our AIS programs have already been implemented by the Spanish government."

"Hmmph. In my day, Cambridge was a hotbed of radicals and traitors." Stern snorted dismissively.

Mari wasn't sure what to say to that so he murmured, "I can assure you that isn't the case these days, in my experience."

The warning look Stern sent his way made his insides

squirm again.

"SIS never did manage to prove that your ancestor was a double agent, Gale. That doesn't mean that there won't be people in the Service watching you closely. I'll warn you once only that I want no such trouble from you," he said.

Mari tried his hardest to look innocent. Inside, though, he was privately fuming at the suggested smear on his relative's honor.

"Is that meant to be an incentive or a threat?" he wanted to know. "Amelia wasn't a spy, Brigadier Stern. She considered Britain her home."

"That may as well be, but the Finns were in league with the Nazis during the war, Dr. Gale. Don't imagine that her handlers were naïve." Stern did not smile, but there was maybe a hint of a twinkle in his gray eyes all of a sudden.

"She grew up in London and was nothing if not loyal to her family and her homeland, sir." This time, it took more effort to be polite. Mari shook his head at the inference that his maternal ancestor might ever have entertained such inclinations.

"It's true that nothing was ever proven, but Professor Pallant was a clever lady and an enormously skilled Elemental. The last Remote Viewer known to modern history." Stern sounded almost wistful. "Her gift was quite something to behold, or so Grandpa told me. We could send coded messages all over the world by the telegraph, but the professor could physically talk with — and spy on — people on the other side of the Atlantic. Very disconcerting sometimes, I'd imagine."

Mari managed a tiny, bitter smile. "She was burned out by the time I knew her," he said, the words soft and sad. "I was only six when she died."

"My condolences," Stern said more gently. "You barely had the chance to know her."

"I remember a white-haired old lady, with a sharp tongue," Mari told him, lost in thought for a moment. "She didn't suffer fools, gladly or otherwise. Music was her great love — the radio was always on in her lounge. She once told me she saw angels dancing on the airwaves and she was so sure that I almost believed her. My mama said she was touched, but not by angels." He sighed and straightened his shoulders, sitting back in the leather and chrome office chair and crossing his left leg over the right knee as he steered the conversation back into safer waters. "The gift we have is a fragile thing, Brigadier Stern, sir. If we don't use it, we run the risk of losing it. Overused, it doesn't last. So, let's talk about your terms, shall we?"

"We are not at liberty to offer you permanent employment, Dr. Gale," Stern said with a smile that seemed to hint that this pained him. If Mari's bluntness caused offense, he did not let it show. "But we can provide substantial financial remuneration for your time and effort on our behalf. The contract here is for two years, with the possibility of an extension, depending on the work you are engaged in at its conclusion." He took a sheet of paper out of the folder on the desk between them and passed it over to Mari. "These are the figures involved. Naturally, you will be expected to keep the nature of your duties for us to yourself. At the end of your contract, should you require protection or anonymity, we will provide it, for you and your closest kin."

"Am I allowed to tell my family who I work for?" Mari asked, his eyes widening at the breakdown in his hands as much as at the idea that he might need protecting.

"You may tell them where you work but the nature of your employment must remain classified, for security reasons. You understand that?" Stern lived up to his name for a moment and Mari nodded, feeling about ten years old again.

"May I have some time to think about your offer?" he asked.

The brigadier looked surprised, but he acquiesced. "Certainly, Dr. Gale. This is not a position that we can easily fill. You possess a certain skillset that only comes our way once in a blue moon. Take as much time as you need." He consulted something in his files with a small frown. "Before you go...were you aware that Cambridge Laboratories have you down in their records as Ms. Isla Marjine Gale? An administrative error, I suppose."

Mari blinked at him for a second, then his tongue unglued itself from the roof of his mouth. "Really? I... erm...yes. Well, I never. A typing mistake, most probably." He laughed. "That's what comes of being saddled with a forename no one has ever heard, or is able to spell. Do you need me to ask if they will resend it?"

"Not a problem. Your identification documents check out, so do your other references, and the evidence of my own eyes will suffice, I'm sure." Stern chuckled. "We look forward to your decision, Dr. Gale. Thank you for your time today."

The rest of the interview process was blessedly short, and within the hour, he was trotting back down the steps from the vast glass fortress and heading for the river. Mari heaved a sigh and pinched the bridge of his nose, fending off a headache, as he began the hunt for a taxi. His mind was buzzing with a mess of nervous energy and confusion, re-running the conversation with Stern in his head over and over. Had he been convincing? Did he even want the job? He wanted to go home and get changed, maybe call Jake and see if he wanted to go for a run.

A smile twitched his lips again as he thought of Jake Chivis, part-Irish, part-Native American and a fellow Elemental. Jake had been a detective with the Detroit PD in a former life, before SEWN—the Six Elements Worldwide Network research program—had brought him to London, throwing him together with Mari as if that was their destiny.

Chivis was a trained inquisitor, even without his Elemental talents. His element was Fire and his gift was enabled through physical contact with material objects. Just a simple brush of Jake's fingers could open up a gateway into another life, sucking him into the memories of the last person to touch an object. This included contact with people which, Mari conceded, could be a problem. If he accepted the job with MI6, the nature of his work would be classified. Even if he managed to keep his mouth shut, and not discuss business, there remained the possibility that Jake might one day pick up a stray memory from him, although thus far he had never done so.

Mari sighed. *One step at a time, Mizz Gale.*

He struck lucky halfway across Vauxhall Bridge when he managed to get an empty Hackney to stop for him in the slow-moving traffic. At the far end of the bridge, though, he turned off to the right and headed down Millbank. Suddenly they were taking a more circuitous route than Mari was expecting, for the second time that day.

"Is there still a problem? You're going the wrong way," he said, feeling his heart jump with the excitement of the unexpected diversion. Maybe it was just that his thoughts were filled with the seductive intrigue of life as a spy for Her Majesty's Government, but the sudden rerouting was alive with possibilities in his mind.

The cabbie grunted. "Be here all day, if we go that way. Road's been cordoned off in both directions all morning. Some silly mare set herself alight near Bessborough Gardens. Emergency Services are all over it. News crews will be down there as well by now."

"Did they get to her in time?" Mari asked, shocked by this.

"Dunno, guv. Probably one of them suicide bombers gone wrong, innit," the cabbie speculated. "There's all sorts of nutters about these days. I'd send 'em all back where they come from. Reckon this one's gone to meet her maker at least."

Mari wrinkled his nose irritably, as a thousand heated retorts sprang to mind. He was not in the right mood for a political argument today, though, and settled in his seat, biting his tongue, resigned to an unscheduled tour of the Thames embankment. Thankfully the cab driver did not press the issue. His smartphone vibrating in his jacket pocket made him jump, but a glance at the familiar caller ID soon put a smile back on his face.

Chapter One

When Jake had first moved into his London flat, he'd been leery about living above a bar, thinking that it would become a problem due to noise or obnoxious behavior. As it turned out, he rarely noticed the bar noise and, for a place that was a notorious cruising joint, there was very little in the way of trouble. Jake chalked it up to their intimidating leather-bear bouncers and the manager's low tolerance for drama-prone twinks.

At the moment, he was carefully navigating a narrow wooden staircase on behalf of said manager. The stairs led up from the bar cellar and Jake was balancing three cases of beer in his arms, shadowed by Manny, who ran the place.

"Those are the last. Thanks, mate, I don't know what I would have done without your help," Manny said.

Of the two other barmen who were supposed to be helping with the delivery, one had called in sick and the other had disappeared a couple of days ago and no one had seen him since. Normally it would have just meant some extra work for Manny, but a week ago he had slipped and taken a tumble on the very stairs Jake had just navigated and his right arm was in a cast and a sling. Jake had been on his way to the grocery store when he'd seen him struggling and offered to help.

"No problem," Jake told him, grunting as he set the cases down. "Saves me a trip to the gym later."

"Ha! Well, if you want to save yourself the membership fees I'll let you haul the cases up twice a week."

Jake chuckled. "Maybe, until you get your cast off, anyway."

"You should come back tonight. We're doing a Best Chest Contest. Place should be packed with fit blokes flexing." He was looking Jake up and down in a way that left no doubt he was getting an early start on watching fit blokes flexing. "You should enter."

Jake grinned and shook his head. "No, thanks."

"Well, come in for a pint anyway, it's the least I can do."

"I might," Jake hedged. "I don't know if Mari's got plans for us tonight."

"So bring him. I guarantee you'll both have fun."

"I'll call and ask if he wants to," Jake said, to be polite.

* * * *

At least Jake thought he was only being polite. When Mari eagerly agreed to a night out, even if it was only downstairs, Jake had to wonder if maybe he'd been stifling Mari's social life. Work kept them both fairly busy and while they liked to jog together in the mornings, the majority of their time together wasn't usually spent in public places.

"Hello, gorgeous," Mari said effusively, dipping his head to drop a kiss onto Jake's lips when he showed up that evening. "You look good enough to eat."

Funny Mari should say that when it was Jake's mouth that was watering just looking at him. While Jake couldn't really remember a time when Mari wasn't smartly dressed, he'd certainly put some extra effort in tonight. His nearly white blond locks were artfully messy and he wore a silvery, near-translucent tank top under a fitted, tan leather jacket and teal jeans that Jake already wanted to peel him out of. He returned the kiss and slipped an arm around him, telling himself it was just a friendly arm, not a possessive one.

"Good enough to eat, huh? Well if I'm the meat and potatoes, you are definitely the dessert. How did you even get those pants on?" Jake teased.

Mari glanced down as if he'd not even realized what he was wearing.

"Spray job. They'll be harder to get off," he said, as if he'd read Jake's mind. Mari was already bouncing on his toes to the beat of the music spilling out from the open door of the bar. They were play a remix of Curtis Mayfield's *Superfly* and Mari chirped, "Old school! Love it! I haven't danced in ages. I think I forgot how."

"Should I remind you?" Jake asked as they walked in. He snagged Mari around the hips and moved in closer with a sexy sway and shimmy.

"Mmmh, I haven't dated a man who wanted to dance with me...*ever*." Mari chuckled but moved his hips in time with the swing of Jake's, nudging up against him. He leaned in close, speaking directly into Jake's ear to be heard. "There is an awful lot of leather going on in here, don't you think? I feel underdressed. Or overdressed...not sure."

"Even if I dipped you in liquid latex and rolled you in metal spikes, you would stand out. Blending in isn't your thing, Ilmari. You're too hot for that." Jake turned him in a swirl between the clusters of people standing around the bar.

"Guy Upstairs! We was wondering when you'd get brave enough to come on in," one of the men at the bar whooped, eyeing Jake up meaningfully before his attention shifted to Mari. "Hello, Blondie. Is he treating you right then, this quiet guy?"

"He's not so quiet when you get to know him." Mari laughed. "And yes, he's a gentleman."

"Don't get many of them in here," observed a shaven-headed chap.

"Jake! There you are. Glad you could make it. What can I get for you two? You want a beer, or are you tired of lugging them around?" Manny asked, coming up to their spot at the bar.

"A beer sounds great, Tanglo, if you got it." Jake looked at Mari. "What would you like?"

His partner scanned the pumps along the bar then the chill cabinets behind it. "Bottle of Estrella, thanks," he decided, his eyes traveling over Manny, splint and all. "What did you do to yourself?"

"Fell down the cellar steps," Manny said gruffly, shifting under that intense stare.

"You're s'posed to tell the hotties you did it fighting a bear." The shaven-headed customer laughed.

"He'd be spoilt for choice in here, I guess," Mari said, and Jake chuckled at the glint of mischief in his eyes.

The other man winked at him. "Too true. All the chickens are too scared to come in tonight."

"Is that right?" Mari asked, slipping onto a bar stool. "Why's that then? Can't be the terrible music."

Two bushy eyebrows crept up their companion's forehead and he looked over at Manny, who was suddenly busy with other customers.

"Did he not tell you tonight's the club's BDSM night then?" He chortled. "Guess that's one way to get newbies in here."

For a moment, Mari's perfectly composed face was totally unreadable. He touched the neck of the bottle to his lips and blew into it gently. His sky-blue eyes flickered to the awkward form of Manny behind the bar then back to Jake's face, failing to hide his surprise.

"I take it they don't just order a pizza and talk about complicated knots?" Mari said, with the barest twitch of his lips.

The bald fellow smirked. "You can sign up to hitch yourself to the switching post later tonight if you want," he offered, his tone teasing.

"Well, that would be awkward." Mari fixed him with that stare, the one Jake knew had already melted the resolve of bigger guys than their barfly. "I might need some help with that. Complicated knots and everything, you know."

He winked and the hairless guy reddened a shade. The guy was clearly considering that proposal and Jake was on the verge of pointing out that Mari was teasing.

"Maybe you coming in tonight weren't such an accident

after all, eh?" The guy laughed at last, breaking the tension. "New faces are always a big draw. You boys are new to the scene, aren't you?"

Mari shrugged one shoulder, pursing his lips as if he was considering the question.

"Maybe some of us are," he said at last.

Mari kept looking at him, stealing tiny glances from the corner of his eye. Jake imagined the wheels in that beautiful complex head of his spinning at light speed. He sipped his beer and hid his grin, keeping his expression unreadable. Jake didn't consciously try for aloof and mysterious, but it got Mari so wound up sometimes that he couldn't help doing it on purpose, once in a while. Of course, the fact that Mari usually wanted to get into his head in the more physical sense only reinforced the behavior.

Jake leaned close to his ear, letting his lips brush over the shell. "Want to dance?"

Mari took a good swig from the beer bottle in his hand then slid down from the stool, still holding his drink.

"Well...come on," he said, with a devilish grin. "What are you waiting for?"

They moved to the nearest clear area. Jake slipped his arms around him and pressed up close, giving him a kiss before he let him have his space again. He could not help remembering how Alex had been so surprised that not only did he like to dance, but he wasn't half bad at it. His ex's unspoken implication — that he was just too straight-laced and uptight to enjoy grinding on a dance floor in a crowd of sexually charged men — had not been lost on either of them.

Jake hadn't realized how much he'd missed dancing, either. He had always been a physical guy and getting lost in the modern-day version of tribal dance was without a doubt something he could get into. Of course, watching Mari move, like he was made out of silk and slinkies, was an added bonus. He wondered what exactly was going on in that clever head. Jake had not missed Mari's interest in the conversation at the bar, nor the way he'd tried to be so nonchalant about it. He still wasn't sure if that was all it came down to—just an interest—or if Mari really was turned on by the idea of playing whipping boy.

Whatever the attraction, Mari seemed in his element, fit enough to out-dance just about any man in here. There was a fierce joy in him as he writhed and slammed his way around the compact dance floor, drawing in fellow participants and bemused onlookers alike, most of whom seemed more surprised than Jake at his wholehearted enthusiasm.

Jake was having a good time and had just started to work up a sweat when Mari touched soft lips to his ear, shouting to be heard over the music.

"Wonder what's downstairs then?" He nodded toward the back of the dance floor where a flight of steps led into the basement, and from which a red-gold light glowed like it was the entrance to Hades.

"Are you asking that because you don't know, or because you want to let your inner exhibitionist run free tonight?" Jake asked, equal parts amused and aroused by the idea.

"I have an inner exhibitionist?" Mari looked at himself as if he expected a mini-Mari to pop out of his belly like the Alien. "All my days! That would be something. Do you think I make a habit of hanging out in fetish bars, Jake Chivis?"

"You tell me," Jake teased. "Do you want me to sign you up for a flogging?"

Mari just chuckled and caught his hand, bringing it up to his lips to brush a kiss across his knuckles. He grinned as he let Mari tow him along in his wake, snaking through the thrashing bodies on the dance floor, down the concrete steps into the lower reaches of the bar. There was another chamber opposite the store room where Jake had earlier been heaving crates. The door to this room stood open, decked with a cartoon poster depicting a Charles Atlas type, in a golden posing pouch, that advertised the club's impending Best Chest Contest. The music was still audible, but louder still were the sharp cracks of leather on bare skin and the rhythmic groans of the clientele who had come to the basement for their punishment and pleasure.

The shaven-headed man from the bar was already there, bent over a bench with his leather pants around his knees as an older guy wearing a peaked cap, a black PVC posing pouch and a pair of biker boots swatted his bare arse with a wooden paddle. The hitching post he'd spoken of, an upright affair with two sets of iron rings and a square iron base, was occupied by a muscular, bearded man. He was nude except for a pair of white briefs, and they'd been tugged down at the back to expose his pale cheeks. He was fastened with his wrists together, over his head, and his feet apart, straps around his ankles attached to either end of a fixed wooden spreader bar. A younger man, with elaborate tattoos all over his powerful upper body and tight black jeans over his lower parts, was swinging a short-handled flail almost lazily at his buttocks, the leather strands striking skin with a rippling sound that nonetheless made the tethered man moan and sigh.

Beside him, Mari uttered kittenish growling noises as he watched the way the stranger flexed and pulled on the restraining bonds each time the lash fell on his bared flesh. Jake made a casual sweep of the room, but he was much more interested in Mari's reactions than the actual goings-on. Mari's fingers were still wrapped around his and they squeezed tighter at the sounds of flesh being smacked. It was marginally quieter down here, but Jake still leaned closer to speak in Mari's ear.

"So, you're into all this?" he asked, less teasing and more curious. "How come you didn't tell me before?"

"You never asked," Mari said casually. His eyes were still fever-bright as he watched the stranger at the hitching post take another lazy slap of the flail. "And it's not the sort of thing that you can drop into polite conversation, is it? 'How's your mother?' 'Oh, she's fine. She says, when are you going to strap me to the bed and whip me, Jake?'" He waved his free hand toward the post. "Wonder how much something like that costs."

Jake nearly choked on a sharp bark of laughter, then cleared his throat at the brief disappointed look Mari threw him.

"Do you mean him, or the post?"

"He is rather cute, but where would we keep him?" Mari said, poker-faced. Jake wondered if he was getting his own back for Jake laughing at him when he turned back again, openly admiring the inked designs on the Dom's well-developed torso and powerful arms. As his client came down from the endorphin rush, the guy was admiring Mari too—rather brazenly, Jake thought.

"Bet he'd win the Best Chest, don't you?" Mari speculated.

"Maybe I should ask if I can borrow his flogger," Jake said, with a sudden hot spark of jealousy. He wasn't sure if he was joking, even as he said it.

For a moment, Mari looked as if he might be struggling to breathe. The inked man unfastened his client and began making arrangements for the same time next month, as the satisfied customer pulled his clothes on. Judging by the damp patch in his tighty whities, before he'd pulled his trousers up over them, he'd found the experience stimulating. When Mr. Muscle-n-Tatts headed over toward them, Mari cleared his throat and swallowed hard.

"Hi there. Are you interested in something in particular? Haven't seen you down here before. What do you like?" the Dom asked, very open, very friendly.

Mari made two unsuccessful attempts to speak and Jake had to nudge him with his elbow.

At last, his voice gone attractively husky, his lover managed to murmur, "I've...um... I've never done this professionally before. Does it...hurt?"

"As much or as little as you like. You can handle the paddles and floggers first," his guide offered. "Get a feel for the weight of them, what you think might feel nice on your skin. That's what nights like this are all about, educating new clients."

"It's…more the bondage that's new to me," Mari said, as shyly as Jake had ever heard him speak. "I *know* what feels good on my skin."

Jake turned his head trying to get his attention, since this was news to him. Mari was not taking him on, his fascinated gaze remained fixed on the hitching post. The Dom responded with a warm smile. He could have been trying to sell windows or a car instead of an intimate BDSM session.

"You like the idea of being tied up, though?" he said in a calm, soothing tone. "A lot of men enjoy that. No need to be shy. We're all like-minded guys here. Is this your boyfriend?"

Mari nodded, no hesitation. In spite of the surge of jealousy, Jake got a warm glow inside him at that simple admission.

The Dom managed a playful pout. "Shame. He's very cute, though. Lucky boy. Does he want to paddle you? Or just watch and fuck you when I'm done?"

Jake wanted to protest, he really did, but he bit his tongue. It wasn't that he had a problem with the spanking, or the bondage, or even—to a limited extent—the publicness of the situation, but he wasn't sure how he would handle seeing another man touch Mari like that. He'd never been a particularly jealous or possessive person, but as he tried to picture Hot Tattoo Guy strapping his Mari up and whipping him, his brain utterly rebelled at the idea. However, he could tell Mari was turned on, and if Jake refused he knew Mari would be disappointed. Worse, he might start to overthink and figure that Jake had him down for a pervert or something.

He tried to catch Mari's eye again but his adorable mate was looking just about anywhere else except at him. Making up his mind, Jake said, "No, if he wants a paddling, I'll give it to him."

Mari turned toward him sharply, his bright, aquamarine

eyes filled with curiosity. He looked rather startled by Jake's vehemence.

Their inked host murmured, "Uh-huh…possessive, much!"

"Seriously?" Mari asked him, ignoring the Dom. "You're up for that? For spanking me, I mean?"

Jake had to fight down the feeling of absurdity that wanted to bubble up as nervous laughter, certain that it would be taken wrong. He wasn't so sure he should do this. While he wasn't prudish about exploring kink and he got off on really pushing Mari's buttons, the last thing he ever wanted to do was hurt him. He had never in his life struck a lover – not even Alex, who had pushed him to the limits of provocation – and playful swats were about as far as any physical roughness had gotten. Jake could sort of see the appeal in turning Mari over his knee and slapping his arse as he squirmed there, but using an actual wooden paddle on him was not really in his comfort zone.

He could tell that Mari saw him wavering.

"Um, sure," he murmured, before Mari could get out one of his patented 'forget it!' head tosses.

"I'm not going to push anyone," their host added quickly, picking up on the tension between them. "That isn't what we're about. But if you wanted to explore your options somewhere less public, I can give you my number." He turned away for a moment toward the wheeled equipment case and produced a card which identified him as Colm Fleming. The company name on his card was The Headmaster Ritual and the backdrop to his details was a soft-focus image of a darkened room with a pair of cuffed wrists and a pale cane in motion. Very artistic, if you liked that kind of thing. "I do photography as well," Colm offered, with a helpful smile. "Not weddings and stuff, but some portrait work. Mostly abstract."

"Aren't you the entrepreneur?" Mari teased, seeming to recover some of his composure, but he took the card with a nod. "Can I have one for Jake as well?"

Colm looked at Jake curiously then back at Mari. "You don't live together?"

"We've not been seeing one another very long. You know how it goes." Mari smiled but he reached out to snake the fingers of his right hand through Jake's left as Colm handed them another card.

Jake smiled too. He wasn't sure if he was disappointed or relieved that Mari seemed to want to postpone the experiment.

"If you're not gonna…?" A young guy had come over while they were talking and he looked from Jake and Mari back to Colm, then gestured toward the post.

Mari waved him toward it with a magnanimous gesture but he nodded at Colm. "I'll ring you. I'd like to talk things over with you, but maybe in a less…hectic environment?"

"Sounds good to me." Colm grinned at him, then reached for a set of cuffs as the lad was getting his shirt off. "I'd best get cracking here. Pun intended."

"Yes, you'd better," Mari agreed, and Jake didn't miss the way he admired the toned body revealed by the young penitent's shucking of his shirt. When his gaze moved to Colm's face again there was a hint of his natural mischief back there. "Thanks for this," he said, waving the card then tucking it into his pocket as he turned away.

Was that flirting? Was he flirting with the guy? Jake tried to rein those thoughts in but he couldn't help it. Mari had a habit of flirting, but it had never bugged Jake before. Jesus, they'd managed to go to one bar for an hour and already he was devolving into Neanderthal territory. He realized something else. It had never really bothered him when he and Alex had gone out and his ex had spent all night coming on to strangers. Then again, he'd known Alex was doing it to get a rise out of him. That was not Mari's way, at all.

"You want another drink?" Jake asked, by way of keeping himself from hauling Mari out of there and grilling him about whether he wanted to sleep with Mr. Whips and Tattoos.

They had to step to one side as a sweating, agitated-looking guy pushed by them on the stairs in an obvious hurry to get down to the basement for some chastisement. Though he looked chastised enough already, in Jake's opinion.

"If you do," Mari said, then exhaled a huff that might have been regret and might have been relief. "Unless, of course, you just want to put me over your shoulder and carry me out, Mr. Caveman. I wasn't giving him the come-on. So you can stop looking daggers. And don't deny it." He pointed a slender finger at Jake as he opened his mouth. "I could see you thinking it. Yes, he's very cute, but he's not really my type. I do like his toy box though."

Jake snapped his mouth closed then pushed a hand through his hair and let out a sigh of his own. He had always pitied guys that acted like possessive jerks and here he was being as transparent as glass, all but snarling at anyone who got too close to Mari. "I'm sorry. I was aiming not to be obvious. I'll try and refrain from clubbing you over the head and dragging you out by the hair." He managed a sheepish grin.

"In that case, it would be my pleasure to have another drink with you, Chivis." Mari chuckled, slipping a hand around the nape of his neck and towing him in for a brief, firm kiss.

They made their way back up into the bar and as they were weaving their way through the crowd, Jake heard someone shout, then screaming coming from the direction of the basement.

The red and gold lighting seemed to be flickering and Mari yelled, "Can you smell something burning?"

Jake noticed the smell just as Mari was saying it, and turned his head. A curl of pale smoke was winding up from the basement stairway, not thick but noticeable.

"Shit!" He grabbed Mari's arm. "Get out of here. Hurry."

Jake gave him a push toward the front exit then shoved through the crowd, trying to get to the stairs.

Chapter Two

Mari moved instinctively the way that he was urged but, as Jake let go and turned back into the sudden rush of panicked bodies, he stopped and looked over his shoulder. Men were pushing by him, streaming past like a churning river forcing its way around a standing stone.

Colm had reached the top of the stairs, sweating and soot-streaked. He was shaking his head and pointing down into the basement as Jake reached the doorway. Manny, the bartender, was shouting and trying to keep order as his customers ignored him, shoving their frantic way toward the narrow exit door. An alarm bell added its insistent clamor to the shouts and screams. In the midst of all the chaos, Manny tried to cajole him toward the door – as well as he could with one arm – but Mari dodged by him and pushed his way through to the basement stairs where he had seen Jake disappear into the swirl of smoke with Colm. He grabbed a beer-soaked towel from the bar and pressed it over his mouth and nose as he hurried to the cellar where the conflagration seemed to be contained. As he got there, he saw the reason for Colm's panic. He and Jake were trying to manhandle the unfortunate client up the stairs, still hitched to the flogging post, which they had detached from its weighty metal base. They had got his ankles free of the spreader bar but the lad was semi-conscious from smoke inhalation and the two men were struggling to haul both him and the wooden post up the stairs. Mari pitched in, grabbing the top of the post, and the three of them carried the client out of the smoke-wreathed cellar. Colm turned around as they reached the bar area, where the air was clearer.

"My kit!" he yelled, and disappeared into the smoke again.

Mari's eyes went wide. "Idiot! What's he doing?"

"Colm!" Jake bellowed after him, startling Mari into almost dropping the man they were trying to help out. He couldn't remember having heard Jake even raise his voice before, and wouldn't have guessed that he could sound that loud, or that angry.

"Damn it! Mari, can you get him out of here on your own?" Jake called over the incessant rattle of the fire alarm.

"You're not going back down there." Mari dropped to his knees, tugging on the straps around the man's wrists, releasing him from the post as fast as he could. The guy had passed out and Mari knew it was important to get him away from the smoke as soon as possible. The smoke coming up from the stairs was thick and dark. The acrid smell had the sweet sickliness of charred meat. "What the fuck happened?" he shouted.

But Jake was already on his way down the steps again, Mari's towel clutched to his face.

Mari swore under his breath and grabbed the unconscious client by his wrists. With no concern for his modesty, he hauled him, semi-naked, across the dance floor into the fresher air coming in from the street. The fact hadn't escaped him that, but for his own hesitancy to experiment, it could well have been him that Jake had been struggling to drag up the stairs. He didn't have time to wallow in self-congratulation though.

Manny met him halfway to the door and helped him pull the lad to safety. At the entrance, he waved his mobile and shouted, "Fire Brigade are coming."

Mari nodded to him, catching his breath in the cooler night air, then ran back inside, ignoring the cries ordering him to stay where he was. Jake was still in that basement and Mari wasn't about to leave the only man who had ever made him feel worthwhile to a horrible fate. Not alone. He grabbed two more bar towels and sprinted for the stairs. Partway to the basement, he hit the thick wall of black smoke and found himself gagging and half-blinded by it. Up in the club it had just been a few wisps of gray swirling around, down here it was choking. He could feel heat coming up to meet him and hear the crackle of flames, even if he couldn't yet see the actual fire. Using the wall as a guide, he eased himself to floor level, almost sitting on the steps, where the air was clearer. The stench was horrendous though, almost enough to make him physically sick.

His eyes were watering so much that Jake slammed into him before Mari saw him, trying to pull Colm's limp body back up toward the stairs. He coughed and swore, something else that Mari wasn't used to hearing from his lips.

"Fucking idiot! Get out! Get out! Now!"

Mari threw one of the towels at him and ignored the insult, grabbing Colm's hanging arm and pulling it over his shoulder. Between them, towels masking some of the smog, they managed to drag Colm back up the stairs before flopping to the ground beside him on the empty dance floor. Mari's eyes were streaming and his head spun as he gasped and choked, fighting the impulse to just black out. Jake coughed painfully into the wet towel, like he would spit his lungs out. Colm was scarily still, eyes closed, scorched lips parted in a soundless gasp.

A searchlight panned through the swirling smoke and suddenly Mari was aware of metallic-sounding voices and the sliding blue lights of a fire tender outside the bar. Strong hands gripped his arms and pulled him upright, then off his feet, and just like that he was floating under again, losing consciousness. He gasped Jake's name as the blackness sucked him down.

* * * *

Mari came to his senses in the back of an ambulance, the

world swaying like crazy around him, and instinct made him reach out.

"Jake!" The word hurt his throat and he coughed violently. Someone pressed a mask over his nose and mouth, telling him to breathe slowly, and he tried to push it away but felt weak as a baby. The rapid, frightened pounding of his heart hurt like hot spikes in his chest and he felt dizzy, almost drunk, and unable to get his breath. He grayed out and when he woke up again he was in a still, quiet room with white walls. For a moment, he thought that he was dead. When he turned his head, though, his ears filled with the shush of oxygen cylinders and the beeps of nearby monitors. His pulse quickened as he recognized Jake stretched out on the single bed beside his own. Jake's eyes were closed but his chest rose and fell in a jagged rhythm. Like Mari, he wore an oxygen mask over half of his smoke-blackened face.

Mari murmured his name again and Jake's honey-gold eyes fluttered open. Relief surged through him like a spear of pure adrenaline.

"Fuck! Thank goodness!" he croaked.

"Mari." Jake's voice sounded raw and he winced. "How long...?" He was stopped by a coughing fit that made his eyes water. When it subsided, he rasped, "Are you okay?"

"Uh-huh." Mari exhaled with a weak nod. "I think so. I feel weird but... What happened?"

"Not sure." Jake still sounded husky and sexy, even tucked firmly into bed and wrapped in a mask. "Colm kept yelling that one of the clients...he caught fire. Just like that. Just burning up. It was that fast." He sucked in a gulp of oxygen, then coughed for a full minute.

Mari blinked at him, moving the mask from over his face so that he could speak. "What? How? Did someone...?" He ran out of air and took another gulp from the mask before trying again. "Did someone attack him?"

"That's what didn't make sense. No one touched him. He just...*whoosh*, went up." Jake started to push himself up on one arm, moving like he was a man three times his age. "I need to question Colm."

"No…stay put." Mari told him. Just pushing the bedcovers back felt like a marathon task. And Jake had been down there longer than him. "It's not going to make a…make a difference if you wait until you're stronger, Jake."

He succumbed to a fit of coughing and pulled the mask back over his nose and mouth, gulping the oxygen gratefully. A dark-skinned fellow in green nurse's scrubs came in, and the argument became academic. He bullied Jake back into bed while checking his clipboard, then told Mari off for inciting him. Mari rolled indignant eyes but the medic was unfazed, and just wagged a finger at him, admonishing him again.

"The guy that came in with us?" Mari asked him, through the mask. "Is he okay?"

Their nurse turned to look at Jake then back at him with a sudden, brilliant white smile. "You fellas got him out, right?"

"Stupid ass went back in," Jake rumbled, his voice barely more than a rasp. "Did the fire spread? Did they get it out before it got upstairs?"

"That's the weird thing," the nurse told them, shaking his head. "Didn't spread at all. Nothing else in the building was damaged, 'cept by the smoke. But the guy still down there was charcoal, man. You know. Nothing to resuscitate."

"That's not possible," Mari huffed. "Is it?"

"You'd be surprised," the nurse said.

Jake nodded, looking thoughtful. "If the fire is hot enough, it could be," he croaked. "Had to be a real hot burn, though. Did they find any accelerants?"

"That's up to the police and firefighters to find," their medic answered in a tone that all but said Jake shouldn't worry his pretty head about it.

"I was…an…arson investigator," Jake said between short, painful gasps.

"I think the operative word there, is 'was', hot shot," their nurse pointed out. "The police and the Fire Super will want to have a word when you're up to it, though."

"We're up to it," Mari insisted, though his pulse was hammering in his throat again and he just wanted to close his eyes and sleep. "Can we talk to them?"

"Course you can, sweetheart." The nurse nodded. "All in good time. You fellas just lay down, though, and stop trying to be heroic on my watch, right?"

Mari subsided, exhausted by just that brief exchange, but he wasn't placated. However, the heavy feeling in his chest pulled him under and he slept at last, succumbing to the bone-deep weariness.

* * * *

It was still dark outside when the Fire Service Superintendent turned up to interview them. Mari noticed how Jake chuckled at the widening of his eyes but he couldn't help it, zoned-out on smoke and medication or not. Superintendent Sullivan was at least six foot four, and filled out his pristine uniform to perfection. A close-cropped thatch of dark red hair hugged his scalp and his sea-green eyes were somewhere between fierce and inquisitive as he confirmed their names and the time of their arrival at the bar.

"All right, you two," he said in a gruff tone. "Whose barmy idea was it to go running back into a burning building?"

Mari raised his hand like an imperious child. "Actually, we were already in there when the fire started."

"Had to make sure everyone was out," Jake told him.

"You did good, in that case, mate," Sullivan said, nodding. "In an enclosed environment like that you were lucky there weren't more casualties. Either of you see what happened?"

Mari shook his head. "We were upstairs. We'd just come from the basement. There was nothing burning then. It would have been pretty obvious." He coughed and reached for his mask again, sinking back down on the pillows.

"How many people were down there when you came

out the first time?" the fire officer asked, making notes in a pocket book.

"Seven or eight, maybe," Jake croaked. "Have you spoken with Colm Fleming? He was down there when the fire started." Jake didn't mention that they had been chasing after him when they'd gone back down the second time and Mari didn't remind him.

"We're still waiting for Mr. Fleming to regain consciousness," Sullivan said with a nod. "You probably saved his life though, so he owes you a drink...quite a few drinks, I reckon. How long would you say it was between you coming back up from the cellar and the fire starting?"

Mari looked at Jake, trying to remember through the haze. "Um...about, three, four minutes, perhaps? We were at the bar, trying to get a drink. No more than four minutes."

"Have you determined the cause of the fire yet?" Jake asked him. "I don't remember seeing any candles, no open flames. Have they tested for accelerants yet?"

"Our accident investigators are still down there and the police have SOCO all over the place," Sullivan said. "They can't find any trace of flammables, no gas leaks, no combustible substances beyond lubricants and condoms. The amounts don't account for the ferocity of that blaze. So what we are trying to figure out is, what the hell created a localized inferno like that, in the space of what...? Four minutes, tops?" He looked at Mari, who nodded his affirmation of the time scale. "Are you sure there was nothing else?"

Mari looked at Jake again, for once lost for words. He could still visualize the density of the smoke and feel the cloying stink in the back of his throat.

"He was the accelerant, the dead man," Jake said quietly. "He was burning when we went back down there. I could smell it, like charred meat. He was well alight."

"Nothing else in the room was touched," Sullivan clarified, with a nod. "The other man that died was killed by smoke inhalation. No marks on him."

"It was blinding," Jake agreed, shaking his head once or twice. "You couldn't see a thing. I was lucky to find Colm before it was too late for him."

"Someone was stuck down there. Fuck! I thought... I guess I just thought those who could run for it did." Mari felt rather sick as it began to sink in, just what a narrow escape they'd had. If he'd gone for Colm's suggestion... If he'd let the man tether him...

Mari steered his thoughts away from that idea. Sullivan made another note.

"We spoke to the licensee and he said that you left the bar with him, then went back, Mr. Gale."

"Dr. Gale," Mari corrected him absently.

"Well, Dr. Gale, you're a very lucky man. I hope you've learned enough to stay out of a building when you can see that there's a fire in progress." Sullivan directed a look his way that made Mari feel about five years old.

"I went back for Jake," he protested. "He's... We're... together."

"Yes, so I gathered," Sullivan said, bland tone matching his bland expression, which were both to be expected right before someone said something like 'to each their own'. "I think that's all the questions I have for now. Thank you for your time, Dr. Gale, Mr. Chivis." Sullivan gave them each a nod and took his leave.

They were both silent for a few moments after he had gone. Jake removed his mask at last and cracked a smile.

"So, we're together?"

He might have been teasing. It was hard to tell, given his hoarse voice. They had never sat down and discussed the terms of their relationship, beyond the fact that they were seeing each other pretty regularly.

Mari shrugged one shoulder then winced. He ached everywhere and not in a good way.

"What would you call it?" he demanded. "I screw you nearly every day."

He flopped back against the pillows, reaching for the

oxygen mask, and took another good gulp of air before turning his head to look at Jake again. "I thought you were going to die in there. I thought we both were."

Jake didn't say anything, he just gazed at him until Mari started to feel nervous, then he pushed himself upright and swung his legs over the side of the bed.

"Should you be getting up?" Mari asked, figuring Jake had to be feeling as rough as he did, if not worse.

Jake didn't answer. He just took the two steps separating their beds and nudged Mari.

"What are you doing?"

"Scoot over," Jake said, nudging him again until Mari made room and Jake slid down beside him, putting his arm around him and snuggling up close.

"You should be using your oxygen," Mari scolded.

"Share yours," Jake told him, making no move to go back to his own bed.

Mari took the mask off, put it over Jake's face for a moment, then his own. "This is ridiculous."

"You told Colm I was your boyfriend," Jake said, nuzzling Mari's shoulder.

He was amused. "Do you have a problem with that, Chivis?"

Jake kissed the back of his neck. "No. No, I don't. Not at all. I kinda liked it."

"Well, then." Mari inhaled a long slow breath and handed the mask over again. "We go out together. We stay in together. We go to bed together, quite a lot. I'd call that boyfriend stuff. You even offered to give me a good spanking. Well above and beyond casual acquaintance, I reckon." He managed a hoarse chuckle and settled down in the curl of Jake's warm, strong, comforting body, liking the closeness of his broad chest, firm belly and thighs against his back and legs.

"Running back into a building fire to come and get me. I'd say that's boyfriend stuff," Jake said. "And I'll be more than happy to deliver that spanking, when we're both up to it, for not staying out."

"Ooh…macho mucho!" Mari snickered, high on oxygen and Jake. "Some Arson Investigator you are. Isn't the first rule of fire safety meant to be get out, stay out, call the fire blokes out? And don't tell me you are the fire bloke. Not valid. And…it's a good job I did come back for you. You'd never have got back up the stairs with him on your own." He held his hand up for the mask again, coughing drily.

Jake placed the ventilator over his face with a gentle hand.

"They will probably want to keep us here at least a day," he told Mari. "Smoke inhalation damage can range from asymptomatic to mild coughing the first few days, it's after that that there's danger from infection."

Mari cupped his hand over Jake's, holding it there, covering his face for a while and leaning his head back against his shoulder. He closed his eyes and murmured incoherently into the mask.

"What was that?" Jake whispered in his ear.

Mari let him move the mask half an inch and repeated it.

"They said romance was dead."

Jake kissed his temple and put the mask back over his nose and mouth. "Well, apart from being in bed with you, the night certainly didn't end up how I planned. Do you think you should call your mom, or just wait until we get out?"

Mari tucked a fingertip under the lip of the breathing apparatus, shifting it enough that he could turn his head to kiss Jake's lips. "She knows I'm spending the night at yours. I think she'll be asleep, though I have no idea what time it is, or what they did with my phone, actually. I'll ring her later. And I don't think I can move. I feel…floaty. Hold me."

"I am holding you," Jake said with a soft, sleepy-sounding chuckle. He wrapped his arm around him tighter though, and made him put the oxygen mask back over his face. "Relax, Ilmari, I've got you."

They both drowsed for a while like that, snuggled close

together. Sometime later their nurse returned and made tutting noises. He didn't chase Jake back to his own bed but he did bring the other oxygen tank over so that they weren't reliant on just the one. After that, they both slept more deeply.

Chapter Three

After a night of observation and oxygen, Jake and Mari were both checked over by the attending physician and pronounced well enough to leave, with the stipulation that they follow up with their own doctors in a couple of days. Mari called his mother, as soon as he was reunited with his cell phone, to explain their unfortunate misadventure and spent the next twenty minutes convincing her that he was fine and would be home shortly.

"She wants to speak to you," Mari said at last, handing his cell over.

Before Jake could even say hello, Annabel Gale's voice in his ear was saying, "You should come back with Mari and stay for a few days. I don't think you should be all alone while you recover from smoke inhalation. It could be dangerous. I can look after you both."

"That's very kind of you, Anni, but really…"

"Now don't go getting pigheaded on me, Jake. We've plenty of room for you and I'd feel much better having you here."

"Um, well, thank you…"

"Good. I'll see you soon."

Jake handed Mari's phone back once she had rung off.

"According to your mother, I am to stop being 'pigheaded' and return with you posthaste," Jake told him, trying not to chuckle, as it tended to set off a coughing fit.

"That's you told, then," Mari said with a clever smirk that told Jake he'd been expecting nothing less. "She has a point, though. Your place is going to reek of smoke, and worse, for days. You should give it a while to settle down, and we have bags of space."

He was being practical but Jake could see from the look in his eye that he wasn't entirely displeased by the situation.

"Speaking of which, I need to stop and get some clean clothes. I don't know if what we were wearing is even salvageable," he told Mari, looking dubiously at the plastic bags containing said garments. At least they had been given scrubs to wear, which were better than those backless gowns.

"Jake?"

He turned his head to look at Mari, thinking that was probably the most hesitant he'd ever sounded and, as such, it instantly got his attention.

"Don't you think you should possibly call your family to let them know you're all right? I mean, it's not likely anyone over there is going to hear about a fire over here, but if they did, they might be worried." Mari was studying him with concern in his pale, beautiful eyes. It was that luminous gaze that had entranced him when they'd first met and he was almost swayed by it.

"That's...probably not a good idea," Jake said, at last. "Do you want me to call for a cab?"

He felt bad for so obviously avoiding the subject but he was definitely not in the mood to explain his family to Mari, who looked as if he wanted to interrogate him further but something—possibly the darkening expression on Jake's face—was holding his tongue in check. That was unusual, in itself.

"I'll sort the cab," was all he said, though, and they finished dressing in relative silence.

* * * *

As the taxi pulled up outside Jake's block, the only thing to show that it was the scene of an ongoing incident was the blue and white police tape across the door of the bar and the lingering smell of acrid smoke. As Jake reached for the door handle of the cab, a familiar figure in a dark, three-quarter-length wool coat turned away from the door leading up to his apartment and Mari murmured, "It would appear that you have a stalker."

"Sit tight, I'll be right back," Jake told him, and got out.

Detective Inspector John Cordiline was attached to the Albany Street police station and this was not their first encounter. Cordiline had headed up an investigation into the death of Phil Weston, the younger brother of Jake and Mari's handler at University College London, a few months earlier. The DI cut an attractive figure. He was in his mid-forties, still quite lean, his dark hair neatly trimmed and beginning to turn gray at the temples. He made eye contact with Jake right away, his stormy blue glare sharp and inquisitive as ever.

"Chivis, I was hoping to catch you at the hospital but they said you'd been discharged. Do you have a few minutes to talk about what happened last night?"

"Can you ask while I pack? I came to get a few things but I'm not staying."

"Sure. Understandable, given the circumstances." Cordiline stood by as Jake found his keys and let himself in. The smell of smoke and char was stronger on the stairs but not as bad once they were up in his apartment. Jake turned on the ventilation fan as Cordiline wandered around his tiny kitchenette. "You have somewhere to stay while they sort this out?"

"Why, are you offering up your place?" Jake leaned against the archway into the bedroom and smirked.

The inspector treated him to another penetrating stare. Jake was pretty sure neither of them had forgotten that last time they'd been together in this room, Cordiline had come on to him pretty strong, and Jake had turned him down flat. The question was a joke but he didn't intend it as a cruel one.

"I think there might be a conflict of interests if I were to do that. But there are places a guy can stay if he needs them."

Cordiline shrugged the question off. "In any case, I came to ask you what you remembered about the fire. I heard you already spoke to the Fire Service, but humor me."

"Mari and I were in the bar area when the fire started. We'd been down in the basement about five minutes before, there was nothing down there that I remember seeing that looked like a fire hazard," Jake said, sticking to hard facts.

"You said in your statement to the Fire Superintendent that you saw the victim coming down the stairs into the basement area." Cordiline checked his notes. "Did you touch him at all?"

That was a more tentative question. Cordiline knew what the Fire Chief hadn't, that Jake was able to retrieve memories from contact with people and objects. It had formed the basis for evidence in a recent murder inquiry, though that part hadn't made the papers.

"No. I try not to touch other people when I go out," Jake replied. "The only reason I remembered seeing him at all is because of the expression on his face. He didn't look like your average barfly out for a night of fun. He looked… stressed. That's the best way I can put it. Like, he was really worried about something."

Cordiline made another note in his book then raised shrewd eyes to Jake's. "I wouldn't have said that was your scene. BDSM, I mean. People surprise me endlessly. How do you go on with not touching in a situation like…like that?"

Did he look embarrassed? Jake thought maybe he did, fleetingly, then it was gone and he was studying his notebook again.

Jake wasn't sure if he should feel amused or insulted by the careful way Cordiline was trying to sound nonjudgmental while still judging like all hell.

"It isn't 'my scene'. I'd given the bartender a hand earlier in the day and he invited me to stop in. It was the first time I'd gone there. As for the not touching part, I'm not exactly into public sex, so it wasn't like it was a struggle to keep from groping people."

The detective flicked a glance at him, his expression stoic. Jake figured his tone said clear enough to 'mind your own fucking business', and surprisingly he did.

"So you'd never seen the victim before last night?" Cordiline asked.

"No."

"Did he say anything, that you recall?" Cordiline asked. "SOCO are still trying to identify him."

Jake started to shrug then stopped, trying to remember if he'd heard him say anything or not. "I don't think so. It was loud, there were a lot of people. I don't want to tell you I heard him say something that I might have misheard."

"You think you did hear him speak, then?" Cordiline pressed.

"I can't remember exactly. He did say something to one of the guys down there that was...uh...giving out paddlings. Something like, 'I need to talk to you', or 'I need your help'."

"Do you recall seeing the guy he spoke to get out?" Cordiline was writing again and he didn't look up.

"Hell, I don't know, John. It was a fucking cattle stampede once people saw the smoke. There were people running everywhere. The only reason I went back down was to make sure everyone got out, but by then, the smoke was so thick I couldn't see my hand in front of my face."

"You went back down on your own?" Cordiline scribbled furiously. "Was Dr. Gale with you or did he stay upstairs?"

"He came down afterward," Jake said.

"Would he have seen the guy leave?"

"Maybe." Jake said. "Why don't you ask him?"

"I will." Cordiline looked up at him with a grim smile. "I should let you pack. Don't take any long holidays. We might need to speak to you again. You seem to be making a habit of helping us with our inquiries."

"Yeah, well, I wish I hadn't been around to help you with this one. I could have done without spending the night in the hospital."

Cordiline started toward the door but turned back as if he'd thought of something else. "When you were with the Detroit PD, you were on their arson investigation unit, is that right?"

Jake arched an eyebrow at him. "Been doing your homework, I see. Yes, I was a detective in arson investigation before I left."

"Ever seen anything like this before?"

"Not like this, no," Jake answered. "The two main causes of arson are people that do it for kicks, and people that do it for insurance fraud. Those cases rarely have any bodies involved. When there is a body in an arson case it's almost always a perp trying to destroy evidence of homicide. This... it's like the guy was fine one minute and a blazing torch the next. It happened fast, in front of a lot of witnesses."

"What do you think of the theory of spont...?"

Jake held up his hand to stop him. "Don't say it. SHC isn't real. There is absolutely zero scientific proof. In almost all cases, there is a logical explanation, and in those few where there aren't, it only means that a reason couldn't be determined. There is no such thing as spontaneous human combustion."

Cordiline smiled at his vehemence but he nodded and closed the notebook. "That was my line of thinking, as well. But given that your...experience is outside the normal frame of police investigation, I was just wondering if you had a different take on it. No offense."

"None taken," Jake said, but he was irritated all the same. People without Elemental abilities had a tendency to presume that either he knew everything about every supernatural incident, or that it was some kind of sleight of hand and he was trying to con them. Cordiline was just covering the bases, but it was still annoying as hell.

"You take care. Smoke inhalation is a bitch. See your doctor, and I don't just mean the blond in your cab."

Jake almost missed the twinkle in the detective's eye as he turned away, but he was out of the door before Jake could call him on it. With a huff of impatience, he went to his bedroom, grabbed a bag and quickly stuffed a few necessities into it. He debated for just a moment whether to take the box of condoms sitting beside his bed. He figured sex wasn't likely while they were at Mari's place but he took them anyway, just in case. He grabbed a few toiletries from the bathroom and threw them in the bag as well, then locked up and headed back downstairs to the waiting cab.

Mari was quiet on the way to his house, watching the streets flick by through the window and he settled up with the driver before Jake could even reach for his wallet. They both heard the sound of barking and the click of hard canine toenails on the hall floor beyond the front door as he turned his key in the lock to let them in. Instinctively, Mari dipped to grab the collar around the neck of his mother's stocky brindle and white Staffordshire terrier and murmured a firm admonishment.

"No, Tonka. Stay. Back inside with you. I'll take you for a walk later."

Then they were inside and his mother was sweeping her arms around him, kissing his cheek. Jake recognized the concern in her eyes but she was all smiles as she fussed over her son, sniffing him and shaking her head at the smell of smoke on him, then welcoming Jake more effusively to her home.

"So glad you decided to come, Jake. It's horrible convalescing alone," she declared with the certainty of experience. "Come in and have some decent coffee. I bet they haven't fed you, have they?"

"No, ma'am. Coffee sounds wonderful," Jake said.

"Anni," she reminded him as she always did. "Ma'am makes me sound like the Queen!"

Mari released Tonka, who rushed over to sniff around Jake's ankles and knees excitedly. They had a pretty good relationship, he and the dog, but the barking and sniffing were part of the greeting ritual.

"Easy, mukwa, I haven't hurt anyone or pillaged the

house yet. You can trust me, remember?" He gave the dog an affectionate scratch between the ears and received a snort of acceptance. Tonka's version of a temporary pass of admittance, valid this visit only.

Dr. Gale Senior put coffee on to brew and eggs in a pan while Jake and Mari went to freshen up in the downstairs bathroom.

Mari undressed and shaved first, a towel wrapped loosely around his slim waist, while Jake got into the shower.

"I could get used to this," he observed over the sound of the water. "What was that, you called my dog?"

Jake turned and tipped his head back to rinse the shampoo out.

"Mukwa? It means bear," he said. "He's built like one."

Mari laughed at that. "He certainly is. If he was human, he'd be a proper bear, don't you think? He's totally the man of the house. If I was less secure, I'd have an inferiority complex."

A moment later, he squeezed into the shower cubicle. "Soap my back. It'll be quicker if we share."

Jake slid his arms around Mari, kissing him first. Their plans had not included fires and hospitals last night and he was immeasurably grateful that the disastrous date night was over, and had not ended far worse. When he broke the kiss, he reached for the shower gel on the shelf and palmed a good squeeze of it to soap Mari up.

His lover turned obligingly for him, not shy about showing off that long, lean, sport-toned body that had caught his eye the first time Jake had seen him running in Regent's Park. It was even more glorious in the flesh. Mari had a hard, sculpted frame that filled Jake's appreciative gaze and fit perfectly in his hands. His skin was a very pale gold, the last traces of a summer tan, faded by the chill of a London winter. A couple of fingers taller than Jake, he was slimmer in build, but they fit together very nicely. A dusting of mid-blond hair on his chest and thighs, and neatly trimmed in the V of his abdomen and crotch, alleviated the pale smoothness of his naked body. Wet from the shower, his shoulder-length, ashen mane was a few shades darker too.

"Mmhhhh…that feels good," he crooned as Jake's soapy hands moved slowly over his naked back and that pert, perky bottom.

Jake caressed Mari's hips and circled around to his front with his hands, leaning his chest into Mari's back as he slid his hands up the toned lines of his abdomen. He pressed his lips to the nape of Mari's neck.

"I'm so glad you're all right," he murmured in a rare serious moment. If Mari had been hurt last night, Jake wasn't sure how he would have lived with it.

Mari half-turned in his arms, an odd smile on his lips. He snatched another kiss.

"I'm indestructible, Chivis. You don't need to worry about me. I was more scared for you. When you collapsed at the top of the stairs I thought you were going to die." He wriggled around to fully face Jake, sliding his arms around his neck and pulling him in close. "I couldn't breathe, and it was nothing to do with the smoke. I don't think I've ever felt that way about a man before. You're a liability."

The glint of mischief in his eyes told Jake that last part was a joke.

Jake kissed down the wet column of Mari's throat and ran his hands over his sleek backside again. "Don't think I've forgotten about that spanking I owe you," he said, giving his left cheek a playful swat.

"Mmmhhh," Mari growled approvingly. His pale eyes darkened a few shades, the pupils swelling as he circled his hips against Jake's in response. The heavy silk of his cock brushed lightly on Jake's, stiffening at once. "I'm not going to let you forget. Don't you worry."

Jake chuckled. "It looks like I've hit your On button, and here I was already thinking I'd found it. It's going to be hard, waiting to get you alone."

Mari leaned in close and kissed his neck, his breath a warm breeze on Jake's wet skin. "Oh, I'm sure we can find lots of ways to be alone," he promised in a sultry whisper.

"You want me to turn you over my knee and spank you in your mother's house? You are so kinky," Jake teased.

"Not kinky, just incredibly frustrated." Mari chuckled. "I want you so bad, Chivis. Having you in arm's reach and having to behave is going to be a serious test of my resolve." He stroked his fingers through Jake's chest hair, his expression still very pouty and irresistible.

"Okay, you keep saying things like that and breakfast is going to be exceedingly late, and embarrassing." Jake gave Mari's bottom a squeeze and kissed him again, then deliberately put an inch or two of space between them.

As if on cue, Mari's mother called from the hallway. "Are you two hungry yet?"

"Ravenous!" Mari shouted back, then giggled and tapped Jake on the nose, reaching past him to turn off the water. "Three minutes!"

"Make it five and we might have time," Jake whispered in Mari's ear, earning him another quelling look that would have been far more effective if there wasn't so much answering heat in Mari's expression. He heaved a dramatic sigh when Mari stepped out of the shower.

"You are so naughty, Chivis," Mari crooned. He toweled himself down vigorously then gave Jake a light swat with the towel and tossed it over to him while he wriggled into his robe. "Five whole minutes. Mmmhhh!" He finger-combed his wet hair in the mirror and ignored the look that comment earned him. "When my mama has her afternoon nap, I am going to bang your oh so clever brains out, Detective."

He left Jake with more than a hint of frustration and anticipation at that remark and closed the bathroom door behind him. Jake debated turning the cold tap on and jumping back in the shower for a moment, but it was bound to only freeze his hide and do nothing to ease the horniness.

When he had finally calmed himself enough to slide into a pair of jeans and a sweater, he joined Mari and Anni in the long, open kitchen-cum-day room at the back of the house, a lovely bright space that looked out over their handkerchief square of garden. As there wasn't even a yard behind the block where he currently lived, Jake was coming to appreciate the rarity of such a private green space in the heart of the city.

Mari had donned a pair of baggy cream sweatpants and a mushroom-colored jersey that fit snugly to his body while Jake had been dressing and controlling his desires. He was buttering toast industriously at the kitchen counter, as his mother sipped her coffee in her favorite chair and watched Tonka roaming around the garden through the French windows.

The TV was playing very quietly in the background, a loop of news broadcasts mostly, which Annabel and Mari were ignoring. She sat with her feet up on a padded stool and had a laptop open on her knees. Occasionally she glanced down and tapped the keys. Mari had told him, before she got ill, Anni had worked in Africa with *Médecins Sans Frontières* and she still handled promotional work for the organization, though Mari said she found it tedious in the extreme after a life on the frontline of medicare. Jake did not have to imagine. His desk job at the university was not uninteresting but compared to the streets of Detroit, it was a pale shade of work. He could never figure out how it paid so much more.

"Have some toast," Mari said, with his mouth full, pushing the plate of buttery squares toward him. "And eggs… So good. She makes the best scrambled eggs."

They certainly looked good. Buttery and fluffy-light, spiced up with a crack of black pepper and a hint of oregano. Mari spooned some over the toast, as Anni told him off for talking with food in his mouth. He pulled a face at her and, without looking up from her screen, she said, "You'll stick like that, one day."

Jake smiled at their personal rituals. He knew she didn't baby Mari, just as she understood that their banter didn't embarrass him. Mari was right. The eggs were incredible and filled the growling hole in his belly that was reminding him how long he had gone without food. They had been planning to eat at the club last night, but that had fallen by the wayside and he was ravenous. When they had eaten their fill, Mari towed him over to the long, comfortable sofa and they curled up there with their coffee, glad of the stillness and normality after everything that had happened last night.

Anni glanced over her laptop at them, assessing them in silence. She was her son in feminine form, Jake noted, a few inches shorter, her loose blonde chignon lightened with silver around the edges of her face, but those bottomless blue eyes were his and so was the set of her mouth as she surveyed them both.

"Are you feeling okay? No queasiness? Breathing all right?" she quizzed him.

"I'm fine, Mama, don't fuss," Mari dismissed her.

Jake nodded. He was tired, having not gotten much sleep, even after he'd laid down in Mari's bed last night, but his breathing felt easier today and his throat was less raw.

"We'll be okay, I think," he said. "The MD at the hospital just said to get some rest. He gave me a note for work."

"Well, he had that much sense, at least," Annabel huffed and returned to her screen.

For a while, the only sounds were the *tap tap tap* of her fingers on the keys, the muted voice of the newsreader and the lazy birdsong from the garden. Mari leaned back on Jake and pulled his arms around him as if he was a cozy sweater. His slim, cool hands covered Jake's larger, warmer ones and he closed his eyes for a while, a gentle smile playing on his lips. Lightly his fingertips traced invisible patterns on Jake's arms and hands and he heaved a quiet sigh of contentment.

The stillness was unbroken until his mother reached for the TV remote on the arm of her chair and turned up the volume a notch, murmuring, "I think that's you, again."

They both sat up straighter, twisting about to look at the screen which showed a familiar, smoke-wreathed, early morning street, cordoned off with police tape and a cold and brassed-off looking female reporter, quite evidently far from overjoyed to be spending Saturday morning covering the aftermath of an inconclusive arson attack.

"Police have not yet ruled out the possibility of a terrorist attack but no threats have been received," she was saying atonally. "Investigators have still to establish a connection between last night's fatal fire and the death of a young woman, now identified as Milda Kilis, outside the Lithuanian Embassy, on Thursday afternoon."

"That's what got my cab driver's panties in a knot yesterday," Mari said. "Traffic got held up and he said someone had set fire to herself on the street. Weird."

"You mean you've been at the scene of two mysterious fire deaths in the space of twenty-four hours? Should we be worried, Ilmarinen?" Annabel teased.

"Shut up!" he exhaled with a shake of his head. "Like the cabbie said, this kind of thing's going on all the time, I'm sure. They're only reporting it because they happened so close to one another. They'll find out it's a protest or something, eventually."

"What's the point of a protest if no one knows what they were protesting about?" Jake asked, more to wind him up than anything else.

"Is it my fault they're rubbish at protesting?" Mari said airily.

"Where did you go on Thursday?" Jake inquired, curious because he knew that Mari was not working at the moment, though he wasn't sure if he'd told his mother about this.

"Just an interview," Mari said evasively. "Some government department wants decent coders in a hurry."

"Did you hear back from them yet, Ilmari?" Anni asked him in a fond tone that answered Jake's unspoken question.

"No. Not yet," he said, then uncurled himself and reached for the remote. "Can we watch *Countdown*? This is depressing."

Jake studied Mari rather more intently, but for once there wasn't anything sexual in the look. He wondered if Mari knew how he twitched his shoulder blades when he was nervous, or how he spoke even faster than normal when he was trying to change the subject. Probably not. What he didn't understand was why Mari didn't want him to know about the interview.

Mari changed the channel and Jake filed the question away for later. After a few minutes, when it seemed everyone had moved on from the conversation, Jake asked Mari, "What makes you think they set themselves on fire and someone didn't do it to them?"

Mari made a dismissive sound, his head still tilted to watch the screen. "If someone had set the guy in the basement on fire we'd have heard about it. Like your friend Fireman Sam said, it would have taken some serious effort to make him burn like that. You don't drop a match on yourself and go up like the space shuttle, do you?"

"We weren't down there when he went up. We didn't see it. All we have to go on is what Colm and the others said happened," Jake pointed out.

"So you think they all lied about it? That would be one hell of a conspiracy, don't you think? Isn't that a bit paranoid?"

"I'm a cop, Mari. We're trained not to believe anyone and be paranoid about everything. Besides, witnesses are more unreliable than most people think. They convince themselves of what they saw and, sometimes, it's not what really went down."

"Your stalker thinks we know more about what's going on than we're saying. He was eager enough to question you the moment he could," Mari told him, his tone cooling.

"So you're not allowed to have a night out, are you? What's the world coming to?" Anni chuckled, reminding them both that she was still eavesdropping.

"It was kind of a special night, not your standard 'get blasted and fall over in the gutter' clubbers, Mama," Mari said, unfazed.

"Ah...fetish stuff," she said with a knowing nod. "Flammable? PVC and things?"

"Not that flammable, Mama." Mari twisted about, propping his chin on the back of the sofa to pretend interest in the TV. "Idiot."

Jake blinked at him but Annabel merely adjusted her spectacles to frown at the larger screen on the kitchen wall.

"Toiled. Six letters," she said, returning her attention to her work, and Jake relaxed as he realized they were just playing along with the quiz show. He leaned closer so his lips were just above Mari's ear.

"He's not my 'stalker'," he whispered. "I'm a former arson investigator and an Elemental that uses psychometry. His interest was purely professional."

Mari curled back around him so that he could touch his lips to Jake's cheek and still keep a sidelong eye on the game.

"He went to the trouble of finding out you were there, and who you were with and, of all the people there, he came to you first. He's probably jealous. Probably thinks I lured you into a fetish club and endangered your life. Or maybe that I somehow set the fire myself."

Jake struggled not to break into an amused grin.

"He's the jealous one, huh?" There was no fighting the chuckle that wanted out at Mari's disdainful look. "He doesn't think we torched the place. Although maybe he wants you to think he believes that, to get a rise out of you."

"And why would he want to do that, I wonder?" Mari squirmed around completely and rested his folded arms along the back of the sofa, still watching the screen.

"I don't know. Maybe he thinks you're cute when you're bristling possessively," Jake prodded.

Mari pursed his lips for a moment, not looking at him. "Dildo?"

"Lidded!" his mother said, rather more firmly.

"Sorry...the temptation was too great."

Mari turned his head again and his expression mellowed as he studied Jake. "Cute, huh?"

"He only has eyes for you, child," Anni pointed out. "I can see it, I'm sure anyone else can see it. Jake, am I wrong?"

"Considering that Cordiline didn't invite me back to his when I said I wasn't staying at the apartment, I'd say he got the message that I'm only interested in seeing one person," Jake answered.

Anni turned her head to look a question at her son. "Enough?"

"He's here, Mama, not there." Mari slid back down onto the sofa cushions and slid his arms around Jake to kiss his nose.

His mother smiled and snorted softly. "Take him upstairs, for goodness sake!"

Jake pressed his lips together, trying not to laugh.

Chapter Four

Jake woke the next morning with Mari snuggled around him. When he stirred, Mari moved with him and he felt those plush lips brushing his collarbone, sucking lightly on the skin of his torso at the top of his sternum. Mari's hair was silky where it trickled over his chest as he kissed lower, rolling him onto his back and lipping at the softer skin of his belly.

"This feels so good," Mari said, voice still deep and husky from the smoke. "You and me, here. You're so warm."

Jake combed gentle fingers through Mari's hair.

"Are you trying to spoil me? It's totally working if you are," he murmured back.

"I'm glad." Mari touched his lips to the indent of Jake's navel then ran the tip of his tongue around the rim of it. "This is my favorite place."

Jake wasn't sure if Mari meant in bed or was talking about his belly button so he didn't argue.

"I'm in my favorite place with one of my favorite people and just for these few lovely moments, everything is perfect," Mari whispered, his words flowing like a summer breeze over Jake's stomach, making the muscles of his abdomen clench in anticipation. His cock was already half hard, always an early riser. Mari initially skirted it, kissing down into the hollows of his hips and nuzzling into his groin. When those warm, soft lips began to draw gently on the loose skin around his balls, Jake spread his legs wider, accommodating him.

Reflex made him tighten his fingers in Mari's hair but he didn't pull or push his head down, letting him take things at his own pace. Jake bent one knee to give him some more room between his legs and when Mari drew one ball into his mouth, Jake sucked in a breath then let it out again, shuddering with eagerness.

"Mmm...you do give the most pleasant wake-up calls."

"I'm a man of many talents," Mari agreed in a husky tone. He applied his lips to the neglected nut, crooning his enthusiasm around it before letting it slip from his mouth again. "You have the tastiest nuts, Detective Chivis. I do enjoy eating them."

Jake chuckled as Mari trailed the tip of his wet tongue slowly back up the underside of his cock, wrapping his fingers around the swollen shaft and stroking back the loose furls of foreskin to roll his exploring tongue around the exposed glans. Finally, he sucked the whole crown into his mouth and worked his lips back and forth over it, letting it pop free with a smirk.

"Oh, baby..." Jake exhaled. "You can do that again and again, if you want." He rolled his hips upward, nudging against Mari's lips.

"Mmmhh. I want!" Mari sighed, his breath spilling heat over the wetness of Jake's sensitive cock. He engulfed it in his mouth again, nodding down deeper this time. His hands moved like ghosts over Jake's hips and thighs, fingers snaking through the dark hair of his upper legs and over his groin, before plunging back into the thicker tangle around the base of his cock and sucking him in as far as he could. A quiver of tension rolled through him, under Jake's fingers, as the head of Jake's cock butted up against Mari's throat.

"That's amazing."

Mari made a sing-song sound that could have been 'I know', and carried on nodding his head slowly, sucking on him while his fingers stroked and caressed all over. His eyes were half-closed, still sleepy, long lashes shimmering gold in the light from the streetlamp outside the window.

Jake sunk both hands into his warm, pale hair and chewed

on his lips to stifle a groan as Mari swirled his tongue around the head of his dick. Jake was of the opinion that almost all oral sex was good but he had to admit, Mari did it better than any lover he'd had before. As the wonderful sensations he was creating started to build, Jake had a fleeting thought of asking Mari to move around so they could suck each other off, but it felt so good he couldn't quite summon the willpower to ask him to stop for even a minute to do that. He would definitely make it up to him, he promised himself, as he let Mari bring him right up to the brink then, trembling and gasping, over the edge.

Mari never flinched, even for a moment, as Jake reached his peak in his mouth. That was something else his lover adored about him. He just kept on sucking and swallowing in perfect rhythm, taking everything that Jake had to offer, stroking and soothing him as he came down from that morning high. Only when Jake finally subsided onto the mattress, did he lift his head and slowly lick his lips.

"Well...that's breakfast sorted out," he murmured, wiping his mouth on the back of his hand.

Jake chuckled, still catching his breath, and pulled Mari up beside him, rolling him so he could kiss him long and hard. He stroked his hand down Mari's flat belly and caressed the swollen length of his cock.

"I do believe there may be a second course," he murmured against his lips.

"At least one." Mari chuckled, catching his breath. "I think I could get used to waking up like this."

That was the second or third time Mari had said something similar and Jake had let the others slip by because he wasn't sure if Mari was just enjoying his company or if he was seriously trying to hint at something. Even if he was hinting, Jake wasn't sure where he might be going. Mari had obligations, and they'd only been seeing each other a few months.

Jake moved his hand under the nape of Mari's neck and spread his fingers at the base of his skull, cradling it, and he kissed him again, a slow, sensual kiss that was in no rush, growing in heat and intensity until they broke at the same time, wide-eyed and breathless.

"Your mother was right. I only have eyes for you. We could make this a more permanent thing, get a place together eventually, if you wanted... I love you, Mari."

Those blue eyes looked up at him for a moment too long, intrigued and unblinking. Mari's hands were still easing up and down his biceps and he was twined around Jake, rubbing the soles of his feet along the backs of his legs, pushing himself against Jake's belly.

"You are funny, sometimes, you know," he replied at last in a husky whisper, trailing his fingers around the back of Jake's neck and pulling him down to kiss him again, letting his lips linger over the contact and slithering full length against him. As their lips parted, he sighed. "Don't tease me. It's not fair."

Jake gently tugged his hair until his head tipped back and kissed all along the rapid pulse point at the side of his throat. His other hand curled around Mari's shaft and stroked him slower.

"I'm not teasing you, Ilmari," he murmured, moving his lips up to just behind Mari's ear. "I've been in love with you for quite a while."

Mari tipped his chin forward into his chest to look at him, his face very serious.

"I don't get how you can know that so soon. I mean...yes, I saved your life. I get it that you're grateful and everything. Should I put this down to the smoke or something?"

For several long moments, Jake searched Mari's eyes and, at last, just shook his head ruefully, kissing him again. That was not the reaction that he had hoped for, but Mari was under no obligation to feel the same way. That was always part of the risk of saying it first, he guessed. He had to accept that Mari wasn't ready to say it back. The hard part would come if he never was.

Mari didn't look away at least. As Jake gazed at him,

Mari worried at his lips, mirroring his shake of the head as if he was trying to work Jake out, like he was a puzzle or something.

"You know…when you turned around that day in the park," Mari murmured at last. "I… I kind of didn't really think that you would. It's always a gamble. But I hoped you would. And…maybe I thought that the trade-off for getting you to turn around would be that you turned out to be a complete arsehole. But you…you totally aren't." He added the last few words quickly, like he was keen not to be misunderstood. "You are…the complete opposite of an arsehole. And you are so brave. I really… I just can't say if I'm ready to let someone be in love with me, Jake."

Jake's chuckle sounded strained to his own ears. "You can't tell me how to feel, Mari, any more than I can tell you. I'm sorry, I shouldn't have said anything. It wasn't meant to try and push you." He let his fingers walk through Mari's hair, hoping he hadn't just screwed things up beyond repair.

Mari quickly turned his head to kiss Jake's hand. "You can't push me, Jake Chivis. I don't get pushed around. And I should love you for that, for being so upfront with me. So maybe if someone ought to be sorry then I should."

Jake rarely regretted his words but he wished he could go back and eat them. Not so much because it hurt that Mari didn't return the sentiment, although it did, but because he could have picked a better time and not just let it slip out like it had. He supposed he'd misconstrued all those wistful sighs and hints, thinking that maybe Mari wanted more of his time. What Jake really wanted to do was get up, make some lame excuse about how he needed to get back home, and go lick his wounds until he could face Mari again. But that was rather immature and cowardly.

"Don't worry about it, Mari. Okay?" He kissed his cheek and the corner of his mouth, trying to coax him back into a warmer mood.

"Sshhh… I'm supposed to be the one that thinks too much, remember?" Mari tilted his head, responding to the kiss. "I love waking up beside you. Don't rush things, Jake." He touched the tip of his nose to Jake's softly. "Unless, of course, you want to keep on touching me like you were. Which was really, really nice, I have to say." He wriggled against Jake again.

Jake smiled, relieved for the excuse to forget he'd ever opened his mouth and make Mari forget as well. He made sure he returned every lick and kiss and stroke and suck of his mouth on Mari's eager body. The sounds that he conjured from Mari's throat were a balm to his ego and so was the way Mari came in Jake's mouth, his head twisted to one side to press his face into the pillows, and even they didn't entirely smother the shuddering cry of ecstasy that escaped him. Mari sprawled under him, panting, for about a minute, then making purring sounds as he got his breath back and stroked his fingers through Jake's hair.

* * * *

After crawling out of bed, Jake made an excuse about having forgotten to grab his laptop and, passing on the offer of breakfast, headed home. He didn't think Mari was convinced about his motive but he still kissed Jake goodbye in the hall before he dashed off. Really he just wanted a few minutes alone, but as he was unlocking the front door to his apartment block, his cell phone rang and a look at the caller ID told him it was DI Cordiline. Jake debated just letting it go to voicemail. He really wasn't in the mood to play twenty questions again, but he knew he would have to deal with whatever Cordiline wanted sooner or later.

"Hello."

"Hi… Chivis, I caught you. I did ring earlier. Do you have time to talk or are you…busy?"

"What do you need?"

"Something's come up, relating to the bar fire," the inspector said, an edge to his voice that said he was irritated. "I'd rather not talk on the phone, if you don't mind. Can you meet me at the usual pub in about half an hour?"

Jake hesitated for half a second. It really wasn't his problem, whatever the issue was, but at last he said, "Yeah. I'll meet you." And hung up.

* * * *

"Jake isn't staying for breakfast?" Annabel looked a question at Mari as he ambled into the dayroom from the hall.

"Obviously." Mari rolled his eyes and snagged the coffee mug she held out for him en route to the sofa. He sagged down there and inhaled the scent of caffeine gratefully.

"What did you do?" She sat in the chair opposite, blowing the steam off the surface of her drink.

"Why is it always something that I did? He just wanted to go get his laptop. All right?" Mari sipped his coffee and winced as it burned down. "I don't own him, Mama."

"He seems to me like he wouldn't mind if you did." Anni smiled at him tolerantly. "He's good for you. Not like that last one. He likes you for who you are, not what he can make you be. Can you blame me if I worry about you chasing him off?"

"Don't." Mari curled up on the sofa, one arm around his knees, the other cupping the mug to his chin. "I'm not ready for another relationship, Mama. Yes, I like him, but don't make this into something it can't be."

"I'm just saying." She sighed and picked up the newspaper from the occasional table by her chair.

"Yes, well, don't. You don't know anything about him, or what he would or wouldn't mind. Neither do I, yet, for that matter. And there's too much that he doesn't understand about me, stuff that I'm not ready to tell him, so...leave it. Please." He couldn't look at her and closed his eyes, wishing that the sofa would just swallow him.

He had screwed things up big time this morning. Jake had been so sweet about it but there was no denying, he had hurt him and there was nothing he could do, bar lying to him, that would make things right. And Jake deserved better than that.

The worst part of it was, he already knew that this connection he had with Jake Chivis was the best he'd ever had. Just thinking about Jake made him smile, and being with him left him all a tingle from the pleasure of being adored with such passion. And maybe that was what caused him so much grief.

Tomas, his ex, had been fond of pointing out that he was a classic, tragic heroine – a femme fatale with balls, to put it in Tomas Arregui's blunt vernacular. Mari had fought against that image since returning to England. Tomas had wanted eye candy, a pretty thing to adorn his arm and suck his dick, and Mari had played along, wanting to please him, thinking that Tomas was 'the one' when he was nothing of the sort. He had been an innocent in Barcelona, but that experience had forced him to grow up. He no longer wanted to play games.

Jake was more of a gentleman than Tomas would ever be. Mari already knew that if Jake should ever be as unkind to him as Tomas had been, then it would be his own fault entirely. He had tested Jake's patience so very much in the short time they had been dating and Jake had been unfailingly chivalrous about all his anxieties and issues. Still, there was an imp of the perverse in Mari that loved to poke him with the horrible idea that Jake would not wait forever. He needed to be honest with his Dark Knight or run the risk of losing him.

But if he *was* truly honest, would he still lose Jake? That was the big fear. Would the reality of who and what Mari Gale was send the first man he had ever really cared for running for the hills?

As one hour rolled into two and Jake still hadn't returned, Mari was beginning to think that he'd more than just screwed things up. To top it off, his mother kept casting glances his way as she worked on her laptop through the morning, although mercifully she didn't say anything. At last, come lunch time, she closed her machine down and looked at him more seriously.

"Did you two have a fight?" she asked him.

"No." He was sprawled on the sofa with his tablet in one hand, the other tapping his knee as he pretended to read, even though he couldn't make his brain focus on the words. "Why would we do that?"

"You tell me," she flashed back.

"We didn't fight."

"Well, if you didn't have words, why is he gone and you've been moping all day looking like a kicked puppy?"

"I am not moping." Mari poked at the screen of his tab irritably. "I'm doing research."

"Right!" She chuckled.

"Research. Into the reasons why people might burst into flames, without any rational explanation. Work," he pointed out. "And he wanted his laptop."

"While you're doing research on that, you might also want to research how to be a better poker player. You can't fool your mama, Mari." She looked disappointed. "I thought you liked Jake. Is it really not working out then?"

Mari ground his teeth silently then shut down his tablet and knocked back the last of his fourth cup of coffee. He swung himself off the sofa. "I'm going out. Tonka needs a walk. I'll be back in a while."

* * * *

Cordiline beat Jake to the pub and was seated by the same table, at the back, where they had met a couple of times before when discussing the Weston case. Jake ordered a pint of lager-shandy, although it was too early, in his opinion, for any amount of alcohol, and he probably shouldn't start drinking in his current mood. Cordiline didn't look like he was in the frame of mind where he should be drinking either. The detective's face was set in hard lines, a grim scowl making him look his age for a change. Though lean, he was big enough and his unblinking glare mean enough to give most civilians pause before tackling him, but at the moment he looked so brassed off that just about everyone was giving him a wide berth.

"Who pissed in your Cheerios?" Jake inquired.

Cordiline waved him into the seat opposite and took a pull on the pint in front of him. "I got a visit this morning. Some suits from on high. Didn't waste any breath on formalities, they just bumped me off this case. Can you think of any good reason why MI5 would be interested in a bar fire, Chivis? If the CIA came along and kicked you off a bog-standard arson case, back home, what would you think?"

Jake frowned thoughtfully and said, "CIA doesn't really get involved in active criminal investigations like that. It'd be NSA, or FBI, maybe, depending on what they think is happening. Either way, though, if the alphabet stew is getting involved, it can't be a good thing. They didn't come on board, just kicked you off the case? They've got to be thinking some kind of terror cell was involved, or maybe a military-grade weapon? It's hard to say without more info, but those would be my first guesses."

Cordiline nodded, his expression grim. "That's what I was thinking too. Fuck it, Jake. What did we miss? There must have been something going on there that they knew about beforehand? You live above the bar, for crying out loud. Have you noticed anything odd going on down there?"

Jake snorted. "That depends entirely on your definition of 'odd'. No. There's nothing going on. It's not a front for anything more than a safe place for guys to cruise other guys. I think I might have noticed kilos of heroin or weapons-grade plutonium being run through the place."

"What about…?" Cordiline hesitated a moment. "You've come across some weird shit, right, in your time? I don't mean drugs. I'm talking about" — he lowered his voice and leaned across the table — "the *X-Files* stuff. Is that what you were dealing with in Detroit? Did something get too heavy?

Is that why you got shipped over here?"

Jake was so incredulous he paused for a second or two longer, waiting for Cordiline to laugh and say he was joking.

"Jesus, you're serious? I didn't get shipped over here, I moved because it was time for a change. And I've got no idea what you mean by *X-Files stuff*."

"Don't give me that, you know exactly what I mean." Cordiline sounded gruff.

"If you're trying to ask me if this has something to do with Elemental abilities, it's not like the fucking movies. There aren't people shooting lightning outta wands. No big hirsute man is going to be knocking on your door and telling you you're a wizard, John. It's a lot more subtle than that."

"I wasn't shipped in from the Green Island a week ago, Chivis." Cordiline tapped his fingers against the pitted surface of the table irritably. "But you tell me that it's a coincidence that one day I'm dealing with some Yank who tells me he can touch stuff and see murderers, while his boyfriend mindfucks my computer systems, then a couple months later, they both wind up getting dragged out of a bar where some mentalist just burst into flames?"

"We didn't have anything to do with that guy catching light, John." Jake wanted to laugh but the words were catching in his throat. "Yes, it's a coincidence."

"So, what you guys do — it's not like...you can't control anything you like with your minds?" Cordiline folded his arms, still leaning in close across the table, visibly conscious that what he was asking sounded crazy.

Jake wiped a hand over his face and took a breath before he answered, "If I could 'control' stuff with my mind, you think I'd be living above a bar and schlepping off to work every day? Give me a break. Best case, I'd be rich and living on an island somewhere, but more likely, if there was anyone that could genuinely do something like that, the government would have them installed in some deep op, or bumped off. I've never met anyone that could read minds or control other people's thoughts. The few that have claimed they could do that were outright frauds, scamming audiences. Don't even try to tell me you haven't done your homework about Elementals. You're probably already aware just what kind of abilities have been proven and what is Hollywood make-believe."

Cordiline gave a slow nod. "You're not denying it, though, there are guys out there that really can play with fire. There've been tests and whatnot. Guys that could burn stuff without even being in the same room."

"Those were not government-sanctioned tests and they are unsubstantiated. If, and that's a big huge *if*, there are any living fire bugs out there, they are keeping that shit to themselves."

"But it's possible," Cordiline pressed.

"If it is possible, and I'm not saying it is, then it's extremely rare. Pyrokinesis is not a talent you can even be registered for."

"Unlike psychometry."

"Unlike psychometry," Jake confirmed.

"Which is also an ability that occurs in the Fire Elemental bloodline."

Jake looked at him hard. "Are you trying to say something, John?"

"You tell me. You're the Fire Elemental, not me." Cordiline tapped his fingers on the table again. "Look, I like you, Chivis. I want to trust you, but I need to know what's possible and what isn't before I let go of this case and walk away. Is it even conceivable that what happened in that basement the other night wasn't an accident? Could someone have gone down there and torched that guy... with his mind, I mean?"

Jake took a sip of his pint then set it down. "It's about as likely as spontaneous human combustion, and you don't need telling what I think of that. Is either one of those scenarios possible? I can't say it's totally impossible, but we're talking a one in a billion chance. There are stories about elementals that were strong enough to do something like what you're talking about, but it's been years, generations, since the bloodlines were that strong. There aren't very many of us, and our abilities tend to manifest in predictable ways. A strong Fire Elemental is likely to be clairvoyant—they get perceptions from things that most people don't see, either through touching objects like I do, or using an altered state to see past or future events. Some of the less strong Fire Elementals may get random precognitive dreams. Once upon a time we might have also had the ability for pyrokinesis, but that was a long time ago."

Cordiline kept tapping throughout the explanation and Jake realized it was a nervous habit. He took so long to think about what had been said, and Jake was just about to ask if that was all Cordiline wanted, when he announced, "They were both Fire Elementals. The guy in the bar, and that woman by the Lithuanian Embassy."

This information, Jake knew, was not meant for public consumption, and he also knew that Cordiline could possibly lose his job if anyone found out he'd told someone outside the force. More stunning than the realization that Cordiline had just risked his neck was the information itself. It could very well be a coincidence, but Jake was just as skeptical of coincidence as he was of theories of SHC or Fire Elementals with actual pyrokinesis.

"What? No smart-arse debunking commentary?" Cordiline asked him.

Jake shook his head and drank his beer. "I don't know," he said, setting the glass down. "I just don't know."

From the look on his face, that admission worried the inspector more than any amount of crazy unregistered Pyros running wild around London. Cordiline took another gulp from his pint.

"Tell me if I'm wide of the mark here but...what you and Dr. Gale are, does it...?" He waved a hand vaguely. "Does it augment your...skillset, having two of you? I mean, in nature right," he went on, warming to his theory when

Jake didn't jump in to shut him up right away, "in nature, fire feeds off air, right? So does what you have get stronger when he's with you, does it help you to...focus?"

"Mari's abilities are very different than mine. He comes from a bloodline of Air Elementals. Their strength is gathering knowledge and communications. And again, they are pretty rare. There are legends about Air Elementals that can supposedly do remote viewing, but I doubt any are living today. Mari's knack with computers is right up an Air Elemental's alley. I have no idea how either one of us could make the other one's ability stronger though. It's not like we're physically made out of fire and air."

"Right..." Cordiline hesitated.

If this had been a police inquiry he would have been scribbling that down in his pocket-book to digest later, Jake thought. Bereft of police procedure, he seemed at a loss for what to do with his hands.

"The Suits would have a field day with that, as well. I was reading up on some stuff before I came over here. It runs in families, right? This Elemental thing? He told you his granny was with the codebreakers, did he? Turing and that lot, at Bletchley Park during the war. They reckoned she could do things with her mind that would turn your hair white. Turing's boss didn't like her much, reckoned she was a fake." He sipped his pint again, shaking his head. "Probably jealous! Thing is, I suppose, what I'm trying to say... They know about you. About both of you. Not so worried about you yet, since you're a secret that's hidden in plain sight, so to speak. But these guys, the DIY cremation bunch, they weren't on anyone's books. And if they were out there, how many more do you suppose there are, just like them? I reckon that's what they're interested in, the Suits."

"If they weren't on the books, how did you find out they were Elementals?" Jake asked.

Cordiline looked over his shoulder, as if he was suddenly conscious of how public they were, but there wasn't anyone sitting within immediate earshot. He put his glass down and leaned forward again.

"MI5 have been watching them. This program you guys have been attached to at the university, it's not the first. They ran one years ago, British Military Intelligence put up the funding for it. They said there are files on those people, the burnt ones. Files that just stop dead about three or four years ago, when the government changed and the funding got cut off. After that the trail goes cold, but I did a bit of digging myself after the spooks had gone and it looks like the guys in the Home Office have been keeping them on the radar. Then, a few weeks ago, the trails started going cold again, people that were on the program disappeared. And when they turned up, there wasn't much left of them to question, was there?"

Jake leaned forward and lowered his voice, as well. "What are you doing poking around in military files, on a case you've been kicked off of? Are you crazy? Losing your job would be the least of your worries."

"It's okay. I was careful, covered my tracks and all that. But I wanted to find out what was going on. This is still my patch, Chivis, even if the spooks are moving in on it. I've got a right to know what's going down here." Cordiline looked angry, put out by the intervention. "And…all right, I'll admit it, I was worried about you. Worried that you might be involved somehow, or that they might find ways to make you involved. I wanted to make sure you were okay. In a professional capacity, you understand."

Jake laughed and it came out more of a soft wheeze. "I'm touched, Cordiline, I am. I'm not involved in any way, although if I were in your shoes, I could see you've got no reason to take my word on that. Listen, I've had one case, when I had just gotten promoted to detective, where the Feds stepped in and it pissed me off too. So don't think I can't relate, but you have got to take a step back from this. You get caught working the case when you've been bumped and some brass tack might put you on the wrong side of the bars. It's not as fun as porn makes it look."

That won him a half-smile and the cop took a longer swig from his nearly empty pint glass. His look was more speculative as he said, "You're right. I can't go sticking my nose into this without landing my arse in hot water. But… your friend can, can't he? Nobody would even twig that he'd been there."

Jake straightened his back as he sat up. "No. No fucking way. I'm not asking Mari to put his ass on the line like that."

Cordiline looked a shade put out at his flat refusal but he held his hands up in surrender. "No one is asking that. He could do it, we both know it. He took great pride in rubbing the Met's collective noses in the fact last time he helped us with inquiries of any significance. Don't you reckon he would love to have a go at cracking the best security in the country? Course he would!"

"Oh, I've got no fucking doubt he would. You stay the hell away from him with this idea," Jake warned him.

They stared at each other for a few seconds and Cordiline shifted his gaze first. Jake relented.

"Look, I want to discover what the hell happened to that guy, too, and if it's connected to the death of that woman. Your hands are tied but mine aren't. I'll get Manny to let me into the bar and I'll go downstairs and see if I can get an impression off of anything. I'll look into it myself, but I'm not getting Mari into this."

"He's really got to you, huh?" The inspector sighed and finished his pint. "Okay. I get it. I'll keep my procedural paws off your boy, but take it from me, he probably won't thank you for it if he finds out. And you be careful. I don't want to have to send my forensic guys around to sweep up what's left of you any time soon."

Jake pushed himself to his feet and nodded. "I'll be careful."

Chapter Five

Mari donned his running gear then took Tonka's lead down from the hook by the door. Clipping the stout chain to Tonka's equally solid collar, Mari circumvented all the excited bouncing around that this engendered with the deftness of experience. If they had a smaller dog, he reflected, not for the first time, he could have got away with one of those clever extending cords that allowed for less energetic walking sessions. And for stopping to chat to attractive fellow park inhabitants.

Not that he'd looked at other guys much since a certain Mr. Tall Dark and Alarmingly Unpredictable had shown up on the scene.

He was still brooding over Jake's surprising declaration as they set out into the gloom. It was supposed to be nearly spring but the weather outside was as grim and cheerless as it had mostly been for the last few months and he had to coax Tonka to keep up with a more vigorous pace for much of their venture out. Disturbingly, by the time they reached the park, Mari was already out of breath. He stopped and wrapped the leash around the leg of a bench while he coughed his lungs up like a forty-a-day man, then sat down feeling dispirited and tired. It was just the smoke, he told himself, but he knew it didn't account for the unhappiness that even Mama could see.

Would it be so bad? The voice of reason that was Great-Grandmama Amelia grilled him. *Moving in with him? He's kind-hearted and very easy on the eye, and he obviously thinks the world of you.*

He smiled, still unsure why it was that his conscience

always took her matronly tones after all this time. He did find it comforting though. Tonka snuffed his way back to his running shoes and he tickled the elderly Staffie's ears.

"I'm not sure. He's sweet and hot, yes. I like him. I like him a lot."

Tonka nudged his hand and made an agreeable noise somewhere between a woof and a sneeze, as if he shared the sentiment.

Well then, why are you in the dumps, idiot boy?

"I don't know," Mari sighed. "It's all too unexpected. Yes, I enjoy being with him but he values honesty and there's too much baggage in my past that I just can't tell him about yet. But I'm afraid that he'll take what I said the wrong way and he won't wait for me."

He rubbed his face with one hand, leaning against the seat back and gazing around the desolate, damp park as if he expected the answer to come running around the corner. Then, in a curious sense, it did.

The guy jogging along the track toward his bench looked familiar. He was moving sedately, as if this was maybe his first time exercising and he didn't want to overreach himself, but as he came closer Mari knew it wasn't that at all. He recognized him right away.

"Colm! What on Earth are you doing running? When did they let you out?" he called.

The young Dom slithered to a halt with a look of relief as he spotted one of his rescuers and jogged over. Tonka growled at him and Mari gave a sharp tug on his leash.

"Tonk! Behave! That's very rude."

"Last night," Colm told him, still panting and eyeing Tonka warily. "I couldn't stand staring at the same four walls. I figured the fresh air would be better for me. And I could say the same for you. Thank you, by the way. They told me at the hospital that you and your boyfriend came back for me. I was well out of it. Thought I was hallucinating. How do you feel?"

"Sick as a dog," Mari admitted. "I can usually run rings

round this place. Just jogging from the house to here nearly killed me."

Colm was nodding his head in agreement. "I'm not ashamed to admit, I had nightmares last night. That was some fucked-up shit that went down."

"You probably saw a lot more of it than I did. It was all smoke by the time I got back on the scene," Mari told him, grateful for that. His mind was shying away from the idea of what Colm remembered, and he had to concede that it would probably have given him nightmares too. "It must have been pretty quick. Did you see how it happened?"

Colm shook his head. "Not what happened, not exactly. I know what I saw, but it doesn't make any sense. You and the hot guy from upstairs were leaving and Louis came down to the basement. I wasn't really paying much attention to him, I figured Donny would sort him out, but then he started raising his voice. I thought he was just drunk, but I remember it because it's really weird. We don't work with anyone that looks drunk, and Louis was a regular, he knew that. So I turned around to see what the problem was and he just..." Colm shook his head again, unable to say what he'd seen.

Mari swallowed, conscious of how his mouth had gone dry as he listened. "He was burning," he said softly, swallowing again to free his vocal chords. "And no one touched him? Before, I mean."

Colm made a negative sound. "I'm not sure. I was watching you and your guy walk up the stairs and then I was talking to my client for a minute or so, I wasn't looking over at them until he raised his voice. I didn't see anyone touch him though. He...he had this look on his face...for just a second. This look, like he was petrified, and I swear, he stared down at himself and just burst into flame."

Mari's eyes widened in shock at that. And as he pictured the scene, suddenly he realized something else.

"He knew!" he exhaled in horror. "He knew it was going to happen. Oh my fucking days! Did you tell the police that?"

"Are you kidding me? They already think he probably got what he deserved, being a pervert, and we're all perverts too. You think I want them thinking I'm crazy on top of it? I told them I didn't see what happened, that's all."

Mari closed his eyes for a second, trying not to think about the man in the basement. He couldn't recall the details of his face, just remembered how irate he had seemed as he'd pushed by them and the sense of heat that he got from the man, and figured it was because he was in a hurry, flustered... *Terrified*, his brain added, and he opened his eyes again, staring into space. *Conscious of what was coming over him. Knowing he was going to die, maybe?*

He shook himself and put a hand to his forehead, massaging there, feeling the beginnings of a headache.

"You said he was a regular. Did you ever notice anything... unusual about him?" he asked, forcing the halting words out.

Colm shrugged. "I didn't really know him. I saw him at the bar before, I knew his name, but he was into Don's style of discipline. Donny knew him better, I think."

Mari hesitated then asked, "Did Don get out? The guy from the fire service that spoke to us said that another man was killed. The smoke..." He stopped, not trusting his voice.

Tonka licked his hand and whined, and he scratched the Staffie's ears absently.

"Yeah, Don got out. His hands were burnt pretty bad. He tried to get the fire out but he couldn't. I didn't recognize the guy that didn't make it."

Something else occurred to Mari. "Do you know what Louis came to Don for? What kind of discipline, I mean? Did he have a regular thing?"

"I think that's what he might have been getting so upset about. I didn't hear everything, but I'm pretty sure he wanted Don to leave with him. There are certain things we can't do at the club. Certain kinds of play."

Mari's insides clenched with a sense of need that he'd

pushed aside for so long that it rarely troubled him these days. "Such as?"

Colm stared at him for a moment, and his voice was pitched lower when he replied, "You can't draw blood on anyone in any way. No water sports. No actual penetration. Not saying that last doesn't sometimes happen anyway, but not out in the open. We keep things pretty tame at the club. If we like a subbie and they want something more serious, we sometimes invite them over." Colm chuckled without humor. "Sometimes they move in. Not with me though. I'm single at the moment."

Mari drew a slow breath. He wasn't naïve and he knew when he was being baited. "Well I'm sure that situation won't persist for long," he assured Colm in a voice that was steadier than it had any right to be. "So…is there anything you draw the line at, personally? Anything a guy's asked for that you won't do?"

Mari could see the subtle shift in him, from tense and upset to more relaxed, open and curious. He was obviously much more comfortable talking about this than reliving the horrific incident at the bar, and Mari couldn't blame him.

"I draw the line at a lot of things. You wouldn't believe some of the things people want to do that will permanently scar or even maim them. For me, it's all about sensation. Seeing how much a body can take, and how much the person can get off on it, but I'm not dumb enough to do something to someone that they will regret once they've come hard and they're back to their senses."

Mari nodded his head once or twice, like a man coming out of a daze. In a sense, he was. The other night in the bar he had been running on pure adrenaline. Today he was more rational, but the temptation was still hovering there in the form of this sexy young man. Even swaddled in his seasonal running gear, he was ridiculously masculine. And most certainly offering his services. All right, he probably expected to get paid for it, but at the moment, Mari didn't have too many qualms about that.

"Do people ever come to you because they feel bad about something, because they want to—how can I put this?—atone for something, but they don't know how?" he asked, picking his way through the words like they were landmines.

Colm chuckled again. "Ah, so that's it, is it? You want to come to me as the penitent? I can do that, beautiful." He put one foot up on the bench and leaned closer. "I just bet you've been a very bad boy, too," he murmured.

Mari was mortified that he was so transparent. He forced a pout and flashed back, "Did I say I was talking about myself? I think I didn't." He hesitated though because Colm didn't move away, nor did he stop looking at him like he'd just realized it was his birthday. He held those twinkling eyes without blinking. "Yes…I've been bad. I've done something very, very bad and I don't really know what's going to fix it." He squirmed in his seat. "I'm not very good at playing games, Colm. I just want… I want to be punished. I want to feel."

Tonka had slipped beneath the bench as they were talking and he looked up through the slats at the young Dom and bared his teeth silently.

"Why don't you come back to my flat with me and we can discuss your transgressions? I promise it will be up to you what you want to do, the first time."

Mari looked down at his feet for a moment, considering this option, and murmured, "Well, you can show me where it is, I suppose. I take it you're not far away if this is your regular running route." Tonka whined at him again and he dropped one hand to the dog's head, giving him a reassuring scratch. "And you presume there will be other times."

Colm flashed him a smile. "You're debating coming back to mine to cheat on your boyfriend and be punished for it. Of course, you'll be back for more. There's nothing wrong with that. People do it all the time."

Mari lifted his chin at that and pushed himself to his feet

abruptly. Tonka bounced up with him as Mari retrieved the lead and Tonka wagged his tail, insanely happy to be on the move again.

"Other people, maybe. I didn't say anything to you about cheating on my boyfriend," he warned. "Maybe you presume too much. I should take my dog home. He's getting chilly, and I don't think he likes you at all."

Colm didn't seem offended by this, or overly worried about Mari's sudden cold shoulder. He just smirked at him with a hint of amusement and perhaps something a shade darker.

"You want it. You can't hide that. You want to find out what it'll feel like to be bound, to struggle against it, to have a flail biting your skin and being forced to submit to it. It gets you hard just thinking about it. Don't be mad at me for your own desires. Hell, if it's the boyfriend you're worried about, invite him over. I'm up for a threesome. You know how many months everyone at that bar has been panting after the hot guy upstairs? There were some pretty hefty bets on who could land him first. Can't say as I blame them. So, what do you say?"

Mari knew that he couldn't argue with the initial point because just hearing Colm talk of binding and whipping him had him stiffening up in a way that made him glad he'd thought to slide a longer jacket on against the cold. He was startled to feel a flare of emotion that he recognized as possessive jealousy when the Colm revealed how most of the bar was in heat for his man though. He was generally analytical about his relationships. Jealousy was something new to him. And it was ridiculous because Jake had made it very plain this morning that he wasn't interested in being with anyone else.

And in return he had been grossly standoffish, almost cruel. That poured cold water on his erection right way. He knew why he felt bad, why he craved punishment. And he wished that he could just tell Colm to punch his lights out right there in the park.

You're an idiot, child.

For once he could not disagree with his great-grandmother.

"I'll talk to him about it," he said atonally. "I still have your card."

* * * *

Once he had rubbed Tonka down and found him some of his favorite kibble, Mari took a quick, hot shower then changed into something more comfortable than his running gear. Mama was taking her nap and he popped in to kiss her hair and murmur in her ear that he was going round to see Jake.

"Oh, good," she mused with a sleepy smile. "Be nice to him, Ilmari."

"I'm always nice, Mama," he pouted.

She just patted his cheek and snuggled back down with a shake of her head. "You know what I mean."

He did, and that had him grinding his teeth all the way over to Maple Street, unsure of the reception he would get when he arrived but unwilling to sit around and wait for Jake to come to him. If Jake felt slighted, then there was no telling how long that would take. He rang the bell a couple of times and squinted into the darkness of the bar. Blue and white tape still fluttered from the doorframe and a sad little sign told punters that they were closed *due to recent trajic events*. Mari was wondering if Jake was giving him the cold shoulder, or just out, when the object of his deliberations walked around the corner, heading for the flat.

"Mari," Jake said, looking surprised but happy to see him—to Mari's relief. "I was just thinking I should call. I forgot to ring you earlier and I left my phone upstairs. Is everything all right?"

Mari leaned in to kiss his cheek. "Of course, I just wanted to make sure you were okay. Have you been drinking?" He sniffed suspiciously then flashed him a tolerant smile.

"I had a pint. Cordiline wanted to meet with me." Jake

turned the key in the door. "C'mon upstairs and I'll tell you about it."

Mari was prey to that sharp spike of jealousy for the second time in the space of an hour. He thought he could have put up with it being just about anyone but DI Cordiline perving on his man. Then he admonished himself for refusing to let anyone else have Jake when he'd been so reluctant to commit this morning. He couldn't even argue about it without sounding like a prat.

"He's keen, I'll give him that," he said, trying to keep his tone neutral.

"He's not," Jake said, letting them into his flat and closing the door. "He had news about the fire, and he wanted help. He's been removed from the case. MI5 are investigating, or so he was told."

Good! Mari thought, with some relish, but he didn't say it because his brain was still processing the latter part of that revelation.

"Why on earth would military intelligence get involved? Do they think it's terrorism?" he asked, forgetting that Jake hadn't heard what Colm had to say yet.

"I don't know. He didn't know, either. That would be my first guess though," Jake said, heading for the refrigerator. "You want a beer?"

"Yeah." Mari nodded. "It's been an...odd sort of day."

While Jake was raiding the chill cabinet on his kitchen counter, Mari settled on the sofa and told him about his chance meeting in the park with Colm, noting that mention of the sexy Dom roused a satisfying bristle of possessiveness on Jake's part too. That was almost payoff for his own emotional overload. By the time he was done relaying everything the young man had told him, minus the parts about how Mari needed a good spanking and possibly a threesome, he was more serious.

Jake came to sit next to him on the couch and contemplated his beer bottle, which was half empty once Mari had finished relating his run in with Colm.

"Cordiline told me something else," he said at last. "That woman we saw on the news yesterday morning? Both she and Louis were Fire Elementals."

A cold-water shock trickled down Mari's spine as that sank in.

"Like you," he had breathed before his brain could censor it. Again, his treacherous mind replayed what Colm had said about Louis realizing what was happening to him. It had been bad enough before, but when he thought about it, all he could see in his head was Jake. His Jake! He shuddered and took another good gulp from the bottle in his hand, wishing it was bigger.

"Just because they were both Fire Elementals doesn't mean it's connected, Mari," Jake insisted. "It could be pure coincidence, it could be...I don't know. It could mean nothing."

"It could be...what? You were thinking aloud for a minute there." Mari gestured toward him with the bottle. "What else? If it's not a coincidence then something is making them go up in smoke, and MI5 want to learn why. Don't you think that's...odd?"

"Odd isn't the word I'd use. Fucking scary is more like it. There are only two reasons for the government to get involved. Some type of terrorist organization, and did any of those guys last night strike you as terrorists? Or some kind of weapon."

Jake took another long swallow of his beer as well.

"Colm didn't think he was armed. He didn't have a bomb, there wasn't an explosion," Mari said rationally. "He just... started burning, and he— He was scared, Jake." He was quiet for a moment, then added, "I am too."

Jake finally gave up his reflection on the beer bottle and turned to Mari, reaching over and putting one arm around him.

"There's nothing to be scared of, Ilmari," he murmured. "There is an explanation for what happened to them, and I'm sure if the spooks are on it they will find out what that explanation is. There's no use worrying about it anyway." Jake paused, and in an apparent non-sequitur added, "So Colm just found you in the park, huh?"

Mari felt his lips twitch.

"No, he was running. And I was running, as it happens. Well, technically, I was sitting on a bench with Tonka but, you get the picture."

"Mmm, I do. He must have been feeling okay to be out running. What else did Mr. Whiplash have to say?"

Mari made his eyes as wide and innocent as possible. "Why on earth do you think he'd have anything else to say? The poor man was in shock...and still suffering from smoke inhalation. And very grateful to us for rescuing him, by the way. And...okay, he may have flirted with me a little bit. Happy?"

He stuck his tongue out, then reached for the bottle he had set between his feet when Jake put an arm around him, covering his embarrassment by taking a drink.

"How much is a 'little bit'?" Jake asked.

Mari gave an artless shrug. "It's more than not at all and less than quite a lot," he evaded. "And no, I didn't take him up on it. What sort of person do you think I am?" he declared with rather more heat.

"I think you're the sort that's interested in what he has to offer, but is maybe too honest to act on it without feeling really guilty. And I guess I couldn't say much about it if you did. It's not like we talked about it. We barely got around to saying things like 'we're together' only a couple of days ago."

"Damn it, everyone's a fucking amateur psychoanalyst today!" Mari snapped, then recoiled just as suddenly, kicking himself for being an idiot. He curled his arms around Jake's deep, warm chest, burying his face in the comforting citrus scent of his light sweater before he could be pushed away. "I like being 'together', Jake," he said in a muffled voice. "This morning, I might have given you the wrong impression about that, but I really, really do like being with you. I'm sorry I sounded so…stupid and uptight and— You took me by surprise, that's all. I don't know if I'm in love with you, not yet. But I really, really do like you, and you are far too clever for your own good, Jake Chivis."

Jake put his arms around him and kissed the top of his head, making shushing sounds and just holding him for a few moments.

"I already said it's okay, Mari. You can't control the way I feel, and I can't tell you how to feel, either. If you don't feel it, then you don't. I'm not going to tell you to get lost over it."

Mari was at a loss for words for a moment. He looked up at Jake with helpless eyes, soaking for a moment in the heat of his dark golden gaze and contemplating this afternoon's discovery that half of the Fitzrovia gay scene was after his man.

"Even if you did, I wouldn't go away," he said, with some determination. What was the old saying? Honesty is the best policy? "You want to know what Colm told me? Okay…" He exhaled a quick, nervy huff. "He wants us to go to his flat. He wants a threesome, with both of us. He wants to teach you how to tie me up and discipline me properly. I suspect he also wants to fuck me. Or you. Probably you, in fairness. That seems to be the general vibe of his intimations. So, anyway…yeah, that's what he said. Kind of, in different words."

"Uh-huh. And, what do you want to do about that?" Jake asked him.

Mari felt like he might melt under that solemn, imperturbable gaze.

"You're really going to make me say it?" he whispered, shivering again at the memory of how Colm had left him feeling this afternoon.

Jake's lips curled in a tender half smile. "It's only fair, I think."

"It is? In what way?" Mari sat up straighter so that he could look right back into those lovely caramel-colored eyes instead of staring up at him like a hungry kitten.

"I've been honest with you about everything, I don't hold things back. If you think he's got something you need then…say it."

Mari closed his eyes for a moment, deliberating, trying to follow his mama's advice and think before he spoke. Jake was so unflappable, so undramatic, and right now Mari was scared of finding out if it was possible to freak him out.

"Since you don't hold things back," he said in a quiet voice, without opening his eyes again, "if I took your belt off and gave it to you and told you not to hold back, what would you do?"

Jake was silent for so long a bead of sweat started to form at the nape of Mari's neck, even though the rest of him was cold.

"If it's something you really wanted, and if it would keep you from going off to fuck that slimy piece of shit, I'd whip your ass black and blue." Jake's reply was a soft rumble that almost melted his insides.

Mari opened one eye and squinted at him. Was he imagining that deep sensual undertone in Jake's words? The jealousy he was not imagining at all. He was sure of it.

"Is that what you think of him? Interesting. He's quite hot for you," he said, and his words barely trembled, which was good.

Mari slid off the sofa and stood, stroking his fingertips down the curve of Jake's cheek. He was growing hard against his zipper and there was more of a tremor in his chest as he whispered, "Unfasten your belt and take it off, Chivis."

Jake did what he asked, but slowly, although it was hard to tell if it was done on purpose, to build his anticipation, or down to reluctance. Mari certainly didn't see any reluctance in his eyes. They were melting hot and steady as Jake looked back at him.

Mari let him have a small, dark smile. He unfastened the button of his fly and skimmed the zipper down.

"Pull my jeans and pants down," he said, sounding firmer than he felt. Inside, his heart and gut were dancing. "Pull them right down then put me over your knee and hold me there. Rest your hand on the back of my neck. Tell me I've had this coming to me."

His voice gave way and he couldn't control the tremor in that last instruction. Silently he cursed himself. He was shaking hard. His whole body was shaking.

For a second, Mari thought Jake was going to call a halt, not be able to go through with it or maybe laugh at him. He was just gearing himself up to handle that disappointment when Jake reached out with both hands and grabbed the waistband of his jeans and underwear, simultaneously jerking them down to his ankles, making his rising cock bob with some vigor. Instead of grabbing him right away and pulling him down across his lap, though, Jake slid his hands up Mari's legs, running them around to the backs of his thighs and cupping his buttocks.

"Jake…"

"Shh. Let me do it my way," Jake told him, and leaned in to kiss and nuzzle Mari's hip, mouthing across his lower abdomen and making light nips at the tender skin just below his belly button. He licked the spot slowly and kissed him there, then without warning, sat back and pulled him forward. Mari was reminded of the hidden strength he'd felt in Jake when he easily maneuvered him, face down, across his denim-clad thighs. He swung one leg over the backs of Mari's knees and rested his left hand at the nape of his neck, effectively holding him down. Instead of the sting of his belt, Mari felt Jake's warm hand caressing his bared backside.

"You've so had this coming, Ilmari," Jake said, low and gravel toned. He delivered a sharp slap with the flat of his hand that in no way could be construed as a love tap.

The weight of promise in his words had Mari lightheaded and gasping even before that crack across his buttocks brought him back to reality with a jerk. He let his breath out in a rush, a huff that ended in a low moan of longing, his body singing with the crackle of heat that seared out from his slapped cheek and raced like a rapid river to his clenching balls.

"Mmmhhh, yes!" he whispered, his face pressed down hard against the sofa cushion on one side of Jake's well-muscled thighs, and his legs pinioned on the other side. His cock was trapped against the warm denim of one of those strong legs and he wriggled harder, enjoying the rough friction against his sensitive penis.

Jake slapped him again, his hand falling in the same place as the first time, then rubbed him there for a moment before delivering again and again. He didn't quicken the pace, just gave him one stinging slap after another in a relentless, steady rhythm.

Mari squirmed harder under him, tormented by the rain of blows swatting him from one side then the other but never quite reaching the sharp, clean sting of pain that he was becoming increasingly frantic for. He stretched his hands out above his head, bracing them against the arm of the sofa and pushing himself back up to meet the warm strong hand that kept on clapping against his buttocks.

"Ohhhh uhhhh – damn it… Jake…please!" he whimpered finally. "Please strap me…please! I'm so close."

"Shh. You're gonna take it how I dish it, Mari," Jake told him in a low, admonishing tone that was as frustrating as it was arousing.

Mari's cock jumped and swelled at the quiet, commanding authority behind his words. His head was spinning with need. Jake carried on swatting him with his hand, totally oblivious, landing the same firm slaps at the same steady pace for a short while, then coming faster and harder. Mari was so wrapped up in the feel of it, and Jake was so smooth about it, that he didn't even notice a tiny pause between one slap of his hand and the stinging line of fire from his leather belt that followed it.

Mari had thought that he would melt in a puddle of pure

cum when Jake finally stopped teasing him and landed that first hard crack across his cheeks. He had to admit that his lover gave damn fine game, when he got down to it, because by the time he began to swing the belt, Mari was just about ready to burst. His heart was pounding like a jackhammer and he was bucking and rubbing himself so eagerly on Jake's thigh that in the end it only took three cracks of his belt, three delicious stripes across his backside that filled him with their fire, and he was lost. Burying his burning face in the sofa cushion as his loins clenched, he began to spurt hard all over his belly and all over Jake's jeans before subsiding in a breathless heap, relaxation rushing in to replace the tension and need that Jake had beaten out of him. A pleasurable heat raced through him that warmed his heart and soothed all his anxieties at once.

"Ohhh... Thank you...thank you..." he rambled effusively. "You have no idea... So...so...amazing. Thank you."

Jake caressed him, his touch impossibly gentle after what he had just done, while Mari floated down from his hazy bliss. Then Jake slowly turned him over and gathered Mari to his chest, standing up with him in his arms like he weighed nothing, and carried him into the bedroom. He set him down on the bed as if he were handling glass, bending over him and kissing him on the lips, slow and tender.

"You are gonna be so sore tomorrow," he said, planting another kiss on Mari's forehead.

"I don't care," Mari told him with a smile that felt too weak, too shaky. "It will be worth it. Every time I move I'm going to remember how this felt. You are beyond amazing."

He snaked his fingers into Jake's hair and pulled him down for another kiss, feeling dizzying, blissful happiness fill his aching heart.

"Are you going to tell me why?" Jake asked with a bemused smile.

"One day, maybe." Mari kissed the tip of his nose. "Not tonight. It feels too good tonight."

Jake did not push him for the explanation and Mari curled up with him, daring to hope that perhaps this could work out between them after all.

Chapter Six

Mari stayed the night and, for once, Jake was glad that his doctor had ordered him to remain busy doing nothing for the next few days. It was a pleasure to wake up two days running with Mari naked, in his arms, and the prospect of nothing more important to do than enjoy each other's company for the next few hours. Once Jake had carried him to bed last night, Mari's gratitude had known no bounds and, when he was done being grateful, he had snuggled around Jake. They both slept better than they had since before the fire. Mari was still out of it when Jake woke, a tiny smile on his soft lips, even in the depths of his dreams.

Jake slipped out of bed as quietly as he could and went to the bathroom, then to the kitchen to put on a pot of coffee. The apartment still smelled very faintly of char, but it really wasn't as bad as it could have been. The place was insulated fairly well to deaden noise, and that also kept out things like smoke. Either that or he was just getting used to it.

As he filled the carafe with water, he looked over at the couch where his belt was still lying, so innocuous and normal, yet a flood of memories hit him at the sight of it. Last night had maybe been tame by some standards, and it certainly wasn't the kinkiest thing he'd ever done, but he could not deny it had been scorching hot. Now if he could just keep the guilt at bay for doing that to Mari, they would be golden.

He pushed the brew button on the machine and his phone chirped at him from the coffee table. There was a text from Manny asking how he was doing. Jake had given him the number a few days ago, in case he needed any more help. He thought about how to reply for a moment then messaged back that he was fine, asking if he could meet up with him later, which was ambiguous enough.

The aroma of fresh brewed coffee lured his gorgeous genie out of the bedroom and Mari greeted him with a coy smile as he accepted the mug Jake handed over. He settled on his left hip at one end of the sofa, blowing small clouds of steam into the room from the surface of his coffee as he blinked away the last vestiges of sleep. Naked save for his sweater, he made a delicious vision to start the day with.

"I need to get back and pick up my laptop and some other things," he said in an apologetic tone. "I thought maybe I could do some poking around, see what I can find out about your stalker boy's spooks."

Jake stopped himself from telling him not to do that. At best, Mari would give him that patronizing smile and do as he pleased, anyway. At worst, he'd tell him off and go stomping out. Well, he might stomp rather gingerly today, Jake amended with a private smirk.

"I have a favor to ask," Jake said, choosing his words with care. "Could you find out what you can about Louis and the woman from the Embassy, but stay out of any government files?"

"I'm an Interface, not a magician." Mari sighed and sipped his coffee. "I can't produce information out of thin air. I have a first name for Louis and…does Cordiline even know who that Milda woman at the Embassy was yet? I have to start somewhere."

He seemed to register the warning look that Jake was giving him and he stretched his hand out along the back of the sofa, stroking one finger up and down the length of Jake's discarded belt in a provocative manner. He didn't argue any more though.

"I'll see what I can do, Chivis. If you find out anything else from Manny, then send me a message."

Jake tried very hard to keep the surprise — bordering on shock — out of his expression and thought he succeeded quite well. If he had guessed that turning Mari over his knee and spanking him beet red would have made him more tractable, he would have done it a month ago. Of course, it was not beyond the realm of possibility that Mari was just telling him what he wanted to hear so they wouldn't have an argument.

He bent to place a kiss on Mari's forehead and tenderly caressed his hip and backside.

"Thank you, and I will."

Mari tipped his head back and brushed his lips against Jake's.

"He's not to get you moving crates, okay?" he warned. "You're still recovering."

Jake watched him reach for his discarded jeans and tiny, bikini briefs. He set the half-empty coffee mug on the floor as he squirmed into them carefully. If it hurt, he was deliberately keeping it off his face.

He wanted to turn Mari over and look, but he also kind of didn't want to see. He couldn't keep from asking, though.

"How bad is it?"

Mari gave a light shrug. "How bad is what?"

He adjusted himself casually and tugged up the zipper, thumbed the button and rearranged the hem of his sweater over the ensemble.

Jake studied him for a moment then reached out and squeezed his backside. Not hard, just a friendly squeeze, and still Mari sucked in a breath and flinched away from his hand. Jake's face crumpled. He felt like a monster.

"I'm sorry."

Mari caught hold of his hand and took it to his lips, kissing his palm then letting go. "No. Jake. Don't. There's nothing to be sorry about, do you understand? I'm all right. I don't want your guilt. I don't want you to feel that way. If you feel that way, I can't ask you for anything again. I don't want to be the reason for you feeling bad. Okay?"

Jake stood and slid his arms around Mari, making sure they were above the waist, and pulled him up close, kissing him softly at first then with more heat. When they broke the kiss, he bent his head to Mari's shoulder, took a deep breath and let it out.

"Okay."

Gentle as a breeze, Mari stroked his fingers through Jake's hair and kissed his cheek, just a peck.

"Thank you." He eased out of Jake's embrace smoothly and smiled at him with infinite tenderness. "I really do need to get moving. I'll see you later, I promise. Be good."

* * * *

Jake let Manny into his apartment less than an hour after Mari had left. The barkeep was understandably upset, and not just about the fire. The insurance and contractors couldn't even begin to assess the damage until the police released the 'scene', and he had no idea when the bar might be open again.

"I'm sure they will be done with their investigation soon, Manny. Even if it's ruled a homicide rather than accidental, there probably isn't much evidence they'll be able to get from the scene after one or two visits."

"What am I meant to do in the meantime?" The dolorous bartender sighed, running a hand through his hair and shaking his head as if Jake could somehow fix things by magic. "The bills don't stop coming in just because I have a bunch of useless coppers in my basement. I knew that mental case Lou was bad news. Thought he'd stopped coming and I can't say it wasn't a relief." He flopped down on Jake's sofa and worried his already terminal fingernails with his teeth.

"That's what insurance is for, right?" Jake said. "You did have the place insured, didn't you?"

"I just rent it. The owner's in Brazil." Manny sighed again and shrugged, looking forlorn. "The stock was covered but I'm not in hock for loss of earnings. Didn't read the small print." He looked up at Jake with a grimace. "Yeah, I'm an idiot. Tell me something I didn't know already!"

Jake offered him a wan smile and patted his shoulder consolingly. "Well, then the sooner they get out of there the better," he said, edging toward what he was aiming for. "Manny, listen, you think you could let me borrow your key to the place?"

The barman's eyes moved to his and widened. "What the heck d'you wanna go down there for? You drop something the other night? Cops have probably tagged and bagged it, whatever it was."

"No." This would be the tricky part. He knew Manny casually, but other than the last few days while Jake had been helping out, he hadn't had many conversations with him, and Manny had no idea what he could do. "No, I didn't drop anything. You know how I told you I was a cop when I lived in Detroit? Well, I was an arson investigator. I'd like to take a look around, just to see if there was anything they might have missed."

"You reckon they're slacking?" Manny frowned at him. "I dunno, Jake. I mean, I like you and all, mate. Don't take this wrong, but…what d'you reckon you could turn up down there that they've not combed over fifty times already? They've had more uniforms down in that cellar this week than I've seen patrol this street in my whole lifetime."

Jake had been hopeful that his cred might be enough, but he'd also sensed Manny would probably take more convincing than that. He could get the bartender in a lot of trouble, if anyone found out Manny gave him the key to get in. Jake ran a hand through his unruly hair and blew out a breath.

"Because I doubt any of them can do what I can do. Have you ever heard of psychometry?"

Manny blinked at him. "That's like…mind control and stuff, innit?" He looked even more dubious about it.

"No, it's got nothing to do with mind control. It means I can touch a thing and know who owned it, sometimes see their memories from when they last had it." Jake could see a lot more than that, but telling people the extent of what he could do tended to freak them out.

"What's that got to do with my club?" Manny sighed. "We've a good idea who was down there and who owns what already. And, don't get me wrong, Jake. I doubt you're going to get any fun memories out of anything in that cellar, mate."

Don't I know it, Jake thought.

"If there is anything in the cellar that held on to someone's memory of the other night, I might be able to figure out what happened to Louis. That's all I want to do, Manny. I want to figure out what happened to him, what really happened to him, and the investigators can only piece together physical evidence and shaky eyewitness testimony. I can maybe see what actually happened."

"Even if you can," Manny said warily, "how's it going to help? I don't see the bizzies being too convinced by you telling them you're some kind of hocus-pocus cop. They'll tell you to sling your hook."

He was playing with his keyring though, and Jake could see that his curiosity was piqued.

"Look, it can't hurt. I'm not going to take anything or move anything. And if somehow someone found out, I can always say I had the key from before, when I was helping out. You won't get in any trouble, I promise. I need to get in there and see if there is anything left, to figure out what happened to him." And as Jake said it, he realized it was true. It was more than just wanting to take a look around because he'd told Cordiline he would. He needed to figure out what had happened to the man, and to discover if it was in any way connected to the victim in front of the Embassy, because as much as he had played down any coincidence between the two, he could not shake the feeling that they were, in fact, linked. And they were both Fire Elementals. It would be simplest if Manny just gave him the damn key, but if he refused, Jake was already planning on breaking in once it got dark.

Manny unclipped the fob from his belt and pried a set of keys off it, plopping them with some reluctance into Jake's hand.

"The Yale and the long mortice key do the back door, it'll be more private if you go in that way. The brass one does the stock rooms, all of them. This one" — he tapped a darker Yale key with a blue spot sticker on it — "opens the dungeons. Make sure you leave everything the way you found it, all right?"

Jake blinked at him. "Dungeons?"

Manny shrugged. "What would you call 'em? The punters like the ring of it."

Jake's chuckle was more of a wheeze, and he put the keys in his pocket.

"Thanks. While you're here, what can you tell me about Colm?"

"Colm Fleming?" Manny said, as if there were two of them, maybe. "He's okay, nice kid. Works out down the gym on Scala Street — I've seen him there a couple of times. His cousin George runs the tattoo place on the corner, near the Greek bar. That's where he gets all the ink. He's been on the scene for a couple of years, very popular."

Jake's fingers itched to write the info down but he didn't want Manny to think this was anything more than a casual conversation. He'd remember it all anyway.

"Is he with anyone? Or is he not the relationship-type?"

Manny grinned. "Why? You interested? I thought you were fixed up with that leggy blond. He's blown you out, has he?"

Jake felt his lips twist into something that wasn't quite a grin.

"No, I'm not interested in Colm. Not personally, anyway. He was down there and saw what happened. I just want to find out what kinda guy he is, if he's reliable, or prone to making shit up." He also wanted to know if Colm Fleming was looking at Mari with more than just professional interest, but he doubted Manny would be able to confirm that for him one way or the other.

"Nah, he seems pretty reliable. Never seen him out with anyone, but I figure it's a funny trade for a guy in a stable relationship, 'specially if he works from home, innit? He seems to like it, though. Donny O'Brien trained him up. He reckons Colm was a quick learner. Got the hang of it really quick." Manny chuckled. "Some blokes like dishing out the rough stuff. Fills a gap for them, know what I mean? Makes 'em feel more manly."

As if on fricking cue, Jake's belt slithered from the back of the couch onto the seat beside Manny. Jake pretended it didn't happen.

"This Don guy, you don't think he did anything to Louis? You said Lou hadn't been around a lot lately. Did they have a falling out, you think?"

"Not sure," Manny responded, shaking his head. "Don had a big client base. Maybe Lou was seeing someone else. Maybe his tastes got too extreme for Donny's liking. We're not into any heavy stuff here. If the client wants that and the Dom's happy to do it, they fix it up somewhere private. That's down to the individual Dom, though."

Jake let that line of questioning go for the time being.

"You said earlier that Louis was bad news, how so?"

"He was just a weirdo." Manny laughed. "Yeah, so we're all a bunch of weirdos, right? But he was kind of a nutter, like. He was always going on about this underground group he belonged to."

"What, like some BDSM thing?" Jake asked,

"Nah, man. It was a church, or he said they were. Sounded like some fucked-up cult shit to me."

"Do you remember the name of the church?" Jake asked. It was probably nothing, but until he got downstairs to see if he got any impressions off anything, it was hard to tell what might be important or not.

"Yeah." Manny mulled this over for a moment. "I think they were called Birthplace…no, Birthright. Something, like that. Nazi-sounding shit, if you ask me."

* * * *

When Mari got back to the house, Mama was resting and he was able to slip in quietly and change into his dressing gown. He was running a bath when she crept through to check that he was home and kissed his cheek with a weary smile.

"You and Jake made it up then? I'm glad," she said, ruffling his hair.

"We never fell out—he just needed to go home for his things. I told you," he soothed. "Are you all right, Mama? You look tired."

"Just…so fed up of all this, the treatment and the waiting, and more bloody interminable waiting." She pinched the bridge of her nose. "I don't know what's worse."

He smiled humorlessly and pulled her close.

"I do. You're going to get better, Mama. And when you do, it will have been worth all the lost time, I don't doubt it. Get some rest. I'm just going to clean up and then I'll make us breakfast, okay?"

She nodded and left him to his ablutions. Mari filled the tub, added some rose oil and cued up a spiky electronica playlist on his aquatic mp3 then subsided into the hot water for half an hour to soak his deliciously sore backside. The oil wouldn't ease the pain but it did help with the healing process, and he wriggled down in the water with his feet resting on the lip of the tub so that he wasn't sitting on the sorest regions. The comforting throb of the music helped him to drown out the contrasting throbbing of his nether regions and he closed his eyes for a few minutes, enjoying this private moment while he could.

He was still horny, which seemed impossible after last night. Even the music didn't quite shut out the memories of Jake's growling moans as Mari pushed deep inside him, fucking him hard by way of a thank-you for the delicious punishment he had meted out earlier in the evening. Maybe it was the guilt, but Jake had submitted to him three times and Mari had still been horny, still hard. Exhaustion had stopped them last night, but this morning, he felt he could have carried on for hours. Sympathy for Jake and the tightness across his own derrière checked him but, alone in the bathroom with the door locked, he indulged his need, stroking and caressing his pulsing cock under the water, his hand quickening on his swelling shaft as his loins clenched and his balls start to climb up into his scrotum almost too quickly. The memory of last night, Jake's hand on his nape, the vigorous slapping of the other hot hand on his arse, the way he'd been so vigorous, so thorough... Mari was on fire at the echoes of his rough handling. He fisted harder and, as his brain replayed the memory of Jake's belt streaking his cheeks with fire, he exploded with a breathless gasp.

Mari let his body go limp and sank under the surface, his cry of ecstasy stifled by the water. When he emerged again, dripping and shaking with relief, he felt less uncomfortable. It would have to do. He forced himself to his feet and toweled off.

He applied some more oil—his hot skin gobbled it up greedily—before sliding into a pair of loose, soft, cotton jogging pants and a warm hooded sweater then returning to the kitchen to start breakfast. Mama came down to eat but went back up to her bedroom again afterward, complaining of a headache, and he took her a glass of warm milk and some ibuprofen. When he was sure that he had the living room to himself, he sprawled on his belly on the sofa and flipped his laptop open.

* * * *

Wearing a hoodie and conscious of the CCTV camera in the service alley behind his building, Jake decided not to wait until dark to make his inspection of the bar. He doubted anyone would check the camera footage after the event.

The smell of smoke was much stronger inside, as was only

to be expected. Through his training and his career, Jake had gotten used to the smell of a burnt-out building but it had been some time since he'd investigated one. He let his eyes adjust to the gloom for a moment — the only light coming in was through the darkened glass at the front. Jake didn't waste too much time there, figuring if there were any helpful memories to pick up at all, they would be in the cellar. *The Dungeon.*

Looking around the bar, after the chaos of the other night, it was hard to tell anything out of the ordinary had happened there. The place was a mess — with drinks left on tables and at the bar, and chairs knocked over — but there was nothing broken, no water damage or soot up here. It was only at the top of the stairway leading down that there was any sign of a fire. The stairwell was covered in streaks of soot that gave the impression of huge shadowy fingers reaching out of the darkness below.

Jake turned on the penlight he'd brought with him and carefully descended the stairs.

In the room below, the evidence of fire was more apparent. The walls and ceiling were black with soot and there were puddles of water from the fire brigade hosing the place down. He stopped at the bottom, getting his bearings, then continued, slowly letting his light glide over walls and the floor.

It would have been easy enough to track to the source of the fire, even if he hadn't had an approximate idea of where the guy had been standing. The furnishings around the edges of the room were water-logged but for the most part intact. It was only near where Donny had been set up with the padded spanking bench that the fierce blaze was most evident. The bench itself was hardly more than blackened ash, and above it the plaster ceiling was a scorched ruin. The walls nearest the epicenter of the blaze were nothing but char, but about six or seven feet from point zero the char stopped, making a clean delineation. Jake ran his penlight up and down the area, moving to stand on the same spot where Louis had most likely been standing.

The lines where the burning ended were nearly equidistant, which indicated to him the heat of the fire had been intense, like an acetylene torch. Without taking samples and sending them to a lab he couldn't determine if there had been an explosion, but just from the look of things, he didn't think it likely. There didn't appear to be any blowback damage, no shrapnel that he could see peppering the area. It looked like an extremely hot, very clean burn that had scoured the area.

He shone his light down at the floor and crouched. Water and tracks from a variety of footwear could be seen, but also a trace of lighter gray ash that had been mostly shoveled up, judging by the patterns left behind. Jake frowned. That lighter ash was most likely human in origin, but it shouldn't have been there.

When someone burned, depending on how long they were in the fire, there were usually charred remains, sometimes quite grisly remains. It was unusual to find a burned body that had been reduced to just bones, and in those cases, it took a concerted effort from someone to keep a fire going long enough to burn a body that badly. To reduce even the bones to gray detritus was pretty much impossible outside of a crematorium. Even then, it took time, and the result wasn't this fine ash, but a substance not entirely unlike coarse cat litter. All that would have taken a lot more time than the few minutes Louis had been burning.

"What the fuck..." Jake murmured to himself. He was more puzzled than ever. None of this seemed to be adding up.

Looking around, Jake was even less optimistic that he'd be able to pick up any memories here. There wasn't much to go off. Still, he made the effort, slowly picking his way around the space and touching the arm of a couch, an overturned chair, a piece of glass from a shattered beer bottle. As he suspected, he got nothing. Making a spiral around the room until he was back near where the fire damage was most concentrated, Jake was just about ready to give up and go. There was nothing here, Manny had been right. The SOCO team had scoured the place.

He dropped his hand onto the headrest of the charred spanking bench and was sucked immediately into a loud crowd of people.

"Lou, go home. I can't do anything for you." A man that Jake *vaguely recognized from the other night was shouting to be heard over the clamor. He was shirtless, wearing just dark jeans and black leather boots, maybe in his late thirties or early forties. He looked like he took care of himself, although he wasn't too clean cut either, with a hint of scruff on his cheeks and chin, and dark brown hair in need of a cut or possibly just a good brushing.*

"You have to! I need your help. I need the release, you don't understand. I can feel it building up inside me. I need you to take the edge off before…something happens."

Oh, god…he was inside Louis. He had hoped for a bystander.

"Before what happens? You're not making any sense," the *man – Jake guessed it was Donny – told him.*

"Before…before…oh…" He looked down at his chest and put *the hand not resting on the bench to his stomach. No, not his stomach, just above it, at the base of his sternum. As far as Jake could tell, there were no wounds on him. Nothing was thrown at him. He didn't hear any sort of explosion. Louis didn't even scream. Flames burst from between his fingers and his head tipped back, looking up at the ceiling.*

Jake gasped and he let go of the bench just as Louis did in the flashback. The light jumped around on the black-scorched walls from the point of his shaking hand. As Colm had told Mari, no one had touched Louis. The nearest person had been more than arm's length away. Unless there had been someone behind him that Jake couldn't see. But then what? Someone had shoved the end of a flamethrower through his body? Someone that no other person had noticed? That made about as much sense as spontaneous human combustion, which was to say none at all. There had to be something he was missing. He just had to find it. Whatever it was, he didn't think it was down here.

He hurried back up the stairs on shaking legs, then out of the back door, locking up as he went. He would take a shower, change, and head over to Mari's. But first, he sent him a text.

Hi, can you look up a church or group in the area called 'Birthright'?

* * * *

From his prone position on the sofa, Mari squirmed around as his sleek mobile phone buzzed, demanding his attention. He removed one of the earbuds he was using to listen to music while he surfed, so that it didn't disturb Mama while she was sleeping, and reached for the phone. When he saw Jake's name in the message bar, he smiled and towed it over toward him. The message was definitely not a proposal though.

"Birthright?" he mused, studying the brief request for a moment. No endearments. No kiss. Jake meant business this morning. Mari briefly hoped he still had a sore arse, but he got to work at once, calling up his favorite encrypted search engine and tapping in the word.

As he had expected, it brought up a variety of websites and blogs covering everything from the Young Capitalist Venture movement to kiddy porn. Mari navigated a route from site to site, covering his tracks online as he went and recording his observations on the phone.

Most interesting, from the point of view of their current investigation, was a page that initially seemed to be nothing more than a plain blue cover with a white compass design on it and a dark gray login button. Mari had grown up surfing the web and he knew, without questioning his gut, that anything this simple was one of two things—unfinished or keeping a low profile.

He clicked 'login'. Unsurprisingly, it asked him for a

username and password. Less unsurprisingly, it didn't offer him a registration option.

"Private members' club, huh?" he mused, tapping his lower front teeth with a fingernail.

He grabbed one of his memory sticks — a slim, silver thing with a pumpkin-head logo on it — and plugged it into the laptop, tapping at the keys when it offered him a prompt. The backdoor entry key whirred and clicked for a moment or two, its ingenious program winding a rapid way into the stubborn webpage, looking for access points where users had logged in or out and left their browser open, and the barely audible fan on his processor huffed at the small effort, then a sequence of letters and numbers appeared in the login box, quickly followed by a password which was even more obscure.

Under his breath, Mari murmured a cynical, "Yay!"

The site hung stubbornly for a few seconds and just as he thought it was going to kick him out on his metaphorical backside for his cheek, the innocuous frontage gave way to a more detailed welcome page.

"Bingo!" Mari exhaled, flipping the bird at his screen before exploring the site in more detail.

The member he had hacked must have just logged off because he had recent posts on the site's forums. Mari tracked back through them, making notes of the people he spoke to and any names that cropped up in their conversation.

As he delved deeper, one thing seemed to be beyond doubt. The site was aimed at fellow Elementals, people like him and Jake. Some of the sentiments being expressed were far from sympathetic with his personal views, though. A small frown creased his brow as he checked out all the tabs and the different chat forums available to the 'Birthright' members. It stayed there until long after he had logged out.

He jabbed the button that killed his music player and rolled himself off the couch smoothly, shutting the laptop. Ten minutes later, having eschewed the sexier option of charcoal, skin-tight jeans for a more comfortable pair of eight pleated Paul Smith suit pants in midnight metallic blue, he wriggled into a soft, cream, jersey roll-neck and his dark blue Burberry duffle coat and hit the road, calling Jake en route.

"Hello, sweetie, we need to talk about your web habits," he told Jake's voicemail with a twitch of his lips. "I'm coming over."

* * * *

Jake was at the flat when he arrived and buzzed him up to the landing. His hair was still wet from the shower. Mari sniffed him approvingly then put his laptop on the kitchen counter where he flipped it open.

"I got my ride in to recommend me as a friend," he explained, using the temporary login that the site system had issued him with to access Birthright again, as a bona fide user. He promptly changed the username and password details it had allocated and turned the machine to show it to Jake. "They were quite sniffy about it. I think they prefer Fire Elementals—they're quite macho about different abilities. I'm sure they'd have been happier if it had been you, but I'll give it a few days before I recommend you so it doesn't look too suspicious. Otherwise, it was ridiculously easy. I didn't even have to use my gift—a simple backdoor hack got me in. Which makes me think, there must be other levels I haven't hit on yet. It's like a rabbit warren in there."

His fingers were flying over the keys as he talked, dipping in and out of the different pages and forums as he showed Jake around.

"The gist of it is pretty basic stuff. Elementals as the chosen children of God...blah, blah. If I'd just been surfing it as a personal interest thing, I'd probably have switched off there," he said dismissively. "There's a lot of ranting, here"—he tapped the current screen with a fingernail—"about injustice and how the government has been using

Elementals then pushing them under the carpet, or even 'disappearing' them." He crooked both index fingers around the word, for emphasis. "The forums talk about 'our leader'..." He crooked his fingers again. "So they're organized, to a degree, but I've not got to the root of their organization structure yet. This forum was interesting." He touched on a couple of tabs and a long, multi-threaded chat spilled down over the screen.

"They're talking about the two incendiaries. Louis was the fireball in the bar, wasn't he? And the girl's name was Milda Kilis — she was a Litvak, a Lithuanian Jew, and some of them make a big old thing of that. Get this, not only were they were both FEs — by the way, none of these people ever use proper nouns when a perfectly good acronym will do." Mari uttered a sigh of despair. "They were both members of Birthright. Louis was pretty active on the forums. Called himself Lightbringer, but it didn't take too much digging to figure out who he was."

Mari hit on his name in the chat thread and the webpage took him to a list of Lightbringer's latest posts. "He's been having a rant here, just a couple of weeks back, about how the 'Istablishmunt' is soon going to wish they'd taken FEs more seriously. Not sure why, or what he means by that. I just wish these people would learn how to spell before they plot world domination. Milda was less gobby — she was looking for her father, Mykolas. The family came to London six and a half years ago from a village near Vilnius and she thought he might have got involved with the Birthright people. She seems to have talked to members that vaguely remembered him. Nothing more than that, though."

He looked at Jake and raised one eyebrow inquisitively. "How did you come across these mentalists?"

"I talked to Manny this afternoon, not long after you left. I was asking him about Louis, what he knew about him, and he said he was always going on about this group he was a part of." Jake waved vaguely toward the screen. "He called it a church."

Jake leaned one hip on the edge of the countertop and drummed his fingers as he looked over some of the conversation that Mari had brought up on the forum. Having skimmed a lot of it earlier, Mari hadn't gotten the impression that there were many clues to be found there, but he felt that they were getting closer. It couldn't be simple coincidence that not only were both of the people that burned Fire Elementals, but that they belonged to the same organization and, possibly, knew each other. Connections like that usually meant something, didn't they? It didn't answer how or why they'd burned, though.

"I don't suppose you found any instructions from their esteemed cult leader on where and when to stage a self-immolation?" Jake asked him.

Mari chuckled at that.

"Oddly enough, no. The Big Cheese is conspicuous by his absence most of the time. Clearly, he has better things to do than organize his web presence. Either that or the lack of spelling and punctuation drives him crazy too. I bet we could pin down some of these mouthy chatroom hogs though. Take them drinking, metaphorically speaking — loosen their tongues. Do you want me to maintain a presence in the playground?"

Jake looked at the screen with a thoughtful expression.

"Yeah, it couldn't hurt." He took his eyes off the block of text in front of him and rewarded Mari with a smile that warmed his heart. "That's some good detective work there, Dr. Gale. You found another link between the victims. Now, we just need to figure out what it is about being a part of this group that sets people on fire and we can close the case." Jake leaned in and kissed him. "Have you eaten yet?"

"Just poached egg on toast. I could handle a few more carbs." Mari had to stop himself from purring at the sudden warm feeling Jake's casual praise gave him. He returned the kiss more deliberately to give himself time to think about that. Since when had it been so important to him what another man thought?

Not since Tomas, at least, his conscience reminded him snidely, and he pushed that idea aside. Jake Chivis was nothing like Tomas Arregui, nothing at all.

"Do you feel like going out, or should I order in?" Jake asked him.

"Up to you," Mari said. Then, so that Jake didn't think he was a total pushover, added, "We could go and brighten the day of that pretty Greek lad, Manolis, around the corner if you like. Their baklava is to die for."

He kissed the tips of his fingers and flung his hand out with a chuckle. No matter what it was that Jake was doing to his head, he couldn't say that he disliked it.

Jake was obviously in an indulgent mood. Under ten minutes later, they were seated at a table in the cafe. Mari had a huge vessel of frothy latte and sweet nutty baklava in front of him and Jake had a rich dark coffee and plate of chicken salad that looked about double the size of what would normally be served, Mari noted with approval. They ate at the café semi-regularly and Mari still found it amusing how blatantly the boy behind the counter spoiled Jake and made eyes at him, while Jake remained, for all intents and purposes, oblivious.

Even with a double-sized portion, Jake still tore through his food and all but licked the plate clean.

"Hungry?" Mari teased.

"Starved. I can only live on coffee so long." Jake chuckled and sat back with a satisfied look on his face.

"Well you did burn some energy last night," he acknowledged with a wicked smile. His gaze flickered toward the counter where their waiter was usually to be found watching Jake intently, when he wasn't busy with other customers. Unusually, the lad's dark eyes were focused elsewhere, fixed on the flat-screen TV that played a muted news loop in the background for the benefit of passing businessmen and customers without access to modern amenities.

Mari followed the line of his intent stare. Initially he

thought the story was just recapping the latest news on the two recent incendiary deaths. Then he recognized the scene behind the reporter, currently taped off and devoid of the usual wall-to-wall human traffic. The journalist was standing outside Buckingham Palace, looking very somber.

Mari tapped Jake's arm and pointed toward the TV where the rolling news caption was telling of a third mysterious death in central London in the space of two weeks.

"Looks like things are escalating. I'm pretty sure it wasn't the Queen or there would be nothing on the TV but wall-to-wall sentimental tributes."

Jake leaned forward again, and Mari could see the muscles along his jaw flex, his eyes glued to the screen. The reporter was speaking with a witness, and the line of subtitling across the bottom read *No, no one attacked him that I could see. No one threw anything at him or held a match to him, nothing like that. He just burst into flame.*

"Shit," Jake muttered. "Let's go. I want a better look at those message boards, see if anyone is talking about this anywhere. Maybe find a physical address."

Mari paid their bill and they hurried back to the flat and the absolute shitstorm that had hit the forums on Birthright. From the moment he logged in, it was clear that this was not a normal day in the websphere surrounding the London-based Elementals. Every second post was something along the lines of *wtf is going on?*

Who is gonna b next?

Man, I am getting the fxck out of here!

WHo wuz it? Ani1u no?

Fuk they sez its lyk an epidemik

Mari folded his hands and rested his forehead on them.

"I love the Internet. I see its potential," he growled softly. "But sometimes I want to kill people."

Jake watched beside Mari as the panic unfolded but it didn't look like anyone was offering any answers, only more questions. After nearly twenty minutes, or thereabouts, a new thread was started by someone called Elm1.

Everyone please calm down. We are working to get to the bottom of this. Please do not speculate or offer information to anyone. All will be explained soon.

"Damn it," Jake muttered. He pointed to the screen. "Do you think you could track where that message came from?"

Mari propped himself up again and studied the post for a moment, then nodded.

"It's doable," he murmured. "Must have come from somewhere. It's not stopped them babbling at one another but it's settled things to a degree. Let me surf for a while." He looked up at Jake with a quirk of his lips. "You don't have to watch. It's probably quite dull."

Jake looked back at him as if puzzled, then said, "You have no idea what you look like when you do your thing, do you? I assure you, it's not dull."

"How would I know?" Mari shrugged.

Wrapping his fingers around the edges of the laptop screen, he touched his thumbs lightly to the point where the Elm1 post still sat on screen and closed his eyes. He tipped his head forward and shivered as he tuned out the quiet London sitting room and slid effortlessly out of his own head and into the spreading network of information that was feeding into his machine.

Chapter Seven

Not for nothing was the Internet known as the web. When Mari navigated it, that was how it felt — a maze of different routes and angles of inquiry, all interconnected and running back down to a hub, which was where he stepped in. But it was a web of passageways and choices that somehow became alive when he reached into it, opening up the Interface. It was this gift, more than his talent for code, that had reeled in the recruiters at MI6. They knew about Elemental Interfaces, of course, but the chance to work with one was a rare thing. Not all Interfaces were sane, for a start. Given some of the mentality out there in the web it was hardly surprising. He didn't normally interface like this every day, sometimes not even every month, because it was addictive and the more he succumbed, the more likely he was to join the lunatics. Usually he did it when they had no other option, when it gave him access to the kind of information he couldn't get by conventional means.

It was incredible though. He never felt quite so free as he did when he let go of the real world and slipped into the network. Hackers only followed trails of code and relied on that to get them into two-dimensional websites.

An Interface like him could go beyond the keyboard, stepping out into the ether, leaving his body behind him and becoming one with the streams of information chasing themselves around the globe. It was like stripping off and throwing himself into a fast-running river. The initial cold-water shock made his pulse race and reminded him of all the hidden dangers, submerged rocks and sudden drops over sharp precipices that he hadn't considered before jumping. Like wild swimming, interfacing was not without its dangers. More and more IT security systems were trying to block what he and other Interfaces did. He knew as much because it had been his job, in both Cambridge and Catalunya, to come up with the programs that could keep a determined snoop out. Fast as it was, though, modern technology couldn't yet match pace with organic intellect and human biology. The defense systems, even the AI systems, were only code, after all, a sequence of prearranged algorithms programmed into the system by humans. A clever Interface could work around those instructions if he, or she, had to.

Put simply, interfacing took him away from the mundane world into places that the hackers never even dreamed about. It was like having access to the biggest interactive game in the universe. Little wonder that it was so addictive.

Mari pushed back from Elm1's post and it was like stepping into a stranger's room, moving slowly toward him, running his hands up a man's arms in a careful dance, engaging with him, shoving him back up against his own walls and stroking higher until he could run fingers through his hair and push down into his skull. Of course, that was an illusion. He couldn't quite break through the other side of the web into a person's real life but he could get as close as possible to that. He could slide his caressing hands as far into the message as the tips of the typist's fingers.

When he reached the source of the Elm1 stream, he let his mind open out, viewing the scene in widescreen mode, seeing the ISP points like places on a virtual map inside his head and registering their relative locations, cross-referencing them, checking out the other places on the web that they appeared, tracing the streams of information interacting with them to their respective sources. He loved this, being able to treat the internet like his own private playground. Interfacing meant that he did not just see numbers and addresses. He saw actual places and got threads of emotion and all manner of curious things. He saw a peculiar house like a fairytale tower, set on the edge of a wood. He saw people coming and going. He felt the tide of tension rising and falling from the fingers that touched the other sides of those keys.

Then he slid away from it, letting go, responding as his body called him home.

For a while after slipping into his body, he felt heavy and nauseous, and as he released the screen his head hit the edge of the keyboard. He just lay there for a few moments, getting used to the thunderous hammering of his own heartbeat and the odd noises of the living room. The world felt confining, small and flat after being so free. That was one of the downsides of surfing.

Jake put a hand to the back of his neck, rubbing lightly before sliding his fingers over his hair.

"Are you okay?" he asked.

"Ynnnhhh," Mari said incoherently. It took a tremendous effort to push himself up onto his elbows again. "Okay... good. Yeah. That was...interesting. Sender doesn't touch keys. Elm1 is typed by... I dunno, his secretary? Maybe. She's hot for him. He's quite posh, I think. Nice house. Up near Hounslow, Strawberry Hill? I think that was the area. Dunno if he lives there, or she does, or it's maybe just an office. There's a park. She thinks about taking him for romantic walks there and not doing much walking. Building is tall...higher than the houses around about. She thinks of it like her ivory tower. She can see the park from there. Should be findable." He rubbed his forehead. "It would be very nice if you were to massage my neck again."

Jake moved both hands to Mari's back and dug into the muscles that connected neck to shoulders, pressing hard and rolling his thumbs out as his palms pushed inward and down like he was kneading dough.

"All my days..." Mari groaned softly. "Like that. Yes."

Jake did it again, moving his hands inward toward the top of Mari's spine.

"It's hard to believe you can get all that information," he

murmured, kissing Mari's hair. "And I didn't know it took this much out of you to do it."

"I had to come and go a few times. I was triangulating from her other posts. She does her own social media stuff from the same machine. I worked out the emotional stuff from that—things she posts online to people who don't know what she does for a living. He's called Roy, the guy that she works for. He… I think he works in medicare or something. Family Planning? Something like that. Birthright is a sideline." Mari tilted his head to look up at Jake. "I'm not comfortable with him. Not sure why yet. It's just a gut feeling."

"Considering some of the bullshit he's spouting on that website, I'd be surprised if you thought he was a paragon of virtue," Jake told him. "We need to find out how people get invited into this group, and where they meet up."

"I ghosted her keyboard," Mari said, snuggling down on the sofa cushions again, head in his arms. "Got you onto the database as a friend of Louis'. I called you Nathan Detroit. Hope you don't mind. It was the first thing that popped into my head."

"That'll be good for monitoring, but I want to get closer. I don't believe in coincidence. Two people we know of, that burned for no apparent reason, were a part of this group, and if the reaction we just saw on their message board is any indication, I'd say so was the third. Someone in that organization has some answers and whoever it is, I have a feeling they're not going to be talking about it online. If they have regular meetings, or whatever, I doubt anyone can just walk in off the street." Jake stopped for a moment, still absently kneading Mari's neck and shoulders, his hands very gentle. "Louis is our best bet. There are at least three people on the forums that knew him personally. I'll bet one of them can either tell us how to get in, or knows someone who can."

"So who do you want to quiz next?" Mari murmured, enjoying the warm pressure on his neck muscles, his eyes still closed. "I can go back in and try to find out where Louis sent his comments from if you like, but I'm not sure how it will work out. I never tried ghosting someone who died before."

"No, I think we can find our information the old-fashioned way this time. You still got the number for Mr. Spanks-A-Lot, right? We can ask him if he'll introduce us to Louis' friend, Don."

Mari turned his head to one side, eyeing Jake balefully. "Oh, joy!"

Jake grinned and pulled him into his arms. "He's not my most favorite person, either, but his friend may have more information."

"I suppose so." Mari twisted around under him and craned his neck to kiss Jake's nose. The warmth of his body was oddly comforting after the disorienting sensation of surfing and he was perfectly happy to just lie here for a while. "If this Donny the Dom can tell us anything, it might cut a few corners. I guess I should give Colm a bell then."

Chapter Eight

Jake almost told him to forget about calling Colm. It felt good to just lie here with Mari in his arms, but in the end, he knew he would feel too horrible if someone else died and he'd not followed up on the leads they had so far. He tried not to listen in on the call, though. Hearing Mari sweet-talking another man in that light, flirtatious way of his got Jake's hackles up, coming so soon after the tender intimacy of kissing and holding him. To distract himself, he thought about Cordiline's question, of whether he and Mari being together enhanced their Elemental gifts. Maybe that wasn't true, but it did seem to ramp up their respective appetites for sex. Mari had not been shy about admitting that he had a very strong libido, but since they'd become an item, his hunger was often insatiable. They made love practically every day—often more than once or twice a day. Alex, his last boyfriend, had loved sex but even he had not needed it the way Mari Gale did. Mari consumed him like he needed Jake's body pressed against him to live. In turn, Mari's lust fired up his own appetite. Jake was quite glad that he didn't have to go to work the next day. He didn't think he would have the energy.

* * * *

Colm invited them over and promised Mari he'd round up Don O'Brien so they could talk with him. Standing in front of Colm's apartment building half an hour later, they were buzzed in and greeted by Colm, who was casually dressed in sweatpants and a sleeveless shirt that showed off both muscles and ink. "Donny's on his way over. I should warn you, he's still shaken up about what happened the other night."

"I'm not surprised, so am I." Mari took control of the niceties so Jake didn't have to. "How are you feeling?"

"Ahh...so-so." Colm shrugged. "Still short of breath sometimes, if I try to overdo things. You look fabulous though."

Mari preened and murmured, "Thanks."

Tension rippled across Jake's shoulders and he had to make an effort not to curl his hands into fists. This was ridiculous. He didn't normally behave like a possessive, jealous asshole when he was in a relationship, but a number of factors had his usual confidence shaken. Mari's lukewarm reaction to his dropping the 'L' word, the fact that Mari hadn't automatically turned Colm down on his suggestion of a threesome, and their two steps forward and one step back bedroom tango, all had Jake wanting to take his frustration out on someone. Colm made for a convenient target. Something about the young man just got Jake's back up.

"Thanks for seeing us at such short notice," Jake said in an attempt to be civil. "Since Donny isn't here yet, can I ask you a few questions first?"

"Sure," Colm said, still smiling as he led them into the apartment. "That's why we're here, isn't it?"

"How well did you know Louis Cortez?"

Colm seemed taken aback by his full-on interrogation and he waved them vaguely through to the long sofa in the living room, which, much like Jake's, was open to the kitchen. The kitchen was more spacious than his but less tidy. A step ladder ran up to a mezzanine area over the lounge space that contained a low-level bed and some drawer units. There were tall windows running along one side of the room and a tripartite oriental screen in front of the wall adjacent to the entrance hall. Mari took a perch on the edge of the chocolate leather sofa and eyed Jake narrowly, as if silently warning him to watch his attitude.

"What does Lou have to do with any of this?" Colm asked, narrowing his eyes.

"You and Don were at the club the other night when he burst into flames. He knew you, all right," Jake said.

"I thought you were here to talk about spanking your boyfriend?" Colm flashed back, looking to Mari for assistance.

"I'm sorry, Colm. I should have explained things better when I called. Jake is helping the police with their inquiries," Mari added in a rather less incendiary voice.

"As in, 'they think he started the fire'?" Colm laughed, but it was a ragged sound.

"As in, I'm a trained arson investigator with the Detroit PD," Jake corrected him. "Now, shall we start over?"

Colm's eyes widened. Mari uttered a sigh.

"Jake, Colm didn't set fire to Louis. Cut him some slack."

"We only have his word for that," Jake grumbled.

"I don't have to tell you anything, Jake," Colm said. "But since I can see it's important to you, Louis came to the club nights, sometimes. Like I told Ilmarinen in the park, he's more Donny's client than mine, but everyone was aware of him. He was one of those people who's kind of larger than life, if you get what I mean? He'd get right up in your face if he thought you were ignoring him. That's all I know about him really. He wasn't a personal friend." He got up and walked over to the refrigerator. "Drink?"

"No, thanks," Jake said.

"I'll have a glass of water, thank you," Mari answered, and shot Jake another warning look.

Jake gave a nearly imperceptible shrug.

Colm had fairly thick skin, it would seem, because he fetched a tall, beaded glass of iced water and grabbed a beer then came to sit on the couch beside Mari, taking a quick swig from the bottle.

"So," he said casually, "did you guys talk over what we were discussing the other day?"

Mari sipped his drink and cast a wary glance at Jake before answering. "We've not really had the chance to talk about anything but the fire yet."

"Not that it's any of your business," Jake snapped. As soon as the words were out of his mouth, he pressed his lips together for a moment. Being antagonistic was the last thing he should be doing if he wanted to draw as much as he could from Colm.

Colm raised an eyebrow. Mari put a hand over his eyes and shook his head.

The young Dom just gestured toward Jake with the neck of the bottle and said, "Actually, it's how I make a living, so…that's not quite right. Look, Jake, I'm not trying to steal your guy, okay? He's very cute, yeah, of course. And if you two have problems with the whole bondage thing then I'd like to help you get around them. Because that's what I do. And if Ilmarinen wants to try it out, then I want him to have a good experience. But you do seem to me to have a problem with this, if you don't mind my saying."

"No, I don't," Jake said, making an effort to keep the growl out of his voice. He didn't quite succeed and he took a breath. This was already not going well and it was his fault. The man had done nothing overt and yet he couldn't shake the feeling of wanting to wrap his fingers around Colm's throat when he talked about wanting to tie Mari up. He wondered if this was how Mari felt whenever he saw Cordiline and suddenly some of his attitude toward the detective made sense. "The only thing I have a problem with is you hitting on him when I'm not around."

"Jake!" Mari exhaled tersely.

"I didn't hit on him," Colm said. "I just asked if he wanted to explore BDSM, and I did ask him to invite you, as well."

"You don't think propositioning him for a three-way counts as hitting on him?"

"I don't think that at all," Colm told him coolly. "I could see that he was worried about how you might react and I suggested that he brought you over, too. I thought it might put his mind at ease."

"Please don't do this," Mari said in quiet desperation. His eyes were wide and alarmed.

"It's okay, I'm not going to fight him," Colm said, flashing a reassuring smile at Mari. "I wouldn't want to damage him. He's too cute for that."

The sudden flash of rage Jake felt at the subtle mockery took him completely by surprise. He'd fought long and hard to learn how to let things like that roll off his back, to not let the hot temper inside get a toe hold and push him out of control. It had been several years since he'd had the urge to pummel someone with so little provocation. Scathing words formed on his tongue but he could feel Mari's distress like a physical presence in the room and he took a breath and let it out. "Look, I came here because I want to find out why a man is dead. Why a few people are dead. Let's just focus on that."

Colm looked from Jake to Mari and back again, a frown creasing his forehead. "Okay, okay…" he sighed. "Look, I was only trying to help. And I'm not sure what else I can tell you about the guy in the club. Lou was a loose cannon, you know. He had medical issues, I think. Psychiatric issues, maybe. Donny might be able to tell you more. I think the whippings helped him to keep his moods under control, kind of like you seem to think the bondage will help you out." He turned his head again, smiling encouragement at Mari. "It soothed him."

Jake purposely ignored the way he tried to divert the conversation.

"Why do you think he had medical or psychiatric issues?" he asked, keeping his tone polite and neutral in spite of his frustration. "Did he tell you that, or is it something you assumed because of his behavior?"

Colm narrowed his eyes just a fraction but he didn't lose his temper.

"It's the way he was with people, quite short, almost autistic-spectrum short. He wasn't wired for personal space. If he wanted something then he'd just be right there in your face, demanding it. When he came to see Donny, it was usually because he was frantic about something and he needed a good hard thrashing to settle him down. Once he'd got it he was fine again. Quiet, actually. It was…odd."

"Sometimes physical chastisement has that effect," Mari said cryptically. "It's like a safety valve. Did you ever talk to him?"

"Not really. He wasn't my client, like I said. He didn't seem very interested in small talk for the sake of it."

"Did he have a temper?" Jake asked. "Did you ever see him get in a fight with anyone?"

"Not a physical fight, no." Colm took another swig from the bottle in his hand. "He would shout at you if he thought you weren't taking him seriously enough, but Donny had a handle on him. He could usually settle him down pretty quick."

"Did you get the sense that if Donny wasn't there, keeping him calm, that he might have crossed the line though? You know how some people just 'feel' like they're ticking time bombs?"

"Yeah, yeah, that's just how he was," Colm conceded after a moment's thought.

Jake fell quiet again and Mari asked him, "What? What are you thinking?"

Jake shrugged. "I'm not sure yet. It just seems odd. I've known a few other Fire Elementals and usually by the time they get out of their teens they have a handle on the temper thing. It only comes out like it would for anyone else, not randomly. An out-of-control adult Fire Elemental is…really odd."

But what he was actually mulling over was that, yet again, he'd come so close to letting that fire inside him spill over, burning away his control. He'd not struggled with his gift like this for years. Why was he finding it so hard now? Was Cordiline right, and Mari's element of air was stoking up the fire inside him? If that was true, did it mean that they were already doomed as a couple? Had Mari been right to reject his declaration of love?

He pushed that thought away angrily. It was not something that he wanted to entertain.

Colm looked back and forth from one to the other of them while they spoke, as if he was watching a tennis match. When neither of them said anything else, he asked, "What's a Fire Elemental? Is that different from ordinary mental?"

Mari chuckled. "You could say that, yes."

Jake was about to ask him what he knew about Birthright, but the buzzer went off and Colm got up to let Donny in. The other Dom was older, probably in his late thirties, his dark, short-cropped hair running to gray at the temples already, though his face was tanned and smooth apart from some creases around his slate gray eyes and the solemn line of his mouth. He had a number of facial piercings which made him look quite fierce, though his demeanor as he came in and shook hands with them both was anything but. Those eyes were tired and haunted.

"Thanks for coming over," Mari told him, swinging back into diplomacy mode. "It must have been a terrible few days for you. I hope you're feeling all right."

Don assured them that he would be okay and Colm got him a beer without asking if he wanted it. As he sat down on the couch and took a long pull on the proffered bottle, his hand shook.

Jake took a seat across from him, his demeanor gentler with Don than he'd been toward Colm.

"I really appreciate you coming out to talk with us," Jake started. "We're trying to find out what exactly happened to Louis Cortez. Colm says you knew him better than he did. Did you know him long?"

"About two years or so, maybe longer." Don sighed, sounding like he'd answered these questions before, which he probably had.

"I know this is hard, but I was wondering if you'd noticed a personality change in him during that time?" Jake pressed him. After a pause, Don nodded.

"Yeah…since you come to mention it, I reckon over the last…maybe nine months or so, he's been like, kinda hyper. Like they maybe changed his medication or something and it wasn't agreeing with him. He was in the army, once upon a time. I reckon that gave him an outlet for his frustration. Once they demobbed him, he didn't know what to do with himself. He missed that discipline. So, he came to me to get it in a different sort of way." He tapped the bottle against the neat, clean nails of his free hand. "Lou could be blunt with people, and when they took it the wrong way, he would fly off the handle with 'em. But he wasn't violent, not normally. Just the last few months when he's been round to see me there's been a look in his eyes, like he's not all there, you know? Kinda creepy. I've been glad to get him done and out of there lately."

"Was he different the other night? Did he do or say anything different that you noticed?" Mari asked, keeping his tone gentle and persuasive.

Don looked him up and down briefly, as if he could see through his clothes, then shook his head. "What, apart from doing his best impression of a roman fuckin' candle, you mean?" His laughter sounded bitter and brittle.

Jake waited until he'd taken another swallow of his beer before asking, "Did he talk to you about this group called Birthright?"

Don made a rude noise through his nostrils and shook his head again but it wasn't a negation of the question so much as a look of bewilderment.

"I knew he was involved with some bunch of mentalists. Thought it was a political thing at first. He'd come and tell me stuff that this mate of his had been feeding him. Elitist bullshit, most of it, I thought. Master Race stuff. I told him it sounded like the sort of bollocks I quit the rat race to avoid hearing. Lou didn't like that, not one bit. Gave me a proper dressing down about it."

"Do you know when he got involved with them?" Jake

asked.

Don thought about it for a while. "Not exactly, but I'd guess maybe a year ago? Maybe not quite that long. He'd been recruited, he said, for other stuff, before the Birthright bastards came along. I remember, once, him telling me that the Government bought him out of the army so they could experiment on him. I just thought he'd stopped taking his pills."

"Right," Jake said, thinking again. All of this fit in with the time that Don also noted his personality change. "He ever tell you where Birthright meet?"

Don gave him an appraising look.

"Why're you interested in them? I'm telling you, they're nothing but a bunch of fascist arseholes." He paused. "You think they got something to do with Lou going up like a torch? Don't see how that's possible."

"Neither do I," Jake admitted. "But I think there's a connection, maybe. If so, I'd like to ask them some questions. Did Louis ever say anything about meeting with them in person?" Jake asked again.

"It was kind of hard to tell what was real and what wasn't with him, sometimes." Donny pulled a face and took another long glug from his beer bottle. "I think they must have been somewhere here in London 'cause he talked about them 'sorting things out in this shithole city', a lot. But I dunno. He mentioned some bloke's name but I can't remember it. Something short, Dave, or Ray, or something."

Jake blew out a short breath and ran a hand through his hair. He had been hoping Don could tell him more about where they might meet up or mention someone Louis had befriended from Birthright so he didn't have to ask Mari to sort through their message boards again, but it seemed to be a dead end.

"Anything else you can think of, anything Louis might have said about Birthright? Anyone he might have been seeing, maybe, that would be able to tell us about them?" Jake asked without much hope.

"No," Don said grimly and emptied the bottle. He tilted his head and stared at Mari again until he retreated uncharacteristically behind his tumbler of water, gulping some of it down.

"You two cops, then? You don't look like a cop." Don glanced back at Jake. "Him, maybe."

"No," Mari said, his voice very soft. "I'm not a cop. Just an interested bystander."

Jake gave Don a wry smile. "Not exactly, either. I'm not working officially, and I'm not on the force here. I have a friend who is, though, and I'm just helping to get him some information."

That was mostly the truth. If Jake dug deep enough to find anything interesting, he would pass the information on to Cordiline.

"That figures. If you were with the boys in blue, you'd have greased my palm first." Don laughed darkly and nudged Colm for another drink. The younger man had been unusually quiet while this interrogation had been going on and he hopped off the sofa and crossed over to his cooler to grab another beer. He held up a second bottle and waved it at Jake, an inquiring look in his eye. Donny was looking at Mari again like he was a winning lottery ticket someone had just dropped.

Jake's phone buzzed in his pocket and, when he looked down, he saw it was Cordiline.

"I need to take this," he said, standing. "Back in a minute."

He dropped a kiss on Mari's forehead on his way to the door. Mari's hand caught the back of his neck and he returned the kiss, on his lips, with rather more heat.

"Jake, where are you?" Cordiline asked when he answered the phone, down in the foyer of the building.

"I'm at a witness's house, digging, why?"

There was a pause before Cordiline said, "I'm not sure I should have asked you to get involved. Shit is happening, Jake. You need to watch your arse."

"What? What's happening?" Jake demanded.

"I can't talk about this on the phone. Meet me tomorrow, same place. One o'clock. Stop investigating, Jake."

"John, what...?" But Jake was talking to a dead air. "Damn it!"

He turned around and headed back inside.

"...it's not as if I've never been able to do it," Mari was saying, with a wave of his tumbler. "I had a pretty high sex drive. But I kind of went through a lot of major upheavals in the last ten years or so, and the dyspareunia only really became an issue when I was in Barcelona and in a serious relationship."

"You must have been an early starter." Don laughed. "You're what...twenty-three? Twenty-four?"

"Twenty-seven," Mari corrected him. "But, yeah. I was... precocious."

"So where does the flogging come in?" Colm pressed him. "How did you figure out you liked it?"

Mari sipped his drink and for a moment he almost looked coy.

"I had a...kind of a mentor, I guess, when I was quite young. My parents were ardent pacifists, I have to add. Neither of them has ever lifted a hand to me. But before I went to university I lived with my father in a big house in Malaysia, that was owned by... I guess he was a kind of local bigwig, he was very well respected. And I was pretty much raised and looked after by his staff while Papi was working. It was one of his guys that first leathered me." He chewed on his lips for a moment at the memory. "I can't even recall what I'd done, but it brought the household into disrepute in some way. And I got strapped, five times, across the backs of my legs. I was kind of stunned by it at first, but the more I thought about it..." He stopped and took another sip.

"Did you want him to do it again?" Colm chuckled.

"Not at first. I mean, it hurt. And I was kind of brassed off that he'd even dared lay a hand on me." Mari laughed. "But the memory of it stayed with me. I cheeked him out a few times afterwards to see if he would do it again."

Both Doms laughed at that. Donny asked, "So you've never been spanked by a pro?"

"No one even flicked a switch at me in the heat of passion for the last eight years or so. Until..." He waved his free hand casually toward the door, letting Jake know he was aware that he'd returned.

"I bet you were ready to burst." Colm gave a husky chortle. He had taken advantage of Jake's brief absence to slide onto the sofa beside Mari and was watching him like a cat watching a small rodent. "I don't know how you've stood it for so long."

"I'm made of granite," Mari said.

"I'd be prepared to bet you're certainly not," Don said in a surer tone. "Not when you're strapped up tight in a sling with a guy either end of you."

"Not the sort of thing that happens every day though, is it?" Mari pointed out to him.

"You want to get tied up, you just say the word. You're talking to the professionals," Donny promised, his expression growing more serious.

Mari twisted around in his seat, looking for Jake, and beamed when he saw him, still and watchful in the doorway. His expression sobered almost instantly.

"What's happened?"

"I don't know exactly. Cordiline didn't want to talk on the phone. He wants to meet up tomorrow. Something's got him spooked, though."

"You sure he doesn't just want to hold hands under the pub table again?" Mari managed a playful wink and Jake rolled his eyes.

"No. He sounded freaked out. I've never heard him sound like that."

"So, why don't you relax. Have another drink, and forget about it 'til tomorrow," Colm suggested. "Have some fun with us while we strap Mari up and show you how to fuck the daylights out of him."

Jake sighed, moving back into the room. "Sure, why not. We'll see how long it takes before I beat the shit out of you."

"You were right, he doesn't like you, does he? Sorry, mate." Don laughed and Mari poked Colm hard enough to make him wince.

"Told you!"

"Ahhh, c'mon, Jakey, you know you want to see him wriggle," Don cajoled, chuckling as he drained his beer bottle and patted Mari's knee.

Jake fumed in silence. If this went on much longer, he was going to make them both regret his coming here. And possibly do something that he would regret, too.

"We're leaving." *Fuck not being a jealous asshole!*

"That's up to him, Jake," Colm said, pointing at Mari who looked startled but was uncharacteristically silent. Jake held out his hand.

"Mari, are you coming with me? Or not? Your call." There was so much more that he wanted to say, but he would not issue an ultimatum. There could be no going back from that sort of emotional leverage and he wasn't prepared for what he would do if Mari said no.

For a moment, he thought that Mari might just do that. The look in his pale eyes was guarded and hard to read. He didn't seem angry, but Jake thought he was confused and that seemed so out of character that it fired up his defensive ire again. Then Mari eased himself to his feet in a graceful, fluid way that extracted him from under Colm's possessive arm without having to push him away. Colm rose too.

"What are you, his dog or something?" Colm protested.

Mari just shook his head in response. "Colm, don't."

Jake got in his face before he could say more. "You want to sit back down, trust me, Mr. Fleming."

"This is my flat, you don't tell me what to do," Colm said, losing his cool for the first time.

"Colm...sit down," Donny told him, tugging at the leg of his sweatpants. Don was still watching Mari, who had shifted so that Jake was between him and Colm, but so subtly that it didn't seem like he was sidling away. "Sit. It's not up to us, or Jakey here. It's up to Mari. What do you want, sweetheart?"

Mari looked from him to Jake, and for a while he seemed to be holding his breath. When he let it go in a rush, the words spilled out of him like water, "I think we should go. I need to lie down."

"I got a bed right up there you can go lay down on, princess," Colm said, reaching past Jake to Mari. His arm brushed Jake's and in a disorientating blink, Jake was looking at someone else, in a different room, with the thump of loud club music playing overhead.

He was laughing, one tatted-up arm bent and resting on another man's shoulder as he watched himself and Mari walking toward the cellar stairs.

"You have the devil's own fucking luck! Every fucking queen and randy slobbering bitch in this place have been wetting their panties over the guy upstairs for months and the one night he comes in with that blond piece on his arm, they're straight over here talking to you."

Jake could feel the way Colm's mouth grinned at the comment.

"Guy Upstairs is fit as fuck, but a bit uptight if you ask me. Now that pretty-boy slut he's banging… I'd have me some of that. Did you see him? He was practically backing himself up onto my dick!" He laughed.

"Don't get all big about it. They both walked away, didn't they?"

"For now, maybe. Bet you any money he'll be back though. I know his type. Guy Upstairs is gonna have his hands full trying to keep that one happy on his own. If I play my cards right, I can shag both of them!"

"And if you don't?"

"If I don't, I'll still bang that blond queen when his boyfriend ain't lookin!"

In the background, Jake had been half-hearing a heated conversation growing louder and there was a scream. Colm turned his head and Jake was ripped back into the present.

Jake sucked in a hard breath. The whole memory had only taken a few seconds but left him shaking with rage. Colm had his hand around Mari's arm and Mari was trying to extract himself without physically shoving him away. Something inside Jake snapped and all his hard fought for control melted away in an instant. There was no thought. His hand slammed into Colm's chest, knocking him back a couple steps.

Colm swung at him. Jake blocked him easily and jabbed him once in the gut, and again with his left fist to the jaw. It was over by the time Mari grabbed his arm, pulling him away. He was shouting something but Jake couldn't hear him through the white noise in his head. Colm crumpled onto the sofa. Jake looked at Don, eyes blazing, but the older Dom just held up his hands in surrender.

Jake stood over Colm, fists still clenched. "Motherfucker, you touch him again...you come near him again, I will take your fucking head off."

Mari was still tugging at him, his face a picture of incredulity. Jake finally turned and took his arm in a firm grip, propelling him toward the door then slamming it shut behind them. He was so furious he couldn't speak, couldn't think, couldn't do anything but march Mari away from there as fast as their long legs would take them, down the steps and out into the street. The air was cooler on his face and his head felt less like it might explode.

"Jake..."

Jake ignored him, pulling him along.

"Jake..."

"Don't fucking talk to me."

"Jake? Are you mad at me?"

Jake stopped. He stared at Mari, utterly incredulous.

"Are you fucking high? What the fuck do you think? You want to go back there on your own, well fine, you go right ahead. Don't let me stop you." He turned, his hand still on Mari's arm, and started walking again.

Mari let himself be towed for a few moments longer. Then he stopped in his tracks and the loss of momentum tugged Jake around to face him. He opened his mouth to growl, "What nuhhh...?"

Mari's mouth covered his and swallowed the words as he kissed Jake savagely.

"That was amazing," he breathed as their lips parted wetly. "I am so horny for you."

"You are out of your mind, do you realize that?" Jake murmured, some of the anger robbed from him by Mari's kiss. "You're not pissed off that I didn't leave you there with the low-rent Marquis de Sade and Caligula?"

"They were just my teasers. You're the stud," Mari whispered in his ear, nuzzling into his hair. "You were so forceful. It was very stimulating."

There was mischief in his sparkling blue eyes as he drew back to look at Jake, still twined around him, pulling on him like a climbing vine, pressing himself close. It told Jake that Mari wasn't exaggerating about finding his burst of temper stimulating.

"So violence turns you on, does it?" Jake huffed softly. He had not really been angry with Mari to begin with but he was still furious over the glimpse into Colm's private plans for him. Even so, he shouldn't have punched the man, but Mari's seeming reluctance to leave had poured gasoline on his fire. "Mari, if you engineered that scene upstairs so you could get me to beat the shit out of him..."

"No! I wouldn't do something like that." Mari's eyes widened, full of innocence.

Jake took him by the shoulders to look at him.

"Do you really want to have sex with them?"

"No. I..." Mari heaved a weary sigh. "What they were offering got me excited but I think that if you had gone and left me there, I would have been too nervous still," he admitted unhappily. "Don't be too hard on Colm. He was playing the game. He didn't push me. It's my fault if I didn't give him proper rules to play by."

Jake blew out a frustrated breath. "You don't know the man, Mari. And after what I saw when he brushed my hand, I really don't want you to."

Mari took Jake's hands in his, folding long, strong fingers, which were a match for his own, around them. He turned them to kiss Jake's knuckles gently. "You saw a memory?"

Jake pressed his lips together and nodded. "He was talking about us, to someone at the club when we were walking away that night, before the fire—talking about you, and what he wanted to do to you. It wasn't nice, what he said."

Mari blinked at him, but the mischief had faded from his wide blue eyes.

"That's...that's very noble of you, Jake. I appreciate it, really. You don't have to defend my honor, though," he said in a more earnest tone.

"You're right, I don't have to," Jake managed, through gritted teeth. "But maybe someone ought to have done before. It makes me angry that guys like that...that they think they can take advantage of you so easily. And sometimes, you don't seem like you know how to stop them." The words were out of his mouth before he could censor them and he wanted to take them back. He tensed, half expecting Mari to slap him and walk away.

"No one is going to take advantage of me, Jake," Mari soothed him, instead. "Only you, if you want to."

"I'd never do that. Not unless you wanted it, too." Jake knew he sounded defensive, but he could not stop himself. He needed Mari to understand that he would never be in danger from him.

"I know. Forgive me." Mari's expression was suddenly gentler. "You're my hero."

Jake held one of his hands but turned the other so he could caress Mari's cheek, sliding his fingers along his jaw and into his hair and looking into his eyes earnestly.

"Don't fuck with my head, Ilmarinen. No games, okay? I'm not going to demand fidelity because I've seen it fuck up too many relationships when it's what one person wants and not the other. If you want to mess around with someone else, fine, but don't be coy about it. Just tell me. Because trying to guess what you really want is going to lead to me punching someone else in the face, and while that seems to be turning you on, it's really not a good idea to test my control. And, yeah, that sounds like some cheesy line from a comic book, but you don't understand how hard I have fought to be who I am, instead of what I could have been."

Mari opened his mouth to say something and this time it was Jake who kissed him to shut him up. He wrapped his arms around Mari, pulling him up close and letting him feel some of the passionate heat simmering just below the surface. He slid his hands down to cup and squeeze Mari's arse, swallowing his gasp and pushing his tongue into his mouth, grinding their hips together until he was sure he'd scattered every last thought in Mari's head.

"Let's go back to mine," Jake murmured huskily in his ear when their lips parted again.

This time, Mari did not argue with him.

Chapter Nine

Jake and Mari walked several blocks in silence. From time to time Mari slowed to check his phone or fire off a text message. It wasn't exactly abnormal behavior for him but he was awfully quiet and, by the time Jake had cooled down, he noticed it.

"I'm sorry about tonight, Ilmari. Are you okay?" he asked at last.

"Uh-huh." Mari nodded, flashing him a tight smile. He was quick to explain though. "My grandmother is here. She called Mama yesterday. I didn't even know she was coming over. I asked if everything was okay and Mama said it was and not to worry." He hesitated briefly. "Jake. You know when someone tells you something and you know it's not right...but you don't want to argue?"

"Yes?" Jake said warily.

"I'm scared," Mari told him frankly. "I told her I'd come home and she just said not to. Like it didn't matter. But I'm still scared. My grandmother lives in New York. She's not popped over for tea and cake."

He looked briefly lost and stared at the phone in his hand as if he was expecting something more from it.

Jake put his arm around Mari and pulled him closer, kissing his cheek.

"I can't say if your feeling is on the mark or not, Mari, but honestly, that would worry me, too." In fact, it did worry him, but he didn't want to come out and say it like that. "Maybe you should head home. I can go with you, if you want?"

Mari shook his head at once.

"Jake, ten minutes ago, you were furious enough to punch a man. You really do not want to meet my grandmother right now," he said with a roll of his eyes. "I just hope she's not being a bitch when Mama's feeling awful."

Jake grinned at him. "Unless she's threatening to tie you up and whip your arse, I don't think there is any danger of me punching your grandmother."

That won him a skeptical laugh.

"I wouldn't put money on that. And you do realize, don't you, that you just ruined that fantasy for me. Now every time I think about taking a spanking I'm going to imagine her doing it." Mari sighed. "Thank you so much."

"You should stop in there at least," Jake said, still grinning at him, unfazed by his lover's quiet dismay. "If you don't want me to meet her, I can go home and you can come over for your spanking later, or tomorrow, if you want?"

"Well if you're desperate for punishment, too, it's not far out of our way." Mari sighed. "She is not like my mother though. You can call her Ma'am all you want. She'll enjoy that."

Jake took his hand and gave it a reassuring squeeze.

"Don't worry, Mari. I'm sure it'll be fine." He smiled, getting lost in his own thoughts for a few moments while they walked. "I wish you could have met my grandmother. She's...she was, really cool. I loved spending time with her when I was younger."

Mari looked interested. "You know, I think that's the first time you ever told me anything about your family, voluntarily. I was beginning to think you were left under a bush or something."

Jake's smile turned rueful. "Might as well have been." He could tell Mari was dying to ask him more but he was not in the mood to get into that whole mess. He was never in the mood to talk about his family really, so he hoped Mari would just let it drop.

"Why have you never said anything about them before?" Mari poked him, reluctant to let go of the bone once he had it.

Jake heaved a sigh. "My grandmother is the only one of any of them worth mentioning, and she's been gone thirteen years. It's just not something I want to talk about."

They were walking again and Mari slipped a comfortable arm around his shoulders, the situation at Colm's apartment evidently forgiven, as he murmured, "I can't imagine that. I mean, I know my family is pretty dysfunctional but they're good people on the whole. I love them, even Grandmama, truth be told. They'd do anything for anyone, so long as it didn't interfere with work too much."

If he was bitter about that it didn't creep into his voice. The way he said it was weary and matter-of-fact, as if it was something that he was resigned to. Jake was already accustomed to Annabel Gale's schedule. She was rarely idle, even though he knew that she was supposed to be taking it easy. Mari had never gone into the details of her illness with him but if it slowed her down, he dreaded to think what she had been like before. Whenever he went around to the house on Albany Street, Dr. Gale senior was invariably writing or researching something, constantly busy.

"I guess it's paid off. Your mother has her own place here and all," he pointed out.

"The house belongs to Grandmama," Mari said with a shrug. "We rent it from her. I imagine that's part of the reason why she's here. She hasn't lived in London for years but she never got rid of it. It was making a shedload of money for her before we moved in. Not that she needs it. So, you stayed with your grandmother a lot when you were a kid, did you? What was she like?"

Jake recognized that as Mari shutting the door on something he didn't want to think about. He guessed it would be right there in his face soon enough.

"She was tough," Jake answered after a moment's thought. "Fearless. She wouldn't back down from anyone. Not even...well, no one. Women are— I don't want to say they aren't treated with respect, but the Bodéwadmi leaders are usually men. The elders, the council members, the spiritual leaders, almost all are male. My grandmother was respected, though, and not just because she was a fire keeper. She was smart, a survivor, and she had endless stories, and a way of telling them that made them stick. When she spoke, you really learned something." Jake shook his head. All those memories were bittersweet. She had been his one shelter when he'd been a child, the one adult in his life who he'd been able to trust. "When I was a kid there were only a dozen people in the world that spoke the Potawatomi language, and she was one of them. She got the council to listen to her about preserving the language and teaching it to kids so it wouldn't be lost."

"Potawatomi?" Mari queried.

"Potawatomi is what the Ojibwa and Ottawa called us, and that is the tribal name the US government recognizes. Bodéwadmi is what we call ourselves. It means 'keepers of the fire'. Several hundred years ago, the Ojibwa, Ottawa and Potawatomi formed the Council of Three Fires, an alliance between our peoples. The Ojibwa were called the Older Brother and are the 'keepers of the faith', the Ottawa were called the Middle Brother and are the 'keepers of the trade' and the Potawatomi were called the Younger Brother and are the 'keepers of the fire'. Most people take that to mean the keepers of the hearth, the ones that protected the home territory, and also the ones that maintained the meeting place, the place of peace. I think it also might have something to do with the prevalence of Fire Elementals in our bloodline."

Mari looked interested. His wide, aquamarine eyes were utterly serious, his attention fully focused on what Jake was saying. He supposed, given Mari's initial response to the revelation that he was part Native American, that he didn't know any more about their culture than most Europeans, but he knew that Mari was smart enough to be curious about other lifestyles, even if he was sometimes blunt to the point of rudeness about the things he didn't fully comprehend. A part of what he liked about Ilmarinen Gale was that he didn't hide behind a façade all the time. He would say what he thought, even if what he thought was patently wrong. Mari was open to learning experiences, though—if you could argue your point convincingly, he always took it on board but he wouldn't pretend interest in something for the sake of it. That made him easy to talk to sometimes, and other times it was a pain in the ass.

Jake steeled himself for one of his lover's casually old-fashioned reactions but Mari said, "Maybe there is something in that. Amelia always said that the Fire Elementals came from Greece and the Mediterranean, but she thought that because of the volcanoes, primarily. When Paracelsus first categorized us, he called the Fire Elementals Salamanders, like the lizards that live in volcanic fissures. He believed that they—you—shared that ability to channel the earth's molten flame into something positive, the same way that the lizards use it to heal and grow. But there are places in the States where the planet's crust is just as thin. Look at all the hot springs and stuff that you have out there. It stands to reason that your people would have a similar affinity with Fire. In Iceland, there were other Salamander tribes but a lot of Water Elementals too. He called them Undines. When I was small, I used to mix them up and call them Sardines and Amelia always told me off for it." He chuckled at the memory, then slid his hand down Jake's back and put one arm through his so that they could still walk close. "Was your grandmother an Elemental as well?"

Jake nodded. "She was, and my grandfather. He was a lot older than she was. He died when I was two or three. I don't really remember him."

"Was she your maternal grandmama or your father's mother?" Mari asked, still digging since the floodgates had opened.

"She was my dad's mother," Jake told him, seeing no harm in him knowing it.

"What about him? Your father? Did he have any gifts?" Mari probed.

Jake sneered. "My dad? Yeah, he had a gift for being a drunk asshole. There's a cab, let's ride the rest of the way. You're sounding out of breath."

Which was not really true, but Mari did seem to have been hit harder by the smoke inhalation. Maybe that had to do with being an Air Elemental. Jake evaded answering any more details about his family, and he was certain Mari knew that was what he was doing but, thankfully, he didn't argue or press for more.

* * * *

Tonka bounced all over them the minute that Mari let them into the house and Mari dropped to a crouch, play fighting him and making a fuss of the dog while Jake got the door shut and unbuttoned his coat. The other door, at the end of the hallway, was open a crack where Tonka had scurried through from the breakfast room, and an unfamiliar Transatlantic voice called through from there.

"Is that you, Ilmari?"

"Yes. Only me. And Jake," Mari called back, pushing himself to his feet as the door opened wider and a tall, pale, glamorous woman in a bronze tulle twinset stepped into the hallway. Her white hair was scraped up into an immaculate chignon and her makeup was flawless.

Jake thought she could be any age over forty. By his reckoning, if Mari was twenty-seven, his grandmother, by rights, had to be in her mid-sixties at least. She certainly didn't look it. Apart from a few lines around her piercing blue eyes and broad, fine-lipped mouth, her skin was amazing.

"Annabel didn't say you were coming back tonight," she said, those eyes roaming over Jake, assessing him like a cop, before returning to her grandson.

"I didn't tell her I was. Nonna, this is Jake Chivis. Jake,

this is Angela Arthur, my mama's mama."

"Hello," Jake said, extending his hand. "Nice to meet you, ma'am. Mari says you're living in New York? I hope your flight was smooth on the way over."

Mari's grandmother shook his hand but before she could say anything in return, Tonka, who had been busy sniffing Jake's shoes up until that point, decided he wanted a closer inspection and made to jump up on her. Jake snapped his fingers and pointed at him before his paws hit her leg.

"Sit."

He had been working on the sly with the dog to teach him some better manners and was gratified when the mukwa sat, right away, without laying a paw on Mari's grandmama. Angela raised one perfectly shaped white eyebrow and nodded once.

"You have a way with dogs. That will come in useful."

"I like animals in general," Jake said, reaching down to give Tonka's head an affectionate pat.

"Good," she said, as if this cemented her decision. "Because he needs to go for a walk, I believe. His leash is on that hook there, Jake. Ilmarinen, I need to have a word with you."

Mari winced, looking like he'd just been told off for begging crumbs from the table. Tonka licked Jake's hand and barked when he heard the 'w' word.

Jake hesitated. He suddenly didn't want to leave Mari here alone with this formidable woman, but, of course, that was ridiculous. For all that she was fierce, Angela was his flesh and blood. What harm could she do? Obediently he turned to get the leash. He gave Mari a sympathetic look and wondered how the old dame would react if he swept Mari into his arms and kissed him.

"C'mon, mukwa, let's go stretch our legs, shall we?"

Mari turned back and blew him a kiss as Tonka bounced around his feet, then flashed a rictus grimace at him.

"Thank you," he mouthed, then—aloud—added, "He doesn't need to go far at this time of the night, he'll only get cold."

Which was clear shorthand for, *Help! Don't leave me alone here!*

Jake gave him a wink to let him know he wasn't about to leave him at the mercy of his grandmama for long, and headed out the door with a happily prancing Tonka at his heel.

"Well, what do you think, mukwa?" Jake asked Tonka after they had gone about a block. "Did we leave Mari in the lion's den?"

Tonka was too interested in sniffing and snorting at everything to answer him. Jake thought it was a pretty good guess though. That was one woman who Jake had no doubt would steamroller any opposition. She'd gotten Jake neatly out of her way like he was a teenager who had overstayed at his friend's house. Even though she was rather brisk, and Mari seemed petrified of her, Jake kind of liked her already. He admired women who had backbone. It seemed to be a family trait in Mari's line.

He took Tonka on a good stroll, making it shorter than the long walk Angela was banking on but longer than Mari probably wanted. On their return, he debated knocking to be let in then decided, since he had the family dog in tow, it was probably okay to come in through the back door from the garden.

When Jake let himself in, Mari was sitting in his mother's recliner with a glass of whiskey in one hand—which he almost threw over himself when the French door opened unexpectedly. He was alone, the look on his face pensive. Jake slipped out of his jacket, and came back to the kitchen where Mari was wiping Tonka's paws with a strip of toweling and admonishing the over-affectionate Staffie for his attempts to lick him.

"Stupid dog," Mari said affectionately. "No, I don't want you to kiss me. You're supposed to protect me, not run away at the first opportunity."

"He's not dumb, he just knows a better offer when he sees

one," Jake teased, kissing Mari's cheek. "Everything okay?"

"What's the opposite of okay?" Mari asked him wearily, but he nodded and pushed himself to his feet, depositing the towel on the counter and sliding his arms around Jake's shoulders. "What an evening! I have such a headache. I need to lie down. Will you stay?"

"Uh, do you think that's a good idea? I mean, you've got family here." Jake wasn't afraid of anyone's disapproval, but he didn't want to create any further tension in the house.

"Family will take a sleeping pill and, believe me, will not rise before ten a.m.," Mari exhaled testily. "All my days! I love my kin but sometimes they test my patience. Mama is resting and she doesn't mind, you've stayed the night before. Tonka loves you, as I believe he's already demonstrated. I'm not asking you to make me scream the street down, but I really don't want to sleep alone tonight. I'm so wound up. If you really don't want to, I can't make you stay, but I would be grateful," he petitioned with a tiny, helpless smile.

"You don't play fair," Jake told him. "How am I supposed to resist that?" He planted a soft kiss on Mari's mouth. His lips tasted smoky from the single malt. "All right, I'll stay and protect you from marauding dragons."

"Mmmh...my white knight." Mari tilted his head and touched his lips to Jake's again. "You're too kind. Come on, let's get comfortable. Do you want a drink or anything?"

"No, thanks. Let me clean up. I'm beat. It feels like today has gone on forever."

When Jake came back from the bathroom, they went up to Mari's den. The neutral, minimal-furnished space, with its bank of computer monitors and its neatly made bed felt like a haven after the chaos of the last few days, but it still seemed strange to come up here with him, especially knowing they weren't alone in the house.

He watched Mari strip, tugging off his light sweater and the T-shirt under it and dropping them over the foot rail of the bed before popping the button of his trousers and easing them off his lean hips. His butt still had flushed stripes crisscrossing it from their adventures of the previous night, and when he wriggled into bed, he quickly turned so that he was lying on his side, facing Jake's half of the bed. The crisp cotton of the pillowcases and duvet cover rustled enticingly.

Even when he was sleeping alone, Jake usually slept in the buff, but it remained strange to strip and climb into bed with Mari here. It shouldn't have been, really. They were both grown-ups and, had they been seeing each other for longer, Jake probably wouldn't have felt weird at all. He followed suit, though, pulling his clothes off and laying them over the chair. When he turned back to the bed he saw Mari was watching him with sultry eyes and grinned at him.

"You look absolutely naughty when you stare at me like that."

"You know I'm bad news," Mari said, reaching for the dimmer over the bedhead and lowering the lights so that they were shrouded in comfortable shadows but still able to see one another. "Even when I'm supposed to be behaving, you put wicked thoughts into my head. It's so unfair. I don't stand a chance."

"Mm, good. My evil plan is working." Jake chuckled as he climbed in and pulled Mari close, kissing him once, twice on the lips and combing his fingers into Mari's hair gently, rubbing at the base of his skull. He almost told him he loved him again, the moment was warm and intimate and felt right, but he pushed the words away. To say that, when Mari wasn't ready to say it back, felt too much like he was coercing him into something. Instead he asked the more pertinent question.

"So, what did your grandmother want to say to you?"

For a moment, Mari was silent and Jake was just beginning to think that was the wrong thing to say and he had clammed up when, in a very small voice, he replied, "She and Mama have had a discussion. She— She has given me the house. Well…the paperwork, anyway. We need to see her solicitor and sign things but…anyway. That's basically why she's here."

He did not look especially overjoyed at this bequest.

"And you're unhappy about that because…?"

Mari looked back at him with a warning shake of his head. "Do you want to think for a moment about the implications of her gift? No one gets a free ride in this family, Jake. We treat one another decently but we make our own way, on the whole. I'm not her next of kin. I'm not even her next to next of kin. She— She tried to give Mama money today, for the next phase of treatment. It's not going to be cheap, any of this. The house is…insurance. I mean, we pay her rent, but it's nothing compared to standard rentals in London. Needless to say, Mama did not accept her offer of financial easement." His mouth was a hard line and the discomfort was visible on his face, even in the shadows.

Jake fell silent and caressed Mari in soothing circles for a while, not quite knowing what to say. People were strange about money. Whether you grew up rich or dirt poor, you still ended up a bit peculiar about it.

"What kind of strings are attached to her signing over the house to you?" he asked at last, guessing that there must be strings, if Mari was so unhappy about this development.

"As you would expect, I am not to make Mama homeless, as if I would even consider it. I am to stay here for as long as she needs me to. If I sell, then I am to sell back to a member of the family, if anyone is still alive to buy it off me. She thinks this means, whatever happens, she has in some way funded it. It quiets her conscience. She can swan back across the pond and feel magnanimous and not have to think about it. Not have to feel guilty."

Mari rarely got angry but Jake felt the scathing heat of his words.

"At least she does have a conscience then, if she needs to throw money at it," Jake said, trying to find something positive in the situation.

"That will be small comfort to Mama if—" He stopped talking and cleared his throat, then took a short, harsh breath. "What sort of mother looks the other way when her only child is—? When it might be her last chance?"

The final words came out hardly more than a husky whisper but he did not break. In the shadows, his pale eyes glittered with indignant rage.

Jake touched his face gently, tucking a lock of pale hair behind his ear as he thought about what he should say. The safest bet would be to say nothing, but he hated seeing that angry pain in Mari's eyes.

"You can tell people they should or shouldn't do something or they will have regrets, but it seldom changes them, Mari. All you can do is make sure you are the person that you want to be."

"I wish I was the man that could tell her to fuck off back to New-fucking-York and take her fucking paperwork with her." Mari said it neutrally enough, but the restless fury prowled under the surface of every word. "If Mama was healthier... Damn it! Damn it, damn it!"

He reached around Jake, pulling himself closer and curling into his arms. For a while, he was quiet and still.

Jake held him, running his hands up and down his back, and said nothing. There was nothing he could really say that would make any of it better. In the end, Mari slept, coiled in his arms like a small, golden dragon, so quiet and contained that Jake was almost afraid to move in case it disturbed him. It took Jake a long time to find sleep.

Chapter Ten

Mari woke in the warm curve of Jake's arms the next morning while the house was still blissfully quiet. Tucked away off the main street, it provided a sense of stillness that was rare in London and very different to Jake's bustling thoroughfare. When Jake's lips began a slow exploration of his naked body, Mari smiled, running his fingers through Jake's dark, tangled curls, remembering that before they had found out about Angela's arrival last night, Jake had been ready to take him back to the flat and do bad things to him. At least, Mari had hoped so.

Only when Jake had kissed his way around to Mari's back and down to the base of his spine, presumably getting a glimpse of his backside, did Jake pause, running a tender hand over his abused skin. He did not apologize again for putting those marks there, but he did bend down to place careful kisses on his hip and cheeks. Mari sighed his approval, letting him know it didn't sting too much.

"There, now you can't say I never kiss your ass," Jake said, moving around him and lipping his way steadily up Mari's ribs.

"You do the sweetest things," Mari crooned. He wriggled at the stinging sensations of Jake's fingers running over his tenderized flesh. "And you can kiss my sweet behind any time."

He reached back and raked his fingers through Jake's thick, mahogany-colored hair with a playful grin. There was heat in those honey-gold eyes and it warmed him to the core. He had been with his share of men who had just wanted sex — and made him want it, too — but Jake edged things up to another level. What he found himself doing with Jake Chivis went beyond simple, uncomplicated fucking, and he loved it more than he could say.

There was hot passion in Jake, no doubt about it, but he was also a deeply sensual lover and human being, and he seemed to delight in drawing out every gasp and moan he could with his lips, hands and body. One of those hands now stroked Mari's cock and Jake's soft, warm mouth kissed his collarbone and chest, sucking and biting his tingling nipples until Mari was ready to beg for more. Then he urged Mari gently over onto his belly and spread him out across the bed, straddling his thighs, a long, heated presence warming his naked back and the cheeks of his bottom. Jake leaned over him to whisper kisses over his neck and run his hands up and down the long, hard muscles of his back, sending shivers of pure delight through Mari's whole body.

"Do you like back rubs as well as neck massages?" Jake asked, his words barely a murmur against Mari's ear, reminding him of how good his hands had felt on Mari's neck and shoulders last night.

"Uh-huh…" He needed every ounce of willpower in his body to just breathe that small acknowledgment, because nothing felt sweeter than getting kneaded and worked until he was ready to melt.

"Good." Jake's fingers pressed more deliberately into his muscles, rolling and kneading across his shoulders, along the ridges of his spine and into the dip at the small of his back. He wriggled as he felt the pressure of each fingertip, the heat of Jake's palms pushing down on his body, working him until he could just surrender himself, then and there. Jake's warm hands covered Mari's ass, rubbing more gently there, and Jake bent forward again, kissing a path back down Mari's spine to the point where his cheeks parted. He exhaled a heated breath that rushed along the shallow abyss between them, tickling and caressing each pore until his skin felt alive.

Mari sucked in a corresponding gasp at the sweet

sensations between his legs and burrowed his face into the pillows, stifling the moans that wanted out when Jake touched him there. In his head, he knew it was too soon. He was still sore from the vigorous thrashing, but his heart wanted to explore the delicious urges that night on Jake's sofa had woken in him. He'd known that his Jake was strong, but not that he was capable of being so rough, and so incredibly assertive.

Jake's explosion of fury last night had taken him by surprise. He was used to the simmering rages that his lover kept on a short leash, but physical violence was unexpected, and not what Mari had been anticipating at all. He wondered if he should be more afraid, but at the same time knew, deep in his heart, that he would never fear Jake. Not even when that rage within him was out of its cage and roaring free. Mari was astonished and impressed by the level of control his lover had maintained thus far, if that was how he felt inside most of the time.

Mari wanted to twist around, to throw Jake down on his back and take him again, but he also wanted to know what was on Jake's mind, so he held still, enjoying the touch of his strong hands. They had experimented plenty of times with ways around his inability to take Jake's cock in his arse. Unlike most of his lovers, Jake had been incredibly kind to him. He never got impatient with Mari because of the annoying quirk of his body that tightened him up so hard when he wanted sex that it was impossible for him to be a submissive lover. Mari still did not understand why his treacherous body did this to him. It was not unpleasant, submitting to Jake's touch and his kisses. He felt perfectly relaxed in Jake's warm hands. Fear was not at the root of his malaise.

Jake's lips were at the very base of his spine then the warm, wet tip of his tongue drew down the valley of his cheeks, just dragging lightly along his skin. Jake's hand moved lower, to the backs of his thighs, still kneading and caressing his muscles as he pushed them farther apart and settled between. Each move he made was slow and deliberate, in no way hesitant.

Jake stroked his hands from the backs of Mari's knees, upward again to just under his bottom, his thumbs delving deeper between his legs, pressing up right behind Mari's balls, opening him wider so he could slide his tongue down to the taut stretch of skin behind them. Mari tipped his head back, unable to breathe in the swathe of the pillow, and caught a ragged huff of breath then another, shuddering uncontrollably at the delicious frisson of arousal conjured by Jake's tongue. He dug his fingers into the soft pillow and whimpered in his eagerness, unable to remain silent as he was licked and teased in such an intimate fashion.

That was all the encouragement Jake needed. His hands moved up to Mari's buttocks and pulled them open, his hot breath fanning over the sensitive skin between, just before he licked Mari there, the firm, wet tip of Jake's tongue circling lightly around his ring.

"Ohhhh...fuckkkkkk!" Mari chittered, tunneling into the bunched pillow again, clenching his teeth because he was afraid that either they would start to chatter and he would wind up embarrassing himself, or he would scream the house down and wake both Mama and Angela in the process. He writhed like a serpent, his body moving in time with the spasms of electric need whipped up by that gentle tongue-teasing. His cock was so hard that he was fighting the urge to let go of the pillow and just jack himself off until he burst.

Jake made a soft hum of pleasure and wriggled his tongue back and forth, teasing him, testing him with small, probing darts. He kissed and tongued Mari until he was thoroughly wet. The tip of a finger joined his tongue after a while, pressing down on his opening. Mari thought he was going to asphyxiate for a moment and lifted his head for a gulp of cooler air. He nudged his hips back, pushing against that firm intrusion, loving the tickle of it in the dimple of his ring. Said ring squeezed hard but Jake thankfully wasn't deterred and Mari whined more urgently at the silken rub of that warm, wet fingertip in its grasp. He spread his knees wider and fought for breath.

The pressure of Jake's squirming digit against his defiant hole increased until it breached the clench of his stubborn muscles, a millimeter at a time.

"Pass me that bottle of lube, babe," Jake whispered over Mari's shivering skin.

Mari's hand shook so much that he almost dropped the bottle twice but he somehow managed to get it from the drawer by the bed back to Jake's free hand, then wondered what the hell he thought he was doing. How many times had he been here, in this situation, so turned on, so hopeful, needing this so much that he thought he would die if it didn't happen?

Then crushed by the immensity of the inevitable failure.

Jake wondered why Mari couldn't commit to a loving relationship, but how could he be the perfect partner when they couldn't even make love? No matter how many times Jake reassured him that it didn't matter, Mari knew different. Maybe Jake could be patient with him now, but sooner or later the frustration and impatience would kick in, the way it had done with his previous partners, and that would lead to frayed tempers and angry scenes. Then Jake would push him away, just like Tomas had. Okay... maybe not as viciously as Tomas, but they would still be forced apart because he couldn't be what his lover needed. Mari didn't think he could take all that again. He had loved Tomas so madly, and his vicious rejection of everything that Mari was had crushed him and left him wounded for years afterward.

"Jake..." he exhaled, as he felt his boyfriend's strong fingers close around the bottle. He held on as if that would save him from the humiliation when, once again, Jake failed to get inside him. "Please..."

"Sshh. It's gonna be all right," Jake whispered, flipping the cap open. A cool drizzle of lube trickled between Mari's cheeks around Jake's finger, letting him slide it in deeper until he touched on Mari's hot spot. Another trickle of slippery gel, and Jake was easing that inquiring digit in and out of him, almost turning his sphincter inside out, it was gripping him so tight.

"Uuuhhhhh...ohhhhh...please!" Mari whimpered, driving his fist into the pillow and practically bucking them both off the bed. That touch inside him was like a spike of fire, twisting and tickling over his neglected prostate until he wanted to scream. "Duuuuuuuhn't stop!"

Jake was not fool enough to stop and obviously had every intention of turning Mari inside out too. He curled his finger just a fraction, pressing it deep then withdrawing, but not completely, and kept it up until he could add more lube, then a second finger, that burned like hot iron as it stretched him hard.

"That's it, baby, I know how that feels... Don't hold anything back, sweetheart. I so wanna feel you come like this," Jake murmured as Mari hid his face deep in the pillow again, forgetting how to breathe, forgetting everything but the excruciating presence of Jake's slowly thrusting fingers inside him.

Mari tried his hardest to ride it out, to let Jake stretch him but—damn his stars, and damn his stupid body—it hurt too much. He curled up defensively, feeling like he'd been staked, gripping the pillow to him with one hand and slamming the other down flat against the mattress, over and over. Mari felt as if he would choke on the word but it spilled out of him like bitter poison, no more than a breath, in deference to his sleeping progenitors.

"No-o-o-o-o-o...nonononono...too...too much!"

His face was on fire as he muffled it in the cool bed linen and tried not to sob with frustration. How was it possible to be so turned on but still so tight? How could he want it so much, yet it hurt like that? He couldn't fathom it. Didn't want to fathom it. Why the fuck could he not just be normal? It was so unfair.

Jake had taken his hands off him the second Mari had tensed up, so gentle that he'd not even felt Jake withdraw, and it was a few moments before Jake reached for him.

"I'm sorry, Mari. I'm so sorry," he whispered, and the words were too warm on his skin.

It took Mari a short while to compose himself enough for words. There was so much going on in his head in those fleeting seconds. He was angry, hurt, shocked, disappointed...more than disappointed, he was gutted almost to the point of despair. Why did he let himself hope, every time, that it could work?

"Don't— Don't apologize. Not your fault," he managed to exhale. "You were...it felt amazing, Jake. Really, too amazing. It just...it got too much, too soon. That's all. My fault. My stupid body!"

He shook his head once or twice, a jerky motion like his neck was broken, unfolding, disentangling himself—and half-turning, reaching for Jake, wanting to kiss him. He needed Jake to know that he wasn't being blamed, that he still wanted him, still longed for him.

"No. Not your fault," Jake insisted, pulling Mari into his arms and enfolding him, pulling him tight. To Mari's surprise he could feel that Jake was shaking too. "I didn't mean to hurt you, that's the last thing I'd ever want to do, Mari. Not the spanking thing, I know that's something you liked, but I know you can't... Your condition... I shouldn't have pushed. That is my fault."

"Stop it." Mari was still shaking his head slowly from side to side. He cupped Jake's face in his hands and kissed him to make him stop talking. When that seemed to have the desired effect, he wrapped himself around that glorious, hard-muscled body and pulled him in close, stroking from his dark, loose curls, down over his strong shoulders and that lovely, mahogany-furred chest, drinking him in with his eyes. "Look at you. You are so fucking gorgeous, Jake Chivis. You deserve a lover who is not a fucking mess," he whispered. "But I'm sorry, you've got me, with my myriad of hang-ups. And—may your gods help you—I am not letting you fucking go."

He stopped talking for a moment because Jake was looking at him rather oddly, he thought. There were certainly questions in those honey-colored eyes, but whatever it was that Jake was wanting to say he must have decided to keep it to himself. Instead, he slid his fingers around the back of Mari's neck and pulled him closer for a scorching kiss.

That helped Mari's dented erection and he drew Jake down into the kiss with as much enthusiasm as he could muster, still throbbing from the shock of the sudden burst of pain on the back of so much pleasure. He turned his head, rubbing his nose up against the side of Jake's, pressing his mouth onto those soft, warm lips and devouring them as if they were his benediction. If he lost Mama *and* ruined this, he promised himself grimly, he would throw himself in the fucking Thames and everything else could go to rot.

"Touch me again," he breathed with determination, as their lips parted and he was able to catch some air. He kept his voice low, his words soft but adamant. "Do what you were doing before. Before I freaked out. Do that, but do it harder. Tie me to the fucking bed and shove my socks in my mouth if I struggle, but don't stop doing it."

Jake's lips parted and Mari could tell he was getting ready to protest, to say something like *you don't have to do this*. He must have seen something in Mari's face, though, because the protest died before it got past Jake's teeth.

"Turn on your side," Jake said, his voice gone hoarse, sliding in behind Mari once more and settling them both in a comfortable position. Jake kissed and lipped along the back of his neck, nuzzling into his hair. He slid a hand down to cup and knead Mari's arse, harder than he had done before. A searching finger wiggled between his cheeks at last, but Jake didn't push it in him right away. He tickled and teased around his ring again while he nibbled, kissed and licked on his neck and shoulders.

Mari turned his head, seeking Jake's lips and kissing him

with renewed hunger as he ran one foot back and forth along his mate's upper leg, enjoying the gentle friction of their two bodies, in constant motion on the bed. Now that they were intimate again he could feel the silken brush of his companion's stiffening cock against his right cheek and he pushed back against it, rubbing gently so that it was caught between his bottom and Jake's abdomen, stroked on both sides.

"Lube me," he whispered. "Please."

Jake reached for the bottle and, a moment later, Mari felt the cool slickness touch him, but it wasn't cool for long. Jake worked it in, warming it up as he stroked his finger over Mari's flexing ring. Still he didn't push it inside him. He was rolling his hips though, very obviously enjoying the feel of Mari's backside rubbing along his shaft and Mari was in no hurry to deprive him. He could imagine well enough how sweet it should feel to have that lovely, big cock inside him but there could be no rushing this goal. Mari was in no doubt of that.

"My beautiful, horny, sexy man," he murmured, like he was reciting a spell. "That feels so very good. So hot. You make me forget what I am. I lose my mind when you touch me like this. I feel like you could make me be anything you wanted."

"I only want you to be who you are, Ilmari," Jake sighed along his cheek, finding his lips again to kiss him and sliding into him—at least sliding a finger into him. That would have to be enough. Jake kissed him hard and pressed down on his gland, working it with the pad of his fingertip. All the slow languor and build-up of a few minutes earlier were replaced by a fierce heat, stoked by Jake's thrusting, wriggling finger.

Mari's answering gasp sucked most of the air out of his mouth and sealed it with a ravenous kiss. His body undulated in time with the caress on his prostate though, riding that steady intrusion. He reveled in the delicious kiss and the waves of alternating heat and cold that spilled out from the firm caress on his internal ignition. If his body was some kind of engine, then that fleshy button—the spot he liked to think of as his 'cc' spot, his climax central—was the ignition, for sure. His earlier pain was forgotten as he pushed down on Jake's massaging finger and a throaty coo of ecstasy spilled out of him when they broke the kiss.

"Uuuhhhhhhhh, Jake! Yesssss!"

Jake's other hand pushed into Mari's hair, gripping hard, holding his head back.

"Touch yourself," he urged huskily, nipping at the corner of Mari's jaw. "Do it for me."

"Jake…" Mari had to swallow twice. His mouth was dry and he was trembling so fiercely, his cock so hard. "I'm— I'm going to come all over the bed if I do that, Jake."

"I can't think of anything that would be hotter," Jake told him.

Mari closed his eyes for a moment. The pleasure of that touch inside and the roughness of Jake's grip on his hair left him dizzy. He braced himself with one hand flat on the mattress, the other he curled around his rigid cock, very, very lightly caressing its curving length just beneath the glistening head. His glans was swollen, flushed with heat and pleasure, leaking its slick spill down his shaft. The intake of breath it summoned roared like a rushing wave between his ears and he thought he was going to melt. He was an inferno down between his hips, the touch of Jake's flesh melding into his own, swallowed by the swelling surge that pushed out from that tiny bud of nerves and tissue. Such a small thing…

He was wrong. It took three or four strokes of his fingers to release that wave from his clenching, rolling innards.

Mari squirmed about violently to mash his lips to Jake's again, muffling his cry, as he came harder than he had ever managed on his own. Or with just about anyone else for that matter.

Not that any of that mattered. Not right now.

The pulse-pounding orgasm seemed to go on and on,

and only when the last spasms were tapering away did Jake withdraw his probing finger. The thick, hot length of his shaft was there a moment later, but his intent wasn't to try to press it into him. Jake rubbed himself in the crevasse between Mari's slick cheeks, his hips bucking smoothly, his arms tightening around Mari, holding on like he wanted to squeeze the breath out of him.

"Uuuhhhh! Ohh, fuck, you are so fucking beautiful...so, so hot..." Jake groaned. He bit down on the muscle running down from Mari's neck to his shoulder, a few soft, desperate grunts accompanying the hot spurt of cum on Mari's back.

For his own part, Mari only realized just how much he had frozen in the moments between his climax and Jake's when he felt the wet pulse of his lover's orgasm splash against his skin. In that instant, he went limp in Jake's arms, panting softly, overwhelmed. As the powerful bands of muscle pulling tight across his chest and belly relaxed, he twisted like a knotted rag in that loosening embrace and let his lips brush over Jake's mouth again, smiling at the torrid rush of his rapid breath.

"All my days..." he whispered shakily. "I just saw heaven, Jake Chivis, and I don't even believe in heaven or hell."

Jake uttered a weak chuckle, between his ragged gasps. He kissed Mari with so much tenderness, smiling when their lips parted and gazing at him with a wealth of heat and emotion in his eyes that made Mari want to melt all over again.

* * * *

Mari saw Jake off for his meeting with Cordiline after a quick coffee and a brisk shower in the downstairs bathroom. He lingered over the kiss goodbye on the doorstep, not caring who saw them and pleased that Jake did not seem to care either.

"Did you two have breakfast yet?" Mama asked him with a fond glance, making him jump as he came back from the front hallway still wrapped in a haze of bliss.

"I thought you were asleep." Mari fought down the sudden guilt. "Did we disturb you?"

"No, I was awake early. He stayed the night?"

Mari nodded, looking sheepish and ducked her attempt to ruffle his hair.

"What? You're a grown man, Ilmari. I know you like him. What you do is your business." She laughed. "But you shouldn't throw him out the door without breakfast. That's just rude."

"He has things to do. And so do I." Mari shrugged her objection off as she followed him into the kitchen. He turned on the washing machine where he had earlier stuffed his sticky bed linen, and put more coffee on to brew. He did not want to think about Jake's upcoming meeting with his tame policeman.

His mother scrambled eggs and he made toast and they moved around one another in the companionable silence they had become used to. This morning, though, he could feel an edge to it and when they were finally sitting by the French windows enjoying the first whisper of watery sunlight, along with breakfast, she said, "You know that you don't have to do what Angela says, don't you?"

Mari's heart sank. He had hoped to avoid that particular conversation for a while, but it had to be faced sooner or later. A sigh shivered out of him.

"I know. But it makes sense, doesn't it? She's trying to be practical."

"And you are mad as all hell about it, as your sweet Jake would say." Anni pointed her fork at him. "Don't even try to argue. I know you, Ilmari. If you don't want to do this, then tell her."

"Mama, don't…" he protested, not knowing which way to turn.

"Don't what? Look, I know what she's doing, and so do you. If you don't want to dance to her tune then this is the only chance you get to turn the score, Ilmarinen. You do not have to stay here for me, you know that. Don't you?" Her eyes burned cold and he looked away, a hard, bitter lump in his throat all of a sudden.

"You know it's not as easy as that," he said, keeping his tone as flat and balanced as he could. "Mama, it could be worse. She's offering me something that most men my age would jump all over. A house, a lifestyle…"

"A leash," Anni said bitterly. "Something to pull you into line when you want your own way."

He put his plate down, the food half-eaten.

"I thought we raised you smarter than this, Ilmarinen," she told him, and the fire roused in his belly again.

"You raised me to be independent," he said. "You think that because you've always refused her money then I should too. But maybe one day I'll need it. Maybe one day you will too. It doesn't mean we have to like it, but she's right and she knows it. I don't like that any more than you do, Mama, but it's true. The next phase is going to cost nearly half a million, and I have no idea where that is going to come from if you don't let her help. At least this way we don't have to worry about the rent money."

"We'll apply for a research grant. Or I'll wait for another study to come around," she said stubbornly.

"And if you don't get it?" He shook his head at her. "No."

"I'll rob a bank." She flashed him a dry smile. "Ilmari, sometimes we have to accept that we're out of options."

"No," he said again. "No. I don't accept that. Your specialist says there are new drugs and you are going to fucking well take them."

"Mind your language, young man." She waved the fork at him again and he lowered his head in shame. "I see what she's like, Ilmari, that's all I'm saying. I fought tooth and claw not to be owned by her. Yes, she's my mother. Yes, I love her, just as she loves me, in her own way. But I will not be in debt to her. And I will not see you go down that route for my sake."

"I have work to do, Mama," he told her.

"Did you tell her you were sacked by the university?" she asked, and he regretted mentioning work.

"No. And they didn't sack me, Mama. I'm just between departments at the moment, that's all." He narrowed his eyes at her. "But I didn't say anything."

"Good." Her lips thinned. "Don't. She'll only use it as ammunition. She and Papa and Emmanuel Karden were thick as thieves once upon a time."

He rose to his feet and kissed her hair on the way back to his room. "Don't fight with her this morning, please, Mama."

"Of course I won't. My only mother comes all the way from New York to see me and I fight with her. Perish the thought."

He held her gaze, shaking his head again at the gleam of devilment in her eyes. "I love you, Mama."

"Back atcha." She bumped fists with him. "Go and do... whatever you're doing. And try to stay out of trouble while she's over here, okay?"

"Of course," he promised, and crossed his fingers.

Back in his room, he logged into his laptop and fired up the processor he had built in one corner of his bedroom-cum-study. Though not huge, the room was spacious and well laid out enough that he could store most of the important books, files and portable trappings of his lifestyle up here. It was a small retreat, a place to come when the world got annoying. He had three monitors on the long L-shaped corner desk and they were all connected to his PC. One shelf above them was devoted to an array of removable hard drives, all labeled and color coded. If he had to run for his life at any point, he knew exactly what he needed to grab first.

In a drawer under the desk in a lockable box, he kept an assortment of smaller flash drives which housed the various access programs he had constructed over the past twelve months. He renewed them constantly. Web security was forever changing and the loopholes and hacks that worked one week might be obsolete the next. That had been an important facet of the job he had recently surrendered, and it was so much a part of him that he was not about to relax his routines overnight. So he kept his hack profiles up to date.

But the job he had been offered revolved around a very different set of infiltration techniques. What MI6 wanted was a talent so rare it elevated him, if not to a unique status, then at least to a most desirable one in the ranks of the Secret Service. That skill too was something that needed exercise and regular work to keep up to date. The gift he had could easily be burned out from too much casual surfing or grow unpredictable from not enough use. The balancing act between those two poles was, as he had told Brigadier Stern, a precarious one.

He flipped two of the seventeen-point-five-inch monitors on, then opened his laptop and, while the CPU was booting, crossed the room and locked the door. Mari wasn't too worried about his mother knowing what he did in here — she had watched him grow up with the skill — but he didn't want his grandmama walking in on him while he was 'off the grid'.

On one monitor, he ran the news channel, scanning for further reports of the recent incendiary deaths in London, on the lookout for anything else that corresponded to the incidents at home or further afield. The other monitor opened on the Birthright homepage. He used the login he had created for Jake in order to access a couple of chat forums there and spent an hour or so talking to people about the burnings and gathering intelligence. Sometimes he doubted that intelligence had much to do with it, but there were members out there with a modicum of common sense, if nothing else, and he focused on them, asking discreet questions about Louis Cortez and the other people who had died. The victim outside Buckingham Palace had been a fellow called Karl Devenish, who had worked for a Swiss banking corporation in Canary Wharf.

Two or three members of the forum speculated that Karl had been a coke head and something of a loose cannon. He had been unmarried but engaged to the daughter of a South African business magnate. Links to his social media profiles produced photos of Karl looking tanned and smug on various immaculate beaches, in expensive restaurants and posing at the wheel of a canary yellow Lamborghini Aventador. Mari rolled his eyes, unimpressed.

Bored with this casual cyberstalking, which he could do in his sleep, he interspersed the cruising of Birthright and its motley assortment of members with some private research. Using the laptop, he typed in *"Chivis"* + *"Michigan"* + *"Potawatomi"*. As the search results scrolled down the screen, his eyebrows rose.

"Well, well, you dark horse," he exhaled in a soft, reverent tone.

It was a way past two in the afternoon when he finally surfaced. Investigation of some of the leads that his initial search on Jake unearthed had required sub-ethical practices, but Mari was less troubled by the conflict with his personal ethics than he was by some of the information this had yielded. He had needed to engage a muffler program in order to link up with the records of the Social Services in Battle Creek, where his precious Jake had been born, just over twenty-nine years earlier. Once he had a homepage up for them, he was able to surf their database. That immersion unearthed details of an unhappy parental marriage and an even less happy childhood. Jake's mother, Kaylee, had fled the family home after enduring twelve years of drunken violence, and filed for divorce. Mindsurfing cached welfare records provided Mari with the information that she'd left her fourteen-year-old son, Jake, behind, and the social services had continued to monitor his situation for four years.

He didn't need to do much more than standard web searching to follow Jake's father, Biyan Chivis. He tracked the bastard through various local newspaper crime columns and police reports chronicling his acts of pilfering, larceny and drink and drug fueled violence, culminating in a drunken car wreck that the local press referred to as vehicular homicide. A young couple and their two infant children had died on I94 up by the Goguac Lake when he'd hit their car head-on in his pickup. That had earned him a protracted stay in prison, up in Ionia. He was still there, as far as Mari could deduce, though he was due for parole in a couple of months' time.

Mari returned to the regional newspapers and searched for Jake. They reported the contrasting tales of a local-boy-made-good, as Jake progressed through the force – in considerably shorter paragraphs than his father's activity had warranted, Mari noted with some irritation. A Bachelor of Science degree in Criminal Justice was reported with a small graduation photo in the *Battle Creek Enquirer*, and there was an article in the *Calhoun County Journal*, from nine years ago, reporting his enrollment with the Detroit PD at the remarkably young age of twenty. Mari tapped his fingers on the desk, mulling over whether or not he should delve deeper into Jake's work record, then pulling back. He wasn't worried about being traced but it felt wrong, curious as he was. Instead, he backtracked and traced his lover's younger life, back and forth between his father and grandmother in Battle Creek, and his mother who had cleared off to Ann Arbor – and given some of the social service reports he'd read already, he could hardly blame her for that. There was a new husband, revealed by state BMD records, and two half siblings, still at school. No room for the son she'd left behind, a son now old enough to earn his own way.

Mari closed the lid of his laptop and pressed the heel of his hand to his forehead, his emotions wrestling to come to the surface. He pushed them back down. There was no time for any of that. How was he supposed to pretend to Jake that he didn't know this stuff?

Serves you right for snooping, fool! His conscience gave

him a good old poke in the ribs and he acknowledged that maybe it was time to call a halt. Jake must be done with his tame detective, surely. He fished for his phone and sent him a brief message.

Everything okay? x

Less than a minute later, he received a text back.

Yes. Just leaving for home. Do you want to come over?

Of course, he sent back, a smile curving his lips. *I'll bring Tonk, he needs a walk and he's pining for you, pack leader.*

See you soon.

Jake sent the message with a smiley face. He did not text anything about his meeting with Cordiline, but Mari hadn't expected him to. He would probably hear soon enough what was going on.

Mari got changed and slipped his running shoes on because it had been too many days since he'd had proper exercise, and sex did not count. The fact that he was dressed to dash meant he didn't have to hang around and make excuses about where he was going, or juggle the question of whether he was he planning to take lunch with Mama and Angela. Tonk looked wildly enthusiastic when he rattled the short chain leash too, which counted in his favor.

"Won't be long," he lied cheerfully, and headed for the door. Pretty soon, he was striding along Cumberland Place to the park, where he was able to really stretch his legs, and he ran down as far as the St. Andrews Gate before returning to the main thoroughfares and heading for Maple Street. It felt good to run, even if he was wheezing by the time he got to Carburton Street and had to slow down again. He paced himself the rest of the way, having no desire to turn up on Jake's doorstep looking a total wreck.

When Jake buzzed him up to the flat, Mari thought he

sounded breathless too, and was concerned until he walked in the door. Tonka bounced up at Jake right away, his whip-thin tail wagging furiously. Mari took in the sheen of fresh sweat on Jake's bare arms as he stood in the doorway, shirtless in just a pair of cotton leggings that hugged his strong thighs very nicely.

"What have you been doing to yourself?" he asked, though a part of him was rather jealous too. Had Cordiline come over here? Had they fooled around?

He admonished himself for the thought but there was no denying that the detective inspector never bothered to disguise his appreciation of Jake's physique, even when he knew Mari was watching him.

"Wouldn't you like to know?" Jake waggled his eyebrows at him, then laughed and pointed to the archway that led back toward the bedroom and bathroom. Mari thought he was pointing directly at the bedroom and was about to make a comment but Jake took a couple of steps and reached up to the bar that was secured near the top of the archway. "I haven't had a chance to go to the gym or run in days. Figured I'd get some reps in while I was waiting for you to get here."

Mari couldn't hide the merry twinkle that crept into his eyes as he turned that information over in his head.

"Right... Like you do," he murmured. "So, how many did you manage then?"

Jake chuckled. "I don't count. I think. Do you want anything?" he asked. Tonka was already sniffing around the kitchen and noisily lapping water from a dish Jake had put out for him.

Yeah. You, you gorgeous bastard! Mari thought, but didn't say aloud.

"You *think*?" he said instead. "How does that work? You mean you think in a kind of rhythm, or you just contemplate your muscular navel?"

Jake curled his hands around the bar and folded his knees so he hung for a moment before pulling himself up to his chin, then lowering back down as he released a breath.

"I think. About stuff," he said, doing another pull up. "Cordiline was reprimanded for involving a" – he let his breath out as he lowered himself and pulled himself back up – "civilian in an active case. A case he's been" – another breath, another pull up – "removed from. He warned me that people are watching." Up. Down. "And told me to stop investigating."

Mari tracked him slowly, following the motion of his body, adoring the way the strong, hard muscles of his chest and arms stood out in stark relief under the golden skin each time he pulled himself back up. He wanted to run his hand over Jake's body but was worried it would make him let go.

"Watching? Who's watching? And why are they watching us and not whoever is killing these poor firebombs?" he asked indignantly.

Jake continued his work out as he answered Mari's questions.

"Your Feds. The MIB. Or in this case, MI5," Jake said as he exhaled. "As to why they are watching us...instead of investigating what happened...there are only two possible reasons." Jake did a couple more pull ups before he unbent his knees and stood, still clutching the bar above his head and looking at Mari intently. "They either have abso-fucking-lutely no clue at all where to look, or they already know what's going on and just want to make sure no one else figures it out."

Mari pouted and Jake asked, "What's wrong with that theory?"

"You stopped," Mari said, disappointed. "Next time, don't wear yourself out before I arrive."

Jake let go of the bar, took two steps and gave him a shove, just a playful push. Mari pushed him back, and suddenly they were wrestling one another, which was almost one-sided because for all his height and run-conditioned body strength, he lacked Jake's overall muscle tone. Pretty soon, his lover was picking him up and carrying him back toward the bedroom whilst Tonka watched curiously from the rug and Mari berated the dog for not running to his assistance. Instead of striding right in and throwing him like a he-man onto the bed, Jake hoisted Mari into the curve of the archway and said, "Grab the bar."

"You are joking, right?" Mari snorted but he reached up and wrapped his fingers around it. He was tall enough that his feet easily touched the ground when Jake lowered him, even holding onto the makeshift workout bar. He looked over his shoulder. "Um...fail!"

"You never did a pull up in your life?" Jake laughed softly.

"Not since college, and I wasn't all that hot at it then. I preferred watching other guys do it." Mari winked at him.

When he made to release the bar, Jake's fingers closed over his hands, keeping them there.

"Uh-uh," he admonished. "Did I say to let go?"

A flash of heat ripped through Mari at the proximity of Jake's hard body and the strength in the hands that folded over his, making him briefly forget all of his worries about what he had discovered this morning. He pushed himself back against the hot, firm body behind him, but obediently kept his fingers curled around the rail above his head. That made his cock twitch and he chided himself silently.

Not why we're here! Is it?

He got a sudden vision of a smaller, leaner, teenage Jake, grim and angry, all alone, working out furiously in the yard in a bid to be bigger and stronger than the man whom welfare said was using his mother as a punching bag, and probably him too. Mari's mood sobered at that thought but he didn't let go of the bar.

In all his life, Mari had never been struck physically by either parent, in anger or even in jest. He could not even say that he understood how someone would cope with such a thing. Dawdling, taking time to get home from school, anxious for his mother but dreading what would come when he got there. Papi was older than Mama, and a confirmed pacifist. Mari had only seen his father get rolling drunk once in his life and that had been at a party. Mama liked a drop of single malt sometimes but she never drank to excess. As a medic, she had seen how it ruined lives and was way too much of a control freak to let that happen to her.

A spark of understanding flared in his brain. That was why Jake didn't drink. Well, not enough to get drunk anyway. Mari had put it down to a provincial puritan upbringing. Good school, good grades, police academy, sobriety badge. It wasn't about any of that. Jake just had no desire to turn out like his father.

Oh, my poor man, he thought in dismay. *I fail you all the time, don't I, Chivis?*

Jake's thoughts were certainly not running parallel to his own, if the distracting way he ground his hips into Mari's backside was any indication.

"You are so beautiful," Jake growled huskily against the nape of his neck. "I was thinking, I could tie your hands to the bar." He slid his own hands down Mari's arms and sides, all the way to his hips and thighs, then back up until one hand cupped his balls and the other caressed his chest. "Then I could give you the switching you want."

"Chivis, my backside is still sushi from your last adventure," Mari teased him, primarily to try to disguise the pulse of pure heat that idea sent through his treacherous body. "If anything, you should be on your knees kissing it better. But if being watched by the Secret Service gets you this hot then maybe we ought to have tried attracting their attention before."

How hot is the idea of fucking a spy, then, Jake Chivis? his mind added sneakily. Not that he could make it part of their lovemaking routine, even if he said yes to the job offer. That still bugged him. What kind of a relationship could they have if he was keeping secrets already? If half his life was a secret?

"Mmmm... There's an idea," Jake murmured over his skin, warm hands caressing his hips and buttocks. He gave Mari a little swat on the hip that made him jump but, before he got the chance to explore this game further, they were interrupted by a brisk rap on the apartment door. Jake froze for just a second, then released Mari's hands, shushing Tonka, who was barking and growling protectively.

"No buzzer from downstairs, and that was a cop knock if I ever heard one," Jake murmured into Mari's ear, making his heartbeat quicken. "If I get arrested, bail me out, please."

He turned away before Mari even had his singing nerves under control, much less his body.

Jake snagged a T-shirt from the back of a kitchen chair and pulled it on as he crossed to the door and gripped the knob. He gestured at Tonka with one hand.

"Sit. Shush." Amazingly, Tonka sat and stopped barking, although he still had a low rumbling growl vibrating his chest, as he watched Jake and the door intently.

From his vantage point under the arch, Mari could see two people on the landing when Jake opened his apartment door, a man and a woman, and even though they wore no uniform, Mari could tell they were some sort of authority. Dressed in well-fitting understated, dark suits and standing ramrod straight with identical serious frowns, they almost looked like movie caricatures.

"Can I help you?" Jake asked, his tone polite but wary.

"Mr. Chivis?" the woman asked, in a formal way that made Mari's hair stand on end just as much as Tonka's. The question, and the careful way it was framed, made Mari think it wasn't really a question. They weren't from the Met, he was almost certain. They would have flashed badges straight off.

Jake didn't answer them immediately. Mari could just see the edge of his profile and the way he was taking in every detail before giving them information. Finally, he said, "I've already got a vacuum cleaner, thanks."

"May we come in?" the man asked. He was younger than

the woman, and a couple of inches shorter than Jake, dark hair trimmed close to his scalp, skin that was the color of light caramel, dark brown, puppy-dog eyes. His expression was as neutral as the question.

The woman was probably in her late thirties or early forties, of a height with her colleague, dark blonde hair cut into a severe bob and a sharp, peppermint-green gaze that took in everything at a sweeping glance — the room, the dog, himself and Jake. Her lips pursed and Mari noted a sheen of lip balm but not much else in the way of makeup. She wore loose-cut trousers and a fitted jacket that enhanced the natural curve of her slim figure.

"That depends on what you're selling," Jake told the young man, folding his arms.

Mari's lips twitched and he suppressed the smirk, his posture unconsciously mirroring Jake's, arms crossed loosely over his chest, grateful that his long, hooded sweatshirt covered the persistent semi in his pants.

The woman sighed, reached into an inside pocket of her jacket and produced her badge.

"I am Intelligence Officer Sarah Vallance. I work for the Security Service. I have been in communication with DI John Cordiline at the Albany Street division of the Metropolitan Police." She nodded toward her partner. "This is Officer Neil Partridge. Let's start again, shall we, Mr. Chivis? May we come in?"

Jake took a step back and let the door open all the way.

"Welcome to my castle, Officer Vallance, Officer Partridge. Would you like anything to drink?"

"No, thank you," Vallance said curtly, following him in.

Her gaze shifted momentarily to Mari then down to Tonka who was watching her with his ears flat. The burly terrier growled again and Mari murmured an instinctive, "Tonk. No!" This served to quell him for the moment.

"I take it you're the officers that have booted Cordiline off the case?" Jake said, closing the door behind them.

"Detective Inspector Cordiline is fully aware of the

implications of this case, Mr. Chivis," Vallance told him. "He understands the potential threat to national security, and has agreed to allow Security Services to deal with any new information."

"Uh-huh. And to what do I owe the pleasure of your company this afternoon?" Jake asked.

"We understand, from DI Cordiline, that you were a detective with the Detroit PD in the States," she said.

"That doesn't sound very much like a question or an explanation," Jake prompted her.

Vallance gave him a thin smile. "You specialized in arson investigation. You also assisted the Met on a murder case recently, in which you and Dr. Gale" – she glanced at Mari, tipping her head in his direction – "were instrumental in uncovering the evidence and building the case against Helen March."

Mari lifted his eyebrows. "You have been doing your homework."

"We did consult on the case, yes," Jake said, his tone casual enough to make Mari look at him and have to suppress another smirk. "I take it Security Services aren't interested in Helen March, though."

"Not exactly," she said. "We have been looking into an organization called Birthright. Have you heard of them?"

"Yes, but I'm sure you can tell us more," Jake told her. "I know there have been three people in the news recently that have burst into flames for no logical reason, and at least two of them belonged to this Birthright organization, which spouts a whole lotta elitist Master Race propaganda on its website."

"Three. All three of them," Mari said, and when Jake looked at him in surprise he offered a helpless shrug. "I didn't get a chance to tell you earlier."

Jake nodded and returned his attention to Officer Vallance. "That's about the bulk of it, which isn't much. So, I've answered your question. Mind telling me why you're paying me a visit?"

Officer Vallance glanced at Mari, a laser beam shrewdness in her gaze, then turned her attention back to Jake.

"Dr. Gale is correct. All three victims belonged to Birthright. All three were also Fire Elementals, like yourself, Mr. Chivis." She let that sink in for a moment. "We have been monitoring the operations of Birthright. The organization was founded by a man named Roy Corrie. He has been recruiting men and women with Elemental talent to his ranks for the past few years. Some of these people have come from the UK, most have been drawn here from further afield."

She looked at Mari again. He held her stare.

"If you have something to say, spit it out," he said at last.

It was her colleague who spoke. Partridge had been quiet so far but he said, "We know that you hacked Birthright's database two days ago. Why did you do that, Dr. Gale?"

Mari rolled his eyes and unfolded, moving away from the door to come and sit on the sofa. Tonka came to him right away and he fussed with the dog's ears gently.

"I got tired of waiting for an invite." He frowned then and fired a cold look at Partridge. "Have you been watching me?"

"Dr. Gale, SIS has been watching you for a long time," Vallance said without any humor.

Mari kept his expression as carefully blank as he could. He wasn't entirely surprised, but to have it confirmed gave him an unpleasant swooping feeling in his belly.

"Given your recent assistance with the Met, your current proximity to the case and your respective talents, we decided it behooves our department to step in before the pair of you get much deeper."

"Uh-huh, I'll just bet," Jake said. "Let's cut to the chase. Are you here to tell us officially to stop investigating Birthright?"

"If we were, would you listen?"

"I guess that depends," Jake told her. "I want to know what happened to those people, why they're dead and how it happened, so that it doesn't happen to anyone else. If you already know those answers and there is a good reason why MI5 hasn't put a stop to whatever Birthright is doing to them, I'll consider listening to what you have to say."

"We could just have you arrested, Mr. Chivis."

Everyone went silent. She said it calmly enough, as if to say that she could, but frankly she couldn't be bothered to go to all that trouble. Mari didn't miss the undertone of the threat, though, and he was certain Jake didn't, either.

"You could, but I take it you're not going to," Jake franked his guess after a moment. "What is it exactly that you want, Officer Vallance? If you're not here to tell us to stop digging, and you're not here to have us arrested?"

"The fact that you are trained in police work, have already established a connection with the organization, and most importantly, that you are an Elemental with psychic ability puts you in a very unique position," she said, like she was winding up to give him an award or something. Which Mari was pretty sure she was not about to do.

There was another long moment of silence. He heard Jake inhale and slowly exhale. He wasn't sure he could breathe yet himself.

"You're looking for a mole," Jake said quietly.

Vallance nodded. "This is a matter of national security," she continued. "I'm not at liberty to give you a full debriefing until you've agreed to meet with our director. I can tell you that Corrie was previously involved in an experiment much like the one in which you are both currently engaged. When we had a change of Government a few years ago, funding for that project was axed and Corrie dipped under the radar for a time."

This confirmed what Cordiline had told Jake. "Last year, not long after he reappeared," Vallance continued, "Birthright sprang up and began discreetly recruiting. Corrie has minimal contact with most of his members, though. Hardly any of them have even seen him, let alone spoken to him. He's reclusive and very paranoid."

"So you want someone to sneak in there and become his best friend? That's going to take some maneuvering, if you don't have an Elemental operative," Mari said, as the cogs began to turn in his head. "But, oh...wait! There are Elementals out there who aren't directly involved in Birthright...yet."

He met her shrewd green eyes and held that look.

"You are well-aware that MI5 knows you exist, Dr. Gale," Vallance countered, with a shake of her head. "The Service is grateful for the work you did with Professor Karden's unit. But we do need someone with a level head on his shoulders, someone who knows how to operate under deep cover."

"Are you saying I'm not level-headed?" Mari experienced a spark of indignation, not only that they had been spying on him but that they'd already dismissed him out of hand. He opened his mouth to argue, but Jake beat him to the punch.

"No, they are just ready to take advantage of someone that's already had police training and is in a perfect position to infiltrate the target organization. Is that about right?" he speculated.

"Cordiline said you were smart." Vallance nodded at Jake. "You've already made the initial overtures. We can help you get on the inside."

Mari stared at her, his heart quickening as he processed the logic of her request. They weren't here to warn him off. They had come to recruit Jake. His Jake! Who was currently looking from one to the other of them, drumming his fingers slowly on the countertop as he mulled over the proposal. Damn it, he hadn't even told them to fuck straight off, which meant he was seriously thinking about their offer.

"If I agree to work for you," Jake said, and Mari prayed silently that he was not about to go there. "I want the full debrief. You guys are holding out. If you can't tell me everything, your boss can. I'll sign whatever privacy agreements you need me to, but I need to know what I'm walking into. Is it a weapon? Did he steal it? Is that why you're looking at him so hard?"

"Chivis..." Vallance and Mari both spoke his name at once, then glared at one another. There was a silent warning in the SIS operative's light green eyes and Mari sat down on the urge to set Tonka on her.

Jake held up a hand to stop them declaring all-out war. "Mari, it's okay. Vallance, I know, you can't divulge information. Tell you what, though, you set up an appointment with your superiors. I'll talk to them. But if they want me to play ball, I want some answers first."

"I can do that," she said, and Mari's spirits sank.

Jake nodded once.

Mari shifted on the sofa, pulling his knees up to his chest. He knew how bored Jake was with his office job, even if it was the chance to start a new life in England. Still, he had a very bad feeling about this deal, but he couldn't be sure if it was just anxiety on Jake's behalf, or something more. He was desperate not to see his lover get hurt, and — by extension — he felt guilty, because he'd firmly erased his right to object when he'd refused to admit to Jake how he really felt. Jake seemed keen to do this, and it wasn't his place to tell him what to do or how to go about it, so he kept his mouth shut. It took every ounce of his willpower though.

Thankfully, Vallance and Partridge took their leave after that, the former saying they would be in touch to set up the debriefing. Mari held his breath as Jake closed the door and locked it, resting his forehead against its surface for a second before turning around. His expression was serious but his warm amber eyes were lit with eager excitement. Mari's hopes were quashed in that instant. He felt sick.

"They know what's going on!" Jake exulted, coming over to drop down on the sofa beside him. "They have the truth about why those people lit up. I know they do. And we're going to find out."

Mari remained quiet for a moment but his mind was

working overtime.

You. They want you. They know what you are, a Fire Elemental, like the people who went up in smoke. Screw that. They know I'm already in communication with Birthright and it would be easier for me to get involved. What the fuck are they up to? Why do they want you, Chivis?

If they hurt you…

He screwed up his nervously tapping fingers into fists for a moment and refused to consider that eventuality. Tonka hopped off the sofa and went around him to Jake, licking his hand. Jake patted Tonka's head and gave his ears a rub then turned and tucked the edge of his finger under Mari's chin, lifting his face.

"You're mad about something?"

"Not mad. Suspicious," Mari said. "If they know where these people are and what they are doing, why ask you to go in?"

Jake shrugged. "Because I'm a Fire Elemental, and it would appear that MI5 don't have one of those."

"I'd be very surprised if they did," Mari grumbled, shaking his head. "I'm already opening channels of communication with Birthright, Chivis. I don't like the idea of this at all. What if they're just using you as a test rodent…or bait?"

Jake smiled at him. "Of course, they are. It's no coincidence that Louis and Milda and the guy outside the Palace were Fire Elementals, or that all of them belonged to Birthright. Something is being done to them. My bet is that our new friends know exactly what that 'something' is, but for some reason they think that barging in and arresting people isn't going to make it stop or –" Jake paused for a second, obviously thinking over the options and possibilities. "Or they are looking for someone or something else. Maybe this Corrie character is just a front? Or maybe he has information they need and they know they won't get it by dragging him into the lockup?"

"And you're okay with this? You're okay with them using you?" Mari asked, an incredulous edge to his voice.

"It's…" Jake paused. "Mari, I was planning on going in to find out what's going on anyway. If they tell me what's happening to these people beforehand, it puts us one step ahead of the game. I don't see it as them using me, more like I'm using them for their intel and backup. It's a job. Just because I don't carry a badge anymore doesn't mean I don't still think like a cop, or stop wanting to put bad guys behind bars where they can't hurt other people."

"Chivis," Mari said slowly and deliberately, "people connected to this group are bursting into flames at the slightest provocation. Don't you think that going in there is a wee bit…irresponsible?"

Maddeningly, Jake's concerned look faded into a grin.

"Aww, Ilmari, you do care," he teased, and when Mari rolled his eyes, Jake pulled him into his arms and kissed him. Not a peck, either, but a hot press of lips and tongue as his strong arms pulled him up tight and held him close.

"People are dying, Mari. I can't just ignore that," Jake said when their lips parted. His voice was still persuasive and soft, almost sad.

Mari sucked in a long breath then blew out a rueful sigh.

"Irresponsible…with a social conscience and a killer body. What did I do to deserve you, Jake Chivis?" He hesitated for a moment. "Please don't do anything…flammable. I don't think I could handle telling your mama what became of you."

He kicked himself before the instinctive words were even out of his mouth. *Stupid! Stupid!* Jake didn't exactly reel back but his whole countenance changed, the warmth in his eyes disappearing and his smile suddenly looking painted on. Mari winced and pulled away.

"You don't have to worry about doing that." Jake's tone was bland.

A small frown settled between Mari's eyebrows and he reached up to touch Jake's cheek. Okay, Jake didn't know what he had learned, but the comment had still been well out of order. If he had been in any doubt as to whether they'd rebuilt family bridges after Jake left home, though, Mari had his answer right there.

"I'm sorry. I didn't mean to upset you," he said, keeping his voice as neutral as possible. "I know you don't like to talk about family stuff. I care, and I can't help wondering why."

Jake's expression softened again and he forced a smile that he obviously wasn't feeling. "It's all right, don't be sorry. Since my grandmother passed away, I've not been close to my family, that's all. They've got their lives and I don't fit into any of it. If anything did happen to me — not saying it's going to — but if it did, then the cops can tell them, or they can hear it off the news, or whatever. If any of them even bothers to look. Don't waste your time on a phone call. I doubt they'd care much one way or the other, unless someone thinks they might get money out of it."

Mari chewed on his lips for a moment, stroking his fingers into Jake's hair. He felt bad for bringing the subject up but at least Jake didn't seem to be mad at him. That was a relief.

"I'm so angry with them for making you feel like that. You don't have to tell me if you don't want to talk about it," he breathed, and felt like a heel for saying it, much as he wanted to know Jake's side of the story. "But I am sorry, Jake. If I didn't have Mama…and you, I don't know where I'd be."

Jake kissed the tip of his nose.

"It's not what anyone did…well, not really. Mom moved away when I was a kid and got remarried, had more kids, and I guess she just got wrapped up in her new life. I don't blame her. Her new husband wanted her to cut ties with the past, and that's what she chose to do."

Mari curled around him, touching his face where Jake had kissed it, then leaning close to rub his nose against Jake's in a tender reassurance. It was the first time Jake had really opened up to him about his past.

"Couldn't she take you with her? Or did you want to stay at home?" he asked, picking the words with care.

That cold look flickered in Jake's eyes again and his lips twisted into a harsh sneer that didn't suit him.

"Neither one of them really asked my opinion on where I wanted to be, but I wouldn't have moved that far away from my grandmother. She lived on her own, so leaving her behind wasn't an option. Besides, Mom probably figured, if she left me with him, he wouldn't try to follow her."

"All my days!" Mari shook his head slowly. "Why on earth do some people even have children? I can't understand it. At least your grandmother loved you. She saw the stars shining in your eyes the way that I do."

He touched his mouth to the softness of Jake's lips, needing to be close to him, to somehow let him know how very important he was. The other morning, he had hurt Jake badly by rebuffing his startlingly sudden declaration of love. It had been a moment of defensive instinct. He could not stand for Jake to know how afraid he was of having his heart broken once more. Though he hoped deep down that Jake would never hurt him, or reject him the way Tomas had, a small part of him still found it hard to trust Jake with the truth. Even so, Mari did not want to hurt Jake like that again. Not if he was going to walk alone into the dragon's lair.

Jake's chuckle sounded only slightly bitter, but he returned Mari's kiss with tender warmth.

"I asked my grandmother once, if she just let me hang around her place because she felt guilty about raising such a piece of shit son. She boxed my ears and set me to chopping enough cords of wood to last her all winter. That was her way of saying she loved me, though, and I got it. It wasn't her fault how my father turned out."

"That's a funny way of showing someone you love them. Maybe I should get you to fix things next time you come round to the house," Mari murmured thoughtfully, then chewed on his tongue, wondering if he'd said too much. Sometimes the words slipped out of him before his brain could edit them and left him fuming at himself.

"Why is that? Are you feeling guilty about something?" Jake teased, kissing him some more.

"What would I be feeling guilty about?" Mari returned the kiss, suddenly reminded of the fact that they had been busy when Vallance and her lapdog had so rudely interrupted.

"I'm sure we can find something for you to feel guilty about, something you need to be punished for." Jake winked at him and he felt his face grow hot.

"My! Is this the man who was so anxious about hurting me that he had to be practically ordered to take his belt off? What's come over him?" He chuckled, leaning back and looking at Tonka as if he expected the terrier to answer him. Tonk wagged his tail and looked adoringly at them both.

"You did." Jake wiggled his eyebrows. "If memory serves, you came all over me, and it was really hot."

Mari struggled to breathe for a few seconds. Jake wasn't the only one who had found the experience incendiary. Thinking about it still had him melting, days later. He hadn't come like that in years. It was as if Jake had somehow discovered the key to make him new, to let him start over again. Maybe this time, he could get things right.

Gently he planted another, more lingering kiss on Jake's mouth then, as their lips parted, whispered, "I could come over you again if you really want me to."

"Sounds delicious…but no belt tonight. Not until your butt heals up some. Also, I think we'd have to lock your mukwa in the bathroom so he didn't try to kill me, and that's hardly fair."

Tonka already recognized this word as a term of endearment created especially for him and he hopped onto the sofa and licked Jake's face, keen not to be left out.

Mari laughed. "There's a lot of love in the room this afternoon."

Jake grabbed Tonka's ruff with both hands and gave him an affectionate rub while he tried to keep from getting his face washed. He looked at Mari once he had the dog settled, though, and it was easy to read the curiosity in his eyes. He seemed on the verge of saying something, but he must have decided not to because he looked away again before he got the question out.

"No, I am not suggesting we sleep with the dog," Mari said, deliberately misreading his hesitation and leaning in to kiss his forehead. "Much as I adore this crazy mutt, I am not about to share my bed with him."

"Are you staying tonight, or do you need to go home?" Jake asked him, and the moment of danger passed.

"I guess I ought to take him back at some point." Mari sighed, tickling Tonka's ears. "He's an old man, they're creatures of habit. Plus, I imagine he's gonna be getting hungry before too long."

He leaned against the sofa back with a wistful smile in Jake's direction. *I'm hungry, too…so very hungry. But not for food.*

"You don't have to run right home, though?" Jake asked, reading that expression perfectly.

Mari pursed his lips, pretending to think about it. "Well, I do still need to tell you what I found about Devenish, the Palace firebug."

"Can you tell me in the bedroom?" Jake grinned at him and Mari found himself nodding in amused agreement.

Chapter Eleven

Vallance met Jake outside a long gray fortress of a building on the north bank of the Thames and took him in, not through the huge arched entrance way he had been eyeballing warily, but via a more discreet door closer to Lambeth Bridge. She avoided small talk and accompanied him to the seventh floor, where he was parked in a small, nondescript room with a view of the Thames and the leafy South Bank. The bland, magnolia office contained a bare, light oak desk and two plastic chairs. Vallance set a stack of papers in front of him to sign — all saying, basically, that he agreed to keep his mouth shut — and left the room. A young man in a decent suit brought him a cup of surprisingly good coffee.

He was scratching his name on the last of the papers about ten minutes later when he was joined by an older man. Jake guessed him to be in his late fifties, although he might have been younger and just prematurely aged from the job, or maybe the smoking. The smell of cigarettes hit him — together with a vivid memory of his old man, smoking like a chimney stack in the corner of the kitchen, back home — as soon as the guy walked in the room. He was plain, brown hair running to gray, even features, average height and build, in a dark suit that was neither expensive-looking nor sloppy.

He extended his hand and Jake shook before he took the seat opposite him.

"Pleased to meet you, Mr. Chivis. I'm Officer Ashcroft. I understand from Officer Vallance that you have agreed to come on board as a consultant on our current case involving the recent deaths of Milda Kilis, Louis Cortez and Karl Devenish."

"You could say I have a vested interesting in finding out what happened to them," Jake said.

Ashcroft smiled and nodded. "Yes, I believe you do. Three Fire Elementals apparently bursting into flame for no reason, in very public arenas."

"Apparently," Jake repeated. "But you know the reason?"

"Not exactly. If we knew for certain what had happened to those people we wouldn't be here in this room together. We are closing in on an answer, though. All three victims were also associated with an organization called Birthright, as you and Dr. Gale have already deduced. That is certainly more than simple coincidence."

"You're calling them victims. You don't believe they set themselves alight on purpose?"

Ashcroft smiled again, just a small quirk of his lips.

He unlocked a desk drawer and drew out a folder that he laid in front of Jake. "These are the Fire and Rescue Service Commissioner's reports on each incident."

Jake opened the folder and started to scan through the pages, noting certain areas that were highlighted. No accelerant was found at any of the scenes. Unsurprising, though, considering the intensity of the blaze and that the bodies were completely consumed. No reports of any sound of explosion or the discovery of shrapnel that might have indicated explosives were used. No official determination of cause of the fire on any of the three reports. All three avoided any mention of spontaneous combustion but they certainly read like a conspiracy theorist's wet dream.

"Until a determination can be made one way or the other on how the fires started, we are treating these cases as unplanned and the people that died as victims."

"Victims of what?" Jake looked up from the reports at Ashcroft.

"We're not sure yet, but we believe it has something to with this man." Ashcroft brought out a photograph from the drawer and laid it on top of the folder. It showed a man with short, reddish brown hair, dark, intense eyes and an angry sneer.

"Roy Corrie is his name. Five years ago, he participated in a government-sponsored research program, studying Elemental talents. Shortly after the program ended, he disappeared. There are surprisingly few intelligence records on him. He has no passport and he is not registered for Council Tax or Utilities in any London borough. A few years later, he surfaced on the National Insurance records again when he obtained work at a clinic in Kensington. Our sources believe that he must be paid cash in hand, as he doesn't have a bank account, either. Around the same time as he gained employment, we think, he founded Birthright." Ashcroft brought out another photo and laid it in front of Jake. This one showed a handsome black man, his face narrow and his smile broad. "This is Aled Mustatti. He is a fellow Elemental and Corrie's mouthpiece."

"Was he part of the 'research program' too?"

"No. We believe Corrie met Mustatti shortly after the program was canceled, possibly to ask him for help. Mustatti works in public relations. Currently, he is the press officer for a well-known pharmaceuticals company. He and Corrie put their heads together and came up with the idea for Birthright, an unaffiliated meeting place for those with Elemental ability."

"Mustatti's an Elemental too?"

Ashcroft nodded. "They both are. Mustatti, we believe, is an Earth Elemental, though unregistered here. Corrie is a registered Fire Elemental."

Jake frowned at that and looked down at the photos, and the files below them. "What was the research program looking for?"

Again Ashcroft flashed that small smile, as if he were pleased with something Jake could only guess at. "It was an experiment to enhance Elemental abilities."

Jake felt a muscle twinge in his neck, he looked up so

sharply.

"When the experiment produced no tangible results, it was eventually shut down," Ashcroft explained.

"How exactly did they try to enhance Elemental abilities?"

Ashcroft steepled his fingers. "There were various methods, as I understand it. Certain mental exercises, sensory deprivation, sleep pattern changes."

"And of course none of that worked." Jake chewed on his lips, thankful, not for the first time, that Weston's experiments at the university were less intrusive.

"Right. As I said, the experiment produced no measurable results in improving Elemental ability."

"You said Corrie might have gone to Mustatti for help. What kind of help?"

"Corrie believed the experiment actually lessened his ability." Ashcroft sighed, lowering his eyes to the photograph for a moment. "After he made very vocal complaints, he was given the best medical attention our government could provide, along with a battery of psychological evaluations. It was never determined if his loss of ability had anything to do with the program he was involved in, or some other factor, but he remains adamant that the experiment was the cause. He is an angry man.

"Aled Mustatti worked in PR for the energy industry at that time, then moved into the medical sector. We believe that is how they met. Corrie enlisted him for his promotional skills. He uses Mustatti to generate fear of the government and regular authorities among his members."

Jake turned this over for a moment.

"He's been burned out," he said slowly, still thinking. "So he's pissed off about that, wants someone to fix it, but nothing will. You think he's trying to find a cure? The cult he's developed are his guinea pigs? And somehow he's figured out a way to make Fire Elementals meditate their way into combustion?"

"That's all conjecture, Mr. Chivis. The connection between the victims is undeniable. What, exactly, is happening to make them burst into flames, is what we need to determine and we believe the answer lies with Roy Corrie and Aled Mustatti."

"Why not just pull them in for questioning?"

"Beside the fact that we can't prove he's done anything wrong...?"

Jake smirked at that. If MI5 believed this man was somehow detonating people remotely, he doubted they would let a silly thing like 'proof' stand in the way of them hauling him in.

"We also need to consider that Corrie and Mustatti maybe aren't working alone," Ashcroft finished.

"And if you just take them out, or haul him in for questioning, you might never know. Until more people start randomly catching fire. So you want me to go in and find out, not only what he's doing, but if he's working for anyone specifically. What if it turns out he did have help? If he's managed to do whatever it is he's done with, say, the help of a foreign government?" Jake asked.

Ashcroft smiled. "Like perhaps the US government? Are you asking if I expect you to betray your own country? I assure you, if Corrie is indeed working as a US agent, your government would want him captured and punished just as much as we do."

"Uh-huh. I'm not FBI, you know. I was just a local cop."

Ashcroft moved a file folder by his elbow so that it was in front of him and opened it. Reading aloud he said, "Jake Chivis, two times decorated officer with a commendation for exceptional service and medal of valor with the Detroit PD in Detroit, Michigan. Promoted to detective in the special arson investigation unit after five years' service, one of the youngest officers to achieve detective rank." He closed the file folder and looked at Jake. "You left the force with a one hundred percent closure rate on your caseload, plus several cold cases solved. I can put some of that exemplary record down to your psychic abilities but I would be willing to bet that a lot of it was also due to exceptional police work.

I am also willing to bet that, despite a lack of Federal Investigative training, with the right support you are more than capable of a deep cover operation, and furthermore, given your less mundane talents, uniquely qualified for this operation in particular."

"Were you a cheerleader in a former life? Or do you just like stroking egos?" Jake asked.

Ashcroft laughed. "Ego stroking never hurt anyone."

Jake blew out a breath. He could feel the beat of his pulse, too fast, in his throat. "Okay. I'm in. On one condition."

"And what would that be, Mr. Chivis?" Ashcroft smiled as if he had an idea what Jake was going to ask for. Either that, or he was already pretty confident that he could get Jake to work for him, no matter what.

"I need Dr. Gale's help. Not going in, but I need him to be in the loop. He can find information that no one else can, not even your best IT guys."

"Do I need to remind you of the confidentiality agreement you signed before coming into this room?" Ashcroft asked.

"No. And I'm sure Mari would be willing to sign one too. If I can't bring him in on this, I'll keep my mouth shut and go home. He's an Elemental too, he's the best at what he does and I need him on board."

Ashcroft seemed to consider this for a moment. At last he nodded.

"Okay, there may be some operational issues that need resolving first, but I'll speak to the people concerned and have the documents prepared for him to sign, if he is willing to help us." He passed Jake a card with an address on it. "Here is the meeting place. Your cover story will be that you met Louis Cortez at the gym he used, and he invited you to the meeting, before his unfortunate accident. Once you're accepted as a member, take your time. Don't push to speak to Corrie. He's paranoid and he's crafty. It may take a while before you gain his trust. Once you have his confidence, make note of anyone he talks to, see if you can discover anyone he's grooming for 'enhancement'."

Jake put the card with the address in his pocket as he stood. Ashcroft stood as well and handed him a cell phone.

"There's a bug in this device that will allow us to monitor your location and listen in. I highly suspect you won't be able to carry it in with you to any meetings with Corrie, but it's worth a try."

He pressed a buzzer on his desk phone. Jake took the mobile and put it in the same pocket as the calling card. He shook Ashcroft's hand and the door opened. The guy who had brought their coffee returned and Jake was shown out.

* * * *

Mari tried not to spend the morning brooding over Jake's meeting with MI5, but it was not an easy thing to do. He had looked so eager yesterday when he was thinking ahead to whatever it was the Security Service wanted him to do. Mari had got the distinct impression, when they'd been investigating the murder of Professor Weston's brother, that Jake missed police work. A desk job, even in security, was never going to be enough for him. This was the kind of thing he had been trained to do. He had a degree in crime busting, for crying out loud. Was it unfair of him to insist that Jake tread carefully to please him, when he was considering accepting a job that might be at least as dangerous? One that he would not even be able to share with Jake?

When he came down for breakfast, Angela sidelined him, and managed to distract him for a time with her assertion that she knew what was best for Mama. Mari listened and nodded and told her what she wanted to hear. Mama was quiet and disengaged throughout their exchange, but afterward, he got the impression that she was disappointed in him. That put fire in his belly and helped him reach a decision. Leash or no leash, he would have a degree of control over their life.

At eleven-thirty on the dot, they met with Angela's

solicitor in Westminster, Mari quite sober, in a dark blue suit he usually wore to funerals, and at eight minutes past twelve he walked out onto the street as the owner of a one-million-pound property in Fitzrovia.

It was a curiously numbing experience.

Mama didn't speak to him when he got back and he didn't have the stomach for an argument, so he changed into a T-shirt and leggings and took Tonka for a longer, harder run than he had been used to of late. He pulled up, wheezing painfully, near Cambridge Mews and leaned on the bench there, catching his breath for a while. It was about then that he spotted a familiar tattooed figure jogging casually toward him, and cast his eyes skyward.

Oh, please, no. Not today!

Colm had a bruise over the lower left-hand side of his face that had to hurt. He looked sheepish as he slowed and stopped.

"Um…hi. How's it going?" He looked around anxiously and Mari thought he knew why.

"It's okay. He isn't here today. I'm…yeah. About the same." He pushed himself upright and nudged Tonka with his foot when his guard dog peered around his legs to growl at Colm.

"I'm sorry about the other night," Colm said quickly. "It kinda got out of hand. I thought you were up for it, though. You seemed like you were enjoying yourself, y'know, flirting with us and stuff. Is your fella always so uptight? "

Mari smirked. "No. I guess Donny must be right. It's just you. Do guys punch you a lot?"

Colm looked disgruntled. "Now your bloody dog's at it. I reckon they're a good pair, your boyfriend and your dog. Has he managed to get it up you yet?"

Mari raised an eyebrow, beginning to see what irked Jake about the man. "And you wonder why people punch you? Look, Colm, no offense but have you ever considered thinking before you open your mouth?" He turned and tugged on Tonka's leash when the burly terrier seemed preoccupied with what was in the nearby refuse bin. "I have to get home. Y'know. Things to see, people to do."

"I'm sorry," Colm said again. "Look, Mari, I'm… I was really hoping we could give it another try. But, if you and Jake have already figured out how to make you relax, I guess I should just butt out and leave you alone."

Mari hesitated. He wanted to just wave his hand and be done with it but a part of him was curious about whether Colm genuinely could fix him or if, as Jake suspected from his flashback, he was just another chancer who wanted a crack at his arse.

"Colm," he said in a more serious tone. "Look, I'm not saying Jake was right to punch you. That was out of order, but you and Donny were too. You knew you were winding him up."

"I guess," Colm said mildly. "But we genuinely did believe you'd talked to him about it."

"I did," Mari protested. "Jake's protective though. And…I kind of like that. I want a solution to my…my problem. But if it's good with you, I do really want it to be Jake that takes me first, if it's going to happen."

Colm looked curiously at him. "You told us the other night, when he was outside, that you weren't a virgin. Was that just bluster?"

"No," Mari said, shaking his head. "That was true. But I told Jake I'd never been with a guy that way. It was a long time ago and it only happened a couple of times. I was a different person then. I don't know how to explain it to him. Easier to say I never tried too hard."

"What do you mean? You don't love him like you loved Mr. First-Time?" Colm laughed cynically, but Mari just shook his head and turned away.

"No. That's not what I mean."

Colm caught up as he walked away. "Whoa, whoa, whoa…don't do that. What do you mean? Did your first force you? Is that it?" For a second he looked angry. "You were raped, and you'd have let us make you go through it again?"

"No," Mari said with more vehemence. "I don't want to talk about this here. But if it makes you feel better, I liked him — my first. I respected him and he didn't make me do it. I wanted to. I just…I was very young, and curious, and I never really wanted to again. Not for a while. So now you know something no one else does. And if you don't mind, I have to go."

Colm didn't pursue him this time, to his relief, but by the time he got home his chest hurt and he felt no better. Mari heard voices coming from the day room and he hadn't even closed the door before Tonka was pulling at the end of his leash, panting excitedly. He unclipped the lead and Tonka's nails clattered on the flooring as he barreled off.

"There you are, where have you been, mukwa? Off running around the park, hmm?" Jake's voice carried back to Mari.

He managed a weary smile at the sound and poked his head around the door into the kitchen.

"Hi. I didn't check my phone. Did you call? How did everything go?" he asked, thinking that Jake looked so alive, so excited and pleased with himself, that it wouldn't do to be negative about his choices. It was up to him how he lived his life.

Jake moved over to him and kissed his cheek.

"It went well. I have an address and a plan…which I can tell you about later," he added quietly.

"Sure," Mari said. "I need to shower, anyway. You can keep Mama entertained, can't you? Make sure Tonka wipes his paws before he goes near the furniture. I'll not be long. Hi, Mama, no Angela?" he added lightly.

"Shopping," Mama said and pretended to be interested in something on her notebook.

Jake watched Mari head for the bathroom before he took Tonka into the kitchen and wiped his paws on his strip of towel. Mari's response had sounded rather too casual. They might not have been seeing each other all that long, but it had been long enough that Jake could tell when he was hiding the fact that something was bugging him.

He waited until he was sure Mari was in the shower before he sat on the sofa across from Anni's chair, scratching Tonka's ears as the dog plonked himself down on the floor beside him and tilted his head back for pets.

"Did you and Mari have an argument?" Jake asked after a moment.

"What makes you think that?" she asked in that same atonal voice that had just dismissed her son. She jabbed at the same key a couple of times, as if it had irritated her.

Jake smiled. Mari had the same tendency to punish his laptop if he was frustrated or annoyed about something.

"Look, I've not been around for long, but I've never known him not to come straight to you, when he comes home, or you not to ask how he is."

Annabel Gale lifted her head and looked at him very directly. "Hmm, you can take the detective out of the force, but you can't take the Force out of the detective. You pay too much attention sometimes, young Skywalker. Ilmarinen is my son, but he has a lot of his father in him too. My ex-husband thought he knew what was best for all of us. He was not always correct," she said cryptically.

"Mm, yeah...I can see that about him," Jake responded with a soft chuckle, keeping his voice low just in case. "On the other hand, he may not get it all from his father." He risked a sly grin at her.

"You have been spending too much time with him. He's a bad influence," she said, pointing a finger at Jake. "To answer your question, we did not argue, we had a difference of opinion. I asked him not to do something and he went ahead and did it anyway. I thought children were supposed to have some respect for their parents."

Jake was quiet for a moment. "So, he signed the papers then."

She looked surprised and Jake gave a half-shrug.

"He's been worried, so he talked to me. You know he only agreed because he cares, don't you?"

Annabel looked back down at the screen in front of her as if there might be answers there. At last she said, "I know he cares. There are other ways to care. This is not a house, it's a noose."

"Only if he lets it be one," Jake murmured back. "And it's too late, anyway, so you might as well forgive him so he doesn't wallow in guilt. I'll even say pretty please with sugar on top."

Anni leaned back in her chair and closed the lid of her compact notebook as if it was fragile. Her eyes were very blue, like Mari's, and like her son she wore her emotions very plainly on her face. There were shadows of frustration and hurt there, but a lot of affection too.

"You know, I was beginning to worry about his choices," she said softly. "He's made some very strange ones in the last few years. I worry that he doesn't know his own heart sometimes. And I worry that, in trying to do things for my sake, he will sacrifice himself again. But you are a choice that I approve of, wholeheartedly, Mr. Chivis. You are good for him. Convince him that this is a bad idea, please. There are other options open to us."

"Before I agree to do that, I'd have to know why exactly it's a bad idea," Jake said.

"You've met my mother," Anni said tersely. "I don't want him to wind up like her, bitter and preoccupied with money. And if she gets her claws into him, she will try her damnedest to mold him into a clone. I swear, I'll have him committed before I let her do that."

Jake's eyebrows crept up in genuine surprise. "Anni… have you met your son? If you think he's going to let anyone manipulate him, you don't understand him as well as you think you do," he protested.

"Jake, I know you care about him, but there are things you don't know," Annabel said in a low voice. "My boy is smart, but when it comes to his emotions, he's sometimes divorced from reality. He's not made smart choices in the past, and he lets his heart rule his head. That's got him hurt badly before. Ilmari is very dedicated to seeing me get well. It isn't the first time that he's tried to be something specifically to please someone else, and I worry, in the pursuit of this goal, that he'll lose sight of his own priorities."

"What do you mean? There is no way Mari is going to change so drastically that money becomes his top priority. This agreement, this house, it's a means to an end for him." Jake leaned forward and gave her his best cop stare. "He's going to take care of you one way or another, and when he's done with that, he'll still be standing on his own two feet. You raised him to be a very competent man. Don't be mad at him for being what you taught him to be."

She opened her mouth to say something else but, at that moment, Tonka uttered a sharp bark and trotted back toward the kitchen and she looked up, her expression masked with a guileless innocence. From the doorway into the back hall, her son exhaled a sigh.

"Jake, don't let my mother wrap you up in her logic," he said mildly, and padded barefoot across the tiled floor to one of the cabinets where he located a box of Tonka's favorite kibble and poured him a bowl of food before coming through to sit down on the arm of the sofa beside Jake. He was clad in loose cream flannel trousers and a light-colored hooded top that he sometimes slept in. His hair was still wet, about three shades darker than its usual pale ash hue.

"I thought he was holding his own very well, actually," Anni said brightly. "He's a keeper, this one."

"I know that," Mari told her. "Don't tell him that though. He'll get a big head."

He reached across and ruffled his fingers through Jake's hair. Jake might have made an innuendo-laden comment at that but kept a lid on it.

"Are you two going out tonight?" Anni asked, and Jake noted there was more warmth in her voice than there had been earlier, when Mari had come in from the park.

"I don't know. Are we?" Mari looked a question at Jake. "Or should we stay home and play charades with my grandmother?"

"Angela is taking me to the theater," Anni said, raising her eyebrows in an expression so like one of her son's that there was no doubting their blood bond. "She hasn't told me what we're seeing yet, so I'm holding out a vague hope that it won't be too awful."

"So we have the house to ourselves for a while? That's very thoughtful of you," Mari teased her.

Jake pressed his lips between his teeth and tried not to laugh. He remembered that he had an assignation tonight, though, and wouldn't be able to take advantage anyway.

"I can't stay long. I have a meeting to go to at nine."

"Alcoholics Anonymous?" Anni asked cheekily.

"It's his sex addiction group," Mari said before Jake could open his mouth to argue. "Hard to believe but he could barely walk in a straight line before he started going."

Jake rolled his eyes and again had to bite his tongue to keep from saying something totally inappropriate in front of his boyfriend's mother.

"It's to do with work," Jake said, which technically wasn't a lie as, he considered, he was working with MI5 on this case. "And speaking of which, I need you to look up a few things, if you don't mind?" he asked Mari.

"Good grief, they're making you burn the candle at both ends. Don't burn yourself out totally." Anni set her laptop aside and pushed herself up from the chair with a sigh. "I suppose I should go take a bath and try to make myself beautiful."

"You're always beautiful. You never have to try," Mari told her, demonstrating that their rift was a transient thing.

Jake smiled, feeling his heart grow warm as she cupped the back of her son's head and kissed his hair.

"Correct answer. Don't get yourself into trouble, Ilmari."

"Trouble? Me?" He feigned a look of hurt.

"You know what I mean," she warned. "I don't want the police knocking on our door at all hours."

"He's already here, Mama," Mari pointed at Jake.

"Behave!" she reiterated. "And, Jake, don't work too hard, all right? I'll see you tomorrow, maybe."

Jake watched her go with a fond smile. He liked Anni as a person, but he also sort of envied Mari his easy relationship with his mother.

Speaking of which, Mari was looking at him with undisguised eagerness and he shook his head, waiting until Anni was out of earshot. Mari opened his mouth to say something then, but Jake held up a finger. He took out the phone that he'd gotten from Ashcroft, went into the kitchen and put it in the refrigerator. Mari had followed him and looked at him like he was worried he might be unhinged. Jake led him back to the sitting room.

"I just didn't want anyone listening in. It's bugged. I'm supposed to take it with me tonight. Are you ready to hear the whole story?"

"They bugged your phone? Class!" Mari looked at his fridge as if he suspected it of making plans with the phone, then hopped onto the sofa and pulled his knees up to his chest, hugging them there like a schoolboy. "Come on then, what did they say?"

"First, this is all classified. I had to sign about three dozen pages of confidentiality agreements. Technically I'm not supposed to tell anyone any of this, but I told them I wouldn't work with them unless I could bring you in on it, so you'll get the paperwork too...if you agree." He didn't wait for Mari to say yes or no because he figured the answer would be yes, and he was going to tell him anyway, so it really didn't matter. Normally he wouldn't have broken that agreement so easily, but he knew Mari. If he didn't tell him, the moment he was out of the door he'd be on his computer digging, and more than likely he'd find what he was looking for.

"Damned right, I do!" Mari told him, a glint in his eye

that said wild horses wouldn't have dragged him off Jake's trail if he'd had to go in alone. In that much at least, he was vindicated.

"Five years ago, there was a government-funded experiment researching Elementals. Guess what they were trying to do?"

"Incinerate innocent people?" Mari ventured with cutting sarcasm.

Jake mussed up his damp hair and grinned when Mari swatted him.

"No. They were trying to find a way to enhance Elemental abilities. They didn't have any success so they axed the experiment and disbanded the program. Roy Corrie, the head of Birthright, happened to be a part of that program. Since he was a participant in an experiment to enhance Elemental abilities and, suddenly, Fire Elementals close to him are becoming highly flammable, MI5 strongly suspect he's continued on his own with the experiment and somehow succeeded, in a way, where the initial experiment failed."

Mari's eyes widened. "Oh, my days! At least Professor Weston isn't unscrupulous enough to put us through anything dangerous," he breathed, thinking aloud. "So...Corrie was one of the first guinea pigs? Were they deliberately trying to create Pyros, or just enhance known abilities? And how did Roy escape a fiery end, if that's the case?"

"Well, for one thing he's a Fire Elemental himself, so my guess is that he was waiting to see if it worked before attempting it personally. Also, Ashcroft said he's burned out what minimal ability he had to begin with." He waited a moment while that sunk in with Mari and those big blue eyes got even wider. "Uh-huh, you got it. Corrie doesn't want to give up on the experiment because he's hoping it'll bring back his 'power'. Gives a whole new spin to the 'birthright' thing, doesn't it? Ashcroft wouldn't say with certainty that they were looking to produce Pyros in the original experiment. If I had to guess, I'd say the Government's first try was with Air Elementals. From a security standpoint, that makes the most sense — trying to enhance an Air Elemental, I mean."

"How so?" Mari was wearing a curious half-smile.

"The most common ability among those with Air Elemental blood is astral projection with a very limited range. Floating up around the ceiling or taking a walk around the house while your body sleeps in bed," Jake pointed out. "But if they could take someone that could astral project say, forty feet, and turn them into a remote viewer, someone who is awake, aware, and fully functional... Imagine sitting here in London while a part of you is off spying, four thousand miles away... Or if they could enhance someone to your level as an Interface, even? Just think, if they had their own lab of hackers that could tap in and pull any data they needed at any time, and get it without leaving a trace behind? And if they managed to turn an Air Elemental into a teleporter? Or make him able to apparate objects? That's in the realm of Legendary ability, just as much as pyrokinesis, and much more useful."

Mari whistled softly through his teeth. Jake saw him shiver though and knew that he got it.

"My great-grandmother used to talk about the Legendary class of Elementals," he said in a reverent tone. "She said there were Elementals still, when she was a girl, that could do things with their minds to turn a person's hair white. Of course, her own hair was already white, and I was only five when she died, so I just thought it was a fairy tale. Angela always said that such things were fables, and my Grandmama Amelia was away with the fairies, but then, Angela isn't from an Elemental bloodline. My grandpapi thought it could be possible, though, that the old bardic songs and poems made mention of people that might well have been Elementals."

"It's hard to say. There isn't much documented proof beyond the stories and fables." Jake sighed. "But people got the idea for those stories and legends from somewhere. Who knows what the people with Elemental blood were capable of when you go back generations and get closer to the source?"

Mari leaned back against Jake's shoulder, a warm presence all down his left side. He still had his arms wrapped around his knees but he tilted his head to look up at Jake with a smile.

"Maybe in generations to come, kids will talk about us like we were the stuff of legends as well." He chuckled wryly.

Jake kissed the top of his head. "Maybe. I don't know if that makes me relieved or sad."

"Well, in theory, at least you won't be around to worry about it," Mari said, in practical-mode. He snuggled closer. "Shame you have to go out tonight. I hope we can manage an hour on our own, at least."

"I think I have an hour or two to spare, maybe." Jake grinned and pulled him closer, kissing him hard.

Chapter Twelve

Jake took the Circle line to Goldhawk Road and, as he left the tube station, found himself on a busy main street dedicated in part to shops selling exotic, multi-ethnic fashions and colorful bolts of cloth. Where the tube line crossed overhead, there was a line of uniform railway arches beneath, many of which had been converted into storage lock-ups and garages on either side of the road. Facing those stood a row of neat terraced houses. He leaned against the railings outside one of them and studied the nondescript unit on the opposite side of the street, wishing he smoked. Smoking gave a handy excuse to be outside loitering and not looking like you were casing a place. Fortunately, it was a busy street, not far from Shepherd's Bush Market, and even though it was getting late, there were still enough people around that he didn't look like a stalker as he pretended to check his phone and watched people, in singles and pairs, enter the nondescript lock-up between a motor shop and several other anonymous arched doorways. Their security didn't look that tight. No one was stopped, they were all just casually strolling in. No key cards or secret passwords required. If he believed he had an ounce of intuition in him, it would be trying to tell him this was the perfect set up for a super-villain's lair.

"Close enough," Jake muttered under his breath as he crossed the street. It was time to see if anyone would freak out at an unfamiliar face.

Considering Birthright was a secret underground group, allegedly bent on Elemental purity and breeding super-humans, it was remarkably easy to just walk in and wander around. There was no one on the door at all. He understood right away why Louis had called this a 'church'. It was set up with rows of folding chairs all facing the front 'altar' area where a lectern was set up. No one was sitting in those chairs yet—they were all mingling and chatting. Jake moved among them slowly, eavesdropping here and there, but mostly they were all talking about their week, their jobs, their kids, mundane stuff.

"Hello, I haven't seen you here before," a woman said to him just as he was turning. She was petite and blonde and had a smile that looked like it belonged on an advertisement for toothpaste.

"Hi, I'm Nathan," Jake said.

"Nathan..." She tilted her head as if sizing him up. "I know I would have remembered your face. Who's your sponsor?"

"Ah, well, you don't remember me because this is my first time here. My friend Louis was supposed to be my sponsor, but...well, I'm sure you heard about the accident. He was going to meet me here tonight," he said regretfully. "I figured even if Louis is no longer with us, well, he made it sound like a welcoming group."

Her unnaturally bright expression crumpled at the mention of Louis and she almost reached out and took his hand then stopped herself just short of doing it. That was interesting. Not all Elementals had his gift for touch recognition, but she respected that it might be a possibility. Even if she wasn't a Fire Elemental herself, she had been around Elementals enough to know that it was not always polite to touch without asking. He made a mental note of that.

"Oh no. You knew him? That's too sad, Nathan. What happened to him, and to Milda and Karl...it's so scary isn't it?" she whispered, softly enough not to disturb those nearby. "Everyone in the group is talking about it. People are wondering if it's some kind of virus that only affects Elementals. That's not...it's not a European accent. Are you here as a student, Nathan?"

"Yes, I'm American. Hoping to make London my permanent home eventually. So, what kind of Elemental are you?" he asked, keeping up the friendly facade.

She laughed and Jake thought it sounded as fake as her smile had been, although her concern and fear about Louis had seemed real enough.

"Oh, me? I'm a Water Elemental, but my gifts aren't very strong," she said, almost apologetic. "My great-great-grandfather was a powerful Water Elemental Healer, though."

"Oh, I haven't met one of those before." Jake beamed at her, encouraging her to continue, even though he thought his face was going to hurt later.

"Really? We're quite prolific, I think," she told him.

"Ah, I didn't know that. Small-town boy. I didn't really have anyone to tell me about my ancestors, so you'll have to pardon my ignorance. That's part of the reason I'm here. I want to learn more about us."

She gestured toward one of the seats and came to sit down beside him, ignoring the curious looks from some of the other members of the assembly.

"I'm Claire," she said. "You've come to the right place. I'm so sorry that you didn't get to know Louis better but I'm sure you'll soon feel at home with us. So you don't have much in the way of family? I was adopted, but I went looking for my birth mother as soon as I was old enough, and she eventually told me about what I was. As soon as I found out, I was just so excited. I did my family tree and found out about my inheritance. I always knew I was different, somehow. And I think that must have shown, because pretty soon I was getting involved with the committee here and helping out in all sorts of ways, and today I'm pretty much a lynchpin in the organizational side of things. It's been so much more than a job to me. Birthright is like the family I never had. I hope you come to see us as your family, Nathan. Really I do."

"I feel at home already," Jake said, doing his best not to sound bored. "So, there are more Water Elementals than other types? I didn't know that. What about Fire Elementals like me then? I know that Louis was one too. They must be the second most numerous?"

Claire opened her mouth to say something, but as she did, another voice spoke up right behind him.

"No, they are quite rare."

Jake turned in his seat and looked up at a tall man with skin so dark it was blue-black. He had solemn eyes and his thatch of tightly curled ebony hair was cut close to his scalp. Aled Mustatti. Jake recognized him at once from his photograph.

"Statistically Earth Elementals, such as myself, are the most numerous," he told him, "although there are nearly as many Water Elementals. Air Elementals such as Tansy over there" — he pointed toward a tall, red haired woman — "are fewer to come by, and Fire Elementals are truly rare here. I'm so pleased that you have joined us. My name is Aled, I coordinate these meetings. Pleased to meet you…?"

"Nathan," Jake said, extending his hand to shake and bracing himself in case he picked up any random memories. Aled gripped his hand briefly and Jake breathed again when he didn't get sucked into the past. "Nice to meet you."

Aled flashed a hint of a very white smile. He had one gold tooth on the upper mandible, about halfway between front and back on the left side. Jake registered it in the way that he mentally registered anything that might aid later identification. The smile was gone as quickly as it came. "Claire, shouldn't you be handing out the agendas?"

She bobbed to her feet and nodded, looking disappointed. "I was just doing it. I'll maybe see you later, Nathan?"

"Sure," Jake said, in a not quite flirty tone. When she'd gone he returned his attention to Aled.

"What happened to my friend Louis was horrible, and seeing as how I'm a Fire Elemental too…well, I thought Birthright might be the closest thing to experts on

Elementals," Jake said. Self-preservation was a universally understood motivation.

"You share the fear of some kind of contagion then?" Aled looked interested. "Let me set your mind at rest. It is no virus, at least, not in the sense that most people understand a virus. And you are safe amongst us here. Louis... I know he was your friend, and I have no desire to speak ill of the dead, but he ran with some unsavory people. He did himself no favors, I hope you understand."

Jake almost asked him how he knew it wasn't a virus, but he let the moment pass. He wasn't sure what would or wouldn't spook them, and asking too many pointed questions wasn't a good idea. He needed to just play good little sheep and follow along until he could ingratiate himself with Mustatti and see if he could eventually meet with Corrie.

"That's a shame," Jake said. "He seemed like a decent guy."

Aled inclined his head in acknowledgment. "We are about to begin our session, Nathan. You must excuse me. Perhaps we can talk later? Enjoy your visit."

Jake watched him walk away. Everyone began shuffling around and taking seats when Aled moved up to the lectern and waited for quiet before beginning to speak.

Jake had thought he was prepared. He'd been expecting some kind of superior race rhetoric, maybe with some Jesus-hugging and bible-thumping mixed in. Instead Aled talked about the necessity to dig into family histories, genealogy sites and the like, to understand how Elemental bloodlines developed and worked. He spoke of the need to cultivate political clout in the battle to have the world acknowledge Elemental abilities as valid and ensure their rights to privacy and civil liberties. Jake found himself drawn into the talk almost against his will. And really, stripped of all the racial separatist bullshit on the website, the rest of what Aled said only made sense. Having his abilities considered valid, making sure no one locked him up or burned him at the stake, were a big part of why he'd agreed to come to London and work at the college. Elemental abilities were still barely understood, and what people didn't understand could easily be used to frighten them.

After the speech, sermon—whatever you wanted to call it—was over, everyone stood and mingled some more. Jake was figuring that he'd gotten about all that he could out of the evening and was edging toward the door when Claire and about half a dozen other women surrounded him.

"Hi, so you're Louis' friend then." A tall brunette with green eyes batted her lashes at him. "No wonder he didn't tell us about you. I'm Tara."

"Claire says you're Nathan," a small, curvy lady with dark blonde hair and a too-earnest grin added. "I'm Lisa, nice to meet you."

"Hello," Jake said to the general assembly.

A small chorus of 'Hi' and 'Hello' echoed around him as more of Birthright's mostly female members congregated in a rough circle, all competing for his attention.

"I'm Sarah. Where in America do you come from? My cousin lives in Utah."

"Hello there, Nathan. I'm Jinny. You are so tall."

"Wow, we've never had an American here before. I'm Elise. I love your accent."

He was admired and cooed over like an exhibit in a petting zoo, though he was grateful that no one crossed a line and touched him.

"Claire also says you're a Fire Elemental?" Tara asked. "Do you have ability?"

That was definitely getting personal and Jake chuckled nervously, not needing to feign it at all. He was used to keeping that part of his life fairly private but he supposed letting it drop that he could use psychometry could only help him in his aim of getting closer to Corrie. "I do, it's a small thing, though. I sometimes can tell who handled an object last, when I touch it." He could do considerably more than that, of course, but he didn't need to tip his whole hand.

"Wow, that must be useful," Jinny cooed, her eyes roaming over him like he was wearing a great deal less.

"Don't let him touch your hand, Jin," the woman called Elise bitched with a smirk that didn't quite reach her dark blue eyes.

Jinny glared back at her but Jake didn't have time to feel embarrassed for her.

"Are you single, Nathan?" Sarah asked.

"Um, I..."

"Lisa's single. Maybe you two should go have a coffee together sometime."

Lisa blushed, to her credit, but added, "There's a really nice place near mine, up in St. John's Wood. If you wanted to."

"Um, I..." Jake stammered, casting around for a good excuse. "I'll have to take a rain check I'm afraid. I have some work I have to catch up on." *On a Saturday night, no less. Smooth, Jake. Smooth.*

Lisa's smile was brittle but she took it gracefully enough and Jake made a mental note of the ones that seemed particularly pleased he hadn't taken his pick of the lot yet.

He expected to get cruised at a bar, but in no way had he been prepared to be so blatantly sized up by what amounted to a ladies auxiliary group. They'd all but asked him if he wanted to sire their babies. Apologizing that he really needed to get home, he made his escape at last and waited until he was in the back of a cab before he texted Mari.

Is it okay to come over?

* * * *

Mari was sprawled on the sofa on his belly, with his laptop open in front of him, a tablet propped up beside him and Tonka stretched out on a blanket, a long warm presence against his right-hand side. He had spent the

199

evening surfing the Birthright website but things were rather quiet online, given that most of their members were at the meeting in Shepherd's Bush. When Jake texted him, his spirits rose immediately and he sent back an enthusiastic reply. Fifteen minutes later, he was letting Jake in through the French doors from the garden and greeting him with a hug. Tonka, who had been asleep for most of the evening, woke up at the sound of Jake's voice and bounced around his feet like an excited puppy.

Jake had hugs and kisses for Mari and ear and jowl rubs for Tonka, which settled them both down. Mari did note that Tonka made no attempt to jump up on Jake, and he didn't have to grab his collar to hold him back once. That was interesting.

Before Jake had a chance to tell him about anything that had happened, the mobile phone that Ashcroft had given him rang, making them both jump with its old-fashioned ringtone. He answered it on the second ring, putting it on speaker so Mari could hear.

"Is anyone with you, besides Dr. Gale?" Ashcroft asked.

"No," Jake said. "What? You mean you're not peeking through the windows?"

Ashcroft chuckled. "If we were, we wouldn't be talking. You did well tonight. Claire Pollard likes you. She's Corrie's PA, keep her sweet. And keep working on Aled Mustatti. He'll be key in getting you an interview with Corrie."

"Right. I figured that," Jake said.

"If Mustatti doesn't pan out in a few days, we can try a different angle. Claire is possibly not as trusted, but she has access to a lot of his files." Ashcroft paused before adding, "And she seemed keen to get to know you better."

"Oh, really?" Mari mouthed, fluttering his eyelashes.

Jake rolled his eyes. "I'm not going to hop in bed with Claire to get to Corrie, just so you know."

There was another, longer pause on the other end.

"How about Aled?"

"What?"

"Never mind. Let's hope it doesn't come to that. I'm thinking, just the fact that you're a Fire Elemental will be enough temptation to get you an interview, at least. We'll discuss more protocol when that happens. Good work, Chivis, and good night."

With that, he hung up and Jake walked into the kitchen to chuck the phone back into the refrigerator. Mari trailed him, then pushed him back against the fridge door and ran one hand across the firm biceps under Jake's shirt.

"Well, that was interesting. I presume Claire is Butterfly Girl, the one I was surfing. MI5 have been watching her too, I see. But who is Aled?" he asked slyly. "Is he cute?"

Jake gave him a look, which Mari supposed was intended to be a warning, but only made him grin.

"He's Birthright's head brainwasher. And, it doesn't matter if he's *cute*. I'm not sleeping with anyone just to get in to see Corrie."

"I'm glad to hear it," Mari said, sliding around him again with a possessive smile. "I'm not in the mood to share. Especially not with someone employed to fuck with your head. So, did you get a feeling off him? Like they're up to no good?"

"I didn't get any memories off of anyone. Everyone seemed to be pretty aware of personal space and careful about not touching anyone else. They were mostly just friendly." Jake shrugged and Mari thought he looked uncomfortable. "Perhaps overly friendly. There must have been half a dozen women sizing me up like they were all thinking about having Fire Elemental babies. It was creepy as hell."

Mari shivered. "What a revolting idea. Do you suppose they're encouraging that sort of thing? A breeding program, I mean? I know there's a lot of talk in the forums about Elemental women only dating fellow Elementals, but... ewww!"

"I hate to say it, but, yeah. I think that's exactly what they are aiming for." Jake made a face that showed his distaste at such an idea. "I mean, my grandparents were both from Elemental lines, but that's not why they got married, or at least not the only reason. These women acted and sounded very much like...like bagging an Elemental guy was an achievement. And not just any guy with Elemental blood either. From what they were saying, it's possible I was the only one there that was a Fire Elemental."

"Well, you are quite rare specimens," Mari murmured, the tip of his nose just about touching Jake's. "Especially up here in northern Europe. Don't Salamanders tend to thrive in hotter climates such as Africa, or places like Iceland and North America, where they have hot springs? It must be a rush for them. Or maybe they just wonder if sex with a Fire Elemental will be like Russian roulette, only with a potential incendiary bomb rather than a loaded gun. Some women get off on that kind of thing, so I've heard."

"Really. So you've heard, huh? No experience of that yourself?" Jake swatted his ass playfully, and Mari flinched, tightening his fingers on his broad shoulders. Jake immediately looked contrite, sucking in a hiss of breath through his teeth and exhaling, "Oops! Sorry."

"No, you aren't." Mari was conscious that his voice had gone husky. His backside was tingling fiercely and he rather liked it. "Are you asking whether I like the element of risk, or whether I've been with women who did?"

"Hmm, well, I'm pretty sure I know the answer to the former." Jake chuckled. "And I wasn't going to ask about the latter, but since you brought it up...?"

Mari shrugged. "I've dated women. Are you surprised by that?"

"Only dated? Or...? How long ago?" Jake didn't sound accusatory, or freaked out, just curious.

"I went out with a girl when I was doing my Master's over here at Cambridge. And when I first came back to London, three years ago, I was seeing a girl who worked at the university but she got another job in Cardiff and we kind of fizzled out," he volunteered, with a half-smile for

Jake's frustrated curiosity. "Yes, I had sex with her. Happy? There wasn't really much chemistry between us, though. I couldn't see myself settling down and being with her until we both got old. But all the guys that I hooked up with in that period wanted me to sub and it wasn't what I was after at the time. Did you ever try it? With a woman, I mean."

Jake blinked once and it was like a shutter came down behind his eyes.

"Sort of. I don't think it really counts. It was a long time ago."

"If you did it, it counts," Mari told him, then touched the side of his face gently. "It doesn't change who you are, Jake. Why would you think it wouldn't count?"

"It wasn't my idea. I don't think it was really her idea, either." Jake huffed. "There's a lot of cultural stuff about rites of passage, and being a man and all, that isn't determined by an arbitrary age for us so much as puberty and maturity. My dad was already on my case all the time about how come I didn't have girlfriends, and when was I going to stop being a pussy boy, and shit like that."

"He sounds charming." Mari was privately fascinated, though—it was the first time Jake had offered up any real insight into his father without being prodded.

"What's the opposite of that?" Jake grunted. "So, anyway, one day he brought this woman home from the bar with him and... How to put this, I knew if I didn't do at least something with her he'd probably fucking kill me, because he was already thinking there was something wrong with me."

Mari's eyes widened in astonishment. A flush of sudden anger on Jake's behalf heated his face. Ridiculous, he knew. It had happened years ago, and he couldn't change it, but Mari was still indignant on Jake's behalf.

"He brought you a whore because he thought you were queer? All my fucking days! Did she know how old you were?"

Jake shrugged. "Probably. I don't know. I didn't get my

height for another couple years after that, so I probably looked like any other gawky kid to her. Anyway, it wasn't great, but she wasn't mean about it. I pretty much knew then, if I ever had any doubt, that I preferred guys."

Mari let his fingers slide down Jake's arms, taking hold of his hands and drawing him back toward the sofa. He sat, pulling Jake in to sit beside him. Gently he guided Jake's fingers to his lips, kissing them.

"Wow," he whispered huskily. "What a baptism. She didn't tell your father, I take it?"

Jake had an odd smirk on his face.

"No. She was decent, and she knew what he was like because he practically lived at the bar. She must have had some pity in her because when she was leaving I heard her tell him there was nothing wrong with me and just give it a year or two and he'd probably have some gorgeous grandbabies." Jake laughed and shook his head. "I think it was just about the nicest thing anyone had done for me. It was like, two or three months without any beatings from him, he was so proud."

Mari chewed on his lips as he slid his arms back around Jake, holding him close, horrified and fascinated in equal measure. Of course, he knew about the beatings but hearing it from Jake's lips sent a spike of very real pain right through his heart.

"He used to hit you? That's...that's horrible. My poor Jake."

Jake brought his arms up but not to pull him closer. He pushed Mari back so he could look at him and Mari searched his face for some clue to his thoughts. It wasn't quite his deadpan cop-face, but still Mari found it hard to read Jake's emotions.

"Don't. Please don't do that. I don't want to be pitied," his lover grated. "It was a long time ago and none of it matters, okay? That's exactly why I don't usually tell anyone anything about when I was growing up. I'm not— I'm not that kid anymore and I'm fine. So no more 'poor Jake' stuff, okay?"

Mari was silent for a moment, mulling this over. He understood that, to a degree. There was plenty that he'd not figured out how to tell Jake, or even if he was going to tell Jake, but he nodded at last.

"It clearly does matter to you. But no, I won't pity you, if that's not what you want. You still grew up to be a fine man, no matter what example he set you. I want to kill him though. Bastard motherfucker!" He seethed.

Jake gave him a lopsided smile and quelled his temper with a kiss. "Don't waste your time or energy wanting to kill him. I don't. Not anymore. It's not worth it."

Mari returned the kiss in a fierce and most un-tender fashion.

"I don't care," he breathed when their lips parted. "He's a vile man. He doesn't deserve to have a son like you. That's so wrong."

Jake smoothed his thumbs over Mari's cheeks as warm hands cupped his face. "He doesn't really have a son. I left. As soon as I could. So did my mother. He's got no one."

"Good!" Mari snapped, the anger still seething in his veins. "I hope one day he realizes what he's done." He closed his mouth for a moment then ventured, "Is that why...why you didn't feel comfortable? When I asked you to take your belt to me? Oh, my stars! I never even thought! I'm such an idiot. So sorry!"

Jake had to physically put his hand over his mouth to get him to stop. Mari got a hot rush of pleasure from that firm compression over his nose and lips. That too was interesting and he didn't fight it right away.

"Shh. No. No, that's not it at all. I was worried about hurting you, and about making sure it was a good experience for you. That's all. There is absolutely nothing to be sorry about, Mari. I don't dwell in the past. I've let all that shit go." Jake released him and he almost wanted to beg him to cover his mouth again. Then pull his clothes off.

"You say that like it was such an easy thing to do," he said instead. "I wish it was. How on earth do you manage to be so calm about it? That would drive me crazy. I had such a placid childhood next to yours but there are so many things that I wish I could just… I don't know…just put them in a box and put the lid on and lose them, I guess." He closed his mouth as he realized he was talking too much again.

Jake's short laugh had a jagged, bitter edge to it.

"Who said anything about it being easy? I was very pissed off at everyone and everything for a long time. It took me a long while to get to the point where I even realized I had a choice. I could be angry the rest of my life and let the shitty way my parents treated me make me someone I didn't want to be, or I could walk away from it and be who I wanted to be. I didn't want to spend my whole life angry and bitter." He pulled Mari closer and kissed his temple. "Memories don't matter. They are just the past."

"You are astonishing sometimes, Jake Chivis," Mari told him tenderly. "You came halfway round the world to escape from your past and you act like it's nothing. And I can see that it isn't, at all. But I still want to be more like you. I want to let go of my demons and be what you deserve."

He leaned in close, pressing his lips to Jake's again in a long, hungry kiss.

Jake kissed him back, sliding his hands into Mari's hair and not resisting the passion Mari spilled over him. When their lips finally parted again Jake said, "You are perfect just the way you are, Mari. But I know you're not happy with yourself. I'll do everything I can to help you get rid of those demons, as long as it makes you happier."

Mari sighed and curled around him, wishing it was that easy.

Chapter Thirteen

Mari woke up at about half past seven and padded down to the kitchen for coffee. Jake was still sound asleep, his face very still and peaceful, dark curls mussed around his quiet features. After last night, Mari could hardly blame him. He made Jake a mug of the strong dark brew just in case he woke but he was still dead to the world when he returned to the bedroom. Climbing quietly back into bed, he snared his laptop and skimmed the news with one earbud tucked in, then logged back into Birthright as NathanD.

The forums were quiet at this time of the day, but he scrolled his way down the various chat threads that he had contributed to, either as himself using the name Sky Larkin, or with Jake's alias. There was some speculation about the new man at their group meeting the previous evening, which was only to be expected, he thought with a proud smile.

On the whole, the commentators were so overwhelmed by Jake's appearance that they were less on their guard than he might have expected, meeting a stranger for the first time. Claire, who was Corrie's secretary, was his official cheerleader already. Mari leaned back in the pillows, feeling curious, and touched his fingers to her final post on the subject of the 'newbie', letting himself sink into the network of messages and follow the trail of her posts back toward their origin. She was awake, he realized with a start as he found the source of the messages, her fingers still flying over the keyboard. Today wasn't a work day but she was posting various missives on behalf of Birthright's unofficial press office whilst she had her breakfast. It was almost like looking through a one-way mirror, only he couldn't see her, just read the emotions she described with her fingers. If he concentrated hard enough he could feel the touch of her fingertips on the keys, fast and light, in a hurry to get on to the next message, and the next.

In between posting press releases to the website, she was cruising the forums the same as him, adding comments, asking questions and…he realized after he had been monitoring her for a while, posting them back elsewhere via another medium. She must be on a laptop or tablet and using a mobile phone simultaneously, he decided, given the stop-start nature of her keypad activity. He backed off, trying to get a clearer view of the network of messaging that spiraled out from her and decided that she was talking to at least three others.

Mari returned to her thread activity and traced back from each of them until he had a clear route to each device and he was able to speed up and down each connection, hunting out the communication process. She was talking to a forum user who identified as AMINO2 on the forums, but given a pinch of detective work, chasing threads and phone calls back and forth, he was finally able to put a real name to… Aled Mustatti.

Well, well… I like a clever nickname. Am I Number Two? It looks that way, Mr. Mustatti.

Aled was watching Claire, observing her posts, not always commenting but checking into the threads that she posted in, curious about what she had to say. Mari was glad that he'd decided to check in this way. At least the spy in the system could not see him. Aled too was wide awake, watching the threads like Claire, keeping an eye on his boss's empire. A shiver slid through Mari's fingers, running up to the base of his spine and calling him back into his body. He lay there for a while, staring at the ceiling, recovering his physical sense of self.

He decided that he would give it a moment then maybe tap back into the threads and play Aled's game, just watching what was said. Corrie's second in command was checking out NathanD's most recent post.

As he watched, three people replied in rapid succession.

NathanD: Thanks for the welcome everyone. It was an interesting evening and I'm glad I got to meet some of you.

Butterflygrl23: It was nice to meet you too Nathan!

Fairylights: Yes, so glad you came last night. It's good to see a new face.

PreciousPearl: Yeah, and especially such a handsome one. ;)

Butterflygrl23: You've got your own fanclub already lol.

Mari shook his head. Jake had not been exaggerating about how keen these women were. It looked as if he wasn't the only one that thought so either. The envelope at the top of the screen lit to let him know he'd got a private message, and when he checked it was Aled.

You are very popular. Don't let them scare you off. Would you like to meet for lunch today? -Aled

"Hmm…" Mari drummed his fingers against his kneecap as he wondered how best to field that request. The fluttering female members of Birthright seemed content to flap around Nathan for the time being but Aled was more direct. Plus he was a fast track route to Corrie. Jake, he knew, would say yes without a moment's pause.

Hi Aled. They're just curious about the new boy. They don't scare me. And in any case, I have a partner already who would have them for breakfast if they tried. Lunch sounds good. You buying?

He hit reply. There, that kept Jake in Number Two's good books but let him know the score without giving anything away about his orientation. Jake ought to be pleased with him.

Speaking of which, Jake was just rolling over and blinking his eyes open as Aled was messaging him back with the details of where and when to meet him.

"Hey, beautiful," Jake murmured, looking up at him from where he was still snuggled up with the pillow.

Mari preened at the compliment and reached over and ruffled his hair, thinking that Jake looked so gorgeous this was definitely a morning experience he could get used to.

"Morning, handsome. You slept well last night. And you have a date this afternoon, so it's probably a good job you got your beauty sleep. There's coffee on the side table, if it's not gone cold."

Jake pushed himself up and reached over for the mug, sipping tentatively, then taking a bigger gulp and sighing appreciatively.

"Perfect. Did you say I have a date? With who?"

He slid back into the pillows, a warm smile pulling at his lips as he watched Jake enjoying his morning brew. Even the idea of sharing him with another man couldn't quite spoil the pleasure of being here beside him first thing in the morning, still warm and tingling from their lovemaking the night before.

"Mustatti wants to take you out to lunch. What do you think about that? He's extremely keen to protect you from the harpies that have been lusting after you on the forums." He smirked at Jake's bemused expression.

"What? Seriously? What have you been up to this morning already?" Jake chuckled. Mari turned the laptop toward him and Jake quickly scanned the various messages, including the private message that Aled had sent him.

"Butlers? Where's that?" Jake asked.

"Near Hyde Park," Mari told him. "He's definitely out to impress if he's taking you there."

Jake looked at him from the corner of his eye, a tiny smile twitching at the edges of his mouth. "You're not jealous, are you?"

"Rabidly," Mari admitted with a nod. "Their waiting list

for a table is weeks long. That's why I also let him know that you're claimed already."

Jake nearly choked on a laugh. "You did what?"

Mari scrolled up the screen to show how he had replied and Jake chuckled again.

"I can't believe you're jealous," he said, but he didn't look upset about that. Just the opposite. He turned his head to catch Mari's lips in a brief, sultry kiss. "So, you've staked your claim, have you?"

"Well, it seems only fair. I saw you first," Mari pointed out reasonably. "And if he's after you then he needs to know that I will fight him tooth and claw for you. Just so he's prepared for that, you understand. It would be very unsporting not to warn him."

He was grinning, loving the look on Jake's face and wondering about that at the same time. It had been forever since he'd been this way about someone, like he would fight and die to keep them by his side. It was a strangely primal urge, and yet it was almost innocent too. He liked the glow of warmth it gave him, deep within.

Jake closed the laptop and nudged it aside so he could pull Mari down further on the bed and roll half on top of him. He framed his face with his hands and gave him a coffee and cream flavored kiss.

"You realize, if I have to seduce him he's going to think I'm a cheater," he said when their lips parted, his eyes lit with impish glee.

"Damn!" Mari exhaled, though he wasn't feeling remotely apologetic. "What a shame! In that case, you're just going to have to behave, aren't you?"

"And here I was thinking that you liked the whole bad boy game. Oh, wait, I've got that backwards, haven't I? It's you that's the bad boy." Jake winked.

Mari relaxed into the soft caress of the pillows and reached for Jake, stroking his hands slowly over his naked skin, enjoying the feel of that sleek, hot body pressing down on him. His fingers traced the lines of the beautiful, intricate tribal tattoo that ran from his shoulders to the small of Jake's back while they shared a long, slow, lip-melting kiss.

"I'm not bad, I'm just smart," he said with a teasing smirk, as they both came up for breath at the same time. "I can't help that. It's genetic."

"Oh, well, in that case, I guess the spankings I had planned for you later aren't necessary." Before Mari could respond to that, Jake dipped his head to Mari's neck and sucked on the tender skin, running his hands up his chest to tweak his nipples at the same time.

A hot shiver rushed through his skin and Mari gripped Jake's hips tighter, rolling up against him, growing harder in response. He had promised himself that he would not get carried away by the imagined pleasure of Jake's hand or his belt cracking down on his arse but it was impossible not to feel it. A low moan of need rumbled like distant thunder in his chest and he whimpered eagerly.

"Mmm…you taste amazing," Jake whispered along his skin to where his neck met his shoulder. He pushed his thigh more firmly between Mari's legs, pressing down as Mari rolled his hips up and pinching his nipples more roughly. "Somebody likes the idea of a spanking," he said.

"Nnnhhh…ohhhh!" Mari yelped, torn between denial and wanton submission. Each time Jake teased his nips, he felt as if he would just melt in a puddle of cum. His body arched and he rubbed up against Jake more intimately, almost squirming out of the loose sweatpants he had donned to fetch coffee and holding his throbbing cock against the silken skin of Jake's belly.

Jake helped him by yanking down his pants, curling his own hips so his stiffening erection could press in the hollow of Mari's hip. He kissed and licked and nipped at the side of his throat and when Mari squirmed some more, Jake caught his wrists and pinned him down on the bed. A fierce spike of fire surged through him in response and he almost cried out then bit down hard on his lips and moaned instead.

"God, you are so fucking hot." Jake breathed warmly over the wetness he'd made on Mari's neck.

When Jake's strong hands wrapped around his forearms, Mari thought for a few seconds that he might embarrass himself by begging Jake to take things further. He turned his head, swallowing Jake's husky endearments by covering his soft, warm lips with his mouth. Mari was so light-headed that he imagined he could reach orgasm just by being held down like this and kissed so possessively that he wanted it to go on forever. Jake's fingers tightened on his wrists, his breathing deepening with his kiss as he responded to Mari's reactions. He moved his knee, nudging Mari's legs wider and settling so their cocks lay side by side, sandwiched between their bellies. He didn't attempt to slip his cock down any lower but his movements and the weight of his body on top of Mari's were certainly stimulating.

"Oh, Jake...oh...so good!" Mari panted between kisses, keeping his body moving so that he could rub against the velvety firmness of Jake's erection. He struggled, but not hard enough to break the hold that pinned him down. "That feels...mmhhh...wonderful... You are so wonderful!"

Jake ground against him, creating even more friction. He sucked the lobe of Mari's ear into his mouth, nipping it lightly with the very edge of his teeth and blowing out so his breath tickled over the ridges and dips. Mari was just a smidge taller than Jake, but Jake was wider in the shoulders and built a shade heavier. He didn't have to try hard to make it feel like he could hold Mari there for as long as he wanted to.

A shift of his hips and instead of rubbing alongside one another their cocks pressed underside to underside.

"Uhhh, babe...please tell me you're close?" Jake murmured against the shell of his ear.

Mari exhaled a helpless whimpering sound as he squirmed harder. "J-Jake... I luhhhh...love... I love the way you make me feel. Like you can make me come just by touching me and holding me down with your body. Makes me think...how good it would feel to have you inside me. Oh...oh, fuck— Jake...I'm gonna come."

Jake bucked harder and faster, the hot, hard length of his dick rubbing along Mari's enough to bring them both off. He smothered Mari's lips with his, silencing his cries with a passionate kiss, pushing his tongue into his mouth just as the first scalding splash of cum spurted and, a moment later, Jake shuddered and came with him.

Mari craned his neck, pushing his own mouth up into the kiss, stifling the yelps of desire that wanted out of him with each jet of semen. His tongue writhed between Jake's teeth and his body wormed sinuously against the hard muscles and velvet flesh of his lover's hot body. If this was as close as he could get to becoming one with his man then he knew he would take it, each and every time, any way that Jake wanted him to.

Jake sank like a dead weight on him and finally, with agonizing slowness, released his wrists, caressing down his arms as their kisses grew softer and more languid. He lifted his head after a few moments and smiled at Mari a smile that melted him further still.

"That was really hot. I would'a pinned you down sooner if I'd know how much it would get you off." Jake grinned wider, then kissed him, pouring so much tenderness into that kiss that Mari wanted it to last forever.

"All my days, Jake Chivis!" Mari panted as their lips parted, feeling weak with pleasure and relief. "You can force me into the mattress like that anytime you want. You are so strong. I love the way that feels. Like you're just taking me over, completely."

His hands, finally freed, snaked around Jake's body, pulling him closer and holding him tight as he rubbed his face against Jake's head and neck like a friendly cat. Jake kissed his cheek and pushed his fingers into Mari's hair, just kissing and holding him for a few moments as they both floated down. His voice buzzed soft and reassuring over Mari's skin.

"Mari…you know I'd never…I'd never really do that. I'd never force you into anything you didn't want."

"I'm not going to let you do that, don't worry." Mari chuckled and his words sounded strained and hoarse, but in the back of his mind a treacherous voice cried out, *Don't listen, Chivis! I want to belong to you, to be possessed by you, body and soul.*

He could not say the words, though, partly out of a fear that Jake would think he was weak and silly. And partly because the admission made him awkward and he had no desire to feel that way when Jake had just made him feel so good.

Jake kissed him again and he was quiet for a while, then whispered, "You would tell me, wouldn't you? If I did something that was too much? Going too far?"

"You would never do that," Mari told him, convinced of it. "I know that already. And I think you would know it, anyway, if you did."

Jake feathered kisses over his jaw and his cheek and the bridge of his nose before covering his lips again.

"Good. I'm glad you trust me. Because I do want to explore this more with you. I might tie you up, or hold you down, or spank your ass, but you will always, always be safe with me, Mari, I swear to you."

"Well that's worth knowing." Mari sprawled beneath him, catching his breath, enjoying the view. "Chivis, I'm not a quivering snowdrop. You're not going to grind me under your big old policeman boots, so stop being so protective. I'm not going to let you go too far. Okay?"

He reached up, stroking his fingers tenderly along the curve of Jake's unshaven jaw. Never in his life had any man made him feel so conflicted, so full of longing and yet so frustrated at the same time. Mari sensed a curious vulnerability in Jake Chivis, a need to belong, to find his place in the world. He wanted to be able to give Jake that space but at the same time he was fearful of ruining what they already had.

So it was with some trepidation that he murmured, "I'm not your mama, Jake. And you're not your father. You never will be that person. And I will never be afraid of you. I will never run away, and I will never flinch from telling you what you need to hear."

I will be a pain in your gorgeous ass for as long as you can bear me, Chivis.

"I know, I know you're not delicate. I'm trying not to be overprotective. It just freaked me out for a second, when you said that thing about forcing you. Playing around, maybe. I'm sorry. I know it's dumb. I know you didn't mean it that way." Jake kissed him gently. "I'll leave it alone. Do you want to hop in the shower with me?"

Mari touched noses with him as they broke the kiss.

"You're not going to harm me, Jake. And yes, I would love to soap you up and get you hot and slippery. How perfect!"

* * * *

Since Jake didn't have to be anywhere until that afternoon, and Mari didn't have anywhere pressing he needed to be, either, they took the opportunity to have a leisurely shower and breakfast, then Jake went home to change and they met in the park for a run. Mari had managed to squeeze some run time in during the last week, but Jake was starting to feel like he'd forgotten how.

The lack of ability to fall into his usual stride and the burning in his lungs pissed him off enough to push harder and longer than he might ordinarily have. Mari kept pace with him, reaping the benefit of having made himself run as soon as he was able to stand.

"So, have you figured out what you want to say to Mr. Birthright this afternoon?" Mari asked after they had loped along in companionable silence for a while.

"Yeah. I figured I'd ask him what he's doing that sets people on fire," Jake panted grumpily.

"Nothing like getting straight to the point," Mari conceded with a grin. "What if he denies all knowledge?"

Jake's laugh sounded like a wheeze. "I'm not really going to ask him that. I'm going to ask him if Corrie will deign to speak with me yet. And maybe if he has any theories about those that have gone up in flames."

"He'll think you're a journalist," Mari huffed. "Or a cop."

Jake slowed and came to a stop, putting his hands on his knees as he tried to drag air into his lungs for a few seconds. He had a small coughing fit, which hadn't happened since the first night when they'd been in the hospital.

"Well what...am I...supposed to...ask him? Smarty pants!" Jake panted.

"You could ask him what Birthright is doing to protect its Fire Elementals, given that you have a vested interest," Mari said, pulling up a few strides ahead then coming back to rest a hand on Jake's shoulder. "Enough of running for one day, I think. You're not ready for this yet. Let Number Two buy you dinner and do most of the talking. See what he wants to tell you, since he's got seduction in mind."

"How do you figure that?" Jake asked. "He probably only wants to schmooze me 'cause I'm a Fire Elemental. He's probably straight."

"But of course, what did you think I meant?" Mari winked at him. "Though the way your Mr. Ashcroft was talking the other day, I think he's kind of hoping you guys will ball so he can listen in."

Jake rolled his eyes and started walking beside Mari.

"I think you're projecting. I'm pretty sure you'd be the one wanting to listen in," he teased.

"I know what you sound like when you get in the zone," Mari reminded him, blue eyes sparkling with mischief. "I'm the one trying not to think about you bent over a table for him. You are going to remind him that your boyfriend knows where he lives, aren't you?"

Jake laughed and slung one arm around him, leaning in to peck his cheek.

"There will be no bending over of any tables," he assured Mari with a grin. "And my boyfriend is not supposed to know where he lives. If he does make a pass, which he isn't going to, but if he did, I will tell him that I am too busy keeping my boyfriend away from other guys that want to string him up in handcuffs and a gimp mask to run around with anyone else."

Mari laughed at that, shaking his head in denial, but he didn't argue for once. Before they went their separate ways again at the park gates, he turned and curled one hand around the back of Jake's head, pulling him in for a quick, fierce kiss.

"Don't do anything random," he warned softly. "I don't want to have to come in and rescue you. You did take your phone out of the refrigerator before you left, didn't you?"

Jake gave him a searching look, a small smile on his lips, before he answered, "Yeah, I've got it. I'll call you when I get done."

* * * *

Mari had not been kidding that Aled was out to impress him with the choice of restaurant. It was one of those places where you needed to be a member to get in, unless you were a guest. The maître d' didn't need to look at a list. Jake gave his name, or rather the name Nathan Douglas, which he had adopted because it sounded more neutral and forgettable than his online handle, and he was led into the dark paneled opulent dining room. He was glad he'd worn a nice suit. He couldn't be faulted there. Although he had felt a tad guilty while he was getting dressed. It had been some time since Mari had seen him in anything but jeans and a T-shirt.

Aled was already waiting when he arrived, sitting at a small round table in a curved booth made of the same dark polished wood as the walls and inlaid with brass-studded, red leather upholstery. Corrie's adjutant was also smartly attired in a dark blue suit that flattered his broader figure, set off with a pale blue shirt and a midnight silk tie with tiny golden candles on it. He rose to greet Jake and extended a hand politely.

"You keep good time. Mr. Corrie likes that in a man," he said with no trace of false warmth in his voice. "Come…sit down. What would you like to drink?"

"Just coffee," Jake said, directing this half to Aled and half to the maître d', who was still hovering. He nodded and took off, and Jake sat opposite Aled.

"Nice place," he remarked.

"It is." Aled inclined his head toward the menu cards, also bound in dark red leather. "I hope you haven't eaten a large breakfast, the lunch menu is very good. And Mr. Corrie is footing the bill. He will not hear of you skipping a meal on his account."

Jake hid an amused smile. Maybe Mari was right. Maybe they were trying to seduce him, but not in a 'bend over the table' kind of way.

"Well, then, I hope I will get the chance to thank him in person."

Aled smiled, the kind of smile that businessmen the world over were well accustomed to. It was an expression that said, we'll see how you trade before we put all our cards on the table.

"As you know, Mr. Corrie is a busy man," he said. "But he is certainly quite keen to find out more about you, Mr. Douglas. It isn't often that we get visitors from the States to our group, less still that they turn out to be full Fire Elementals. Quite a rare treat for us."

"You said it before, that Mr. Corrie is a busy man. What exactly does he do that takes up so much of his time?" Jake asked.

Aled raised the tumbler of clear liquid in his right hand to his lips and took a swallow before speaking. It was not a nervous gesture, Jake recognized those well enough, but he was deliberate in taking his time with the answer. Aled seemed well accustomed to thinking twice before he opened his mouth. Little wonder that his reputedly paranoid boss liked having him around.

"He is engaged in drawing up schedules for the education of potentially gifted group members, even as we speak," he said with another of those businesslike smiles. "But there is a lot of work done behind the scenes to keep our kind safe from...exploitation. Mr. Corrie is hands-on where fundraising and publicity for Birthright are concerned. He is very serious that we don't send out the wrong kind of message to those who don't understand what we are about. Mundane society still has no accurate grasp of the reality of Elemental skills, nor the potential for those who possess them. In times gone by, we were seen as freaks of nature, to be pointed at and exploited for gain, or feared and hunted. The recent...incidents have been unfortunate and bad press for us among those who know what we are and what we can do. Very bad for business if you happen to be a Fire Elemental, as I'm sure you are well-aware, Nathan."

For half a second, Jake debated asking him why he thought those Fire Elementals had gone up in flames, but he was conscious of what Mari had told him and decided to take his advice instead.

"So he's trying to do damage control in the publicity department. That makes sense. It sounds like he's really on top of looking out for Birthright. Does he have a plan, or an idea how to protect us from it happening again?"

Aled huffed a short, humorless laugh.

"Don't you think we're working on that, Nathan? The whole of Birthright, from the top to the very humblest of our members, wants to know why this is happening. Mr. Corrie has people working on that twenty-four seven. And that's why he wanted me to speak to you. We've been studying our Fire Elementals closely since the first incident last year, and we feel that we're getting close to an explanation."

"Hold on..." Jake interrupted him, a frown creasing his brow. "Last year? How many people have been affected by this already?"

Aled folded his hands on the table between them. He held his tongue as the waiter brought Jake's coffee and asked if they were ready to order. Only once they had given the man their requests and he had whisked himself away to the pass again, did Aled continue.

"Including the three on the news recently there have been five, one just after Christmas and one in October last year. The first was not a member of Birthright. The second had connections with us, but had not come to meetings. We were...studying him. Mr. Corrie saw some potential in him."

"What kind of potential?" Jake asked.

"He had the gift of psychometry," Aled said. "That's where a person is able to determine who last held an object. Sometimes they get a name, sometimes just an idea of what the person looked like."

Jake made sure his expression didn't waver. He was being set up. He was certain Aled had already heard from the women 'Nathan' had spoken with at the meeting and knew he had ability. It was not at all hard for Jake to resist telling him that he could do far more than just tell what the last person to touch an object looked like. He had never liked to tell people about what he could do. But he was supposed to be making himself a tempting target. *Damn.*

"Yeah, I know what psychometry is," he said. "I sometimes get impressions of people from objects, as well."

"You do? Well that's good to know. It's been a while since we've had any new blood with conspicuous gifts," Aled said with a thoughtful nod of his head. "We attract a lot of misfits, Nathan. I won't soften that with the sort of PC flannel that you will hear in most social organizations. Many of them come to us harboring hopes of being superheroes, when in truth, all they're ever going to be are checkout operators and bank clerks. But what Birthright is good at is nurturing people who genuinely have skills. We can marry people like you up with the kind of opportunities that will set you up for life. I think that Mr. Corrie will be very interested in talking to you."

Yeah, you keep saying that, Jake thought, managing to keep the irritation off his face.

What he said was, "What, you're not going to immediately try and test me? That's unique."

"Why would we do that?" Aled's answering smile was warmer this time, as if he sensed some of Jake's frustration and even understood it. "We're having lunch, Nathan. This isn't a job interview. If you're going to work with us then I would much prefer that you do so of your own free will, and without feeling that you need to jump through hoops to impress us. Natural talent is a very rare thing. I also understand just how difficult it must be for you, meeting me in a strange and very public setting like this, not knowing what kind of horrors lie around each corner, each fork, each knife, every door handle and bathroom tap. Believe me, we are grateful."

Jake was surprised by that level of astuteness. Even Mari hadn't really gotten it at first, how weird and difficult it could be to always be at the mercy of other people's memories. It would have been easy to like Aled if Jake hadn't known he was deliberately risking other people's lives. Well, he didn't know that for certain yet. How much Aled knew about Corrie's experiments was still a gray area, but he didn't seem like a man who would just blindly follow.

"I appreciate that," Jake said. Their food arrived and Jake was not above thoroughly enjoying the meal, despite the circumstances. Everything was cooked to perfection and looked and tasted excellent. If this were a date, he'd be ready to take Aled home. Maybe. Not that he was particularly attracted to him. The pompous way he spoke was annoying.

While they ate, Aled talked more about Birthright and what they were trying to accomplish. He outlined the successes they had already achieved, such as getting a Water Elemental that read auras registered for her diagnostic ability, and another Water Elemental registered as a certified touch therapist. They had helped fund a business that employed Earth Elementals who were able to locate lost objects, and their business was such a resounding success they had plans for expansion.

Jake had to admit, if it wasn't for the Elemental Purity bullshit and the fact that they were somehow responsible for three — no, five, he reminded himself — deaths, people who had died horribly as a result of whatever they'd done to them, they had some good ideals. It was really too bad they were bigoted murderers.

"You seem preoccupied," Aled said and Jake looked up from his plate to find Aled watching him eat. "It can't have been easy for you, coming all this way to the UK and practically starting over in a new life. I don't see a ring, so I'm guessing you and your partner haven't been together for very long. And if she isn't Elemental, then there is always that barrier. Sex is a comfort, but it's no substitute for family. We can give you a family that understands your needs though, Nathan. We can give you some stability while you get used to a new way of life."

Jake raised an eyebrow at that. A part of him wanted to snarl that he'd had his fill of 'family values' but the cop side of him quashed that impulse. Aled didn't need to know about his dysfunctional family.

He ought to just play it straight, and he already knew he could pull that off. He'd done it often enough. He probably should play to Aled's assumptions, as well, as it might make it easier to integrate with them if it took a while to get the information he was seeking. However, he found he was repelled by the idea. More than that, it made him angry to think about having to pretend again. Mari had changed him more than he'd realized.

"What exactly does that mean, 'a family'?" Jake asked.

Aled took a swallow of his drink. "A family can be whatever you need it to be, Nathan. I suppose the way that I mean is in the sense of a support group, a network of like-minded people. I know it isn't always easy for some of us, coping in the mundane world. I meant no offense. Maybe you don't need that. You can speak your mind freely with me."

And do you ask every new member of Birthright out to lunch so you can welcome them to the family, or just Fire Elementals with talent?

Jake smiled and tried to make it a warm expression. "Oh, I don't know. That sounds kinda nice. And, from what Louis told me, you seem to be doing a lot to make life easier for us. I think I'd like to be a part of that," he said, hoping he sounded receptive but not gushing. He had to wonder, though, if he didn't know what was behind Birthright's mask, how easily he might be wooed. Aled was doing a bang-up job of cult indoctrination so far. What a scary thought.

"It's only human to extend the hand of friendship." Aled laughed, amused by this. "Okay, so we can't work magic on your behalf. But we can put you in touch with the kind of people who can help you to make the very best of your talents. If that's what you want." He looked a question at Jake, his expression sincere.

"The best of my talent? You mean like a job? Or…what, exactly?"

"Sometimes it can be that. Sometimes it can be an opportunity, a chance to make your mark as an Elemental in the mundane world," Aled said in that silky voice.

"That sounds…kinda vague. I mean, I'd like to help out, I like what I've heard so far. But I'm not sure my 'talent' is really much of anything special. I've never seen how it's much good to be able to tell who last used a hairbrush."

"And all your friends can, say…pick up that ice bucket there and tell you exactly where the wine waiter was last night, and who he was with, and what they did?" Aled chuckled, a deep, husky sound low in his chest. "I'd say that was pretty special, Nathan. But it should be so much more than just a party trick, don't you think?"

Jake shrugged. It certainly could be, much more than that. It was getting hard to keep playing stupid. "How so? What would you do with it?"

"If we could establish a consistent prevalence for a gift in our people, then it would be one step closer to having acceptance of, say, a talented psychometric in every newspaper and police department. It's a long way down the line, but there's nothing to say that it couldn't be achieved in our lifetimes." Aled shrugged and speared a cherry tomato from his plate. "And that's a drop in the ocean compared to the gifts that our ancestors possessed."

"I can see how it would certainly be more useful, if it were controllable, but it isn't. I can't make it happen, it just comes and goes as it pleases. I don't understand how you plan on making it consistent?" Jake took a forkful of the delicious food on his plate but it turned to ashes in his mouth as Aled began to explain.

"There are…processes, things that we have been working on, a whole raft of contributory factors from sleep, to relationships, to diet," Aled said with the enthusiasm of a true zealot. "It's amazing just what can be done with some work, discipline, and a little…push."

"Really? That's fascinating. I've never met another Fire Elemental who could control psychometry. Have you had a lot of success? I'd be really interested in learning more." *And also knowing what you are really doing to these people*, he added silently.

"There have been experiments, programs run already in this country and elsewhere," Aled told him. He took another bite of his lunch and chewed reflectively, watching Jake's face, then gestured toward him with the fork. For one stomach-clenching moment, Jake thought that he knew why he'd had come here, and this amiable lunch was all part of some elaborate game.

Then Aled swallowed and flashed that white and gold smile again. "You know, initially I wondered if that was why you were here, in London. I know there is another program being run somewhere in the city."

"Nothing so exciting. My company opened an IT support office in London and I fancied a change. Pretty mundane." Jake forced a laugh. "All sounds a bit X-Files to me!"

He covered the tightness in his throat by taking a sip from the glass of iced water beside his plate and carried on eating. Aled laughed too, still watching him quietly.

"Maybe," he conceded at last. "But these projects happen arbitrarily, at the whim of the government. If they decide that no progress is being made, they can pull the finance for a program at any moment, without warning. Where does that leave the participants?"

"That would suck," Jake conceded with a nod.

"More than that, it would abandon them with no support, in possession of a potentially terrifying ability and no greater means of controlling or directing it than they had before," Aled said, warming to his subject. "Birthright is a self-funded organization. Any money that Birthright earns through work or sponsors comes back into our own programs and support facilities. And that, in turn, helps our members to grow and feel free to develop their gifts. Birthright will always be there for you, Nathan."

Having to weigh his every word was tiring. The muscles of Jake's shoulders and neck were so tight he was starting to get a headache. He didn't know if he should still pretend to be eager? Most normal people, the minute money was mentioned became wary.

"Well, that makes sense, I guess," he said cautiously.

Aled smiled again and Jake knew he'd taken just the right tone. "It is natural to be skeptical. But you will see, we have nothing to hide, and you have everything to gain. Come to a few more meetings, get to know our members, our family. There is no rush. We want everyone to feel comfortable and at home within our community."

Damn. He was good. Jake wondered if he was a Psychology major or if the manipulation just came naturally to him. He had just the right balance of push and reassure to lure a supposedly lonely, vulnerable guy into the mix.

When they'd finished their lunch, Aled told Jake when the next meeting was scheduled and gave him his phone number, in case he needed anything, had questions or just wanted to talk. They stood and shook hands and Jake thanked him for lunch, and he was just starting to think he'd done a good job of working his way deeper and got away clean, when Aled said something that froze his blood.

"Why don't you bring your significant other to the next meeting?"

Damn it!

"I...um, I might," Jake said, then turned and hurried away before Aled could insist, or ask more questions. He had absolutely no intention of letting this creep anywhere near Mari.

Chapter Fourteen

After letting Jake run off to his lunch meeting, Mari headed home and took a shower then ran his grandmother to City Airport to catch her flight up to Cambridge, where she had a conjugal visit arranged with his grandfather. Grandpapa Pallant wasn't a jailbird but given how often Angela saw him, he might just as well have been. Mari spent more time with the old boy than his grandmother did, but neither of them seemed particularly bitter about this. In fact, the arrangement seemed to suit them. He often wondered what his grandparents had ever seen in one another, for they appeared to operate in completely different environments. Angela was an investment genius, the daughter of a New York Stock exchange wizard who had made his first million by the age of twenty-two. Thomas was a senior lecturer in Nordic mythology and a Fellow of his old university college, St. John's, never happier than when he was prowling around in a dusty old library or expounding the merits of some long-dead Icelandic bard to a select group of enthralled students, most of whom, bizarrely to Mari's thinking, worshiped him and hung on his every word.

He loved his grandfather dearly but they had almost as little in common as he and Angela. Thomas Pallant had an ingrained horror of technology and any device invented since the 1950s was a complete mystery to him. Mari appreciated that, while it was true not all information could be accessed digitally, there was no excuse for not utilizing any technological shortcuts that did exist. That said, he and Grandpapa always got on well. Thomas and his older brother had been fond of their mother, his notorious ancestress Amelia, and always had some new story about her when he came to visit.

As a result, he didn't dismiss Angela's suggestion that he join her out of hand. It had been quite a few years since he had visited Cambridge, and Jake was likely to be busy for most of the afternoon. Mari had already emailed Ashcroft with a digital acceptance of his invitation to join the investigation into Birthright that morning, but he saw no reason why he couldn't do some more digging on the move.

The flight took just over twenty minutes and within the hour they were in the heart of the medieval city, wandering between the golden walls of college buildings that were, in the main part, many hundreds of years old. Having grown up in the comparatively modern cities of New York and Kota Kinbalu, Mari had been amazed by Cambridge when he'd first come here to study for his PhD, wandering the narrow winding streets with his eyes and mouth wide open. Having since spent almost five years immersed in the place, he was almost as casual about it as a native.

They met for lunch with Grandpapa in the lofty halls at his college, which always made Mari think of Hogwarts. He had studied at the infinitely more modern Cambridge Laboratories on the outskirts of the city, which—whilst prestigious—had none of the olde worlde gravitas of St. John's. Grandpapa Thomas looked in his element there, cutting a tall, elegant figure in his long black robes as he crossed the court to meet them, the sunlight glinting off his silvery curls. Mari knew that he got his height from the Pallant branch of the family. The old fellow was, as ever, delighted to see them and, after planting a kiss on Angela's perfectly powdered cheek, greeted Mari with a vigorous hug.

"Dear boy! What an unexpected pleasure. You look well."

"He has a playmate," Angela said with a smug quirk of her lips. "It's doing him the world of good."

"Well, that's splendid," his grandfather agreed. "No one

should be young and alone in a city like London. What is Karden up to these days? Keeping you busy?"

"He's still a pain in the backside," Mari told him, since it evidently wasn't common knowledge that he and Karden had parted company. "He's recommended me for another post. I can't say much about it, but it made me think of Grandmama Amelia. It's kind of…like what she was doing. During the war, you know."

"Well…" His grandfather blew a huff of breath through his teeth. "She'd be proud of you, I'm sure. Though she'd worry too, no doubt. Things are so much more intensive than they were in her day. I'm sure you know what you are doing, Ilmari. But be careful. Don't let them use you the way they used my mother. There was so much that she could never say about what went on, back in the day. But one day it will come out and the world will know how much it owes to people like you and her."

"She was a heroine," Mari said with a smile. "And she loved that—she never tried to hide it."

"True, but it took a lot out of her, my dear," Grandpapa said earnestly. "She was never the same after the war, so my brother always said. Michael was older than me, he remembers better. They worked her until she was frazzled, Ilmari. It sent her crazy."

"Not completely crazy. She knew who she was. I remember her, when I was a child. She always knew me, and knew how to make me laugh." He smiled at the memory of the sweet old lady who'd shown him how to tap a phone line with his mind and marveled at the potential of the nascent internet technology that her great-grandson tried to teach her.

"True, she was sharp as a tack, but sometimes her head was somewhere else, you know," Grandpa told him. "She would go away to another place, in her mind, and we just couldn't bring her back, not until she was ready. It was like an addiction with her. She loved the thrill of it, of being out of her body, out of the constriction of her failing flesh."

"Grandpapa, you make aging sound so alluring." Mari laughed.

"Just be careful, Ilmari," the old boy replied with a concerned frown. "I don't want to watch you sliding down that same path. I'm glad you have your young love to keep you grounded."

"I'm not in love, Grandpapa. I'm too young for love and marriage and settling down." At the same time, Mari wondered just how true that was. Jake was certainly making him feel and think in ways that were beyond his normal, analytical sphere of emotions.

"We all say that, but someday a special someone will sneak under your radar and...boom! You're torpedoed." Grandpapa chuckled at Angela's expression of tolerant disdain.

"I'm a damned U-Boat now, am I?"

"You know it, woman. You're a menace," he said affectionately, laying a hand on hers. For a moment, her features softened and Mari shook his head at the miracle of it. Love could soften even the hardest of hearts.

Before he knew it, the words were tumbling out of his mouth.

"How did you know that you and Nonna were in love? How long did it take before you realized that it was the real thing?"

"Oh, ho! It's reached that stage, has it?" Grandpapa smiled broadly at the tell-tale flush tinting Mari's pale cheeks. "Well, it's different for everyone, and I can't speak for Angela..." He turned his head to give her a warm smile, that amazingly she returned. "But for me, I think it was that week we spent at an Icelandic poetry retreat just outside Reykjavik." His gaze returned to Mari. "Your grandmama ruined her best heels and she hated every moment of it. But she stayed, for me. I think I knew then that I adored her. And I let her have her revenge by dragging me around every last damned store in New York, the next time we spent together."

"He was a true martyr." Angela chuckled, shaking her head.

"I don't know how I survived it." Grandpapa uttered a long-suffering sigh.

"I think the secret to a good relationship is to always be honest with one another," Angela said, patting her husband's hand. "I may not always have loved the same things your grandfather does but I never pretended to for his sake. Nor did he. We have our own lives and interests and we still have our love. There's only so long you can live a lie before the deception turns to resentment."

She fixed him with a penetrating look and he chewed on his lip, but held her gaze.

"I don't lie to him, Nonna."

"You don't tell him the truth," she countered at once. "Annabel and I talk, you know."

"The truth isn't important. I've moved on since Irfan. And Tomas," Mari said. "I'm not the person I was back then."

"Most certainly not." Grandpapa chuckled, running a soothing hand over his hair. "You must forge your own path, Ilmari. But tell me, are you happy? Are you content as you are?"

He hesitated barely a moment then nodded. "Yes. I'm happy, Grandpapi. Happier than I've ever been."

"Well. That's all that matters, my child," his grandfather declared in absolute certainty.

* * * *

He was still thinking that encounter over as he flew back to London that evening. Angela was staying a few nights in Cambridge and would fly back at the weekend, so he was undisturbed on the journey home. Mari thumbed his phone back on as he passed through the arrivals hall, texting Jake to find out how his meeting had gone.

Do you fancy dinner at mine? You can tell me all about it.

It was only a minute before Jake texted him back.

I just got home. Come to mine first?

Okay. Let me drop the car off.

Mari walked back across to Maple Street after he'd parked up, and it was only just over half an hour after he had texted when he finally arrived at Jake's apartment. The smell of smoke lingered in the hallway as he jogged up the stairs, still wearing the pale green, Paul Smith two-piece suit he'd donned for his trip north.

There was a poster in the window of the bar advertising a party to celebrate their re-opening night, in a week's time. People died but things moved on. He shook his head and told himself to stop being maudlin.

Jake let him in, and when he entered the apartment the faint miasma of burnt timber gave way to a lemony clean scent. Jake wasn't much for clutter anyway, but the place looked spotless and scrubbed. Jake himself was, unfortunately, not doing shirtless pull ups, but he still looked delicious in snug, faded jeans and a T-shirt that was probably a size too small — though Mari had no complaints. Especially not when Jake slid his arms around him and kissed him.

"You look gorgeous. I feel underdressed." Jake laughed.

"Nonsense, you look good enough to eat," Mari promised him, basking in his warmth and the pleasure in his amber eyes. He touched his mouth to those soft lips again. "And I can always take things off, if it makes you feel uncomfortable."

"I think maybe you ought to," Jake said, a teasing grin blooming on his face. He slid his hands inside Mari's jacket and up his rib cage before helping him remove it, taking it to hang on the back of a chair. "That's better," Jake told him, pretending to look at him critically. "I think you need to take a few more layers off though."

"A few?" Mari twitched at the neckline of his shirt and pretended to peer inside. "I'll be down to the bones."

He loosened his tie some more though, tugging it down with a coy sidelong look at Jake through the tumble of his forelock.

"Down to the skin at least," Jake insisted, sliding his arms around him again and kissing him with more heat. He moved his hands down Mari's back and over his arse, kneading gently there and pulling him up close to his body. "I missed you."

Mari lifted his left arm and glanced at his watch. "It's been...eight and half whole hours since you saw me?" A playful grin tugged at his lips though and he felt that rush of heat inside again. Jake missed him. That was good to know. "You can tell me how much you missed me in the bedroom, if you like?"

"That...is...an excellent idea," Jake said as he bent his knees and dropped his hands down to the backs of Mari's thighs so that, when he came back up, he lifted him off his feet and pulled Mari's legs up around his waist at the same time. Jake was already kissing and nuzzling his throat as he turned toward the archway between the lounge and the bedroom.

Mari caught his lips between his teeth to keep the moan of need inside but when Jake picked him up like that, like he weighed nothing, he had to fight the rush inside that made him feel as if he could just float into the air. What was wrong with him? Mari thought that he'd already come to terms with the idea that he could not be the person he needed to be, for Jake, or for any man. The way Jake made him feel, though, was almost unreal. He was ravenously hungry all the time, only not for food, just for the touch of Jake's warm, hard-toned body pressing up close to his own.

It was just a few of Jake's strides from the sofa to the bed. Mari had done the route so often that he could count them in his head. One, two, three, four, five...and down. Jake tumbled on top of him on the mattress and mashed his lips onto Mari's fiercely again. Mari pulled at the belt of Jake's jeans, wrestling it undone, popping the fly button and running his searching hand over the denim-clad swell of his crotch.

Jake was tugging at the buttons of Mari's shirt and pulling it out of his trousers. Mari eased his zipper undone and reached for the hem of his deliciously tight T-shirt with both hands, pulling it up hard to Jake's armpits. "Hands up."

Jake complied and Mari had the T-shirt off his back and tossed aside in seconds.

They dropped back onto the bed, Jake's lips covering Mari's, working them, pressing them open and slipping his tongue between. He reached between their bodies and slid the palm of his hand over the bulge in Mari's pants, cupping and squeezing him lightly.

Mari groaned into his mouth, his hips pushing forward, pressing that protuberance into his groping fingers. After the day of traveling and adulting he'd had, it felt good to be back in Jake's expert hands but he thrust aside the question of whether his feelings for Jake were deepening, or if he was simply making up for a painfully long, barren period in his love life.

He watched Jake's honey-gold eyes darken as he eased his hand into Jake's open fly, massaging him through the soft, charcoal jersey material of his boxer briefs. Jake moaned softly and pulsed into Mari's grasp, closing his eyes.

"I can't think when you do that." He chuckled breathlessly.

"Then don't." Mari snaked his fingers up into Jake's hair, pulling Jake's mouth onto his for another kiss, wanting to be close to him tonight, to hold him. He had a terrible cold feeling, a rush of anxiety that matched the flood of sexual heat that he'd been wrestling with since he'd arrived here. He didn't want Jake to go back into Birthright's lair but he knew that it would be insanity to ask him not to. He would have to explain why, for one, and he wasn't sure he knew how to rationalize his fear of losing Jake, without sounding ridiculous, so he said nothing. Instead he stuck his hand into Jake's briefs and wrapped his fingers around his stiffening cock to fist him hard instead.

Some of his tension must have commuted into his face and his actions though because, after a few minutes, Jake reached down and stopped the determined friction of his pumping hand. He settled into Mari's arms instead.

"What's wrong?" he murmured. "You have something on your mind. I can always tell, you know."

"This is going to sound stupid," Mari whispered, his lips very close to Jake's ear, summoning the courage to speak his mind in the comfortable silence that surrounded them. "But I don't want you to do this Birthright thing. I have a bad feeling about it. At first, I just thought it was nerves, and so on, but I can't shake it. I want you to tell them you can't go in there on your own."

Jake opened his eyes a sliver to look at him and his heart thumped. Mari knew it had been the wrong thing to say, even before Jake opened his mouth.

"Mari, if I don't find out what it is exactly they are doing, the next Fire Elemental they get their hands on will die, just like the others. They've already proved they have no scruples when it comes to getting what they want."

Mari held Jake's solemn stare. "Chivis, you *are* the next Fire Elemental they got their hands on," he reminded him.

Jake smiled at him. "Yeah, but I know better than to buy into their game. I'm not going to agree to jump into their 'program'. I haven't even met Corrie yet, much less gotten close enough to find any information."

"So, you never did tell me, what's your verdict on today's meeting?" Mari propped his elbows on Jake's chest and put his chin in his cupped hands, watching him tenderly.

"If I didn't already know they were batshit crazy, I'd say they were doing a damn good job trying to gain acceptance for Elementals." Jake heaved a sigh.

"Might they be both?" Mari wanted to know. "Well-meaning but deluded?"

"It's possible. I'm not getting a misguided vibe off Aled, though. He talks like a man that doesn't get sidetracked by any old horseshit."

"Do they genuinely believe they're helping Elementals?"

"They don't just *believe* they are helping Elementals, they *are* helping them," Jake admitted. "Unless Aled is lying, and I don't think he was. They are also killing people, and they're aware of that. There were two more victims, months ago, that didn't make the news. I guess because they died less publicly. Whatever they are doing to these people, two of them dying didn't stop them from doing it again."

Mari knelt up with his hands flat on Jake's chest, staring at him. "He confessed that they had a hand in the deaths?"

"No. Not exactly. We were talking about Louis and I asked if they had any theories of how to protect other people. He didn't have any, but he did say they were aware of it happening to two others last year. I don't know for certain that Aled is aware of what caused the fires, but…well, call it instinct, but I think he knows something anyway."

Mari swore under his breath, something that he did very rarely when they weren't having sex.

Jake reached up to stroke Mari's cheek with tender fingers. "Hey, settle down. We knew most of that going into this business. It's our job to find out why."

"You aren't going to be talked out of this, are you?" Mari sighed. It wasn't a serious question. He knew the answer but he still felt it would have been wrong of him not to try.

Jake cupped one of Mari's cheeks with his palm. "Who else are they going to get to do this? Even if they don't get their hands on another Fire Elemental willing to play guinea pig, Birthright has killed at least five people. The first one might have been an accident, but not the others. They knew what happened and they convinced others to follow along, anyway. They need to be put in prison for that."

"If they kill you too, who is going to give them the proof?" Mari wanted to know. He curled around Jake possessively, as if he could physically hold him here, refusing to let him leave.

Jake put his arm around Mari's shoulders and stroked his

hair. "They are not going to kill me. They want to recruit me. I'm not going to tell you it's perfectly safe, but the risk is minimal." He kissed Mari's forehead with infinite tenderness. "I'll be okay, Ilmari."

"They want to recruit you so that they can play god with you. I want to damage them every time I think about that too hard." Mari scowled.

Jake uttered a soft chuckle and carried on stroking his fingers through Mari's hair as if he'd not said anything.

"Why, Ilmarinen Gale, I think you do care after all," he teased.

"Stupid man," Mari responded. "Who else is going to let me fuck him the way you do?"

"I don't think you'd lack for volunteers, if you wanted them," Jake said in a very serious voice.

"I think you haven't walked a mile in my shoes yet," Mari told him. "Don't get yourself killed, Jake Chivis. I don't know how to do bereaved, and I look terrible in black."

Chapter Fifteen

Mari kept his appointment for his first debriefing at Thames House. The Headquarters of MI5, while more staid and formal in appearance than those of their International brethren across the river, were—in his opinion—infinitely less intimidating. He was met, in reception, by a lanky, loquacious redhead named Darren, who took him up to the fifth floor and chatted with him until Ashcroft was ready to see him.

"So, you worked with the AI Security team in Barcelona? That must have been really exciting," Darren gushed while he was processing all of Mari's paperwork, and Mari was sipping a surprisingly good cup of coffee.

"It was...interesting, yes," Mari conceded. His work in Catalunya had been hush-hush, and he still wasn't exactly sure how much he was allowed to talk about it, even to people who knew who he was and wanted to use his skills for the public good.

"My brother was at Cambridge around the same time," Darren chattered on, not dissuaded by his lack of a proper response. "Brent Colquhoun. You didn't know him, did you?"

"It's a busy place. A lot of different colleges. And I was mostly based up in West Cambridge at the Gates Building anyway, so I'm afraid not." Mari smiled at him.

For once, he didn't feel like the office baby. Darren was maybe only twenty-two or twenty-three at the most. He babbled on for a while about his brother and Mari nodded and made the appropriate responses, during the course of which he learned that Darren was really twenty-five and his grades meant he'd studied in London instead of Oxbridge but his fascination with IT and his good degree had ensured him a job here at Thames House as soon as he graduated. After a while, Mari began to appreciate how Jake felt about his ability to talk the back leg off a horse. By the time Ashcroft came to rescue him, he was almost grateful.

"I hope Darren hasn't been too annoying." Officer Ashcroft chuckled once they were safely shut away in his office. "He's a good lad, but painfully keen to impress. He's been looking forward to meeting you for nearly a week. As have I."

"My pleasure," Mari said, accepting his handshake. "What is it that you'd like me to do for you, sir?"

Ashcroft pushed a set of files across the desk towards him. "Birthright was born out of a number of experiments in the 90s and early 2000s," he explained. "I accept that computer technology was not as far-reaching back in the day as it is today, but it would be helpful to know if there was anyone communicating with the original test group that is connected to the current organization, apart from Corrie."

"That might be difficult, Officer Ashcroft. Once a communication has been sent, it's kind of like smoke on the breeze. The echoes of that message only last for a short time," Mari told him, genuinely apologetic.

"In that case, we will primarily need you to monitor communications from Corrie's headquarters," Ashcroft told him. "The man is extremely paranoid and his online security is very good. But as Darren has tried to explain to me, your ability allows you to slip through the smallest of gaps in any firewall system. Is that true?"

"That isn't quite how it works, but yes, he's right. I can touch other people's messages without setting off their antivirus systems, or leaving any trace behind," Mari told him. "Firewalls are no use against an Interface. Basically, what I do is to ride on the backs of messages sent by other people. I can come into his system via any message that's been opened by him. It's…subtle, but it's only useful if the person you're investigating has a data trail. I've been monitoring Birthright's communications for a while, but all I really know is that Corrie has a day job. He works as an attendant for a fertility clinic in Cheniston Gardens, according to his National Insurance records, but I'm not sure what he does there. The man has practically no online presence, which is frustrating. Claire Pollard sends all his forum instructions out. Aled Mustatti deals with most of Birthright's social interactions, meetings and such. But you know that already."

"You can feel all of that from…whatever it is that you do?" Ashcroft looked astonished.

"A lot of it is reading between the lines." Mari tapped his fingers on the desk, then, sensing that Ashcroft wanted some explanation added, "Corrie doesn't have a lot to say, but what he does say is usually angry — letters on his employment files complaining about how people have treated him and the like. He's not very good at interaction. I think that may well be why Mustatti deals with the day-to-day running of the organization. In contrast with Corrie, he's very traceable — Eton then Sandhurst, a spell in the military, service in Baghdad and Afghanistan, highly decorated. He was discharged four years ago and he's worked in public relations since. Devenish, the guy who burned outside Buckingham Palace, is an open book. There is precious little that he doesn't splash about on social media. He liked to talk about himself. Police records identified that he had a serious cocaine habit. He wrote off a Maserati by wrapping it around a lamppost in Kensington High Street last year while he was tripping his head off. If he'd not burned up from mysterious causes, he'd probably still have found a way to kill himself before too long." Mari sensed that Ashcroft was beginning to stare at him in a way that suggested he was talking too much again. He shrugged and ran his fingers over the aged cardboard files. "You still keep records on paper?"

"We find it more resilient than digital files," Ashcroft said with a twitch of his lips. "Yes it burns, but with proper storage, which we have, it's more reliable. Some of the older documentation has been photographed and transferred to microfilm."

"I've never tried to surf a handwritten document before," Mari speculated. "I was just wondering what kind of traces that would leave behind."

"Take whatever you need and conduct your experiments with my blessing, Dr. Gale." Ashcroft nodded to him. "Darren will be your go-between and bring you whatever you require."

* * * *

The wait between Jake's first meeting at Birthright and the second seemed to take forever. The week of forced inactivity had Jake on edge and short of patience. Each day that crept by, he watched the news and waited in trepidation for another report of someone bursting into flames. Fortunately that didn't happen. This was good for more than just the obvious reasons. It meant that it was likely Birthright had no Fire Elementals left among their members. Which in turn meant 'Nathan' would be doubly attractive for recruitment into the inner sanctum, and with luck, it wouldn't be long before he met Corrie.

Mari, meanwhile, was at least kept occupied working for MI5, even if he did grumble over the tedium of trawling through records that yielded nothing of practical use.

Finally, the night of the meeting arrived and Mari helped him with what to wear, although Jake was dubious about his choices — a dark cashmere sweater Jake had gotten a few years ago and was now a tad too tight across his shoulders and dark gray slacks that also showed off his assets just a little too well.

"Are you sure about this?" Jake asked Mari. "I feel like a

sacrificial calf being sent off to slaughter."

"You want to attract attention, don't you?" Mari teased, sliding a hand under the close-fitting sweater. "Trust me, you look formal, but sexy. It's a killer mix."

"Funny, that's how I would usually describe you." Jake chuckled, reaching one hand up behind him to cup Mari's cheek as he nuzzled him. A kernel of warmth dropped into his middle and Jake turned to brush a kiss over Mari's lips. "You are too distracting by far."

"I am, aren't I?" Mari returned the kiss with plenty of heat. "Remember that when those cultists are all trying to jump your bones."

Jake laughed. "Thanks for the wardrobe help. I'll see you after the meeting."

"Take care," Mari told him, uncharacteristically sober as he waved Jake off.

* * * *

"My friends, it is no secret that the statistics are grim. Only one in ten children born to an Elemental bloodline in the last decade exhibited signs of psychic abilities. Those who do are often hobbled through diluted family ties and lack of nurturing during crucial formative years. We all know our history. Most of us know the secrets that were kept, the pressure put on parents to hide their children's gifts. But we live in a different age. It's time for us to reclaim our place and take back our birthright. It is our duty as Elementals to ensure our lines remain strong, to rebuild where they have been weakened, and to make sure all of us reach our fullest potential."

Aled Mustatti punctuated his speech with short, effective pauses and sweeping gestures. When he came to a stop, the rapt audience rose to their feet almost as one, cheering and clapping wildly, whipped into a righteous frenzy. Jake stood with them and clapped as eagerly as those around him. He hid the unease inside him behind a smile. He was figuring out how he could strike up a casual conversation with Mustatti when Lisa — or maybe this one was Elise, he couldn't remember — cut him off before he took more than two steps.

"Nathan! Hi! I'm so glad you could make it again."

"Hi, um…"

"Lisa," she supplied helpfully. "Don't worry, I know you met a lot of us at once. How was your week?"

"Oh, it was okay, not too bad," Jake said, keeping one eye on Aled.

"Good, that's good. So, you aren't working again tonight, are you?"

Jake stifled a groan. How had he forgotten about that? He should have made sure he had another excuse ready. "No, I'm not working tonight but…" He kicked himself silently. "I was hoping to have a chance to speak with Aled. About, you know, the group." That was actually the truth, no matter how lame it sounded.

Her eyebrows came together briefly then smoothed again. "Oh, I see. Yes, I suppose that is a good idea. He probably wants to speak with you as well, I'm sure." She had that bright tone that people got when they were trying to hide how disappointed they were.

"Maybe we could go have that coffee tomorrow night?" Jake wished he could call the words back as soon as they were out of his mouth. The last thing he wanted to do was lead her on, but if Aled proved difficult to crack, it didn't hurt to explore other avenues.

Lisa brightened at once, a big smile threatening to pull a muscle in her cheeks. "That sounds great! What's your number? I'll text you the address."

Jake told her and she started tapping on her phone. "Okay, I'll see you tomorrow."

"Yeah, sure. See you tomorrow," Jake said, sliding by her. He'd lost track of Mustatti but spotted him on the other side of the room talking quietly with a small group.

"You mustn't think of it that way," Aled spoke quietly.

"That is only what our current culture has taught us to feel. There were many other cultures before our modern day that saw the benefit of making sure certain traits were passed to children despite marriages or who was raising those children."

Jake listened unobtrusively and tried to keep his lip from curling. He couldn't hear what the man speaking with Aled replied, he murmured so low, but Aled nodded and clapped a reassuring hand on his shoulder before the three he was talking to moved away. He was about to clear his throat to get Aled's attention but the man turned to him before he had to do anything.

"Nathan, good to see you again."

"Thanks, I enjoyed your talk tonight."

"Did you? That's wonderful." He tipped his head and looked at him. "Some of our members, they have a little trouble at first, seeing the logic behind what we are working toward, not just for those of us already here but for future generations."

"Yeah, I uh, I see that. I wanted to ask you about something you said earlier, when you spoke about helping us reach our full potential. You'd said something like that before, but I always thought, if you have an extra ability, like psychometry, for instance, that you just have it or you don't. The way you make it sound, it's like you could help people, I don't know, practice at it."

Aled nodded. "That's exactly what I was saying. It's a common misconception that we can't improve upon our abilities. Take your ability, wouldn't it be better if you were able to control the images you receive? If you could approach a new place and know that you will only detect the residual energies from objects of your choosing?"

Jake swallowed. What he was saying, it was too damn close to a genie in a bottle wish. Something he'd longed for nearly as long as he could remember. And if it was tempting for him, knowing what he knew, then how much more tempting would it have been to someone who had no idea of the risks?

"That...that sounds really good. You could help me do that?"

Aled smiled. "Indeed I can."

* * * *

Mari was immersed in a pile of dusty documents up on the seventh floor of Thames House while Jake was being courted by the active members of Birthright. He was quite glad that he'd elected to come over in jeans and a sweater now. Even in nitrile gloves, his hands were filthy.

His skin was beginning to crawl too, but not because of the light film of paper dust. As he dug deeper into the files on the early experiments, he was beginning to realize just how lucky he and Jake were to be the subjects of a relatively enlightened research team at UCL.

The experiment in 1997 which had been Corrie's first brush with the government was little short of barbaric. Participants had been locked in sealed rooms, subjected to lengthy sensory deprivation and, in many cases, forced to the very limits of their Elemental abilities. Some had failed to demonstrate any practical skill and had been dismissed from the programs without any visible evidence of support. Some had simply burned out, left unable to use their gifts at all. Mari felt rather sick after reading it all.

"Dr. Gale...? Dr. Ga—ah, there you are," Darren said as he came around the edge of a filing cabinet. He held two steaming paper cups and set one on top of the cabinet near Mari. "I thought you might want some caffeine, working late." He glanced down at the papers in Mari's hand. "Is there anything I can help you with?"

Mari accepted the cup with a murmur of thanks and pushed his glasses back down onto the bridge of his nose as he shuffled through several piles of paper.

"Actually, yes. There is. Do you know what this means?"

He located the report he was after and pushed it across to

Darren, tapping about halfway down.

"It says that the subject was not responsive to EQ8, and suggests referral to a different test group. What's EQ8? Some kind of new examination system?"

Darren took a sip from his own cup. He didn't look down where Mari pointed before answering, "No, it's a classification. Elemental QED number eight." He took another small sip.

Mari looked up at him with a twitch of his lips. He tilted his reading glasses back into his hair. "Translation?"

"That's what they were calling the drug. Or did you want the actual chemical compound? That's classified. You'd have to talk to Ashcroft for that."

For a second or two, Mari just stared at him, the coffee suddenly forgotten in his hand. His heart rate had picked up and he was suddenly light-headed.

"Drug?" he repeated slowly. "What drug?"

"A part of the experiment to enhance Elemental abilities involved several drug trials. None of which produced any measurable results so they were discontinued some time before the program was canceled." Darren frowned. "Are you all right, Dr. Gale? You've gone very pale."

"Do you know what the purpose of the drug was, Darren?" Mari rifled through the pile of papers again, looking for anything else with that reference on it. "Was it aimed at a particular ability? Were they looking for a specific result?"

"I don't know the specifics. I know the aim of the program was to open the subjects more to their Elemental abilities but I don't believe they were focused on just one ability, if that's what you mean. Officer Ashcroft ought to know more." He paused. "I don't know that it matters considering that it didn't work. Is there something wrong, Dr. Gale?"

"In all the years I've been engaged on different trials on Elementals, no one ever jabbed me full of drugs, to the best of my knowledge." Mari exhaled, realizing just how fortunate he had been.

"I doubt they did it without the people involved

knowing," Darren assured him. "They probably had to sign rafts of paperwork consenting to it first. I can find that for you, if you want."

"Later, maybe." Mari forced a laugh that he didn't feel. There was a thread of chill running through him still. Birthright wasn't an officially sanctioned experiment. There was no way they would have access to drugs like this, surely. "I'm thinking," he began, "that this drug trial was what left Roy Corrie with next to no ability...now if that happened to you, what would you do?"

Darren shrugged. "There's not much I could do, if I'd agreed to all the waivers, except be massively pissed off. Maybe I'd try and shout it to the press, if no one else would listen."

Mari made a small note on his phone to search the letters columns of London and national newspapers the next time he was at the British Library. Given Corrie's propensity for venting his rage in pen and ink, it wouldn't surprise him to learn that the man had been indiscreet about his experiences here.

"You wouldn't want to see if the process could be reversed?" he asked, peeling off his thin plastic gloves and dropping them on the table so that he could warm his fingers around the paper cup containing the dregs of his coffee.

"But the drug didn't work. It didn't do anything. If Roy Corrie didn't burn himself out, if the drug somehow did it to him, wouldn't others have been affected by it as well?"

"Hmm...maybe." Mari mulled this over. "Or maybe it has different effects on different Elemental gifts? There's something else though — if this is EQ8, then what were the results of experiments with EQ1 through 7? Can you round up those for me, Darren?"

"Yes. It will take some time to pull all the files. I can tell you now though, all of them failed. I can also tell you most of the material you'll find in the files will be heavily redacted. If you need more than that you'll have to talk to

Ashcroft about clearance."

"Leave that to me." Mari forced another smile he didn't feel. "I can be very persuasive."

Darren reached into his pocket and pulled out a slim mobile, glanced down at it, then back at Mari. "Looks like you'll have your chance sooner rather than later. Officer Ashcroft would like you to come to his office for a debriefing with Mr. Chivis."

Mari's spirits lifted at the thought of seeing Jake, so much so that he was wearing a broad smile by the time he reached Ashcroft's office door, and was shown in at once by his PA. Jake looked tired but still delicious and Mari accepted the offer of an empty seat and dropped down next to him, letting his knee rest against Jake's for a moment, even as he greeted their handler.

"You wanted to see me...us, sir?"

Ashcroft smiled benevolently and folded his hands on his desk in front of him. He wasn't quite the picture of grandfatherly concern yet, but given a few more years and a bit more silver in his hair, it was easy to see how charming he would be.

"Mr. Chivis has had something of a breakthrough with Birthright," Ashcroft announced.

"I wouldn't say that just yet," Jake added. "But I think I'm getting closer." Turning to Mari, he explained, "Mustatti has been hinting at some sort of training program they have to enhance Elemental abilities. He's offered to take me on board. It gets us another step closer to Corrie, and I'd be willing to bet that this enhancement regime is the connecting factor to the victims."

Mari's eyes widened and something swooped in his chest, not in a good way. The feeling was like one of those falling dreams, where his body seemed to drop away and he had to catch himself sharply.

"That's...exciting," he said, searching for a word that would convey his encouragement without giving too much voice to the dread this news stirred up in him. "Progress."

Jake gave him an odd, inquiring look, not convinced at all by his words.

"You sound less than enthralled, Dr. Gale," Ashcroft franked him.

"You tell me if I'm wrong to be concerned, sir." Mari returned his serious gaze. "And while you're at it, maybe you can tell us more about the Elemental QED experiments in the 70s and 90s?"

Ashcroft's smile didn't falter. "I would say there is every reason to be concerned, Dr. Gale. We have citizens dying in horrible, unpredictable fires. That is very concerning. It's also why you and Mr. Chivis have been asked to apply your unique talents to the case. I assure you, we are using every precaution to ensure your and Mr. Chivis' safety," he said, not missing at all where Mari's real concern lay.

"And the experiments?" Mari probed.

"They involved drug trials, if I recall correctly." Ashcroft folded his hands, a small defensive gesture which Mari did not miss.

Mari let his gaze flicker briefly to Jake's face, which was his professional 'cop-face', quiet and unreadable as he took this information on board. Satisfied, he returned his attention to Ashcroft.

"Why were they halted?"

"Ostensibly due to budget cuts." Ashcroft's smile thinned. "However, if there had been even the smallest hint of any success I'm sure funds would have been found. The drug lots failed to produce any results and it was determined prudent not to throw good money after bad. I assume by your line of questioning that you believe there is some connection? I must tell you that's very unlikely. Not only did the experiment fail, but those formulas are classified. Even I don't know what compounds were used in the trials."

"Did the recipients know?" Mari asked. "Or were they just ordered to sign a disclaimer before you shot them full of random drugs?"

He forced the tremor out of his voice but anger simmered now in place of the empty, swooping sensation.

"The participants were not bullied or coerced, Dr. Gale. They were told the drugs were experimental and any information relating to them was classified."

"What were the drugs supposed to do?" Jake asked quietly.

"The idea of them was to reduce natural defenses and open the test subjects to their abilities, as I understand it." Ashcroft gave a patient smile to both of them.

"Psychoactive drugs?" Mari queried.

"Dr. Gale, we weren't pumping them full of LSD and encouraging them to jump out of windows. It was a controlled experiment," Ashcroft said in a mild tone.

"And you didn't think that might be something we should know about before getting ass deep in the alligators?" Jake said just as quietly.

Ashcroft spread his hands. "It's not pertinent. As I said, those trials all failed. Completely. The formulas are classified. I very much doubt…"

"What? That Corrie somehow figured out what you were giving him? That he is mixing up some chemicals in his bathtub that happen to turn people into fire bombs? Do you really think teaching his people some yoga meditations is what's causing them to go up in smoke?"

Ashcroft pressed that affable-grandfather smile on him again but there was some strain showing in the fine lines around his eyes this time.

"Mr. Chivis, like yourself, I think the latter option is most unlikely. But there is no way that Corrie could get his hands on the drug. The compound instructions were all destroyed once the experiment concluded. It's standard procedure."

Mari chewed on his lips, frustrated. Although it was a relief that they weren't using untested pharmaceuticals on Elementals any more, he still felt anxious.

"You'll be careful, won't you?" he said to Jake. "Don't let them give you anything. Not even a pill, okay?"

"I'm always careful," Jake said, more gently then he'd spoken to Ashcroft. "Mari brings up a good point. If I walk into the meeting with Mustatti and the enhancement involves taking some drug, what then?"

"As unlikely as that is, if it happens we'd like a sample, if at all possible."

Mari opened his mouth to tell Ashcroft what he thought of that idea but Jake put his hand over his — just a brief, warning touch, then gone.

"If possible," Jake said, and stood. "If that's all, Officer Ashcroft?"

* * * *

They were back outside when Mari finally gave vent to the explosion Jake could see building in him.

"Have you lost your mind?" he yelped, grabbing Jake by the shoulders and pulling their faces close, heedless of the passersby.

Prickles of warmth tingling along Jake's skin despite Mari's tense words. Part of that heat was simply Mari's touch, but another part was the pleasure of being able to stand here like this with him, in a very public setting, and not care at all who saw them. The feeling of that freedom gave him a fierce surge of joy and he kissed Mari impulsively, then grinned at the incredulous look on his face.

"My mind is still where I left it, last I checked," he said.

"In that case, I can only deduce that you're drunk," Mari grumbled, but his words were more tender now. "How on earth are you going to fake taking medication if they give it to you? Surely they'll... I mean they aren't going to just give you a pill and walk away. What if it isn't a pill? Jake... I'm worried. I'm scared."

"I know you are," Jake said. He didn't try to tell him not to worry. That seemed pointless. As much as he liked working with Mari, he had to remember that his boyfriend was a civilian, not a trained investigator. He didn't have the cop mentality that made him look past the risk to the job that needed to be done. "I'm not going to take any drugs they offer, Mari. If I see a way to steal a sample of whatever it is, if it even exists, then I will. But I'm not so heroic. I'm not going to sacrifice myself to get an answer. That wouldn't serve anyone."

Mari cupped his face in both hands and kissed him so hard that his knees shook. When their lips parted, he breathed, "Please be careful, Jake. I have such a bad feeling about this. I know I'm not a psychic or anything so…helpful. But something doesn't sit right with me. And…I don't want to lose you."

Jake stopped himself from promising he wouldn't lose him. He tried not to be superstitious but some things stuck, and one of them was not to invite fate's attention. Instead he kissed him back more gently and put his arm around him, leading him down to the street level, where they might catch a cab. "Let's go find something to eat. You'll feel better with some food inside you."

Chapter Sixteen

"Relax…breathe deep…let your focus drill down to a single point…"

Aled had a good voice, Jake would give him that. If he'd wanted to take a nap, he'd be out like a light listening to that rich, melodious timbre. Very carefully he peeked from under his lashes at the others sitting cross-legged on the floor of the meeting room. Everyone looked completely at ease, faces peaceful. When he was younger, Jake had tried meditation for a while to help him get a handle on his temper. It had never done much for him. He'd found much more spiritual peace while running than he ever had sitting still.

"I will now count back from ten, and as I do I want you to slowly become more aware… Ten…nine…"

Jake kept his eyes closed and held still, pretending to drift slowly back to awareness. He wondered if anyone actually got anything out of this or if they were all pretending. He'd had exactly one truly spiritual experience in his life, and that had involved a two-week journey alone in the wilderness. Somehow, he doubted anyone got the same brush with something larger while sitting in their living room. Then again, who was he to judge? Maybe they were just better at it than he was.

"And you are now completely here in the present, completely awake and aware," Aled said as he finished his countdown.

Jake opened his eyes. His companions were doing the same, all smiling happy faces, all with the same slightly dreamy looks. It was creepy. Maybe it did do something for them.

At Aled's urging, people got up. There was a little kitchenette off the main room where snacks and coffee were set out. In little groups of twos or threes they took their plates and cups and went back out to graze and socialize. Jake somehow ended up alone with the food and Lisa, in the kitchen. Their coffee date a few nights before had been about as awkward as Jake could imagine. He'd been avoiding her since but she had him cornered now.

"Hi, Nathan. So, did you get anything out of the meditation? Some people really reckon it changes their lives," she said with a giggle that suggested she was not one of those people. She folded a couple of stray napkins then toyed with the food on her plate like she had no intention of eating it.

"Not really," Jake admitted. "Has anyone told you they did? I mean, has anyone you know of been able to enhance their ability with the meditations?"

"A few of them *say* they have," Lisa replied in a scathing tone. "And Claire Bear reckons she's oh so much more 'empathic' since she started doing them. But everyone knows she's just trying to get into Roy's pants."

Jake choked on a soft chuckle. "So, you don't believe them?"

"You've got me." She put a hand over her left breast and gave him a tragic look. "It's hokum, isn't it? Maybe it calms some of them down a bit. But gives them 'powers'?" She wriggled her fingers demonstratively. "No. I don't think so. You either have them or you don't, right?"

"I suppose," Jake said neutrally. "Do you have any Elemental ability? If you don't mind my asking."

Lisa nodded. "I can move stuff." She chuckled at the look on his face. Then picked up a spoon and moved it to the kitchen sink, adding, "Not like that. I mean everyone can do that, if they're not like, quadriplegic or something. I can move stuff without touching it."

"That's not a very common ability," Jake said, actually

impressed.

"Only a couple of people in the group can do it," she admitted. "It kept the kids I was at school with entertained but it's not like, something you can put on your CV, is it?"

"Is that why you were invited to try out the enhancement exercises?"

"I guess so."

"What about Louis? Did the meditations help him?" Jake asked. He was treading dangerous ground with that question, he knew, but he had to start getting closer to the truth sooner or later.

"Louis? He wasn't in the class."

That was surprising. Jake had been willing to bet he had been.

"Oh, I didn't know. He talked a lot about this group and how it had been helping him. I just figured…" He shrugged and gave her his best 'aww shucks' smile.

Lisa actually batted her eyelashes back at him.

"Louis had a lot of one on ones with Aled," she said, lowering her voice and gesturing toward the door with the vol-au-vent pinched between her forefinger and thumb. "They were both in the military for a while. I used to think that was probably why. But they kind of had a lot in common," she added cryptically.

Before Jake could think of a reply, Lisa made her move. She leaned in close and put her hand on his arm, smiling coyly up at him. "I had a good time the other night. I was hoping we could go out again."

Oh, boy. He forced himself to smile back instead of move away, and waited a moment so he wouldn't stammer out something stupid. "I had fun too." He had to squash the impulse to tell her some lie, like he wasn't ready to date, or even the truth, that he wasn't interested in her. He had to keep all avenues for information open right now. Even if he felt like a jerk leading some poor girl on. "Maybe we could go out again, sometime."

"That would be really great," she agreed. "You know,

when you said you were a friend of Louis' I worried at first that you'd turn out to be...like him. I'm so glad you're not."

"Like him?" Jake knew exactly what she meant, but he wanted to hear her say it out loud. He'd already been thinking of her as another potential victim, or at worst an innocent bystander. He had to keep in mind that no one here was above suspicion until he knew what they knew, and what they didn't.

"You know. Or maybe you didn't. He was...what do you say in America? Lou batted for the other side."

"Were he and Aled together, then?"

Lisa made a rude noise through her nostrils. "Those two? Please! I don't think so. I know they both served and they both liked a bit of tail." She chuckled, shaking her head. "But they moved in different circles, Nathan. Aled's ambitious. I know Louis was your mate, and I'm sorry, but he was a proper flake."

Jake pressed a smile onto his face. "Don't be sorry. Anyone that knew him knew that. We should probably go back out and socialize," he suggested. He had more questions, but he needed to go slow with her. If she started to feel like he was interrogating her, she might stop being so forthcoming with her thoughts and theories on the members of Birthright.

"I guess," she said, half mimicking his accent as she slid her arm through his and towed him out into the main hall. "Let's go and party."

* * * *

By the end of the next week, both Jake and Mari were pretty much recovered from the smoke inhalation. Jake was glad for the increased lung capacity, since Mari was making him work to keep up as they ran down one of their favorite routes through the park.

"You're mad," Jake said.

"I'm not mad," Mari answered without slowing.

"You're upset?"

"I'm not upset," he snorted.

After a few moments of silence, Jake said, "I'm not dating her, Mari."

"You're not turned on by women. You told me as much," Mari said simply.

"Uh-huh." Jake let it go. He didn't have much choice, anyway, as Mari seemed intent on running his legs off. By the time they reached the gate, they were both sweat-soaked and panting.

"Come back to mine?" Jake asked.

"If you have the energy for me." Mari turned his head to wink at him. He pushed on so that Jake was forced to keep up.

That was definitely a challenge if Jake had ever heard one. Fortunately, he was up for it and once they were back in his apartment, he proved just how much energy he had for Mari. When they were lying naked in bed and panting for entirely different reasons, Jake asked, "How's the digging going from your end?"

"Excuse me?"

Jake chuckled and kissed his forehead. "The research? Have you found anything useful in the files?"

Mari stroked his fingers over Jake's chest, wriggling back down into the comfortable pillows.

"The drug trials were extensive. The files hint at subtle changes to the formula they were using. Each level built on the one before. Sometimes people disappear from the trial records. Sometimes the scientists just record that there was no conspicuous alteration to the test subjects' abilities. It's all very frustrating." He sighed. "I can't even go off-piste and surf the records. It's very weird trying to surf paper files. Like opening a dusty cupboard with no lights."

"Totally archaic," Jake said.

Mari poked him in the ribs and Jake grinned.

"There may be nothing to find. Don't get too frustrated. We will find out what happened to those people, one way or another."

"The Birthright records suggest that they're carrying out experiments of their own," Mari told him, sobering. "I don't know exactly what, but there are files in Claire's computer that discuss the three Elementals who burned up. They talk about how unsuitable Louis Cortez and Karl Devenish were for some trials. I can't remember the exact wording without my notes but the gist was that Corrie didn't approve of their lifestyles. He reckoned they were incompatible with the current program, whatever that means. None of his e-mails connect. He just fires out random observations whenever something pisses him off and the recipient either knows what the blazes he's talking about, or they have to ask him in person. It's bloody annoying."

Jake laughed. "You're not expected to uncover their motives single-handed."

"I wish I could just find something that meant you didn't have to spend so much time with them," Mari breathed. "And I don't only mean this Lisa creature."

Jake lifted his hand and stroked his fingers through Mari's hair, fighting a small smile. It used to make him roll his eyes in annoyance whenever Alex had decided to play jealous bitch. He never felt that way when Mari let his green-eyed monster show. Maybe because he knew Mari wasn't just play-acting for attention.

"We'll get there. Mustatti keeps talking to me after the meditations, hinting that he can 'take me deeper'. I know I'm getting close to him letting me in on the real deal."

He had wanted to put some more pressure on Aled, but Ashcroft cautioned patience. Work on gaining his trust. Play the wide-eyed rube and let Mustatti lead him. And keep his guilt at not telling Mari that Aled was queer well under wraps. It wasn't important, he told himself, and hoped that was true.

* * * *

Jake finally got the breakthrough he'd been working

toward when Aled called him one morning, out of the blue, and asked to meet with him to discuss the next step in enhancing his ability with Mr. Corrie. He barely had the time to text Mari and let him know before pulling on his clothes and rushing off.

Aled picked him up on Tottenham Court Road and headed west. Forty-five minutes later, they were climbing out of his tidy black Audi on the forecourt of a handsome three-story building on the edge of Strawberry Hill Park. Claire fetched him a coffee which he was glad of, because Roy Corrie kept him waiting for half an hour. She was less flirty with him today and he wondered if she too was jealous of his apparent dalliance with Lisa.

Finally, Corrie put in an appearance, stalking into the meeting room where Jake had been waiting, with Aled in tow. He was a much smaller man than Mustatti but carried himself as if he was taller, very upright and brisk. Corrie was not unattractive, Jake supposed, though not in a way that he personally found hot. He wore his dark hair short and his face clean-shaven. Jake tried to picture him as a super-villain, the evil mastermind behind a plot to make living fire bombs, but he took in the small, watery, dark eyes, fleshy lips and forgettable features, and couldn't quite get there.

"So, you're the Yank that's got half my organization's knickers in a hormonal twist then?" Corrie said by way of greeting. He spoke rapidly, with some kind of regional accent that Jake couldn't place, all flat vowels and nasal tones. "What's so special about you, Mr. Douglas?"

That was a weird way to start out a conversation with someone you were keen to recruit, Jake thought. Instead he replied, "I wouldn't say I was all that special. Maybe it's just the novelty of a new face. You must be Mr. Corrie." He held out his hand but Corrie ignored it, skimming him with his eyes. A half-smile twisted his mouth for a second then was gone. He kept his hands clasped behind his back and started to pace around the room. Jake turned in place, keeping him in his sights, but Aled made a simple, discreet gesture that he should take a seat and Jake lowered himself into a chair.

Corrie abruptly stopped pacing, standing in front of where Jake sat, his body canted forward and his weight balanced on the balls of his feet. His small dark eyes bored into Jake for a moment, then flicked furtively away.

"Claire tells me your Birthright handle is Nathan Detroit. Are you a fan of musical theater, Mr. Douglas?" He huffed, as if this was funny.

"No, sir, my name is Nathan and I come from Detroit," Jake said, keeping his tone just the right side of deferential.

"Why?" Corrie stared at him for a moment, his eyes narrowed to slits.

"Um…I beg your…" Jake began but Corrie interrupted.

"Why did you come from Detroit? What is your reason for being in London?"

That one he could answer without specifically having to lie. "I came here for work. To take up a new job."

Corrie paced away a few steps but came right back, standing over Jake again, looming, or trying to. "What line of work? What is it that you do, Nathan?" The words might have been neutral but the way he asked was almost an accusation.

"I work in IT," Jake answered calmly. The way Corrie looked at him, so intently, had him a bit on edge. He was saved from Corrie's challenging stare by a hesitant tap at the door, even though it was open.

Claire smiled in at them and brought a tray with more coffee, which she set on the desk.

"Here we are," she chirped and handed out the cups, practically placing them in everyone's hand.

"Thank you, Claire," Aled said, in a tone that was unmistakably a dismissal.

"You're welcome. I did remember how you take it, Nathan? Cream, no sugar?"

"Yes, it's perfect. Thank you," Jake said, taking a sip

because she seemed to be waiting for his approval.

He had the oddest feeling that she was trying not to curtsy.

"Wonderful, let me know if you need anything else."

"Yes, yes. We will," Corrie said impatiently.

Claire took the cue and left.

"Mr. Corrie and I are glad you could come, Nathan," Aled said in a more diplomatic tone.

You could have fooled me, Jake thought. Corrie looked wound so tight his teeth might crack. "Thank you for inviting me," he said, instead.

Aled smiled. "I know you've been very interested in our work with Elemental enhancement. Thank you for you for your patience. I know the meditations can sometimes feel like they are not doing much, but I assure you, with practice and diligence, they will help you gain more control over your innate ability."

"I'm sure," Jake murmured. "Is that all there is to it then? The meditations eventually enhance ability?"

"There is more, but we will get to that in a moment," Aled told him. "Did you know that you are the only Fire Elemental with ability currently a member of Birthright? Not the most stable of elements, fire. We've been working recently with Earth Elementals. They make up the majority of our members, but not many have strong abilities. Dowsing, or finding lost objects, come more naturally to some, but we've only one member that has the stronger Earth Elemental ability of telekinesis, and her control of it is very limited and costs her dearly in energy."

Jake figured he must be talking about Lisa but he held his tongue for now, waiting to see where Aled was going.

"But that will change, with time. I'm sure of it. At one time, Earth Elementals were not only the most plentiful of the Elementals but their powers were far stronger. Do you know that there are theories that Earth Elementals were the builders of Stonehenge and the pyramids?" Aled was saying, warming to his topic.

"I think I might have read that," Jake answered.

"Are you gay, Nathan?" Corrie interrupted out of nowhere. "Al says you have a partner." The word dripped off his tongue like pond slime. "Very specific term, that. A partner. Not a girlfriend then. No ring. You haven't got a wife?"

Jake was caught so off-guard by the question, he didn't have time to consider if he should even try to lie. Before coming here, he had decided he probably should lie, if they asked, but if the deception went on for any length of time it might get more difficult.

"Er, does it matter?" he asked, stalling.

"If it didn't matter then would I be asking?" Corrie looked at him like a hawk watching a mouse. The skin of his pale face clung to the strong bones of his jaw and cheeks, thrumming with tension. "Do you always answer a question with a question, Nathan?"

"Only when I find the question irrelevant," Jake said, then bit the inside of his cheek. Shit, he was supposed to be kissing this guy's ass, not getting pissy. "I just don't see how my sexuality makes any difference here," he added, in a milder tone.

Corrie's lips twisted again and Jake thought his mouth looked like it said a lot of cruel things and was permanently bitter about it. That bitterness was what marred his appearance. It made his features hard, and not easy to like.

"I suppose your non-answer is an answer in itself."

Jake had to hold back a sigh. "I suppose it is. I am seeing someone, and he's an Elemental, as well. Are gay people not welcome in Birthright?" Jake asked. He figured if that was the case, this was probably going to be the shortest undercover operation in history.

"We have no official policy on individual sexuality," Aled said, and earned a sharp look from Corrie. "We do encourage our members to date one another, or at least other Elementals. It's not a requirement of course, but if we want to keep our bloodlines strong we have to set sentimentality aside. We were hopeful that your interest in Lisa Channer was more than simply platonic."

Jake had been hazed, called names and heckled mercilessly at various times in his life, for his sexuality, or even his perceived sexuality, but he couldn't ever remember feeling so disgusted by someone's reaction to him being gay before. Did they even realize how fucking creepy it was to be looking at him as potential breeding stock?

If he had been here under any other circumstances he would have gotten up and left, but he couldn't very well do that over something so minor.

"Okay, well, since you know, is it going to be a problem?" His voice seemed to echo oddly in his ears.

"No, of course not," Aled said, again getting the words in before Corrie could speak, and Jake got the distinct impression that, if Aled hadn't beat him to it, Corrie might well have said otherwise.

The head of Birthright looked at Jake with a sour expression. If he thought anything at all, he kept it to himself.

Jake lifted his coffee cup to take another sip, just to be doing something other than sitting there awkwardly, but as he lifted it to his lips he frowned. It seemed to be taking a hell of a lot of effort to lift his arm. He stared at it for a second, started to say something, but his thoughts were swimming. He was suddenly exhausted. He could feel his head start to drop forward and was startled by a loud bang as his coffee cup hit the floor.

Shit…this isn't…right. Mari… I'm sorry.

That was his last thought before the room went dark.

* * * *

The persistent throbbing in his temples was the first thing Jake became aware of. He tried to open his eyes but it felt like he had anchors tied to his lids. He was uncomfortably warm, sweat damp, and his tongue seemed to be glued to the roof of his mouth. God, he hated hangovers. He was still struggling through the heavy fog of sleep when a surge of a different kind of heat went through him. Mari was running his hands down his abs and squeezing his package playfully over his jeans.

Jeans...

He didn't wear jeans to bed. *Wait!*

Jake struggled awake. It took monumental effort to get his eyes to open and everything jerked and spun in his vision making him feel sick. Not his room. And not Mari touching him. He made a sound and tried to push Aled's hands away but it felt like he was dragging his arms through mud.

"Sshhhh... Don't try to fight it. Your body says it's fine," that rich, unctuous voice rumbled to his left somewhere, out of his blurry vision. "And you brought this on yourself, Jake."

"Uhhh...?" Jake squeezed his eyes shut for a moment and when he opened them the room seemed too bright. Aled was a haze of darkness against the blinding white walls, ringed in an aura of silver and gold like a fallen angel. As Jake began to be more aware of his surroundings again, he sensed something else, a kind of mirror presence that emanated from the point where Aled's hot hand was moving over his body.

Without warning, he was dragged into a memory.

Corrie, pacing the room, swearing at him, a sheen of sweat on his high, pale brow, those bug eyes huge and panicky like a startled horse. He heard Aled's mellow voice, like distant thunder, ripple up from his own chest, startling him

"Jake Chivis? He's a detective? Are you sure? He says he knew Louis. He can't be a spy."

"My contact is certain."

There was a pause before Aled said in a relieved tone, "He still knows nothing. And now that we know about him it will be easy to shut him out."

"Don't be stupid, Aled. Sooner or later they will get impatient. We have to act now. Chivis is a Fire Elemental and a powerful

one, he didn't lie about that. We use him as planned. The only difference is now we need to disappear until the surrogate delivers."

"Roy, this is madness. We can't use him."

"Who knows when we might come across another Fire Elemental? And by then it might be too late. This will work, it has to," Corrie said.

Aled's hand lifted from his crotch briefly and Jake was thrown back out of the vision, his stomach lurching, suddenly forced to orientate again. He'd never had such a clear image from simply touching another person, certainly not from being touched through his clothing. What the fuck had they done to him?

"This is all your fault, I'm sorry to say, Detective Chivis," Aled told him in that voice that was as dark and powerful as he was.

It was starting to come together in Jake's foggy mind. His cover was blown, obviously. They knew who he was, and who had sent him. It explained Corrie's barely suppressed hostility toward him. And they had drugged him, then given him the experimental drug. *Fuck.* How had they found out about him? He wanted to punch Aled in the face to get him off but he was still having trouble focusing, much less coordinating his limbs.

"How…?" Jake's throat was so hoarse and dry, the word stuck and he had to swallow and try again. "How did you…? What did you do to me?"

"I think you know that answer to that," Aled said. His hands moved to Jake's belt and tugged on it, popping the buckle open, then the button beneath it. He took the zipper down in short, careful jerks. "Your friends at MI5 were using you, sunshine. No two ways about it. Sorry." He didn't sound terribly sorry though.

His warm hand got to work again, massaging slowly through the thinner material of Jake's boxer briefs. His skin looked pale and Jake realized he was wearing thin, sterile gloves.

"You might be disgusted but your little man likes that," Aled observed with a dark chuckle as Jake stiffened for him, in spite of his efforts to push his hand away.

Someone in MI5 had warned them he was a plant. Did MI5 know they had an informant in their midst yet? Did Mari know? The semi-paralysis was starting to fade and with it some of the brain fog. In its place came a swift and hot surge of rage. He struggled up on his elbows, forcing one arm forward to shove at Aled, although it felt clumsy and slow.

"Get your fucking hands off me," Jake rasped out.

"No can do," Aled said, fending him off easily. "Relax, Jake. Or I'll have to tie you to the bed. I'm just following orders. You're not my type, don't you worry. Given how hard you are already, this won't take me long."

"Orders? Right." Jake snorted.

"Don't flatter yourself." He shoved Jake back down and held him there with one arm across his chest while the other gripped and stroked him roughly. "I don't need to resort to rape. I just want your donation."

Panic surged through Jake on the heels of the rage gripping him as what Aled was saying sunk in. The idea that they'd use him as an unwilling sperm donor was more repulsive than Aled just being a sick creep. Jake shoved against him, still weak and clumsy, but he still managed to land a hand on Aled's face. It was meant to be a punch but ended more like a heavy slap. His momentum was lost though as he was plunged into another memory. His vision telescoped like he was looking down a long tunnel.

Jake watched through Aled's eyes as Corrie lifted a syringe filled with an innocuous, clear liquid and flicked it a couple times before bending and stabbing the needle into his arm.

"He's being watched, monitored." Aled sounded nervous. "If he disappears the Security Service comes looking for us."

"Let them look. By the time they find this place we'll have what we want and be long gone." Corrie stopped and sneered at Aled. "The EQ10 is already in his system. The next part is your job."

"And then? What are we going to do with the detective here?"

"If he lives, he lives. If not..." Corrie shrugged.

The vision ended as quickly and unexpectedly as it had started. It had been absolutely surreal to see his own unconscious body through Aled's eyes. He had barely landed a glancing blow on Aled and hadn't even been touching him when it started. That had never happened before. He had to be physically touching someone, or something, to get a clear read off of it.

By the time he could think again, Aled had already grabbed a pair of restraints from somewhere and had fastened one tightly around his right wrist.

"Don't be an idiot. You're not going to get very far in this state. I'm sorry, all right, Jake. You seem like a decent fellow, in spite of all the lies. But this will be easier for you if you don't fight me."

"Fuck you!" Jake rasped. He threw his weight into trying to get up, get off the bed, get out of Aled's grasp, but he was as uncoordinated as a newborn colt and all his strength seemed to have fled. Whatever they'd given him was not just a normal sleeping pill. This was like trying to fight anesthesia—it wasn't just affecting his mind, it was affecting his body.

Aled overpowered him and attached one cuff to the bed frame. He put everything he had into trying to throw him off but it was like trying to fight against a landslide.

"That's better," Aled said as he got Jake's other wrist cuffed to the bed. "Look, you can do this yourself if you'd rather. I can give you some space. Lay back. Think about your boyfriend. But one way or another, it's going to happen."

"You're a sick fuck! You fucking killed those people. You think I want to let you get your hands on a kid?"

"You don't have a say in this, Jake Chivis. I think you need to start getting your head around that. We don't want people to die. But, in order to protect our kind, we need to do things that aren't always...ethical," Aled said without apology. "Your friends in the Security Service are getting too interested, and someone like you on their side isn't helping the cause of ordinary Elementals on the street. You think they'll be any slower to exploit your gifts? Think again. We want Elementals to be strong for the Elemental cause. They want people to use as weapons."

"You aren't helping or protecting anyone. You're a murderer." Jake glared at him.

Aled's face finally tightened in anger, his dark eyes flashing. "I think you need something to help you relax."

"No!" Jake pulled at the bonds holding his wrists but it didn't help any more than it stopped Aled from reaching into the drawer of the bedside table and pulling out a syringe. His heart pulsed faster at the sight of it and he tried to swing himself of the mattress again, lashing out at the man with one foot.

"You really shouldn't need another dose yet, but perhaps your metabolism has already started to increase. It's one of the side effects." Aled dodged out of range of Jake's boot. Jake tried to twist away again, without success, and Aled jabbed his arm.

Within moments, Jake felt his muscles go slack. His eyes rolled as he fought to keep them open, struggled to stay conscious. His whole body felt like a heavy lead weight, impossible to move. He was slipping in and out, dark one moment, aware of Aled moving toward him the next, dark again, then the other man's hand sliding back into his jeans. This couldn't be happening. He couldn't let this happen. Thankfully, the drug seemed to have killed off his willful erection, at least.

Jake groaned when he saw Aled approach the bed again with a length of tubing and a surgical catheter in one hand. This time, when he blacked out it was a merciful release.

Chapter Seventeen

Mari was sprawled on the bed, his laptop on his knees and a tablet on the bed beside him, spectacles perched on the end of his nose. He heard a tap at his bedroom door and called, "Come in."

Mama opened the door and brought him a mug of tea. She came to sit on the bed beside him, setting the cup on the bedside unit.

"What are you doing in here, child?"

"Just chatting to people." Mari leaned over and kissed her cheek.

It was only half a lie. He had been in and out of the Birthright chatrooms all night and though the mysterious Nathan was a topic of interest, certainly among the female members of the society — no one had seen him since the public meeting. No one but Claire anyway, who reckoned that he had been in to see Mr. Corrie, but had gone home. She speculated on the rumor that he had a girlfriend. Another user was telling the room that Aled said he had a partner already. That was greeted with disappointed emojis all round.

He had also been delving deeper. Birthright's head honchos had contacts running in all directions, and once he was into Claire's phone and laptop it was like being given the key to a whole network. She knew astonishingly little, but she was Corrie's secretary and she fielded his calls, kept his phonebook and distributed his letters and e-mails. And via that network he had all the access keys that he needed. He'd spent the day following the trails of each number and address to see where they led, making notes on his phone as he went along.

"No Jake today?" she asked cheekily.

"He does have a life of his own, Mama," Mari demurred, shaking his head at her.

"Are you seeing him later?" she probed.

"Why? Do you want the place to yourself? Hot date?" he teased.

"I'm just interested." She patted his shoulder as she pushed herself to her feet. "Don't spend all night on that thing, you'll get square eyes."

Once she had gone back down, Mari checked his phone like it was a compulsion, even though he knew there were no messages. He had been listening for them all afternoon. Jake hadn't been in touch since leaving for his appointment with Corrie. That could just mean that he'd got stuck talking to someone, or he was in a zone with no mobile coverage, unlikely as it seemed in central London.

He was anxious though, and had been since Jake left for this meeting. There was no logic to it. He knew well enough that Jake was a trained cop—that he was armed with a tracker and MI5 were watching him—but even so he was nervous.

When there was still no call at half past six, he hauled himself off his bed and swapped his casual wear for smarter jeans and a tight vest and sweater then headed to Jake's flat. Maybe he'd gone home and crashed out, Mari reasoned. In which case, he could wake Jake up with a quick snuggle. He knew the key code for the street door and he had a physical key for the apartment.

The tiny flat was quiet and in darkness when he let himself in, and there was no sign of Jake in the lounge or in the bedroom. Mari flopped down on the sofa with a brief huff of disappointment and flipped open his phone, sending him a message.

Getting worried. Call me. Or text. Or something. xx

As he slid his phone back into his pocket something

chimed quietly, away to his right, in the bedroom. He pushed himself to his feet with a concerned frown and went to investigate.

On the bedside unit, the message light was flashing on Jake's abandoned mobile. Mari exhaled another sigh of impatience.

"You stupid man! Where on earth are you?"

He picked up the device and closed his eyes, pushing down into very simple web of communication pathways that connected with it. Jake did not speak to many people. And he had not used the phone since earlier this morning. *Damn it!*

Mari sat down on the bed and resisted the urge to slam the small cell down on the cabinet in case it broke. He pulled out his own mobile again and scrolled through the contacts until he found Ashcroft.

"Dr. Gale, I presume you are not calling to inform us that Jake is with you," Ashcroft answered without preamble. He sounded quite tense.

Mari's heart sank into his boots. His hand shook around the phone.

"He isn't here. I'm at his flat. He hasn't rung me. I hoped…" There was no point in finishing. Jake evidently wasn't at Thames House. Where was he?

There was a short pause before Ashcroft said, "We have been tracking his phone, of course. This afternoon the GPS signal was scrambled and shortly thereafter the listening device went dead. Either of these things could have been a simple equipment malfunction. Together, it raises suspicions. We've held out hope that he would move from whatever area he was in that was blocking the signal but, when it became apparent that this was not going to happen, we began preparations to find and extract him."

Mari swallowed hard, his mouth too dry. He could feel his heart beating faster than it should.

"Your intelligence knows where he is, right?" he said weakly.

"We are working on it," Ashcroft said, more gently. "We've been monitoring the general area he was in when the signal disappeared."

"Why would it…? Do you think they found out about it?" Mari asked him, trying to figure out in his head, given what he knew about Birthright, how they might react if they thought they were being spied on.

"There are any number of reasons a signal might be lost, as I imagine you already understand. However, some sort of blocking device seems most likely. Combing the area is time-consuming. We have officers working on narrowing the parameters but they can only track so fast." The bland note in Ashcroft's voice was not lost on Mari and his next question confirmed what he was gearing up toward. "If you want to come in, perhaps you can help speed up the process."

Mari was nodding before he had even stopped speaking then realized with a jolt that Ashcroft couldn't see him.

"Yes." He said the word before the other man had drawn breath. "Yes. Whatever you want me to do. I'm worried. It's not like him to keep people hanging. If he was okay I'm sure he would have contacted one of us by now."

"I'll send a car for you," Ashcroft told him. "Faster than waiting for a cab."

* * * *

When Jake opened his eyes again the room was mostly dark. Only a few fingers of light came in through the window from the street lights outside. For that, he was glad. His skull felt like it might split open at any moment. He shifted on the bed and discovered his arms were still bound above his head. Carefully he tugged on the straps. The weakness and confusion that had plagued him earlier were still a problem, but at least he was alone in the room.

He looked down at himself and noted his jeans were zipped and buttoned but he could feel stickiness on his belly under his sweater, coupled with an uncomfortable zinging sensation in the sensitive flesh of his cock, and that sent a wave of burning anger and shame through him. If he got out of this before he burned up… He cut off that line of thinking. Or tried to, but all he saw was Mari's worried face, asking him not to go and meet with these people, not to put himself at risk. And, damn it, even if they didn't kill him outright, he might be living on borrowed time anyway. How long? Years? Days? Hours?

Jake tamped down on the panic again. It was the sedation messing with his head. If he was going to die, he really didn't want to spend what time he had left tied to a stranger's bed. Gritting his teeth, he began to flex the muscles of his arms and legs, like he was trying to bring circulation back, but he was only trying to get them to work right. He eventually reached the point where he thought he could get up, if his hands weren't tied. He shifted and wiggled as best he could, working his way slowly up the bed, then twisting his lower half off to one side, which crossed his arms over his head but gave him some more slack in one of the tethers. It also meant, with some contortion on his part, he was able to reach his wrist with his teeth.

He wasn't quite as desperate as a coyote chewing his leg off in a trap, but he could certainly work on the fastening holding the restraint closed. Before he got that far he felt a wave of nausea and was sucked into a memory.

A pretty brunette assistant, in a leather bustier style top and heavy makeup, smiled at him and handed him a black plastic bag. "I hope you enjoy them."

It lasted just that tiny flash and Jake was grateful. If Aled had used these cuffs with anyone else, Jake didn't want to see it. He tugged and pulled and gnawed at the restraint until finally he got the strap to come free. Jake breathed a sigh of relief as he got the second one off his other wrist and rolled off the bed. He swayed again, getting his land legs back. A quick look out of the window showed him he was on the second story. He'd probably sprain an ankle — if not break his leg—jumping.

Who was he kidding? He didn't want to jump. He wanted to find those two bastards and beat the shit out of them. He turned and half walked, half stumbled across the room. *Shit.* Maybe he should jump. He felt so weak. As he stumbled again, his hand caught the dresser and he was flooded with bright daylight, and two men setting it down in place.

"You owe me at least a pint for lugging this heavy bitch up here, Lou."

"Yeah, yeah. How about I pay you another way?" Louis grinned, reaching for him and pulling him into a steamy kiss.

Jake shook his head as he came out of the memory. It was so bright and so vivid. Every detail picked out. He was in Louis Cortez's house. Well, the cuffs made sense at least. If Corrie and Aled had been planning this from the beginning, they'd have known the house would be empty too.

Taking a few moments to catch his breath and give himself more time to get his strength back, Jake stood and closed his eyes. Sometimes he could go days without picking up anything. Right now, he couldn't touch a thing without getting some sort of impression from it. This was already getting annoying. Was it the drug making him so sensitive? The drug that supposedly didn't work? How long before he burned? God, he wanted to take those two assholes with him if he had to go. It was a terrible thought, but Jake figured it would be justice at least.

* * * *

Mari had arranged to be picked up at home so that he could fetch his laptop and he was waiting by the front window when the unmarked black Volvo pulled up outside. Consequently, he had the door open by the time young Darren raised a hand to knock. The expression on his face was one of brief startlement as he lowered his hand again.

"Doc…" he began, but Mari touched a finger to his lips to

shush him.

"My mother is resting. I don't want her disturbed," he whispered and the young fellow nodded earnestly. In the hall lights his hair was a dark shade of terracotta, and he reminded Mari of one of his old colleagues at UCL, Harry George. He was surprised to discover that he felt nostalgic for the office camaraderie of his last job.

Mari squirmed into his coat and told him softly, "Wait there, I just need to grab my bag."

He ducked back into the front parlor and retrieved the messenger bag with his laptop and tablet, then checked his phone, just in case. There was still nothing from Jake, and he sighed as he pocketed the slender device.

When he went back out to the front door again, a standoff appeared to be in force between Colquhoun and Tonka. The dog had woken up whilst Mari had been fetching his things and come out to investigate. Unusually, he didn't bark, but maybe it was just that he had picked up Mari's scent and knew he had already vetted the newcomer. Colquhoun was backed up to the door watching the Staffie nervously.

"Is he safe?" he asked as Mari reappeared.

"Depends on whether you're trying to steal his favorite squeaky toy or not. Here, hold that," Mari instructed. He passed the man his laptop bag, then turned to the dog. "Sorry, Tonk, no walkies yet. I'll come back later and take you out, I promise."

Tonka wagged his tail uncertainly, then looked up toward the door again and Mari realized with a pang that he was looking for Jake.

"He's coming back, you soft dog," he murmured, hoping it was true. "He just has something to do. You don't think he'd desert you, do you, mukwa?"

Tonka whined and licked his hand and he crouched down to make a fuss of the unhappy terrier before they left, as quietly as Colquhoun had come.

It was getting late in the evening, but the lights were still burning in Thames House when Mari and his chaperon reached the north embankment. He was expected there, because security flagged them through and Colquhoun shepherded him right up to the seventh floor. The open-plan office was busy, with people still working away or trotting back and forth to the printer. He was shown straight through that area to a smaller room, at the back, where Ashcroft was waiting for him.

"Darren has been collating all the tracking information that we have from Jake's phone, up to the point where the signal was lost, Dr. Gale," Ashcroft told him. "Do you think you can use your...gift to pinpoint the current whereabouts of the device?"

"I can tap into the communications networks," Mari explained as he was extracting his laptop from the messenger bag. "If I have access to a device that's been used to make calls or access the worldwide web, I can plug myself in. It's kind of like an out-of-body experience. From all accounts, it looks eerie to the people left behind, but my physical body isn't dead, just...deactivated. If you're going to watch, it's only fair to warn you."

By his standards, it was a short explanation and Ashcroft nodded as he took this on board. There was nothing rushed or flashy about his attitude. Mari wanted to put a rocket under him and make him hurry up and find Jake, but he bit his tongue and forced himself to be patient.

"If you can get me to a phone that Jake has called, using the bugged mobile to contact you here, I can probably trace back to where his device is at the moment," he said instead.

Looking like a child that was eager to see a magic trick, Ashcroft took his own, rather ancient Nokia, out of his pocket and handed it to Mari.

"Jake has called this phone from the cell with the tracking device installed."

Mari took it, trying to decide if Ashcroft was trusting or desperate. Neither idea gave him much confidence but he laid the phone on the desk between them and laced his fingers, cracking his knuckles, more for effect and to focus his mind than for any practical reasons. He framed the phone with his hands then closed his eyes to shut out unnecessary visual distractions. The sounds from the office outside faded as he touched the index fingers of both hands to the screen and his gift reached out, sensing a new network of pathways to explore.

This was not like looking into Jake's phone at all. That had been a relatively simple task, just a few calls spiraling off from the central hub, mostly to his own cell. Stepping into Ashcroft's call history from this battered, unprepossessing piece of plastic was like walking out of a quiet elevator into the heart of New York's Grand Central Station during the rush hour. There were communication pathways running off in every direction, too many signs to focus on in one glance, messages running back and forth and making him duck and dodge to avoid them, or at least that was how it felt.

He took a quick breath and pulled out, shaking his head to clear it, then stepping back in with a clear image of what he was looking for in his head. It took a while to find the sign for Jake's contact in amongst the rest but once he had it, just like locating the right platform to begin a journey, he was away.

He poured himself into that contact and followed the trail of communication traces it left behind until he reached the phone that had sent them. This was the difficult part. The device itself was dead, he could feel as much, and stepping into a dead phone was something like entering the house of a deceased person. There were shadows and memories but there was no new activity. He could still look out of the windows though, metaphorically speaking. Though he didn't see actual places, he could compare the message stream into this device with others around it and draw clues to its location from there.

When he looked out from Jake's phone, absorbing the metadata from its GPS chip, he was perplexed by what he found. Mari was familiar with the feel of Birthright's offices and he already knew that the device was not there. The location was familiar though. He recalled that he had followed one of the threads back from the chatrooms to this place. But which one?

Slowly, he pulled away, letting himself slide back into his waiting body and testing it by tapping his fingers and flexing his legs a couple of times before he opened his eyes. Try to do that too quickly and it was like letting go of a piece of stretched elastic, as he had found out when he'd first attempted it as a child. The backlash had knocked him out cold and his father had panicked and berated Great-Grandmama Amelia for hours afterwards.

When he focused on the real world, Ashcroft and Colquhoun were both leaning on the desk across from him, staring at him like he'd turned purple.

"Well...that was interesting," he said, testing his tongue, which still felt numb in his mouth at first.

"I'll say," Colquhoun enthused, not quite under his breath.

Ashcroft was smiling. "Do you know where he is, Dr. Gale?"

Mari cleared his throat. "Not exactly. But he's... somewhere connected to a member of Birthright that I've checked out recently. The ISP traces feel very familiar. I just need to figure out when I've come across them before, then we can work out where it is."

Ashcroft reached over and shuffled a few folders, pulling one out of the stack, opening it, and handing a sheaf of papers across the table to Mari. "Here is a print out of addresses belonging to Birthright members that we have on file. I don't suppose that will help you much but I have it on a spreadsheet on the computer too. What can we do to help?"

"I need somewhere quiet to work. And I need to hook my laptop up to your Wi-Fi." Mari tapped a finger on the lid of the machine in question. "I can get back to myself from there. It's like laying down string to follow when you take a blind path," he told the still bewildered looking Colquhoun. "When I go back to it from the same machine the traces are still there. I already followed everyone in the chatrooms to see if they talked to people who knew more about what was happening with the incendiary cases. And I followed the traces of the people that burned too. They were dead of course, but they leave…smoke trails I guess is the only way to put it, like the contrails a plane leaves in the sky when it flies over. They don't last for very long but they're there."

"Are you certain you can't use one of our machines?" Ashcroft asked, even as he snagged a pen and scribbled down the Wi-Fi password.

"I potentially could, yes, but it would take a lot longer than just using mine. The trails are already there. I would have to retrace my steps using another machine."

"Understood," Ashcroft said, passing him the sticky note with the code on it. "You can use my office. If you need anything, Darren can get it for you. Please notify him the moment you pinpoint Jake's location. He can get things moving right away."

It always felt odd to surf with an audience of strangers but Mari was able to shut them out once he plunged back into the web of communications again. When he did this he could almost understand what came over Tonka when he was chasing scents around the park, following one trail then stopping when a more interesting smell crossed the track that he was sniffing out. It was not an emotion-based gift like Jake's, he got no senses or feelings from his threads, just the typed — or occasionally spoken — word messages and comments flying back and forth across the vast network that covered most of the civilized planet.

Interfacing this way was not a fast process, more like sorting strands of embroidery silk, picking out the strands that matched with the color he was weaving, putting some aside and others together. Mari knew the shade and thickness of the strand he was after, so it was just a question of going back through the chats he had monitored initially to match it with the one he half remembered.

He had been pinging back and forth from thread to thread, poster to poster, for about an hour when he hit on it, and came back up with such a rush that it made his nose bleed. His heart was thumping violently. As he blinked his eyes open he found Colquhoun peering at him with concern, holding out a handkerchief, and he took it with a grateful smile.

"What happened? Is that what having an Elemental gift does? Melt your brain?" the MI5 officer gasped.

"If you overindulge any kind of habit, it melts your brain, eventually," Mari told him, his words muffled by the hanky pressed to his nostrils. "I think I have the link. Can you find out where Louis Cortez lived?"

"I can do better than that, I can tell you," the young man replied. "It was a place up in Chiswick. He inherited it from an elderly relative. We checked it out after he went up in smoke but we didn't find anything out of the ordinary. Well, at least, not out of the ordinary in a way that would explain him burning up."

"I think that Corrie is using his house as a bolt hole," Mari told him, feeling giddy from the prolonged interface and the thrill of the chase. He pressed the hanky to his nose again and drew it away to examine the scarlet bloom it contained, his mind still whirling. "That's where Jake's phone is."

Let's hope that's where he is too.

Chapter Eighteen

Jake walked as steadily as he could to the bedroom door, still trying to shake off the effects of whatever they'd doped him with and doing his best to keep his rolling stomach from heaving. That would be perfect. Instead of punching him in the face he could just puke on Aled's shoes. Then he would punch him in the face. And then he was going to beat Roy Corrie until he quit seeing red.

Jake grasped the door handle, half expecting it to be locked, but it wasn't. They must have figured between the dope and the wrist shackles he wouldn't be able to get up and roam around. He touched the handle and it was suddenly lighter in the room again.

He was looking down at his own unconscious body and the dark hand wrapped around his cock, stroking him fast and hard. The results came fairly quickly, jetting out through the fine catheter tube that had been inserted into him while he was blissfully unconscious, into a plastic container. Aled detached the bottle then capped it quickly and leaned back for a moment, adjusting the impressive boner in his pants. He lifted the nitrile-gloved hand that had just been stroking Jake up to his face and inhaled deeply.

The memory was gone and he was standing alone in the room. He squeezed his eyes shut and breathed deeply, willing himself not to be sick. *Not his type? Fucking right. Sick fucking bastard.* Jake wanted to kill him, kill them both. He had just about reached to yank the door open when he stopped himself from moving again and took another deep breath.

He had a right to be angry, but that didn't mean he should be. Not at the moment. That wasn't just talking sense into himself, either. Since his teens, he had been able to keep that red rage under control. He literally should not be angry. This rage in him felt wrong, like it didn't belong. He was sweating again, as if he had a fever. Even the thought that he might be getting ready to burn up didn't really quell the fury inside.

It took everything he had to open the door slowly and look into the narrow hallway with caution, rather than charging out like a bull. It was empty and dark, but there was light coming from the stairwell and he could hear voices, low and heated, in discussion.

"I'm not going down for this, Roy," Aled hissed.

"You won't, we weren't followed."

"That doesn't mean we can't be found. I'm getting on that plane in an hour."

"I need more than an hour to fertilize and implant Milda's eggs. Leaving him tied up here makes no difference."

Jake paused as his stomach quivered and acid came up the back of his throat. They had most likely sentenced him to an excruciating death and for what? He stood at the top of the stairs and shook his arms, flexed his fingers, trying to will strength back into his body.

The stairs looked old and creaky — there was probably no way he was going to come down unnoticed. Better to rush them than try for stealth. He should've armed himself with some kind of weapon, but he was afraid to touch anything. The slightest brush was flooding him with memories and he couldn't afford to be lost in one here. He had to make his move before they decided to check on him.

Jake ran down the stairs two and three at a time, hitting the floor as Corrie and Aled jumped up from their seats. Without even pausing, he cocked his arm back and slammed his fist into Corrie's jaw. It lacked some of his usual power but it connected and it rocked his head back. Unfortunately, it also threw Jake spinning into a memory.

I can't get you any more. They are already poking around, a man told him, sitting next to him on a park bench. He was *youngish, maybe around Jake's own age, give or take a few years. He looked vaguely familiar, Jake thought. Pale and thin, with reddish hair.*

"You are in this up to your teeth like it or not!" Corrie snapped. "Don't try and back out now."

"Roy, those people died."

"They knew the risks. We miscalculated, but we found the flaw in the formula. EQ10 will be the one that works!"

Jake fell back as he was literally knocked into the present. He had a face. No name, but he had a face. He knew Corrie's rat in MI5.

His abductor was sprawled on the floor clutching his nose and cursing incoherently. As Jake went for him again, a strong hand grabbed him by the hair and jerked his head back, stopping him in his tracks.

"Not so fast!" Aled warned him. "Don't want you getting too excited, do we? Anything could happen."

Jake's training kicked in automatically. He didn't try to pull away, instead he pushed toward Aled, at the same time he kicked out, popping him in the kneecap, which got him released. If he had been at full strength and speed he would have jumped to his feet and followed up with a few jabs, but he just barely made it up as Aled cursed and fell back. Jake nearly fell again, too. The room was doing spins. He barked his shins on an end table and knocked over a lamp, and the second he touched it he was seeing Louis, sitting with another man, drinking a beer and laughing with him.

The room tilted again, and he could still see the memory, but almost like it was overlaid on the present view. Like a double image. That had certainly never happened before.

He had to escape, he was in no shape to fight. He should have jumped out of the window upstairs when he'd had the chance.

"Stop him!" Roy yelled, still parked on his ass and clutching his nose.

Jake veered towards a doorway that, bizarrely he knew — from the brief moment of flashback — led to the kitchen.

There was a door there. A door that led outside.

"You fucking stop him!" Aled was hopping around clutching his knee, but already moving toward him again.

Jake stumbled for the door and almost dropped through it, then turned and slammed it shut with his shoulder, looking for something to put in front of it. A small bookcase stood against the wall and he grabbed it, spilling contents across the floor and towing it across to wedge behind the door, fighting another of Louis' flashbacks to moving day as he did so.

Bare-assed and spread-eagled against this very bookcase, in the middle of the room, surrounded by moving day boxes, gripping the edges as someone else thrashed his bare behind with a belt. Hard and aching for release, lips parted around a cry for more.

Jake let go and maneuvered it the rest of the way with his elbows and knees. The shelf unit was just high enough to slide under the handle, which thankfully was the lever kind. Moments later that handle rattled against the top of it, to no avail, while Jake was catching his breath. That ought to slow them down at least.

The door frame shuddered as Aled began to throw his weight against it. Beyond the quivering door, he could hear Corrie shouting orders, his voice getting further and further away.

Jake was torn between the desire to escape and the logic that told him he wasn't familiar with the lay of the land outside, or whether he'd be able to get away before they broke down the door or came at him from another direction. Calling for help might make more sense. He looked around the kitchen area for a phone and spotted his mobile on the counter top, disassembled. He didn't see another.

Maybe he could make it to a neighbor's house? He hated the idea of that. So far Aled and Corrie weren't trying to kill him, directly, but he wasn't sure if that would hold true and he didn't want to put anyone else at risk. If he could take more than three steps without falling into someone's memories, that would be a big help.

He was still deciding what to do when the bottom windowpane on the door leading outside shattered. There was a large, heavy, wooden cutting board on the counter and he grabbed it, as the nearest thing to hand, trying to ignore the thankfully innocuous vision of scraping chopped vegetables into a steaming pot.

By the time he was back in the present, Corrie was standing just inside the open door, his arms held out loosely at his sides, his face twisted into a grim mask. Behind Jake the woodwork around the latch began to splinter under the pressure of Aled continually throwing himself against the door. The bookcase squealed a protest as it was pushed forward across the kitchen floor.

"You're in a lot of trouble, Corrie. Don't make it any worse."

"Only if they catch me!" Corrie snarled.

"You burned out whatever ability you had, Corrie. Accept it. No drug is going to bring it back."

Jake clutched the handle on the cutting board, shifting sideways as he spoke, trying to get room to maneuver. The kitchen was almost as tiny as his own and there was nowhere to go. One or the other of them, he might have been able to handle, even in his current state, but if they both got him cornered it was going to be a very short fight.

As Aled came crashing through the kitchen door, Corrie rushed him. Jake brought his arm up, the one still holding the cutting board, and hit Corrie. Aled came at him from the other side and grabbed him. Jake brought the board back around trying to smack Aled, glancing it off his head, but he was slow and weak. He still felt like he was moving through syrup. Aled ripped his makeshift weapon out of his hand with an angry snarl. Even in such a tight space Jake took some satisfaction from noting he was limping and bleeding too, and he didn't waste the advantage. When Aled grabbed for him again, Jake bent and charged back, taking him in the midsection and aiming another kick to his injured knee. Aled howled with pain and fell, but he still had a hold on Jake and took him down, as well.

Jake had time to think that this was not good. No, this was bad, very bad. He couldn't let himself be pinned. He was good at grappling and wrestling, but Aled was taller, probably matched him for weight, and had all his strength. Desperate, Jake got an arm up to punch him but before he got the momentum going, some hard object smacked into the back of his head and left him seeing flashing red and black stars.

"Hold him!" Corrie snarled.

Aled rolled him hard onto his back, straddled him and held him down. Aled's face was a grimace of pain and rage and he gave Jake a quick jab with his fist. Corrie got in the mix, helping to hold Jake down while he pulled a syringe out of his jacket pocket and got the needle uncapped. One of the dancing red stars in Jake's vision settled on the side of Corrie's vein-bulging forehead, near his temple. Jake blinked at it but it only quivered very slightly, not leaping and spinning like the rest.

He blinked again.

"Police! Put your hands up and come out of the building!" a metallic-sounding voice boomed.

Jake didn't think he'd ever been so relieved to hear those words, but he didn't for a second believe either of them were going to listen. Corrie's eyes were so wide and enraged Jake thought they literally might pop out of his skull and he brought the arm holding the syringe down in a stabbing motion.

The shot was deafening in the confines of the house. Blood spattered his face and those buggy eyes looked shocked.

Aled pushed both arms automatically into the air above his head, as the kitchen door was kicked inward and an anonymous figure in a dark flak jacket and visored helmet strode into the room. Without a word, he dragged Aled off Jake and threw him face down on the floor.

The small room was suddenly swarming with armed cops and Aled was in handcuffs. Corrie looked beyond restraints, still sprawled in a spreading pool of his own blood. People in helmets and visors and Kevlar vests were in and out of the house, their footsteps audible in the rooms upstairs as they checked the scene was clear. Someone called from upstairs, "Perps contained, situation under control. Stand down. Stand down."

Then he recognized Officer Vallance, entering through the kitchen doorway, with a more familiar figure on her heels. Mari threw himself into the house, as frantic as Tonka hearing the 'w' word. He dropped to his knees on the kitchen floor and flung his arms around Jake.

"Oh, my days! You're alive. I was so worried!"

Jake sat up, still with his hands raised to the base of his skull as an instinctive precaution, but he was afraid if he tried to move any more than that he was going to vomit. His head hurt from front to back, and that concerned him almost as much as the knowledge that he might very well be a ticking time bomb. He put his arms around Mari and squeezed him, burying his face at the side of his throat and inhaling deeply. He had been so afraid he might never get to do that again. After a few moments in which he allowed himself to clutch Mari tight, he felt he had to at least try to get to his feet.

"Help me up," he told Mari, still clinging to him.

Gasping as if he'd run a marathon to reach Jake's side, Mari crouched to give Jake his arm and began drawing him upright. A guy in the green scrubs of a paramedic joined them on Jake's other side and having checked for Corrie's pulse and shaken his head, he turned his attention to the walking wounded.

"Are you all right, mate? You weren't hit?" he asked, and Jake was conscious of the fact that he was still covered in blood. No wonder Mari was so panic-stricken.

"I wasn't shot, no," Jake told him calmly. He should probably mention his head, but really, even if he had a concussion, he didn't want to spend hours at a hospital when they might be the only hours he had left.

That was such a sobering thought he wasn't sure what to do. He'd been on the other side of the uniform enough times to recognize the symptoms of shock, but understanding the reaction didn't make it any easier to deal with.

"I need to get out of here," he said, to no one in particular.

"Chivis, are you all right?" Ashcroft suddenly appeared from the throng.

Jake wasn't sure if he was all right. He should probably lie and say he was fine.

"I need to get out of here," he repeated, his fingers tightening around Mari's arm.

"It's okay," Mari kept saying soothingly, his hand warm and surprisingly steady over Jake's. "It's okay, you're going to be okay. He just needs some air, Officer Ashcroft. I'm going to take him through into the yard."

"We need to talk to you, Chivis. Don't go anywhere." Ashcroft spotted the constituent parts of the tracking phone they had given him on the kitchen counter and headed toward them with a grunt of disapproval. His redheaded assistant was already examining the pieces carefully, wearing latex gloves.

Jake stopped dead and grabbed his arm. The young man looked up, startled, and both Mari and Ashcroft stared at him as well. Jake started to say something and was yanked into a memory.

"Nice dog, good boy. Just stay right there, okay?" He was looking down at Tonka and the chunky terrier stared back at him in silence.

Jake shook it off, tried to speak and stopped. He squinted hard at the man, who was looking at him like he was worried he might be unbalanced. Jake was unbalanced, but not enough to make a mistake. The hair, skin and coloring were both right but this guy had an open, boyish earnestness to his face that was all wrong.

Jake let him go and looked at Ashcroft.

"I need to talk to you. Outside."

He let Mari lead him out of the door and down the short

path toward the front of the house and the street, grateful for the cool night air on his face.

"You saw something when you touched him," Mari said, but it was not a question.

"Yes," Jake confirmed, turning to look at Ashcroft as the older man stopped beside them. "You have a spy, Officer Ashcroft. Someone told Corrie who I was and who I was working for."

"Are you sure?" Ashcroft looked concerned but calm. "They didn't pick up on something you did? Corrie was excessively paranoid."

"No, they were told," Jake said. "They knew my name, and I saw it, when Corrie touched me. I saw what the man who told him about me looks like. I thought that kid in the house was him, for a second."

"You certainly freaked him out, grabbing him like that," Mari said. "But from a personal viewpoint, I trust Darren. Tonka trusts him too, which sways my opinion, I have to admit. He didn't growl at him, in any case."

"Darren has worked with us since leaving school. I trust him implicitly, or I wouldn't have let him look after Dr. Gale," Ashcroft emphasized. A small frown creased his forehead. "He did have a brother who worked in the scientific bureau. I don't know Brent as well, we've only met once, but they do look alike."

"If you get me a picture I can probably say for sure. He's also the one that's been supplying them with the chemicals to make the drugs they've been testing," Jake told him.

Ashcroft's eyes widened. "Are you sure? I've heard psychometry is often subjective, that you only get suggestions, not clear pictures."

"I do. Crystal clear. Ask DI Cordiline from the Albany Street division of the Met if you don't believe me. I can identify a suspect from the memory I received," Jake said. "Get me the picture. That's all I can do for you. I need to go home."

"You can't leave yet, Chivis. I'm going to need a statement

about what happened."

Jake stared hard at him and tried to ignore the pounding in his head, but the fresh air was doing him some good.

"Sometime between my first meeting with Aled and him calling me earlier today, someone in your employ told them I was working with you. Corrie and Mustatti decided they were out of time to find another Fire Elemental to use as a test subject and their chemical supplier had gotten cold feet. They drugged my drink. When I woke up I was upstairs." He pointed up toward the second floor of the building. "Mustatti told me while I was unconscious they had injected me with their latest chemical cocktail."

Jake could feel Mari tense beside him and heard his sharp intake of breath. He put an arm across his back and squeezed his shoulder just once. Jake had not wanted to break it to him like this but Ashcroft needed to be appraised of the full situation and he just wanted to get away from here as soon as he could.

"If you believe that there's a chance you might..." Ashcroft closed his mouth on the rest of that sentence, then a moment later he added, "It would be irresponsible of me to let you loose under the circumstances."

Jake opened his mouth, prepared to let rip, but Mari's hand covered his lips gently, a cool presence on his hot skin.

"I'm still an agent working under the control of MI5. If I stay with him, then you haven't let him loose, have you?" he said reasonably. "I will make sure he doesn't go anywhere that people might be endangered. Is that acceptable?"

Ashcroft hesitated. "I'm sorry, I can't just let you walk, you understand. Until we can be sure that you're not going to suffer any side effects, we can't let you out of our sight. I will do my best to ensure you are comfortable and have some privacy, though."

Ashcroft seemed on the verge of saying something more, then he just cleared his throat, turned and went back toward the house. Jake faced Mari now but he couldn't meet his eyes.

"I'm sorry…I didn't want to tell you like that."

"Shhh," Mari whispered, cupping his chin in the tips of his fingers and leaning in to kiss him softly on the lips. "From the moment you didn't call me, I expected worse, Chivis. This is a blessing, trust me." He ran his hands down Jake's arms and took both his hands. "Let's go for a walk, hmm? Cool you down."

"Cool me…" Jake looked down at himself. He was wearing a torn, lightweight, summer sweater, no jacket, and Mari had a coat on, so had Ashcroft. He had seen traces of their breath when they'd both exhaled, but he didn't feel cold at all. He dragged his eyes back up this time, looking at Mari, then he wished he hadn't. The pain and the worry he saw in those pretty blue eyes just about broke his heart.

"Yeah, we should probably stay outside," he conceded. "Just in case."

"C'mon." Mari pushed an arm through his and towed him away from the scenes of organized chaos behind them. "I need to keep you alive so that you can identify the mole, right?"

Jake didn't even care anymore, which was ironic since he'd risked his life for the information. He was still unsteady on his feet and his hand throbbed, among other smaller annoying aches and pains. His headache was receding in the cooler air, though. They walked around the block, conscious all the time that they were being tailed and watched by Ashcroft's people.

"Do you think they'd let us go to the park?" he suggested.

"Probably not. Anyway, there are probably muggers and dossers and all sorts around there at this time of night," Mari pointed out, linking arms and pulling him closer as they walked.

"I didn't get any memories from you, when you touched me," Jake said, as he suddenly realized the fact.

"I thought you said you didn't, generally, after you've been around someone for a while?"

"Not usually, no, but…I've been picking up memories

since I woke up…from everything. Literally, every damn thing. The bed, the dresser, the door handle, punching that fucker in the face, a lamp…everything. It hasn't stopped." Jake cut himself off as he heard the sudden fear in his own voice.

"Shhh." Mari touched his lips again, with his fingers first, then his mouth. As they parted he whispered, "It will be okay. I wouldn't say it if I didn't believe it, Jake. It's why they were giving Elementals the drug, to enhance what they could already do. If they got it right this time it makes sense that you're seeing more, feeling more."

He stopped and slipped his arms around Jake's neck, just standing close to him, holding him, their bodies rocking together in the darkness, like a slow dance to music only Mari could hear.

"Promise me something, Mari…" Jake started to ask but Mari shushed him again, and kissed him, and when Jake tried to speak he put a finger to his lips. But this was important, so Jake took both Mari's hands in his own. "Please, Mari, you have to…"

"I don't have to anything. Nothing is going to happen to you, Jake. You mustn't say it. You will be okay." His gaze was quiet and earnest, as if he was willing himself to believe it as much as Jake.

"You don't know that. And if it does, if I start to…to act weird, or something, I want you to get back from me. Don't try and stop it or…or put me out, or anything like that. Just get back where you'll be safe. Please."

"Chivis, hush." Mari shook his head, his expression indescribably sad but his tone not cowed. "You are not going to burst into flames. And if you do…well, I'll stand where I damned well want to. You hear me?"

Jake wanted to argue with him, force a promise from him that he'd keep himself safe, but he knew it was useless and only a waste of time. He had never really been concerned with or afraid of death, and he wasn't so much tonight. Only…he knew that, if he died, he would lose Mari and he couldn't think of anything worse right at that moment.

He wrapped his arms around his lover and crushed him closer, putting his face into the crook of Mari's shoulder. It had been years and years since he'd cried over anything but he could feel his throat tightening up at the very thought of how monumentally he'd screwed everything up. He had been too cocky, too confident that he was smarter than Corrie. And he might pay the price for that, and leave Mari alone and grieving in the process.

He couldn't speak around the lump in his throat, and he didn't want to let Mari go. His shoulders shuddered, and a tear or two squeezed their way out from under his tightly closed lids.

Mari held him close, refusing to pull away, refusing to let go, to be safe, to be anything other than near to him. He steered Jake firmly toward a bench in a nearby bus shelter and drew him down to sit beside him in the darkness. The sounds of London carried on around them, muted, in the background, the honk of car horns and the low rumble and rattle of the underground trains where they passed beneath nearby vents, the sound of music from a distant bar, the closer commotion of Ashcroft's people locking down the crime scene behind them, a mish mash of voices and vehicles and laughter and life going on in the background.

"What will be, will be," Mari told him soothingly over all of that. "Listen to me, Chivis. You are an astonishing human being. In the impossibly short time that I've been with you, you have done things and shown me things that I never imagined. And I can never hope to be as wonderful as you, but one thing I understand. If anyone can overcome this drug and make the best of it, then you can. And I won't let you fight it on your own."

And so they sat together, arms around each other, and they waited. Anxiously at first, but Jake could only be anxious so long before his brain tried to distract him with other things. At one point, he started to doze. He wasn't deep enough to dream, but this all felt dream-like anyway.

If he was fully awake and aware he certainly wouldn't have murmured, "I love you, Mari," before he slipped down on the bench and put his head in Mari's lap.

When he opened his eyes again, he didn't have a clue how long he'd slept, but some hours must have passed because the sky was getting light through the trees across the road. There was a black Volvo saloon parked opposite their shelter. The two men sitting in it were watching them. He felt every ache when he sat up, but he didn't feel the disorientation or the exhaustion tugging at his mind any more. Beside him, Mari was slumped with his eyes closed and his head tilted forward at an uncomfortable-looking angle, chin on his chest. Jake shivered in the cool pre-morning air and wondered if that was a good sign. Surely the fact that he was still here was a good sign. How long did it take before he knew for sure if he was in the clear? He didn't feel any different.

"Mari," he whispered, leaning in and kissing his cheek. "Mari, wake up."

Mari leaned back and rolled his head, groaning. He blinked several times, then seemed to realize where he was and cursed under his breath.

"All my fucking days…! Please don't tell me I just spent the night in a bus shelter. I can't feel my legs!" He reached out though, stroking his fingers through Jake's dew-damp hair, his expression softening and filling with wonder. "You're still here. And you're all wet, that must be a good thing, right?"

"I guess so," Jake said. "I've no idea how long it's supposed to take before I'll know if I'm in the clear, or…if I ever will be." And wasn't that a disquieting thought first thing in the morning? He reached up and touched Mari's face, then nodded toward the Volvo across the road. "We should let them do what they need to do, I guess."

"Well, I can't speak for you, but I hope they let us have a shower and get changed before those Security Service boys start to grill you again." Mari pointed a warning finger at

Jake. "Next time I tell you that something is a bad idea, you better listen to me, Mr. Chivis."

Jake bit the tip of Mari's finger lightly but he didn't argue.

Chapter Nineteen

The waiting servicemen did not take them to Thames House but drove around the North Circular then headed west of London, up the M40 motorway, out into the countryside. The ride was a quiet one. Mari slept again but Jake could not close his eyes—he watched everything, reading signs for places he'd never heard of. Little more than an hour later the car pulled up on the driveway of a large house on the outskirts of Oxford. They were welcomed and shown to a comfortable guest bedroom with an en suite bathroom. There was a message from Ashcroft asking them to come down and speak to him as soon as they were ready.

Jake decided 'as soon as he was ready' would be after he'd joined Mari in the shower and most certainly after they'd had breakfast. He slipped into the steamed-up shower cubicle. It barely had enough room for the two of them but that was okay.

"You know, I think sleeping on a bench in a bus shelter just to keep me company qualifies you for the Awesome Boyfriend of the Year Award," Jake told him, nuzzling the sodden hair that curled at the back of Mari's neck.

"Oh, yeah?" Mari turned his head so that he could brush his wet lips against Jake's. His long, lean body fit nicely into the curves and contours of Jake's within the snug confines of their four glass and tile walls. "What does this award entail, exactly?"

"Umm…how about breakfast? If we can get breakfast. And after that, whatever you want to do today…er, after I speak with Ashcroft. And if they're prepared to let us wander around."

"Oh…we-ell that should leave us…about thirty-five minutes," Mari teased. "I'm sure I can think of something that could keep us entertained for that long."

Jake laughed, still running soapy hands over Mari's naked back and ass. "Where do you think we are?"

"Not sure," his lover replied, leaning back into his touch. "I thought they were taking us to Bletchley Park when we came off the motorway, but that's not a private residence any more. It's not a hotel, either, as far as I could see when we pulled in. Must be top secret! How do you feel about making love in a shower that's potentially bugged?"

Mari turned in his arms and winked. Jake kissed him, running his hands down his long, sleek back and over his firm cheeks but as Mari pressed closer to him he suddenly remembered Aled touching him, waking up feeling sticky and realizing what had been done to him while he couldn't stop it from happening. He broke the kiss off.

"Hold that thought. I need to get soaped up first."

"Oooh…nice!" Mari chuckled, reaching for the shower gel. "Can I help?"

He had a palmful of golden gloop before Jake could object and reached out, running it up and down his chest and belly. Jake had to admit, if anyone could erase the feel of Aled's touch it was Mari, and it seemed fitting. This was who he wanted to be with. This was who he wanted touching him. He leaned in to kiss Mari again as his soapy hands caressed him.

"Stay with me today, when I talk to Ashcroft. I don't want to be apart from you."

"I doubt he would approve of me tagging along," Mari observed, leaning in to kiss a slow, warm line from the lobe of his ear down to his collarbone.

"I don't care. I want you there," Jake said, squeezing Mari tight. Mari held on to him just as tightly and for several moments they remained locked together like that, under the cascade from the shower rose, letting the water sluice over them. When they finally did pull apart again, Mari smiled at him and they shared a wet kiss before turning the water off.

"As long as Ashcroft doesn't kick me out, I'll be there," Mari told him as they toweled off and got dressed.

* * * *

Ashcroft met with them in a downstairs office where he was busily typing while talking on the phone. He waved them in toward a couple of chairs and ended the call abruptly. "Have a seat, please. I'd like to go over the details, Jake, from the time you met with Mustatti forward, as best you can recall."

Jake sat and folded his hands, resting his forearms on his knees. This could take a while—he might as well get comfortable. Mari settled on the chair beside him and Jake felt one of his hands touch his shoulder before Mari put them both in his lap.

"Mustatti picked me up around noon," Jake began. "I didn't get any sense from him that he knew who I was. He kept our conversation to Birthright's plans, and their projects to increase Elemental job positions and usefulness in certain fields. Corrie was hostile, though, when he finally met with me. Not antagonistic exactly, but condescending. He asked about where I was from, what I did for a living and my sexual orientation. His attitude had me a little nervous but I thought he was just full of himself. They didn't talk about the drug or anything experimental, just the same line of rhetoric about advancing Elementals in society, until I started to feel the effects of whatever drug they gave me. I had no indication they knew who I was until after I woke up."

"At that point, what happened?"

"When I came round? Almost right away, I was pulled into a memory of Corrie telling Mustatti who I was, and something about having to lay low until the surrogate delivered. When I came out of it Mustatti called me by my real name and confirmed he knew I was working with MI5."

That was glossing over quite a bit, but Jake was not about to tell him what else Aled had done. As far as he was concerned, no one needed to know that.

"And then?"

The words were very soft and neutral, and Jake looked at him closely for a moment, but couldn't tell if Ashcroft knew he was leaving things out or not.

"I struggled to get up," he continued, "and when I touched Mustatti I got another memory. I saw Corrie inject me with something and then tell Mustatti the EQ10 was in my system. When I came out of that memory, Mustatti injected me with something that put me out again. Later, after I woke from that, I was alone, and I managed to escape from the room where they were holding me. I overheard Mustatti and Corrie making plans to get on a plane, though, I didn't hear where they were planning on running to. Corrie talked about needing time to implant fertilized eggs."

Now Jake saw Ashcroft glance at Mari, who said, "That ties in with what we know about Corrie's work history. He was employed by an IVF clinic. He would know about such things."

Jake shuddered at the memory of Aled's hands on him again, but pushed the thought away. "I ran down the stairs and fought with them, and got another memory. This one of Corrie talking to a man I thought I recognized, about the chemicals needed to make EQ10, and how he thought this new formula would be the one to work. At that point, I realized I had underestimated how much the sedative was still affecting me and retreated to the kitchen where I tried to escape. That was just about the point your men arrived."

Ashcroft gave him a very direct look for a long moment, then said, "From what data we've uncovered and evidence we've found so far it seems their next step was to see if they could make viable offspring from Elementals that had been given the enhancement drug. If you hadn't stopped them…"

Jake held up a hand. "I didn't stop them. They found out who I was, that's the only thing that stopped them."

"Yes, well. Be that as it may, they were stopped," Ashcroft said diplomatically. "Roy Corrie is dead. Aled Mustatti will face charges. At this point, we are still unsure if any other members of Birthright knew the full extent of the willful endangerment those two created, among other charges."

"And the EQ10?" Jake asked.

"Mustatti claims the formula was so volatile it had a shelf life of only a few days. They gave you the only dose they had, in part because they were sure they wouldn't be able to find another Fire Elemental before the drug was no longer viable. We don't believe him, of course, but so far we haven't been able to locate further samples in any of their homes or offices, so he may actually be telling the truth."

And if they did find any, Jake doubted Ashcroft would tell them about it, anyway.

"Why Fire Elementals? Why didn't they give the drug to other types of Elementals?" Mari asked.

"Their files indicate they did, at the start. The only conspicuous results they observed were in Fire Elementals though, for whatever reason. That was apparently as unclear to them as it is to us right now."

Jake closed his eyes for a second, then opened them again. "You're going to study their research?"

Ashcroft stared back at him without flinching. "Of course. We need to know what they did, how they accomplished it, in order to prevent it from getting into the wrong hands. You of all people should understand this, Chivis. If they could make this drug, there is the potential for others to make it, as well. And if that happens, I think we can all agree it would be better to have some kind of counteractive cure already on hand."

The reminder that he still might not be in the clear was enough to keep Jake quiet. Even now he could feel the sheen of sweat at the nape of his neck and how uncomfortably warm and close the room seemed, although no one else seemed bothered by it.

"Are you all right, Chivis?" Ashcroft asked, when he wiped a hand across his sweat-jeweled forehead for the second time. "Would you like to stop? Take some water?"

"Let's just get this done with," Jake said.

"Very well." Ashcroft produced an A4 cardboard wallet with some photographs in it, and laid them out in front of him. "I'd like you to take a look at these and see if any of the men in these photos match the supplier you witnessed in Corrie's memory."

The images were mostly taken from CCTV footage but some, Jake was sure, were ID photos and police mugshots. He studied them carefully even though he knew which one the man on the bench had been the moment he set eyes on him.

"Can you indicate the man you saw in your vision, Chivis?" Ashcroft asked.

Jake took a breath and tapped one of the prints decisively. "It was him."

"You're sure? One hundred percent sure?" Ashcroft pressed.

Jake nodded. "I told you. I was sitting right beside him, close enough to count the freckles on his face. It was him."

"Okay." Ashcroft put back all the photos apart from the one Jake had selected. "I think we're done here. Thank you, Jake. We will keep you under surveillance for a few days, to be safe. If you have any other side effects from the drug, please do notify one of our people as soon as possible."

Jake and Mari both stood, but Ashcroft wasn't done. "Would you mind staying behind a moment, Dr. Gale? I have something else I'd like to discuss with you."

Mari looked surprised and glanced at him, but Jake simply nodded then gave Mari a small smile. He let his hand brush Mari's as he left the room. That earned him an anxious smile in return.

Once the door was closed, Ashcroft took a seat across the table from Mari and invited him to sit again, viewing him over his steepled fingers.

"Dr. Gale, I want to thank you for your assistance in this investigation. Your intervention most probably saved your...partner's life," he said, and there was a hint of a question in the word 'partner'.

Mari nodded, but that had not been a question so he held his tongue for the moment. In his opinion, he had done what had needed to be done to find Jake. He would do it again, and again if necessary.

"Will he be all right?" he asked at last, when Ashcroft didn't speak either, for a moment, but just studied him. "Jake, I mean?"

"Time will tell," Ashcroft said, refusing to cushion the response. "We have full medical staff on hand here to monitor him. We will do everything in our power to ensure he does not follow the same route as the other victims. As you yourself pointed out, all of their other test subjects had various issues with health, mental and emotional stability and substance abuse. Jake seems to have learned to control the more volatile aspects of his Elemental inheritance, and he was not given the same formula as the others. There is hope yet that he might not go as they did. In the meantime, if we find a way to counteract what was done to him we will make that available."

"You're using him as a lab rat?"

"No, Dr. Gale. But it would be remiss of us not to monitor him at the very least," Ashcroft said, with a dry smile.

"So this is your laboratory? Very nice," Mari said, never taking his eyes off Ashcroft.

"It serves its purpose," Ashcroft agreed.

"Was the snake in the grass Darren's brother?" Mari asked him, switching the subject because he knew he would get angry if they continued to argue about the ethics of what had happened to Jake.

"You're aware I'm not at liberty to tell you that, Dr. Gale."

Ashcroft smiled again though, like a kindly priest. Mari doubted that his thoughts were in any way Christian.

"Will Darren lose his job if it is?"

"I didn't invite you here to discuss Darren Colquhoun," Ashcroft neatly diverted him. "I understand, from my sources across the river, that they are in negotiation to acquire your services. Have you made a decision yet, Dr. Gale?"

Mari blinked at him. He supposed it should not come as a surprise that the two branches of the Security Service were watching one another but it did give him pause that Ashcroft was aware of his job offer.

"I...ah... Um... No," he said, kicking himself. Could he possibly have sounded any less articulate? "I was going to tell them this week, but I was...distracted."

"Is that 'no' you haven't decided? Or you have decided and the answer is 'no'?" Ashcroft prompted, sitting back in his chair and folding his arms. He watched Mari with shrewd eyes and he felt suddenly like a child again.

"I...um... I was going to tell them, 'no'," he said, in a smaller voice. "I understand that it's...it's an honor to be asked. And I understand what they are offering, but... I don't need it."

"Good," Ashcroft said, taking him by surprise.

"Good?"

"Absolutely." The fellow beamed at him. "Do I take it, from your response, that this means you are still in search of some form of gainful employment?"

"Well... I suppose so," Mari conceded. In truth, he'd not given it much thought. During the past week, he'd had to come to terms with the fact that he had a boyfriend, whom he'd still not properly assured of his feelings, and he'd also become the owner of a substantial property in Fitzrovia. In addition to that, he was driven to distraction by the idea that said boyfriend might burst into flames at the slightest provocation. "I still have to pay the bills, I guess. And... well...yes."

"Am I entitled to know why you plan to turn down my friends across the river?" Ashcroft asked him.

Mari heaved a sigh. "This is going to sound strange. I do need money, a lot of money. My mother has a drug-resistant form of myeloma. She isn't convinced of that, though. And the new drug trials she wants to access cost a lot of money. MI6 were willing to offer me a serious remuneration package, but they want me to travel all over the world at the drop of a hat, and I need to be here in London while she isn't well. All in all, it just felt…wrong. And I've been shoehorned into both of the jobs I did since finishing at Cambridge. They weren't really my choice. And they weren't really a fit for me. I haven't been happy. I want to do something that feels right."

Ashcroft nodded. "That makes sense. But you also need to work to your strengths. How do you feel about the idea of working for Homeland Security? You wouldn't be a spy so much as an information officer. Your talent for collating info-streams is impressive. And you would be working with Darren and his team. You and he operate well together already. He's told me how keen he is to work alongside you."

Mari opened his mouth, then closed it again, thinking fast. "Is this a permanent contract?"

"Subject to a trial period, like most positions, but yes, it could well be a permanent thing. We might not be able to match MI6 for perks and I doubt we have the budget to send you jetting off around the world every five minutes, but we can offer you a substantial salary and…"

"It would be based in London?" Mari interrupted him.

"Well, yes…sometimes up here, but mainly at Thames House," Ashcroft confirmed.

"What sort of money are we talking about?" he asked, warily.

Ashcroft reached for a pen and scribbled down a number on his jotter, then turned it around. Mari blinked at it for a moment. Then he tore it off and put it in his pocket.

"When do you want me to start?"

* * * *

"What did he say?" Jake wanted to know once they were out of the building and they could finally relax in the lovely gardens, cooled by the breeze from the stream that ran through them.

Mari had come out of his meeting with Ashcroft looking rather pale and dazed and he was unusually quiet, all the way back down to the foyer. He looked sideways at Jake and exhaled a shaky breath.

"He wants me to work for them. He offered me a job."

"That's good. Isn't it?" Jake stopped and rested his hands on Mari's arms. Touching him like this, he could feel that his lover was shaking. He still didn't get the remotest hint of a flashback from him, though.

"I... Yes, I suppose it is," Mari conceded. "I just... I wasn't expecting it. It's very good though. I get to stay in London, with you, and the money will help towards Mama's treatment. I'm... I think I'm in shock."

Jake laughed and put his arm around him. "Congratulations. We'll have to go celebrate as soon as we get back home."

* * * *

Two weeks of semi-isolation out in the country should have been a nice little getaway for them, but seeing as how Jake's every move was watched and monitored, in between sessions with a doctor who made distressed sounds every time he took his temperature or blood pressure, it was not all that fun. At the end of the period of 'observation', the doc told Ashcroft that he figured if Jake were going to suddenly burst into flames, it would have happened by now, and they were finally allowed to return to London.

They were barely through the street-level door to his apartment and climbing the stairs before he pressed Mari up against the wall and took possession of his mouth with all the pent-up frustration he'd been feeling since the night of his escape. Mari's lips felt cool against his own but there was nothing cool in the passionate way he snaked his arms around him and held on tight. They broke off the kiss long enough to stumble up the remaining stairs onto the landing.

Jake wrestled the key out of his jacket pocket and into the lock and they tumbled through the door into the living room. As Jake shoved the door shut behind them, Mari slammed him up against it and kissed him hard, tugging on his belt and getting it undone in record time.

They both kicked off their shoes and Jake popped the button on Mari's trousers and yanked them off his hips. Mari forced his hands into Jake's jeans, pushing them down without even bothering with the fastenings. When Jake gripped his ass and tugged him into the heat of his groin, Mari uttered a breathless sound that continued even while Jake's tongue invaded his mouth. He bucked against him, rubbing his erection on Jake's belly and wrapped his fingers in his hair yanking on it hard.

As they both came up for air, Jake growled, "Bedroom!"

"Whatever you want," Mari crooned, and Jake hoisted him off his feet and carried him there, depositing him on the bed with a huff of satisfaction then divesting himself of the remainder of his clothes. He stood for a moment, watching Mari wriggle on the duvet, as hard and keen as he was.

"You look magnificent," Mari told him as Jake pounced, quickly stripping him out of his jacket and shirt, then kissing his way down Mari's belly to his lean hips and hauling his trousers and briefs off.

"You are too beautiful," Jake growled into the hollow of his left hip, kissing him there, then spreading his legs and caressing with his tongue into the valley of his groin and down to the root of his rigid cock.

"Too...ahhh...too beautiful for what?" Mari laughed, his voice quivering as Jake licked and tickled him there. That little tremor sent steel to Jake's dick.

"Smartass, can't you take a compliment for once?" He chuckled, and lipped his way back up to Mari's mouth. He curled his fingers around Mari's erection as they kissed slow and sweet for a while. Mari's warm hand wrapped around his shaft, mirroring his touch. His fingers and thumb felt divine, easing up and down on Jake's hyper-sensitive cock, stroking and milking him with such finesse that Jake was aching for him in no time at all.

That touch successfully removed all Jake's preoccupation with anything outside of what was happening here and now. Mari's reactions, the sound he made and the way he bucked his hips and crushed his lips had him on fire – in an entirely good way, for once. Jake groaned eagerly, thrusting into the curl of Mari's fingers and forcing his tongue into his mouth with renewed enthusiasm.

"Oh, damn... I really need to fuck you!" Mari panted between Jake's lips as they jacked one another harder.

It was difficult to break off for even a second, as Jake reached a hand up toward the head of the bed and grabbed the box of condoms. He stopped moving with a groan as he tipped the box on end and nothing came out. He flicked the empty box over the side of the bed with an impatient huff and looked down at Mari, those melting blue eyes moving over his face seriously.

"I've gotten tested twice in the last six months and came back negative on everything," Jake told him.

Mari's expression grew slack as he took that admission of his desperation on board. He clearly shared it. "Oh, my stars! This is embarrassing," he whispered in a husky tone. "I... I uh...I haven't had sex with anyone but you for... the longest time. So...uh...yeah, I got checked out when I came back to London, and again, just over a year ago. No problems. I know it seems like a long time, Jake, but...it didn't seem necessary. At one point, I seriously thought I would never get laid again."

Mari stared up at him, eyes wide and full of need. Jake

had gone still above him, holding himself there, he hoped that his perfect, cop poker-face was giving nothing away. Under him, Mari managed a shaky laugh.

"How insane is that? I come to London, one of the gayest fucking cities in the world, and in three years I get laid once. And that was with a woman. I am so crap at this, Chivis."

"You are not. You're choosy." Jake leaned down to kiss him again. He was both touched and a little sad at Mari's admission. His boyfriend was beautiful and sexy, and he never seemed to realize it. What he did say was, "If you were tested a year ago and you were healthy, then that's good enough for me."

He kissed Mari more passionately, running his hand down the front of his body and into the well of his groin again, his fingers skating over his shaft, making him flex and curse under his breath some more.

"Oh, my word, you are amazing." Mari exhaled. "Pass me the lube, Chivis. Or are we out of that, as well?"

Jake snagged the bottle and put it in Mari's hand.

"Still got enough in there for a week, at least." Jake winked. It was more like a few months, he considered, because it was really good, slippery stuff. They'd have to never leave this room to use it up in a week. And wasn't that a seductive thought?

Mari flipped the cap and slicked him up with deft fingers, while still sucking on his mouth like he was some new food source and it was all he needed to live. Jake groaned between his lips as Mari touched and probed at his ass, pressing two well-oiled digits inside him and working them in and out and all over his twitching gland until Jake was bucking and writhing, his loins on fire. Mari finished by drizzling some of the gel over Jake's stroking fingers so that he too was quickly and economically oiled and ready.

"I am so ready to nail you," he growled in a low tone. The urge to dominate a lover wasn't something that overwhelmed Mari often but tonight it was plain that he wanted Jake pliant and submissive and Jake had no intention of objecting. He slid one leg over the top of Mari's and up between his thighs, bucking his erection into Mari's hip while they kissed and teased one another.

"Well, come and get me." He chuckled. "Or do you want me on top?"

Mari's hands moved to his upper arms and when he rolled he took them both over to the other side of the mattress, pushing Jake down on his back and burying his face in the hollow of his clavicle, kissing his throat as he eased up between his legs. While Mari was not as brawny as him, he knew how to use what muscle he did have. When he dropped his hands to the backs of Jake's thighs, pushing them toward his chest so that he could straddle his hips unencumbered, he was totally in charge, and that felt so good after all the tension and frustration of the last few weeks.

Jake bent his knees and let them fall to the sides so Mari could settle more comfortably between them, his muscles relaxing to the point of melting under Mari's touch. For someone who was usually so in control of himself, Jake had not once stinted on yielding to Mari's demands, he always gave himself over completely, and it was a pleasure to do so. Jake wrapped his calves around the backs of Mari's thighs, hooking and pulling him in encouragingly.

Mari uttered a growl through clenched teeth as he wriggled his throbbing cock into place, nudging and pushing, easing himself into Jake and letting the momentum of their entwined bodies do the rest. And, oh…how sweet it felt to do this skin on skin. The friction was just the right side of painful as Mari pressed his hard cock deeper and Jake watched him, loving the intensity in his eyes—the sheer concentration as he thrust himself inside.

"All my fucking days!" Mari hissed out in a rush. "I don't know how people do this with a rubber after trying it bare. It feels so good."

Jake arched under him and lifted his hands to Mari's back, his fingers digging into the tensed muscles there.

"Feels amazing…" Jake panted. "Ahh, fuck, Mari— 'm so hard for you."

He pulled Mari down to kiss him then buried his nose in Mari's hair as their bodies came all the way together. Mari arched his back, rolling his hips with more urgency as he kissed Jake's neck and his fingers gripped his thighs, using them for leverage while he pulsed in and out, harder and faster. Though Jake would never have admitted it to anyone, it felt fantastic to be taken over like this. Mari was making him feel good, and that was better than any amount of drugs and psychotherapy.

Jake tightened his arms around him and his body moved in time with Mari's, falling easily into his rhythm. The hotness of Mari's breath huffed over his ear every time he exhaled and the coolness that came after, when he gasped again, was bliss. Nothing felt this great, nothing in the world.

"Uhh, yeah…ohhhh, do it like that, baby," Jake murmured huskily. The hard length of his cock rubbed between their bellies as they squirmed and bucked against one another. "Fuck, I c-can't hold…just feels so fucking good!"

Jake lurched under him almost violently, and Mari struggled to hold on to him as the liquid heat of his cum spurted between them. He sank down between the spread of Jake's thighs, towing him close, pressing his warm, nude body against Jake's heaving torso as he drove down hard, once, twice, three times more. At the next thrust he was there, coming with a soundless gasp and subsiding in Jake's arms, panting like a sprinter after a hard race. He buried his face in the sweat damp hollow of Jake's neck and shoulder, holding him tightly.

For a while, Jake could not speak, and he didn't want to let go, not just yet. Mari didn't speak right away either, he still held on to him, peppering tender kisses across his brow and temple and making happy cooing sounds of satisfaction.

At last, he murmured, "You are amazing. I'm so glad you're in my life, Mari."

"You are a lucky man, indeed," Mari crooned in his ear. "That felt better than anything I've ever done with any guy."

Jake's laugh was barely more than a wheeze. They fell back into quiet. Lying there, warm and entwined, felt almost as good as the sex, although it probably had a lot to do with the afterglow of said sex.

"You are delicious," Mari assured him, his eyes twinkling with lusty mischief.

"So are you," Jake panted, pulling him close now that their initial lust was slaked. He needed Mari to know how much he depended on him. "Mari…that night, after Corrie was shot, all I could think about was that I might never have you in my arms again… I just couldn't stand it."

Mari's mouth swallowed his in a kiss so greedy that it took his breath away. He rubbed up against Jake, the friction of their two bodies creating a silky lubricant out of their sweat, and Jake's semen, that had them slithering up against each other effortlessly. As their lips parted, he murmured, "You said it again that night, by the way."

Jake knew exactly what he was talking about but kept his expression impassive as he asked, "I said what?"

"When you were slumped in my lap on the bench, you said that you loved me." Mari raised one perfect, tawny eyebrow. "That's the second time. Was it just because you were afraid you might incinerate me?"

A flush of heat rose to Jake's face but fortunately, he thought, it was nothing more menacing than a wave of embarrassment.

"I *was* afraid I might incinerate you, but that's not why I said it." He lifted a hand to push the pale, delicate strands of Mari's hair off his face and kissed him softly. "I meant it. It's not fair of me, though. I don't want you to feel trapped."

Mari glanced sideways then back at him with a crooked grin. "Why on earth would you think that?"

"Because the last time I told you how I felt, you accused me of being delusional and practically ran away from me,"

Jake said.

"You were delusional. And I wasn't terrified then that you'd burst into flames before I figured out how I felt about you," Mari said, leaning back into the pillow with a languid smirk. "You are very sexy when you're all sweaty and flustered, Chivis. Did anyone ever tell you that?"

"I'm glad you think so," Jake said. "And I'm not that flustered, just... Have you figured it out yet?"

"Have I figured what out?" Mari folded his hands behind his head and looked up at him with an infuriating grin.

"You know what. Have you figured out how you feel? About me?"

"Well, yes. You might well go declaring love after you've only known someone a short while, but I've learned to take my time. I'm not good at important decisions, you know. But yes... I've made up my mind." Mari nodded, running a hand through his sweat-damp hair. He suddenly looked rather coy.

"You have?" Jake's heart stuttered for a second. More firmly, he added, "I know how *I* feel."

"So you do. Well, I saved your life, so it's only natural that you'd feel very grateful," Mari chattered on, in that way he did when he was nervous. Jake recognized it for what it was now and he let Mari talk himself out. "Which I'm glad about because... I felt so ill when I thought that something bad might have happened to you. If you do that to me again, I may have to kill you myself."

Jake reached over and brought both hands up, cupping Mari's face, and kissed him full on the mouth. As their lips parted, he grinned down on Mari.

"Is that what it's come to? I almost got myself killed...and you still won't say it?"

Mari thrust his fingers into Jake's hair and pulled him down to kiss him roughly, attacking his lips with a ferocity that left Jake breathless. When they came apart again, Mari's eyes were shining and he murmured, "Would I move heaven and earth, and even make my nose bleed, just to find you, if I didn't love you? Would I kiss you like that if I felt anything less than love for you? You are ridiculously insensitive, Jake Chivis."

"Good, because you are absolutely impossible, Ilmarinen Gale, so we make a fine pair. But I still love you more than anything in the world."

Mari sank back down on him, kissing him like he wanted to inflict an injury. Jake drew Mari into his arms and kissed him back, hot enough to burn away all the boundaries between them.

Breathing Betrayal

Excerpt

Chapter One

Rain *pink-pink-pinked* against the window pane and *drip-drip-dripped* into the pot that Jake had placed under the leak in the hallway. Murky gray morning light greeted him when he opened his eyes. Another drizzly day. He had thought that was just some persistent stereotype, a comic exaggeration—about how rainy it was in London—but so far, this month, it was turning out to be true.

Jake was steadily getting used to the weather. It really wasn't all that different from his native Michigan. He had been told by his colleagues this was an unusually wet November and that when winter finally kicked off, it wouldn't be as severe as he was accustomed to. That was something to be glad about, at least.

The weather was not the only thing he'd had to get used to after moving a little over three and a half thousand miles away from the only place he'd known. London was worlds away from Detroit. It was still alive for one thing, not a dying husk. It was cleaner too, even with more than ten times the population. London had its crime and its dangerous places just like any large city, but even the urban degeneration here had a certain vibrancy to it that was unlike the desperation and decay of Detroit.

Enough of that.

Thinking about home was a guaranteed way to put him in a bad mood. At least he didn't hate his new abode.

The apartment was small and leaky but it was clean and bug free and he didn't have a lot of stuff anyway. Four rooms — kitchen, bathroom, small living room and a closet-sized bedroom that was barely big enough to hold a double bed and the armoire. The kitchen was equally tiny. A small fridge, sink and an ancient two-burner stove. There was just enough counter space to plug in his coffeepot. He was not complaining. The small space made it easy to keep warm and clean and discouraged clutter. It was also paid for, which was another big plus.

He hadn't liked that idea at first. He thought the university should just pay him outright and let him figure out how to deal with the rent and utilities, but he had to admit that having them take care of the bills took some of the worry off his mind. Unfortunately he still had plenty of other things to worry about.

No, he told himself firmly. He was not going to start off the day thinking about home and everything he'd deliberately left behind when he got on the plane. That was over.

Jake dragged himself out of bed and across the living room to the bathroom. After a quick slash, he washed his face, finger-combed his hair with wet hands then threw on some sweats and he was ready for his morning run. There would be time for a shower and food later. Back in Detroit, he would have started his day by driving to the track or the gym to work out before heading to the station house. Here he could walk or use public transportation to get just about anywhere he needed to go. At first the idea of not having a car, of not being able to just hop in and drive wherever he had to go, any time he wanted, had given him more of a panicky, trapped feeling than being an ocean away from everyone he knew and everything familiar. A car was the very first thing he'd asked about, after moving his meager belongings into the apartment. The research assistant who'd been assigned to ensuring he got settled in and had what he needed had told him to give it a week or two and, if he still wanted to purchase a car, the university would arrange it. At the time, Jake had thought there was no possible way he could survive for so long without a vehicle at his disposal, but by the end of his first week he had explored the Tube, the cabs and the buses, got himself an Oyster card and found he could get around remarkably well without having to fight through traffic behind the wheel. He hadn't brought up the need for a car again.

There was a small park only one street over from where he lived, and several right around the university, but they were little more than decorative green space—compact garden squares hemmed in by the tall, dark façades of houses and office buildings—nice for a picnic maybe, but not big enough for a run. Fortunately Regent's Park was fairly close to where he lived and the paths and trails there were perfect. The park was never truly empty but this early in the morning, especially on such a wet, gray day, only the dedicated were out. They all had little earbuds or headphones on and their eyes were fixed forward, everyone in their own private bubbles. No one stopped to say good morning. No one drew him to one side to ask if he could touch their grandmother's wedding ring and tell them if she'd hidden cash somewhere in the attic. It was great. It was almost perfect, except for one thing.

There was one other person from the university that liked to run the same route he did and while Jake didn't see him every morning, it happened often enough that he'd started looking for the guy while he ran. That annoyed him.

317

Running was his time to clear his head. It was meditative. He could tune out and think of nothing. Or at least he could until he started paying more attention to the people he passed than he did the simple rhythm of putting one foot down in front of the other. Now during his morning runs, he was distracted by looking around to see if he'd catch sight of a particular slender figure whose long legs ate up the distance like the wind.

Jake told himself that he was only looking so that he could avoid him, and thereby avoid having to make polite conversation. It definitely wasn't because of the way the ridiculously tight Lycra leggings he wore outlined every muscle in his lean thighs or the way his perfect ass looked so tasty in them. No, not at all.

Jake never had been very good at lying to himself. Even so, admiring that sexy little derrière from a distance was all he would do. He had learned his lesson about getting involved with coworkers. Anyway, it was unlikely he'd see him today, given the dismal weather. He could stop looking around and just concentrate on pushing himself.

* * * *

The park was usually Mari's first call of a morning, though he sometimes gave his running a break when the weather was this grim. Today the rain was that fine, persistent drizzle that evaded umbrellas and invaded just about all items of clothing that weren't a wetsuit. He was used to it, having spent almost the last three of his twenty-seven years here, at UCL, but after the sunshine of his previous job in Barcelona, it was still kind of a comedown to walk out of his front door on a morning like this.

Fortunately the park was just around one corner, and the university campus just around the other, one of the perks of living in town. Papi had wanted to pay for a place out in the countryside, arguing that it would be more peaceful, but his Mama would hear none of it. The London house had been her grandmother's then her father's. He had been renting it out for years while the family lived abroad but now it was finally useful, even if the reason behind its new purpose was a less than happy one. Plus, Mama argued successfully — because no one, not even Papi, would dare to fight with her right now — it was also a short cab ride to the hospital, not an ungodly trek through the suburbs every time she had treatment or saw her oncologist.

He pushed those thoughts away, determined not to dwell on what might be, knowing she would not thank him for it. She had not wanted him to come to London at all, but on that point he had dared to defy her and anyway, he'd already been offered and had accepted the post at University College London. It was a decent job, even if London was not Barcelona.

There was no one quite like Tomas here, but maybe that was a good thing too.

Mari put his head down and pushed on into the clinging miasma of the chill London rain. Tomas Arregui was something else he would rather not think about right now. With the clarity of hindsight, perhaps it had been for the best that the job had come up with UCL when it did. Given longer to chew over the frustration of his on-again, off-again lover, he might well have been driven to do something he would most certainly regret.

Damn it, though! The memory of Tomas was like a persistent tic that wouldn't let go of his hide once its nasty little fangs had sunk in.

He was glad of the distraction presented in the form of another early-morning loper and his spirits perked up even more when he was able to make out the familiar form and easy gait of the new guy who was working with the Web Security Team. Mari had spotted him striding through the park before, though they had never spoken. Lester in the print room said he was American, though Mari thought there was a slightly Hispanic look to his rough-cut, thick black hair and darkly handsome features. Maybe Romani, even? He couldn't be sure.

He was well built without looking chunky, except when he was bundled up in several layers of damp running gear, and almost as tall as Mari's six-foot-two-inch frame, which was a plus. It got embarrassing trying to flirt with men who were forced to look up at him all the time.

Not that he had any idea if Mr. Tall, Dark and Handsome was even that way inclined. But that never stopped him testing the waters. Alicia in his department said that one day some guy was going to punch his lights out for flirting the way he did, as if every man in the world was automatically gay and, by definition, hot for him.

He'd made her laugh with his mock-horrified response. "You mean they *aren't*?"

More books from Pride Publishing

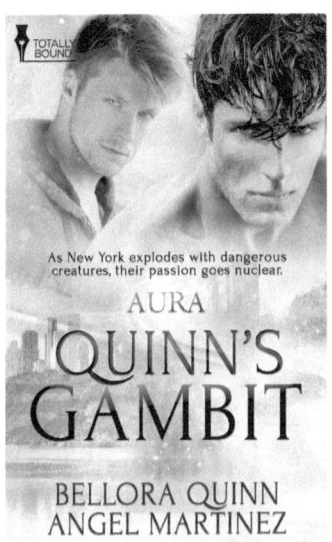

Book one in the AURA series

An unregistered human con wizard and a duty-bound, straight-laced elf cop. As New York explodes with dangerous creatures, their passion goes nuclear.

Finding a killer isn't easy, but someone's got to do it…

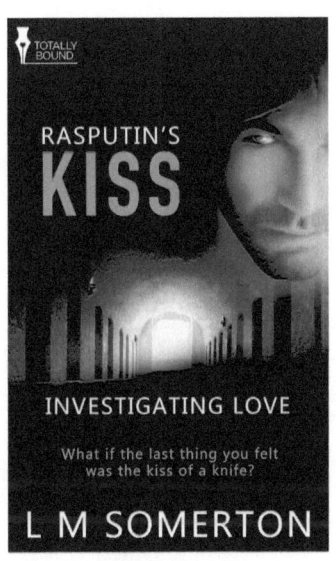

Book one in the Investigating Love series

What if the last thing you felt was the kiss of a knife?

Passion and love bring them together. Murder could tear them apart.

About the Author

Bellora Quinn

Originally hailing from Detroit Michigan, Bellora now resides on the sunny Gulf Coast of Florida where a herd of Dachshunds keeps her entertained. She got her start in writing at the dawn of the internet when she discovered PbEMs (Play by email) and found a passion for collaborative writing and steamy hot erotica. Soap Opera like blogs soon followed and eventually full novels.

The majority of her stories are in the M/M genre with urban fantasy or paranormal settings and many with a strong BDSM flavour.

Sadie Rose Bermingham

A storyteller since before she started school, Sadie also enjoys reading, photography, live music and long walks on the beach.

Sadie has worked as a bookseller, a pedigree editor for the racing industry and a local and family history researcher. Originally from the north of England, she has been working her way across the UK ever since. She currently resides on the south east coast with her long term partner, where she hopes to buy a mobile home and establish a whippet farm.

Our authors love to hear from readers. You can find contact information, website details and an author profile page at https://www.pride-publishing.com/